RECKLESS FATE

HOLLOWS GARAGE
BOOK 5

KATE CREW

CONTENT WARNINGS

Scenes involving domestic violence, comments and references to child abuse, knife violence, police violence, gun violence, death (both on page and references to), murder, and sexually explicit scenes.

PLAYLIST

*Miss Americana & The Heartbreak Prince —
Taylor Swift*
 Bad Reputation — Joan Jett & the Blackhearts
 ANGELS & DEMONS — jxdn
 Chasing Highs — ALMA
 reckless driving — Lizzy McAlpine, Ben Kessler
 Heaven — Julia Michaels
 Angels Like You — Miley Cyrus
 Next Ex — Sueco
 Question...? — Taylor Swift
 Glitch — Taylor Swift
 bloody valentine — mgk
 Black — Dierks Bently
 i'll be damned — gavn!
 Dancing Under Red Skies — Dermont Kennedy
 Afterglow — Taylor Swift
 Death By A Thousand Cuts — Taylor Swift

right where you left me — Taylor Swift
see you later (ten years) — Jenna Raine
Sleeping on the Blacktop — Colter Wall
Blinding Lights — Loi
The Way I Loved You — Taylor Swift
Just Pretend — Bad Omens
Coffins — Bohnes
Yours — Sueco, Bea Miller
Skin and Bones — David Kushner
I Will Wait — Mumford & Sons
this is how I learn to say no — EMELINE
Don't Blame Me — Taylor Swift
Locksmith — Sadie Jean
Religion — Livingston
Half Life — Livingston
But Daddy I Love Him — Taylor Swift

This book is for all the chronic people pleasers who are always putting others before themselves.
You are lovable without sacrificing yourself.
And if they ask you to sacrifice your happiness for theirs, fuck them.

AUTHOR NOTE:

I've been heartbroken that the crew's series is over, but I'm in awe every day of everyone who has been here for the journey. Thank you a million times for reading and loving these characters because your support and enthusiasm have meant the world to me.

Each message, review, post, and shared moment has brought these stories to life in ways I never imagined. I could have never done this alone and you all made sure I never had to!

As we finish this series, I'm filled with so much gratitude and excitement for the future. You have all has inspired me and I can't wait to share what comes next.

Thank you for being a part of this incredible adventure.

ONE

DAISY

WHEN I STARTED COLLEGE, I didn't think it would end like this.

After two years in my sorority, I was leaving, packing up my room and moving back in with my dad until a dorm opened up or until I finished out the last two years of my degree. Somehow my life that seemed so shiny and new two years ago felt heavy and worn out. I kept trying to get ahead, but kept stepping backwards.

Now I'm moving into the room I grew up in, and most likely falling back under my dad's strict rules. Luckily, the house was only ten minutes from campus, but not living here would change my entire experience. I could only hope that a dorm room would open up soon. They said my chances were high within the first two months, but I might not get my choice of dorms or rooms, which didn't really bother me at this point.

Anything would be better than moving home for long.

Dean, my boyfriend of a year, walked in, grabbing another box for me. "Are you sure you want to do this?"

"Yes, I am," I said, for what felt like the millionth time. "I don't want it to end like this, but I think it's for the best. I can't stay here when half the girls have made it clear they don't want me to."

"I mean, I get there's some fighting going on, but what about the fact that you will be further from me, and I will have a thousand fewer chances to actually see you, not to mention getting any alone time with you? You do still have friends here. It's not like they are all mean to you."

I looked back at the photo on my dresser still, the one of the entire house of girls on one of our event days. There were a few girls here I would still consider a friend, but the other half of them had taken the first opportunity to ruin my life. They had a new leader. Sydney wanted my place as president and after she nearly got me kicked out of school for all her complaints, I would willingly hand it over to be left alone. The excitement of joining the sorority had worn off and now I wanted to not be looking over my shoulder every day to see if someone was sabotaging me.

"I'm hoping it's temporary," I said, trying to sympathize with him, but it was hard when I had enough on my plate. "A month, maybe two tops. I'm waiting for a room to open up."

"A month or two? Are you just going to be spending time at the frat house with me, then?"

I knew I made a face, but I couldn't help it. "No, definitely not." I didn't know if I could stomach staying there again. The last time I did, I woke up and puked, the smell in the kitchen so unbearable I couldn't even stomach making a cup of coffee. Not to mention the endless loud noises that left me with almost zero sleep every night.

"What? Why not?"

"I'm sorry Dean, I just don't really feel comfortable sleeping there, and I like my sleep. I *need* my sleep. Which doesn't happen easily when I try to stay the night."

"So what? I'm going to be sleeping at your dad's house? That sounds weird and inconvenient."

"Umm, no to that, too. He's really strict and will never let a guy sleep there with me. I think even if we were married, we would be in separate rooms at his house," I said with a laugh, but when I turned, Dean was sneering.

"So are you saying we won't be spending *any* nights together until you have a dorm room?"

"I mean, maybe? I guess I could try to sleep at the frat house, but could you change the lock code to your room or something? The guys there do not seem to have boundaries."

"No, I mean, even if you do, what is that going to be, like, once a week tops? Daisy, you're not serious right now, are you?"

"I'm doing the best I can. You know I can't stay here. This place is so toxic ,I'm losing my mind."

"Couldn't you stick it out until a dorm room opens up?"

"That's not how it works." I smiled, trying to give a reassuring touch, but he was stiff. "You could always sneak into my room. That could be fun," I said, trying to lighten the mood.

He rolled his eyes and scowled, not meeting my eye. "No, I'm not doing that. If your dad found us, he would be pissed, and then it would get back to my dad, and to coach."

"And we're adults, so I think that would be okay. Come on," I said, grabbing his arm again. "I think it's hot."

"Not when I have so much riding on my dad paying for my school so I can play football full time."

"You literally get drunk every weekend, if not every day during the week, and you don't worry about getting caught with that?"

He stepped back, and I didn't miss the coldness that came over him. "You know, we have a lot of games lined up for the next month and there are events outside of the games that I have to go to. Then, you won't even be nearby, so..."

"So?"

"So maybe we should take a break for a month. You can focus on all these changes, and I can focus on football."

Red hot anger rushed over me like a tidal wave. I knew exactly what he wanted to focus on, and this was the perfect opportunity for him to do that. "And maybe you can put a little more focus on Sydney, too?"

"Daisy, you know nothing happened. She hit on me, I turned her down, the end."

"Fine, if we are on a break, are you going to sleep with her? Are you going to be sleeping with other people?"

"I mean, maybe, I guess. If we aren't together, would it matter?"

"Are you going to sleep with Sydney?" I asked again, each word carefully said, because I knew the answer would make or break us.

"I said 'maybe'. She has texted me a few times. I don't want to tell you yes or no because I don't know."

"That's pretty much a yes." I took a step back. "Okay, then. Get out."

"Daisy, we don't have to make this bad. It will just be a month and then we can talk."

"No need. We're done."

"Wait, no, please. I do love you. I wasn't trying to break up permanently. We just both have a lot going on."

"No, you were just trying to take a break so you can fuck my friends and then keep me around. Get. Out."

I pushed him out of the room and shut the door. I could hear him on the other side, knocking and pacing.

"Come on, Daisy. We can't be over permanently."

I pulled the door back open, peeking out to see him staring at his phone.

"Why?" I asked.

"Because we are made for each other. We are perfect. But no one wants to settle down with the first person they fall for, right? It's different for you. I need the sow-my-wild-oats type of shit."

"Fine, go ahead. I will, too."

He rolled his eyes. "I already know you're not the type to do that or to understand why I would. You're perfect, Daisy. I just want to experience a few more things before I'm settled down."

"I'm not the type to understand? Why not? You think I don't want to sleep with other people?"

"You do?" he asked, eyebrows jumping up. "Yeah, right."

"I'm going to."

"I don't believe you."

"So that's why you wanted this? Because you thought I wasn't going to sleep with anyone else, and you could. Then we would get back together?"

"I mean, yeah, kind of."

"You're disgusting. Get out." I slammed the door again.

"Daisy, I wasn't trying to start a fight."

"Go away!"

"Fine, but we aren't done talking about this."

I heard him walk away and turned back to the room. I had two boxes left and then it was over.

My time here was over, my relationship was over, and at almost twenty-one, I was moving back in with my dad.

My life was over.

TWO
KYE

I KICKED the car into gear and peeled out, already expecting the swing of the back tires and turning to correct it. The car flew around the curve, and I spun the wheel hard as I straightened back out. I was ahead of the other guy, the last turn ruining his speed and improving mine. I told him when he asked for the race that I was good at this one. He thought I was being cocky, but I only wanted him to know before he threw down a thousand-dollar bet.

I went around the last curve, hitting the finish line long before he did, and turning to park by the crew. I nearly lived to race, and tonight was no different. The surge of adrenaline, the feeling of being so in control of my car that no one could beat me, and then winning.

The winning part always got me. I knew there were plenty of things I was shit at doing in life, but racing would never be one of them, and it was proven to me over and over when I won.

And I always won, or gave everything attempting to. It might be a curse. Quinn always said it might be. The way my brain shut down in a race until all I could think about was crossing the finish line first. I would rather run headfirst into a wall than lose. And I would. When the other racer would slow to be safe, I would speed up. Nothing seemed to deter me.

Among the hundred curses I seemed to live with, this one was the one I could handle.

I got out, pushing past a crowd of people, and heading over to the crew, who were standing around their cars. It was the only part about this place I hated, the loud crowds that didn't seem to understand personal space.

"Thank you, Kye," Ash said, grabbing a stack of money from the guy next to her. "Your race just secured my shopping trip tomorrow."

It was race night at the empty lot we used for street racing. Everyone came out with their cars to race along the made-up track in a deserted parking lot. It was a round track tonight, the sharp curves fucking up half the guys here. They wanted to slow down and ease around them. I wanted to speed up and drift around the turn so I could keep going.

The crew knew my attitude about races, so they were betting on every race I did, confident that I would win, and so far, I had won three out of four.

"Thank you, because I had my eye on a new pair of shoes," Ash said.

Fox groaned. "Did you even make enough to buy them?"

"Almost. After the next race, I'm good to go."

"You better win it, Kye, or else I'll have to make up the difference," he said.

I laughed. "Not a problem. I think I can do this with my eyes closed."

"But you're not going to," Quinn said, an edge to her tone because she knew I would try.

"No, I won't."

It's not like racing here would help my chances of getting on Holt's racing team, but it's what I knew. It was a double-edged sword. I loved racing, and this was my way of doing it, but I also wanted to race for Holt, and he didn't approve of street racing. There was a fine line between doing what I loved and risking getting arrested, which could ruin my chances with Holt if he found out.

But it didn't seem to stop me.

Scout sat with Chase on her car with Jax and Carly next to them. Every one of the crew was in a relationship and I was happy for them. I could honestly say that the crew felt complete with Quinn, Ash, Carly, and Chase around.

They were happy and constantly seemed to think I wanted what they had. There was something about people in love that never believed that I didn't want it. I didn't want anyone touching me, and I had no interest in sleeping with anyone. The thought of hands on me alone sent a wave of disgust through me.

I wanted to be alone.

I didn't think anyone but Carly tried to understand that I didn't want someone. I couldn't wrap my head around needing the affection or attention, or even having that much time to give another person. Keeping up with just the crew was plenty for me.

I headed back to my car, not worrying over anything any longer as I got ready for my next race.

My life was good. It was everything I wanted, and I wasn't planning on any of it changing soon.

THREE

DAISY

A WEEK after moving out and breaking up with Dean, I found myself walking up to the lake house, my nerves already fried. I kept trying to remind myself that I was still technically friends with a lot of these people, and the ones here who I wasn't friends with didn't matter.

The panic still welled up in my chest, though. The chronic need for everyone to like me was still trying to burrow under my skin until I did anything to be friends with all of them again.

It had to be an illness. I wanted all of them to like me, even when I knew I didn't like them.

It had been one week since I blew my life up by moving out of the sorority and breaking up with Dean. The domino effect that followed left me on the outskirts of everything. Even the girls who were still friendly to me started responding less and less until my phone sat by me, silent all the time. I knew it had to do with me being gone more. I was out of the sorority house and off campus. The out of sight, out of mind effect, was currently all too real.

I was now a social outcast, and I hated it.

It's not like they had all been the best of friends, but moving out of the sorority didn't mean I wanted them all to cut me out completely. A few of the girls had become close friends over the past few years, and they were taking me moving out personally. The other half were celebrating, taking Sydney's side in the entire mess and making me the villain.

So I came out tonight not only to get my friends back, but to figure out what they were all saying about me. I didn't exactly want to be back on top in the sorority hierarchy, but I wanted to be *something* to them.

It felt like an obsession now. I needed them to like me, to be happy with me, and the idea of them being mad at me and not knowing why was driving me out of my mind. It was either sitting at home hoping they liked and commented on my socials or texted me, or I was going to be here, trying to get attention to stay in the friend group. Sydney was having a party here at her parents' lake house and I knew if I missed it, I would never be relevant again.

I saw Dean sitting out front, and I tried to make a wide berth to stay out of sight and out of his grasp. As much as part of me missed the relationship we used to have, no part of me would be looking to rekindle it.

"Daisy, you came!" he yelled, reaching out for me. "Can we talk?"

I swerved out of his grasp. "Of course I came. And no, we can't."

"Did you come to the game tonight? What am I saying? You always come for me," Dean said with a laugh, his friends joining in. The insinuation was clear, and it made my skin crawl. It was just like Dean to share too many details, twisting our private moments into something gross. Every time I hung out with them, they treated me like I was easy, all because Dean couldn't keep his mouth shut, and told them every detail of our personal life.

"Just leave me alone, Dean. I don't want to talk to you tonight."

"Yes, you do," he growled, grabbing my arm and squeezing tight. "And you can't embarrass me after a win like that. Come on, let's hang out."

"Screw you. We broke up, remember? I'm dating someone else now anyway, so leave me alone." The lie fell out of my mouth so easily that I was grateful. I wasn't always the best liar, but I couldn't stand here alone and pathetic, because I knew he was already sleeping with my friends.

Or at least some people I had thought were my friends.

He laughed, the rest of his group still laughing along with him.

"*Right*, I'm sure. You could barely get me, Daisy. Is he even real or are you just making it up to not seem so pathetic?" he mocked.

The anger and embarrassment burned my cheeks, partly because it was rude and partly because it was true. I hadn't been with anyone since him. And it had only been a week, but I knew he had already slept with Sydney. Dean was so good at making me feel less than him, and even if I knew it wasn't always true, it was now. No guy had even attempted to hit on me in the last week, and the whole school knew I was single.

I felt even more pathetic than when I had walked up here.

I turned, searching for someone, anyone, who looked like they could help. There had to be one guy at this party who was single, hot, and desperate enough to kiss me right now.

This wasn't the night I planned to have, and there was no way I would let Dean laugh me off. I let him do it the entire time we dated. I felt free of that now, and the need to prove that burned through me.

I looked through the crowd and saw him.

Kye Baker, of all people, was walking down the sidewalk right towards me.

All messy blonde hair and tattoos. One ran up the side of his neck and another peeked out from the wrist of his jacket.

People stepped out of his way. The scowl on his face made him look pissed, and the tattoos and piercings didn't make him look any friendlier. He was hot—I didn't know if there could be any question about that — but the hot from afar type. The type of guy you stepped away from because he was unpredictable, ready to fight at a moment's notice, and there was no reason to become a target.

On any other day, I would have stepped out of his way, too.

I knew enough about Kye. We went to high school together, and I knew he and his friends were into…illegal things. I knew he didn't go to college here, so he was probably only at the party to make trouble. I knew his track record with my dad and getting arrested, and one look at him backed up everything I had come to believe. I didn't think my dad could even count the number of times he'd arrested Kye. One of the last times I actually saw him was when he was being arrested, and I happened to be in my dad's car.

Kye seemed to thrive on getting into trouble, doing everything he could to cause chaos, and it seemed to be true tonight.

I also knew that he knew who I was.

Right now, he was the only one paying even a bit of attention to what was happening to me. He also remained the one person here that Dean would not mess with or question further. Even if someone didn't know Kye, it was pretty easy to assume he wasn't scared of a fight.

Kye's eyes found mine, and he cocked an eyebrow at my sudden interest in him. Which was fair, considering every other time we'd run into each other, my face was probably more repulsion than interest.

It felt like enough for me. I hurried down the walkway, headed right towards him. He pulled to a hard stop, that eyebrow still raised as he glared down at me.

I wasn't sure if he felt more surprised that someone stepped in front of him instead of away, or that it was me.

"What are you doing?" he asked, the deep tone obvious that he wasn't happy with my sudden appearance. I was still speechless, taking him in.

He looked more dangerous up close, more wild. The tattoos, nose ring, and intense gaze made a shiver run down my spine. I wasn't someone who hung out with people like him, but there was always a good time to start, and right now I needed someone who would make Dean stop bothering me completely.

And I knew him being single was almost a guarantee.

I reached up, wrapping my hands around his neck and pulling him down to me. "Make this believable, and I'll give you whatever you want," I begged quietly. "Please, I'll do anything."

He didn't say anything but furrowed his brows further.

"Make what believable?" he grumbled. He was so stiff that I had to adjust my arms around him. It was like holding on to a board, and that wasn't going to help me sell this to Dean.

"So glad you made it, babe," I said loudly, moving onto my toes to kiss him. My lips were against his for a second before he reached up, grabbing my face. He squeezed hard, the force of his fingers hollowing out my cheeks, his lips still an inch from mine as he held me in place.

"What the *fuck* do you think you're doing?" he asked, his words a whisper, but the snarl on his lips was clear.

"I'm sorry. I'm so sorry, but I need your help."

"And jumping me is going to help you?"

My heart raced, the panic bubbling up that he was going to reject me now.

This was bad.

This was really bad. Kye rejecting me in front of everyone would be so much worse than it only being Dean.

It seemed to click then as he glanced over at Dean and then back at me, a cruel and twisted smile coming over him. "That's your boyfriend?"

"Ex, and I will give you literally anything you want if you play along."

"Anything?"

I should have stopped right then and there. I shouldn't have promised literally anything to a guy like this, but I was already wrapped around him. The anger and embarrassment would only get worse if I backed down now.

"*Please.*" I begged again

His hand finally loosened its grip on my face. "Interesting that you are so desperate about something, you're coming to me," he said, the deep rumble of his voice making warmth spread over me.

"My ex-boyfriend is a dick, and I would like him to regret the things he has said to me. You are my best bet for that."

He leaned down into me, and I took the opportunity to bring my lips to his. He was frozen, a statue, as I kissed him, and I almost pulled away in embarrassment until he finally moved, kissing me back.

It was so soft, so gentle, that I couldn't believe it was Kye kissing me. I had assumed it would be rough, painful almost, but the hesitation to his lips shocked me.

I wound my hands into his hair, pulling him closer. He hesitated before his tongue ran along my lips. My body started to melt against him, but he didn't seem to mind as he pulled me in closer, nearly holding me up as my legs slowly gave out. I could feel every swipe of his tongue to my toes, the heat burning through me so fast, but I needed more. I was almost crawling up him now, clinging to his body like my life depended on it.

We stayed like that for another second until he pulled away. "Wait," I said on instinct, wanting more.

"Do you like an audience?" he asked with a quiet laugh.

Reality snapped back, and I glanced around. "Damn," I breathed. I had just made out with Kye in front of everyone.

Worse, I liked it. Judging by how turned on I was now, I *really* liked it.

Heat crept into my face, and he noticed. "Oh, come on. Don't shy away now. You meant to do this, now own up to it," he said. There wasn't warmth in his tone, and a new fear churned in my stomach that I had just pissed off the one guy that I should definitely *not* piss off.

He pulled a cigarette out of his pocket but stopped before he could light it. I followed his eyes, turning around to see Dean staring at us, mouth open, the shock on his face making me smile.

At least I got the satisfaction of seeing that.

"Hey, what's up?" Kye said, throwing an arm over me,

each move so casual and comfortable, like this was completely normal for us. Like we really had been dating.

I leaned hard against him, my legs still not recovering. "Do you guys know Kye?"

Anger, or something more like hatred, flashed over Dean's face. I didn't actually know who knew Kye and who didn't. He came around the parties enough that I wouldn't be surprised if they knew him, but Dean hadn't gone to our high school, and Kye kept to himself so often that Dean could easily not know him from any other strange guy that comes around.

"Are you fucking kidding me?" he seethed. "We take one small break and this is what you go find? Some bottom of the fucking barrel loser?"

"You said it didn't matter who I was with and the same for you. Haven't you slept with half my old house at this point?" I asked.

"Daisy, I didn't do anything like that."

"But you slept with Sydney," I said, already knowing it was true.

"I told you before we even broke up that it might happen."

Kye pulled away from me but stayed close. He fidgeted with the cigarette now, and I really hoped he wouldn't light it until I left.

"Hold on, you told her *before* you broke up that you were going to fuck her friends? And you're calling me a loser?" Kye asked, nearly laughing.

"Shut up. No, I told her it *might* happen." Dean turned back to me. "You know I couldn't promise anything."

"And neither could I, so you can't be mad that I'm with him now."

"Yes, I can. I know your dad wouldn't be happy about this

either." Dean came closer now, his friends right behind him, but Kye didn't move.

"Aww, poor guy," Kye mocked. "Are you just mad she already found someone that fucks her better? Or that there's really no use for you now?"

I pinched at his side, knowing that if he pushed it more, Dean would start a fight.

Dean's face turned a deep red now.

"Daisy, do you know what your reputation will be after word gets out that you're with him? Especially after me? Everyone is going to think you're a slut."

"You better stop while you're ahead, Dean. We're going to the party. If you want to keep calling her that and start a fight, just let me know. I'm here whenever." He waved his hand around. "Until then, Daze and I are going to have some fun." He grabbed my arm and pulled me along with him. It wasn't kind or gentle. It definitely wasn't romantic, but I still smiled as he dragged me with him. "Then maybe head home early to have more fun. She can't seem to get enough," Kye added with a wink as we walked by. "Something about football players' dicks being as useless as their brains? Probably one too many concussions and kicks to the groin."

One of Dean's football friends stepped in front of us, and Kye stopped, pulling me a little more behind him and dropping his hand from me. I almost wrapped my arms around his waist but thought better of it. This entire interaction was going to my head as the hottest thing to happen to me in months, maybe years, while he was pissed off that I bothered him.

"Can I help you?" Kye asked.

"You can't say that shit to us," one of Dean's friends said.

"I can say whatever the fuck I want if he's going to

threaten her or call her names. I really don't think anyone is
going to stop me."

Dean and his friends looked back at each other, but Kye
didn't move. The calm scowl across his face left an open invitation for them, but no one took it. I didn't know if I should
back up or lean in.

My mouth had dropped open at some point, not knowing
what to do. I expected Kye could scare them off, but he was
going above and beyond what I planned. The easy way he
dropped right into defending me wasn't helping me find this
any less attractive.

He took us a few more steps past them, and then he spun
me. I gasped as he made one fluid motion and I was up in his
arms, my legs locking around him to gain some stabilization.

"Bye, Dean," he said, grinning as he stepped into the
house. I leaned down, finding his lips again. I was too turned
on to care if he was mad.

We made it to a bedroom, and excitement shot through
me, until he literally threw me down onto a bed.

"I agreed to pissing off one boyfriend, not trying to
convince an entire party that I'm here with the damn prom
queen."

"I just thought —" I stumbled over my words, trying to
get up and face him. "I thought that was enjoyable."

"For who? You? Didn't realize you got off on jumping—
what was it that Dean said…" He grinned, but it wasn't
friendly. "Oh, that's right, a bottom-of-the-barrel loser. I have
to go," he said, pulling out the cigarette and lighting it this
time. "I'm assuming you can get yourself out of here. Or do I
have to be here for that, too?"

"No, I'll figure it out. Thank you."

He stopped at the door, the light flooding into the room and leaving him an outline of black.

"Did you really choose to jump me because I can scare Dean?"

I nodded before I could answer. As much as I wished it wasn't, my body was still on fire, aching for him to come closer again. "Yes," I said.

He nodded, taking a long drag of the cigarette before disappearing into the crowd.

FOUR

KYE

THERE WASN'T much that surprised me anymore. I got used to life handing me the most ridiculous things, and I learned to deal with them as they came. But Daisy Wells, of all people, jumping me last night and kissing me was one of the biggest surprises of my life.

Another girl might not have been as much of a surprise. There were plenty over the years that literally threw themselves at me. The perfect prom queen even approaching me felt ridiculous, but kissing me?

I wasn't a fan of touching anyone, but over the years, I'd learned to handle the feelings that went with it. Sometimes it was pure disgust, my body going cold and clammy, my stomach rolling like I might puke.

Other times, it was pain. Pure blinding pain that seemed to wash over me in waves until I wanted to scream. Pins and needles and knives were skin met skin.

When Daisy threw herself at me, I had braced for either of those, but it hadn't come. I had waited and waited, but I hadn't been disgusted or in pain. My body had quieted when her legs wrapped around me, when her lips found mine for the second time, when her hand pushed through my hair once.

Complete silence.

I shook the thoughts of it from my mind as I pulled into Holt's offices behind Ash, Scout, and Fox. Maybe I had just been too stoned. Yesterday hadn't been a good day, and I knew today was going to be rough so I might have overdone it last night.

That had to be it.

I wished I was already stoned today. Holt had a meeting with us, more specifically for me, because I had been arrested the day before last. I didn't think it was my fault, but Holt didn't seem to care that the other guy actually owed me his car and wasn't giving it up. When I had politely reminded him that he owed me a car, he called the cops for assault.

"This is bullshit and you guys know it," I said, pushing my hat back on.

"It doesn't matter. It's enough that my dad is worried about you being added to the list of racers so today is judgment day," Ash said.

I groaned, following behind them as we made our way up to Holt's office that overlooked the track.

I had been here plenty of times, and even had a talk or two with Holt about cleaning up my rap sheet, but this was the first time, he had called an official meeting.

There had been plenty of back-and-forth conversation about me being one of his rally drivers, with the hope to one day help him expand into different stunt driving. He told me from the beginning he liked the way I drove, and I liked the way he helped Ash and Scout with their careers, but it wasn't until recently that I actually thought I could have a spot as a driver.

It wasn't a job I ever entertained—the idea of being paid to drive a daydream—and I never thought it would actually happen. I was a poor kid from a bad life, even having the chance to own a garage with the crew felt so far out of reach, but it happened. I didn't want to believe this could happen, too. I still agreed to the formal meeting, bringing Ash, Fox, and Scout along to help with whatever shit Holt was going to throw at me.

When we finally sat down at the oversized meeting table, I knew I made the right choice based on how Holt was looking at me.

"Well, I'm happy to see you showed up. I had some concerns you were going to think this was a joke."

"No," I said, sitting up a little straighter. "I know what's on the line this time."

"I wasn't sure based on the arrest *days* ago."

"Dad," Ash said. "You want him on your team, don't start the conversation with insults."

"I wasn't trying to insult him, it's the facts. I do want you on my team, Kye, but the rap sheet you have makes me worried that this isn't going to be a serious career for you, more of a hobby, and I don't pay for hobbies."

"I wouldn't expect you to. The arrests have nothing to do with how seriously I would take this. I'm here for a reason today."

"I already know you can race well. I've seen you drive and think you have plenty of talent, but I can't have any of my drivers getting in trouble constantly. The company's image relies on you being responsible and not causing any worry that you could be a risk on the track."

I could feel my heart rate picking up, that I could actually have this in my life made me shake in anticipation.

"I can do that," I said. "It makes sense that you want any employee or racer to stay straight. I can handle it."

Holt was already shaking his head. "You say that, but nothing you have done has shown it."

"So what?" Fox asked. "You brought us down here to tell him he doesn't have to spot?"

"No," Holt said, shooting him a look. I knew Fox had grown more comfortable with Holt over the years and wasn't worried about saying what needed to be said. Somehow, Holt had come to like him more for it. If I opened my mouth right now, though, I would be out. "I'm saying that Kye needs to prove he can be a stand-up employee off the track before I consider him to be a stand-up racer on the track. No arrests, keep working hard, and show that you can maintain stability in your life. Your friends all seemed to have figured it out. They found their girlfriends, settled down a bit, and it's working out. I don't care what you do, but I need you to show that you can handle this type of responsibility."

"You expect me to clean up my act by not getting arrested and getting a girlfriend?" I asked, my throat tighter now.

"I expect you to clean up the act, Kye, however that needs to happen, and make it clear you are serious about this. Prove that, and we can start working on a strong career for you."

I held back my eye roll. The only thing in my life I *was* serious about was cars and racing. How the hell would I approve that any more than I already had?

FIVE
DAISY

I KNEW there were going to be downsides of going to college in the same town I grew up in. I knew there would be issues with going to a smaller college. I had been right, which wasn't a huge surprise.

First, it was leaving the sorority.

Now, it was being the center of one of the biggest rumors of the week. Technically, it wasn't even a rumor because they all thought it was true, but now everyone I knew thought I was dating Kye. The response has ranged from telling me how terrible of a choice I was making, to asking if they could have his number when I was done, to needing to know all the dirty details. People who hadn't been at the party were even hearing the rumors now.

Above all of that, though, I was at the center of it.

Everyone wanted to talk to me, ask about Kye, ask how we met. The rumors of what happened between Dean and him were out of control, ranging from Kye beating Dean up and breaking his arm to Dean beating Kye up and breaking *his* arm. Each one was only getting more ridiculous, but I realized that the rumors didn't matter. I was temporarily back on top. Everyone from the sorority kept texting me. Some of them even apologized for icing me out.

Who would have thought Kye of all people would help me stay relevant at the exact moment I needed to?

All the good parts of this were adding up, until I realized I needed one thing to keep this going.

Kye.

Which was how I ended up walking up to the garage I knew he worked at, my hands wringing together as I got closer. Kye was only one scary guy in a pack of them, and now I was walking right into their cave.

A guy stepped up to the open garage bay, a sweet smile on his face, as he noticed me.

"Can I help you?" he asked.

I recognized him as the one I saw with the angry, dark-haired girl the day they got arrested last year.

"Um, I was looking for Kye. I was hoping I could find him here." I sounded so nervous. I mean, I was nervous, but I wished I didn't sound like it.

"You are here to see *Kye*?" he asked, his eyebrows jumping up.

"Yeah? Is he here?"

"Oh, he's here. You don't have a car with you?" He looked behind me like he hadn't just watched me walk up.

"No?"

"You don't have a car to fix, but you still want to see Kye?" he asked again, nearly dumbfounded.

"Is that a problem?"

He shook his head, smiling harder. "Not at all."

The smaller red-headed girl that had been with them

walked over. I knew Scout from school. Not that I ever talked
to her, but I knew *of* her at least. "Jax, what's up?" she asked,
the surprise on her face matching his.

"She's here to see Kye."

Her mouth dropped open. "Kye? For what?"

"I just needed to talk to him."

"Did he know you were coming?"

"Definitely not," I said. The nervous laughter that escaped
me only made Jax smile harder, until they both broke out into
laughter, making me more uneasy.

"Maybe I shouldn't have come."

"No, no, no," she said. "We will get him. It's really no
problem. Kye just doesn't get many visitors. Wait here." They
both turned, knocking fists as they disappeared further inside.
I looked to where they were going, but between the cars and
the toolboxes, I couldn't see much.

A minute later, Kye emerged, and I froze. The scowl was
still on his face, but this time he had no shirt on. He was
wiping his hands off, throwing the rag aside as he walked out,
and my mouth watered at the sight. He was already danger-
ously hot, but without the shirt, it was somehow worse. A
mess of abs, tattoos, and grease was in front of me, and I was
trying to figure out why I ever thought this was unattractive. I
always went for the clean-cut, no-tattoos type, and I couldn't
for the life of me remember why.

"I'm not really sure why you're here, but please don't
jump me again," he said, a cocky grin plastered on his face.

"Sorry about that. *Again.* I promise to keep my hands to
myself this time."

He gave a sharp nod, crossing his arms as he looked down
at me.

"Can you maybe sit down or something? I'm already

intimidated enough. I don't need you towering over me like this," I said, leaning back a little more.

He cocked an eyebrow. "I need to sit down so I don't intimidate you?"

"Maybe just lean against the car?"

He blew out a hard breath, walking over to a car and sitting back on the hood. His arms were still crossed and he looked even less happy than before, but at least I wasn't trying to stare up at him. I stepped a little closer, realizing that while I didn't have to look up at him now, from this angle, I had a perfect view of his electric blue eyes.

"Okay, that helps a little, I guess," I lied.

"What do you want, Daze?"

The nickname made my stomach flutter. I usually corrected people, preferring my full name to Daze, but I couldn't bring myself to correct him when it made that shiver go down my spine when he said it.

"I need a favor."

"From me?" he asked, his eyebrows shooting back up. "Are you sure you're in the right place?"

"I am. After the other night, people around the school think we are dating now for real."

"And?"

"And it's working. Dean is jealous. My friends are actually wanting to hang out again. Everyone wants to know about you and I dating."

He rolled his eyes and leaned back on the car, somehow looking hotter as his abs and biceps flexed.

"Again, *and?*"

"*And* I came by to see if you would like to go to a party with me this weekend."

He laughed, leaning forward as a stray lock of hair fell

across his forehead. The nose ring glinted in the sun, and I could see an old scar across the top of his shoulder. He always seemed to look feral. Something about him made me feel unsettled and the wicked smile on his face wasn't helping calm my fears about it.

"Let me get this straight. You used me the other night because you wanted to piss off your boyfriend and I was scary enough for you. Now, a rumor is going around that I'm dating you, and you think that's your ticket back to popularity somehow?"

I nodded. "For now. I mean, I'm sure the novelty of it will wear off, but if you would come this weekend and just, I don't know, hang out with me for a night, it might be enough that people forget a few things that I really need them to forget."

"And you honestly believe I am going to help your image?" he asked, waving a hand over himself.

"I think you are broody and mysterious and people eat that up. You can be yourself and people will fawn all over you for a night."

"They never fawn all over me. What makes you think they will now?"

"Because if you come there with me, there will be a bit of a buffer between them and you, so they will feel a little more open to gawking at you."

"Wow," he said, sounding more excited now. "And somehow you in between will help them like me more?"

"Exactly!"

"Then not a fucking chance." His face fell as he pushed off the car, towering back over me.

"What? Why? Isn't that a good thing?"

"No. I don't want people to like me, especially not those people." He turned, already heading back inside. I couldn't believe he was already blowing me off. I thought I at least had a chance at winning him over.

"But it's just for one night, and I will owe you in return."

"You already owe me."

"Okay, true. Then I'll owe you even more now."

That made him stop. "Owe me how?"

"I don't know. What do you need? You be my fake boyfriend for a party, maybe two, and in return, I'll do something that you need."

He took three large steps back to me, and I held my breath as he came closer. The wicked smile back on his face made my heart stop. "You're a good girl, aren't you, Daze?"

"I like to think so," I said, trying to straighten my shoulders. I still chewed at my bottom lip, worry settling in about what he would ask of me. This was such a bad decision. A guy like Kye could want anything from me.

"And good girls like you have a good image. People like you and just assume you wouldn't get in trouble."

"Considering my dad is the sheriff, yeah, they assume I'm not getting into trouble."

"Then fine."

"Fine? Like you would come with me?"

"Yeah, I'll be your scary fake boyfriend for a night or two if you come with me and be my good girl fake girlfriend for a night or two."

My nose scrunched. "What does that mean?"

He blew out a hard breath and pushed a hand through his hair.

"I need Holt to realize that I'm trying not to be a complete fuck up now because I want on his racing team. I just found out earlier that unless I show him I'm actually taking this seriously, he isn't going to take *me* seriously. I've fucked up one-to-many times, and he seems to think my arrest record is proof that I don't care about my future."

"And dating me would help that?"

"If he thinks I'm being good enough to date the sheriff's daughter, then yeah. If he thinks I'm dating you, he's going to believe I'll be on better behavior and not getting arrested by my girlfriend's dad."

"Then I guess we have a deal. Here," I said. "Give me your phone and I'll add my number. The party is this Saturday. What day do you need me to come with you?"

"I'm not sure yet. I'll have to tell Holt in a believable way that this is a real thing and then let you know."

He handed me his phone, waiting as I put my name and number in it. When I handed it back, though, he was already changing the name from Daisy to Daze.

"You have a problem with my name?" I asked.

"Not at all. You have a problem being called Daze?"

"Not at all," I said, not adding the part where it only wasn't a problem at all *from him*.

"Alright, then, it looks like I have myself my first girl-friend. Lucky me that she's fake," he said. His eyes were heavy as he looked me over once.

"I guess I'll see you Saturday, then?" I asked, trying not to follow up his confession with questions.

"Guess so."

"Would you mind if I text you once or twice before then? Maybe it'll help me feel like you aren't going to eat me alive next time I see you."

That almost got a smile out of him, one side of his lips turning up as he stepped back. "Sure, I can handle a text or two."

I nodded, waving as I headed back out towards the sidewalk. Luckily, the school wasn't too far from here and it was a nice enough day that I walked back.

Which gave me plenty of time to freak out about asking Kye Baker if he would be my fake boyfriend.

Because he said yes.

SIX
DAISY

The weird thing about being so popular for so long was how little alone time I used to have. Now, it was endless hours and even days when I wouldn't hear a word from any of my 'friends' or see them at all. Living off campus was leaving me even more secluded, but it didn't help that somehow, in the breakup with Dean, I had become a social outcast. The texts and calls I had been getting after everyone saw me and Kye together were already dying down, and I wasn't sure if they would pick back up until Kye went out with me again. Not only that, but I was becoming more and more convinced that Dean had completely moved on with Sydney. Not that I cared, but I couldn't understand how my entire life was being handed to her so fast. My boyfriend, my position in the sorority, even some of my friends. I was almost scared to find out what she would be taking from me next.

I paced my room for an hour before I texted Kye, my stomach flipping as I hit send and threw my phone onto the bed.

I was barely expecting a reply, but a few minutes later, my phone pinged.

DAISY

> How deep does this fake relationship go? Do we have to text every day?

KYE

Why would we need to?

DAISY

> I mean, don't we have to get to know each other a little? Won't people think it's strange if we don't know anything about the other?

KYE

Do you think any of your friends are going to question me?

DAISY

> Good point.

> What about Holt?

KYE

Fine…Give me the basics. Where we met, how you managed to get me to date you. All the important facts. Aren't boyfriends supposed to know the girl's favorite color, too?

Does that even come up in conversation?

DAISY

> First, aside from going to school together, we met again at a party. Second, how did I convince you to date me? I'm pretty sure he will be asking me how you convinced me. Good try though. And my favorite color is light blue. It doesn't come up in conversation, but it's always important to know.

KYE

But why?

DAISY

In case you want to buy me a present...
Maybe color coordinate? You'd look good
in blue.

I smiled as I sent it, surprised when his text came back immediately.

KYE

Puke. There will be no color coordinating
and I will wear whatever I want. And why
would I have to wear your favorite color?

God, I'm one day into a fake relationship
and can't even keep this straight.

DAISY

What's your favorite color?

KYE

Blue. Obviously.

DAISY

Obviously?

KYE

My car?

DAISY

Oh right. Do I have to know about that? I
know next to nothing about cars.

KYE

No. Holt will probably believe it more if you
don't. If I show up with a car girl, he would
accuse me of paying one of our friends
to go.

DAISY

When do I have to meet with him?

KYE

I'm not sure yet. I'll see him on Thursday and let you know.

DAISY

Two meetings for both of us?

KYE

Yep.

I sighed, but smiled again. We both needed it if we were going to get my friends back, and him a job.

DAISY

Well then, good luck to us.

Wednesday

DAISY

Alright, I wasn't going to bother you again, but you're not mad at me for what happened at the party, right?

KYE

What? Wanting me to fight Dean? No. I would prefer to fight Dean.

DAISY

I'll circle back to that, but I meant the making out with you part. You seemed mad about it.

KYE

Ahh. Not mad. Just let's keep this fake and not do that again.

DAISY

Okay. I can handle that.

KYE

You sure?

I rolled my eyes. Did he really think I was that desperate and horny that I wouldn't be able to keep my hands off of him?

My lips pursed together as I typed out my lie. Part of me was a little concerned that was exactly what would happen.

DAISY

I'm very sure.

KYE

Alright, prom queen.

DAISY

Don't call me that.

KYE

It's what you were?

DAISY

But I'm not anymore.

KYE

You sure? You still walk around like you're better than everyone else.

DAISY

I do not do that at all!

And you are the one walking around trying to fight everyone

KYE

It's fun.

I rolled my eyes and laid back, pulling the covers over me.

> **DAISY**
> What are you doing?

> **KYE**
> Getting a tattoo

> **DAISY**
> Oh.

> Was I interrupting?

The image of him laid back in a tattoo shop, getting a tattoo with a pretty tattooed girl next to him flashed in my mind, but I tried to shake it away.

> **KYE**
> Not much I can do besides look at my phone while they work.

> **DAISY**
> I guess that's true. What are you getting?

A few minutes went by before a picture came through. It was a cartoon scythe, the words good luck flowing around the blade.

> **DAISY**
> That is morbid.

> **KYE**
> And here I thought I was nailing the inspirational quotes.

Somehow, Kye was funny, and I hadn't been expecting it. He seemed so moody and mean that thinking about him being funny felt strange.

> **DAISY**
> Not quite. A for effort, though.

KYE

Damn. I'll keep trying.

I set my phone aside, trying to ignore the last text. Two hours went by before I broke. I liked texting with Kye, especially when I wasn't able to text any other guys without ruining the lie we had going.

DAISY

Goodnight

KYE

Night Daze

I rolled over, smiling while I drifted off to sleep.

Thursday

DAISY

Are you busy?

KYE

Kind of. Why?

DAISY

I'm bored.

KYE

I'm at race night.

DAISY

Which is?

He sent a picture, a mess of cars and headlights. The girls in the background were beautiful and smiling.

DAISY

Oh. Sorry. I won't bother you more then

KYE

No one said you were bothering. I just will have to race soon, so I might take a while to text back.

DAISY

It's alright. Have a good night.

I flopped back, knowing he wasn't going to respond but wishing he would. I was bored, and talking to him had actually been fun this week.

Twenty minutes later, my phone chimed, Kye's name flashing across.

This time, it was a video of the inside of a car. He must have a stand because the phone went still as the engine revved. Suddenly, the car took off, the phone jumping once before he sped down the road. Then it was over in seconds, Kye yelling something and slowing the car down.

The phone moved again and turned to his face, where he smiled and winked at it.

"I won," he said before ending the video.

I was smiling so hard by the end of it that my cheeks were hurting.

DAISY

That's insane. Good job.

KYE

Thanks.

DAISY

Still ready to be my fake boyfriend on Saturday?

KYE

Where?

DAISY

A party

KYE

Where?

DAISY

A frat house...

KYE

Gross

DAISY

I know, but I'm looking forward to showing up and showing Dean that I'm perfectly fine and happy.

KYE

Are you?

DAISY

No.

There was nothing for minutes. Each one that went by made me worry more. Maybe I said the wrong thing, or maybe he just found a girl to pick up for the night. It was past ten now. It wouldn't be that wild of an idea that he could find a girl at the races and take her home.

I slammed a pillow over my face and yelled.

I hated that I felt rejected over him going home with another girl. It shouldn't matter, and him doing so wouldn't be wrong at all. I couldn't get attached to the first guy that stepped up to play my fake boyfriend, and I obviously knew there wasn't any chance of this turning into something real, but it was hard not to like the attention when he texted me back constantly. I thought that talking to him would be like pulling teeth, but Kye always texted back.

I groaned again and my phone chimed.

> **KYE**
> Want to go for a drive?

> **DAISY**
> Seriously?

> **KYE**
> Yeah? I'm going out, anyway. I have an empty passenger seat.

> **DAISY**
> Are you going to go death speeds?

> **KYE**
> I can try to relax a bit if you're that scared.

> **DAISY**
> Then I call shotgun. When?

> **KYE**
> Already leaving races. Be there in ten.

I looked around the room, tearing through piles of clothes until I sat back. I had to remind myself that we were going out for a drive, not out on a date.

I needed to relax and force myself to realize that I didn't have to be all perfect and put together just to ride in a car.

I pulled on a pair of shorts and a hoodie, not letting myself think twice as I turned off the cameras and slid out the window. There was no point in thinking I wouldn't have to sneak out. My dad would be all over me if I told him I was going out, and he would send the entire fleet of officers to figure out who I went out with.

I jogged down the street until I was out of sight before hitting the app on my phone and turning them back on.

It wasn't a minute later that I heard Kye.

He pulled over, and I jumped in.

"I didn't know if you would actually come out or not. Did you tell your dad you were coming with me?" he asked, already pulling away.

"I snuck out."

He started laughing. "You're, like, twenty years old, and you have to sneak out?"

"Yes, because you know who my dad is, and how he would feel about this."

"Yeah, hard to forget. You know he's going to find out eventually, considering I have to make it clear to Holt, right?"

"Yeah, I know, but I'm also not going to tell him at ten o'clock on a random Thursday. Maybe at a nice dinner or something where you can show him that you aren't a barbarian."

"So no eating soup with my hands?"

I laughed and leaned back, suddenly at ease. The car was comfortably warm, the lights from the dash leaving us in a low glow, and the rumble of the car was more soothing from the inside. That, and it smelled amazing, the musky cologne scent making me take deep breaths of it.

We drove in silence for another ten minutes, Kye seemingly knowing where we were going, but I quickly became lost.

"Where are we going?" I finally asked, losing track of the turns we had made.

"Around? Why aren't you happy? Do you miss Dean?"

The sudden change of topic back to Dean jolted me back to reality.

"I don't know. Part of me misses having such a perfect boyfriend. Like everyone envied me for it. I know how shallow and pathetic that sounds, but it's hard to let go of when that was my entire life the past few years."

"The other part of you?"

"Feels pathetic that I like the image so much that I'm fake dating you to get it back."

Kye laughed, and I lightly smacked his arm. "You can't make fun of me for this."

"I'm not trying to, but it's funny you think dating me helps your image. And honestly, that you even want to hang around these people. I can barely handle people I do like. Why waste my time?"

"You don't have girlfriends? Or want one, at least?"

"No, not for me."

"Boyfriends?"

He shot me a glare but grinned. "Not what I was getting at."

"Interesting. Just sleep around, then?"

"Not quite what I was getting at, either. Do you want to put on some music?"

I nodded, picking a song and snuggling back into the seat. The rumble of the engine became soothing, the warm musk making me close my eyes and enjoy it. My mind held onto the thought that I was in a death trap with Kye, but my body fought it, drifting off as he eased into another curve.

I didn't know how much time had gone by, but suddenly, Kye was tapping my arm to wake me up.

"I figured you should get home," he said, quietly.

"It's one in the morning?" I asked, my eyes going wide when I looked at the clock on my phone. "You've been driving around with me asleep for two hours?"

"I think so? I don't know. I didn't keep track."

"Oh my god, was I drooling?"

He leaned back in the seat, his eyes heavy, and I wondered how tired he felt. He looked good, the easy smile on his face making him less intimidating. It nearly put him into the cute category more than the feral one. "I also didn't keep track of that. I was just enjoying driving, and you weren't really bothering me."

I leaned over the console, putting us a little closer. His eyes dropped to my lips, and I took the invitation to lean towards him more. He didn't move, frozen in his seat as he continued to stare.

"I really can't tell if you want to kiss me or not."

"Daisy," he said, the whisper so clearly a rejection that it immediately stung.

I pulled back fast, the heat creeping up my neck, and I knew I would be red in a second.

"Sorry." I grabbed my bag off the floor, pushing the door open to run home.

"Talk tomorrow?" he asked.

"Yeah, talk then. Goodnight."

"Night, Daze."

I didn't wait for him to pull away before I started back to the house, doing everything I could not to break out into a full run. It was rare for my confidence to waver, but Kye rejecting me was enough to make me want to puke.

Friday

DAISY

Are you still showing up tomorrow?

KYE

Yeah, I'll be the super annoyed tattooed guy in a fast car, hoping that his fake girlfriend says I can go drive instead.

DAISY

Do you like doing anything other than driving?

KYE

Does riding bikes count?

DAISY

Like a bicycle?

KYE

Cute. I mean motorcycles.

DAISY

Yeah, that counts.

KYE

Then no.

DAISY

Weird.

KYE

I would guess that isn't the first time you've called me weird, so what do I care?

DAISY

You would be correct.

Weirdo.

KYE

Prom queen.

DAISY

I'll take that as a compliment.

KYE

What if it wasn't one?

DAISY

I'll still take it as a compliment.

KYE

See you tomorrow...Prom queen

DAISY

See you then...Weirdo

SEVEN

KYE

"I CAN'T BELIEVE you roped me into doing this." I tried to keep an open mind about all of it. I needed to be here tonight so she would come with me to show Holt that I was not trying to completely fuck up my life, but these parties seemed a hell of a lot less fun when I had to be on good behavior.

"I still can't believe you agreed."

She smiled up at me again, and I tried to ignore the way I wanted to keep looking at her smile. Who cared about someone's smile?

"I can't imagine I am going to be welcome at another frat party. I'm sure Dean didn't hesitate to bitch about me to anyone who would listen," I said, clearing my throat and trying to put my focus back on the house.

She rolled her eyes hard, but she still had a smile. "Yeah, right. You are trouble and that's what this place runs on. I'm sure anything Dean could say would only elevate your status with these guys."

"True, and spending my entire night pissing a guy off

while I get to hang around the girl he wants is what fantasies are made of. Think of how mad he is going to be."

Her hand wrapped around my bicep, and I ripped it away. It didn't matter if I didn't have a problem with it last time, my instinct would always be to not be touched, and this was no different.

"Sorry," she said, eyes wide. "Did I hurt you?"

"No. Sorry. I didn't realize you were going to do that."

I almost regretted it when I saw the shock on her face, but I didn't feel bad for long when I knew the pain that I would feel with her hands on me could be worse.

"I thought we could stop for a second. Just kind of get on the same page before we walk in," she said, but I was still lost to the thought of her hand on me, even for a second.

I liked when people were scared to bother me more. It was easier to hide your hate for being touched when people were too scared to touch you, but the way she had so easily reached out to hold on to me made me uneasy. I didn't let people close enough to even think they could touch me, and that let me keep this entire problem a secret. I knew the weird way people acted when I told them the truth.

"About?"

"On if you can play the part well enough, because now I'm a little concerned. You know, kiss me here and there, touch me all night, stuff like that."

"Touching you all night? Is that what I have to do?" I could hear the strain in my voice.

"I don't know, Kye," she said with a laugh. "How have you acted with previous girlfriends?"

I gave a harsh laugh and leaned back on the bench they had near the end of the walkway. People wandered past, but no one stopped to bother us. "If we go off of that, I probably wouldn't be touching you."

"What? Why? I assume you're all over the girls you hang around."

"The girls I hang around are my friends and are also dating my friends, so no, not hanging all over them."

"I meant the ones you're sleeping with."

"Yeah, that's who I meant when I said I probably wouldn't be touching them all night. Listen, Daisy. I'm not..." I groaned, hating to admit anything about myself, especially to someone who would really not understand. "I'm not a very *touchy* person. Like at all. I'm just not good at it, or with it? I'm not mad about last weekend, but thinking about doing it again... I don't want you to get all pissed, but I pretty much keep to myself. It might not cross my mind to do whatever it is you want. I really don't think I can play the fake boyfriend like you are hoping I can."

"Really?"

"Yes."

"That's a surprise. You seemed so good at it the other night. You played the part so perfectly."

"Yeah, maybe an off night or caught up in fucking with your boyfriend. I just don't want you to get the wrong idea."

"No, of course not. You being here for me tonight is enough. I won't expect more," she said, smoothing out her skirt, her eyes suddenly not meeting mine.

"Alright. I'll do what I can to keep up your appearances."

Her smile seemed a little forced, but she still waved for me to follow her.

The rooms were already packed, the music blaring, sending a little thrill of adrenaline through me. I liked the mess and chaos of a party. I could get lost in the crowd and no one would care who I was or why I was there.

I could fight and rage and yell, but people were okay with it.

This wasn't one of those times.

As soon as I walked in, Daisy moved closer, angling herself at my side like she belonged there. I guess for the night, she did. Besides the crew, I wasn't used to someone at my side. My hands twitched at the thought that I would need to touch her. It hadn't been bad, and I tried to remember that, but it also felt stupid to think it could give me that same feeling again.

The pain and disgust at being touched had become so normal and comforting to me. It felt wrong that it hadn't happened when she touched me. And worst of all, in the panic of it all, I was starting to think about trying it again. If it was a fluke, a random night of being high, then I could try it again and stop worrying about it.

Not *if* it was a fluke. I knew it had been, and now I was just driving myself crazy, thinking it wasn't.

We sat down on an older couch, the room of people taking glances at us. I leaned over, whispering to her. "I feel like an animal in a zoo. They are staring."

She laughed, her hand resting on my leg for a second before she realized what she was doing and pulled away. "With those tattoos and that face? Where else should they be looking?"

"I do not like attention," I whispered, not missing the liquid heat that rolled through me as her scent hit me. I couldn't place what it was, the mix of lavender and mint made a strange combination. I leaned in closer, her soft hair brushing against my nose. I wasn't close enough to be touching her, but it was the closest I had willingly been to anyone in months, and it felt more intimate than I liked.

But I still didn't move.

She sucked in a hard breath, angling her neck and giving me more access if I wanted it, but I didn't take it.

As much as I didn't touch or get touched, I watched people. Over the years, I had become just as fluent in the body language of people as someone with more experience. I always thought it helped me navigate *not* being touched and now was no different. I could see that Daisy was okay if I wanted to lean in further, and I thought it was strange that I liked her wanting it.

"You smell amazing," I said.

"I'm glad you think so. I was pretty pleased with my body wash selection," she said with a quiet laugh.

"You're telling me your entire body smells like this?" I asked.

"I would think so."

A feeling that I didn't know rolled through me, making me need to sit back up and roll my shoulders to hide the shake of them. I couldn't say anything, my throat tight and my body nearly shaking as I tried to calm whatever strange feeling was growing in the pit of my stomach.

It seemed like an hour went by as we sat there together before I leaned back in, not able to help myself from getting closer again. "These people are wild, and I don't mean in the way I am. Are those two fighting over *that* guy?"

Her eyes followed mine until she saw the two girls yelling at each other. I couldn't hear what all they were saying, but she seemed to know already. "Oh, yeah. They are constantly fighting over the same guy. Always a different guy, but they are fighting over one."

"Is that what you do?"

"No. I'm more of a one guy kind of girl, and not a guy who would entertain another girl."

"Ahh, but somehow Dean made the cut?" She was so close, and all I wanted to do was sit here, whispering to her all night. "*Fuck*, you really do smell amazing."

It was the smell. It was getting to my head and drawing me in. It had nothing to do with her, just the scent.

"For someone who doesn't want to touch me, you sure are getting close."

"Sorry," I said, pulling back hard. She was right. I always kept my distance, and here I was, leaning back into her.

"No, I didn't say I had an issue with it." The small smile reached her eyes, her amusement with this clear. I couldn't imagine she knew what was wrong with me, but now I was questioning if she found out somehow.

We watched as a girl got up on the table in front of us and started dancing. Daisy watched her and sighed.

"Do you have a problem with her up there?" I asked.

"No."

"Then why the huffing about it?"

"Because sometimes I wonder what it's like to be able to do that, and not care what everyone else in the room is thinking. She doesn't care if we are judging or enjoying it. She doesn't care what we are thinking, she cares that she is having fun."

"Oh, so you are jealous of her, then?"

Her eyes flew to me as though I said something terrible.

"I am not jealous."

"But you are? You want to be doing that and not caring what people think about it."

She was quiet, her eyes not leaving mine. "Maybe."

"Then go."

"Go what?"

"Get up there and do exactly what you want to be doing."

"What would people say about me doing that?"

"They will say, wow, look at her having fun. I better not say shit or her...boyfriend," I said, smirking, "will kick my ass." I pulled out a cigarette and rolled it through my fingers. I needed something, *anything*, to keep me from testing out touching her again.

"You think you can kick anyone's ass and that gives you a free pass to do whatever you want?"

"I think if you're scary enough, people will think twice about sharing their stupid thoughts out loud. Who cares what they think? Do their thoughts change your life?"

"They could."

"Then they have too much power over your life. Do what you want tonight. If anyone says shit, it gives me an excuse to get into a fight."

"You really like fighting, don't you?"

I held out my hand, my knuckles still red and puffy from a fight two nights ago.

"Go," I demanded.

Daisy rolled her eyes, but got up and headed towards the girl on the table. I didn't take Daisy for the partying type, but there she was, letting the girl pull her up onto the table along with her.

I couldn't take my eyes off of her. She was smiling so hard, it had to hurt.

Another song came on and she kept moving. Her eyes would find mine here and there, apparently making sure I didn't leave, but there was nowhere else I could think I wanted to be. I couldn't move, every part of me frozen as I watched *her* move. The same heat flowed through my veins again, warming every part of me until I felt lighter. It felt like a high, the warm, tingling sensation leaving my head feeling a little lighter.

A guy came up, standing in front of me and blocking my view of her. The heat was immediately replaced with rage. It was clear I had been looking at her. I kicked at the back of his leg, hitting it once and planning to do it harder if he didn't get the hint.

I wasn't going to miss a second of Daisy on that fucking table.

He finally saw me, his eyebrows shooting up, and the way his eyes narrowed a bit to let me know he wasn't a fan of mine. When I looked at his shirt, I knew why.

Shit.

He was a part of the football team, which meant he knew Dean. I wondered if that meant he knew Daisy, too.

Which meant that Dean could be coming over any second if he was here.

For the first time in my life, I didn't want a fight. I wanted Daisy to keep enjoying her night uninterrupted and me to keep watching, uninterrupted.

I wanted to keep looking at her dance on the table like she didn't give a fuck what anyone else here was thinking because I was starting to think it might be the first time she had ever not cared.

Like clockwork, Dean walked in, his eyes falling on her immediately, not seeing me sitting here watching his every move.

I took a long drag of the cigarette, shaking the thoughts from my mind.

Of course I wanted to fucking fight. Besides taking off in

my car after this, that was all I needed to want to do, not worry about Daisy and her thoughts.

He said something against her ear, the music too loud for me to hear, but her eyebrows went up and she seemed to prompt him to say more.

But then she looked at me, the hard look in her eyes not giving much away. It was the only sign I needed. By the time I made it to them, he was already reaching out to touch her.

"Unless you want that football playing arm broken, don't touch her," I said, taking another drag of the cigarette.

Dean's eyes narrowed at my words, and he pulled his arm out of my reach. "What the fuck are you doing here?"

I grinned and stepped closer to Daisy. "What do you mean? I like going to parties with my girlfriend. Is that a problem?"

Daisy smiled as she moved to sit down on the table next to me. Dean's eyes raked down her body. The small smirk on his face almost made me punch him right there. He didn't care that I was there. He thought he still owned her. He knew she was better than this for real, and he wasn't buying our lie.

Lucky for Daisy, there wasn't much I wouldn't do to win this game. I stepped closer, parting her legs until they were pressed at my sides. Her arms wound around my neck and she pulled herself closer until our bodies were flush against each other. I hid my flinch, my body going stiff against her, but I ignored it.

The pain didn't come. My stomach didn't roll, but my body couldn't forget years and years of it being there.

Then her lips came to my ear. "Is this okay?"

I wanted to close my eyes as the shiver ran down my back, her breath against my ear almost making me collapse, like I suddenly lost all control of my body.

"Yeah," I said, the words tight.

"While this is already pretty hot, you really don't have to fight him or anything," she whispered.

"Whatever you want," I said, loud enough for Dean to only hear my part.

I tried to keep my breathing calm as she pressed against me, but my heart hammered in my chest.

It shouldn't be happening.

I should be focusing on the fight to drown out the pain of her touching me, but I was drowning out the fight to focus on her hands, her legs, her lips against my ear.

A quiet hum filled my body, and I wanted to scream. Where was the pain, the pure disgust? Where was the instinct to fight her off of me?

She grinned, and I knew the look. It was the same type of look that I got when I came up with a plan.

Her hand wrapped around my neck, and I froze. The long nails she had on started digging in just enough to make me stop thinking straight. Then she leaned in, kissing and biting my neck like no one else was in the room. Her tongue moved up my neck until she bit at my ear.

I didn't know what she was doing that could suddenly make me feel like I was on fire but being drowned at the same time. I stayed there, frozen, trying to get any control over my body, but I could never control it. Usually, it was the pain I was trying to control, but now it was blinding need and confusion.

I couldn't breathe. Her hand had loosened, but it stayed there as she pulled back with a smile.

"I think we have to go," I finally said to Dean, who looked ready to kill me. "*Great* seeing you, though."

I didn't know how I managed to say anything, the words sounding like someone else's voice.

My hand slid under her ass and she clung to me as I picked her up and headed out the door. The crowd moved out of my way like they always did, and she laughed against me as someone yelled out to her.

I didn't know if she realized the show she was putting on was working way too well for me. This was a different type of pain, a lingering burn that seemed to go all the way to my groin. It wasn't like I'd never been turned on before. I had had plenty of times when I needed a release, but I took care of that myself. Those times were definitely never caused by another person, and that included any sexual experience I had.

I didn't like to be touched, and I didn't care to have sex, so what the fuck was going on now?

By the time I set her on the back of my car, I could barely breathe. I pulled back, trying to give some relief to the feeling spreading over me. My lungs were still so restricted, it felt like I couldn't get enough. My chest tightened. The place her hand had been on my neck was still burning, and my dick was now hard and pushing painfully against my jeans.

What. The. Fuck.

She chewed on her bottom lip, her eyes dropping to my jeans, and I could see the smile grow.

"I want to apologize for jumping you again, but I don't want you to think I didn't enjoy it."

My stomach jumped and my groin tightened more. Her eyes on me somehow made me want her to do exactly what she did again.

The panic set in at the thought of her touching me again, and me somehow liking it.

Or worse, that it was a five-second fluke and the second she touched me again would be blinding pain.

"Kye," she whispered. The heated tone wasn't lost on me. It was too much, the teeth, the nails, the lips. I knew what came next, and I didn't think I could handle more after what she just did to me.

What no one had ever done to me.

"We should go," I said, pushing a hand into my hair, nearly ready to start pulling it out. "Unless you need to go back inside longer."

"No. No, that should be fine for me."

"Alright. Come on. I need to get you home, then."

"Oh. Oh, right, of course. Let's go."

I didn't say a word as I got in, waiting for her to get in and pull on her harness before I took off. The car roared as I hit through the gears down the quiet street. If Daisy was scared, she didn't do anything, but unless she started screaming, I wasn't going to slow down.

I needed her out of my car and to put some distance between us again. I needed a break from the buzzing that had filled my head, my body screaming at me to touch her. It was magnetic, my hand twitching on the shifter, wanting to know if I touched her again, if it might be different.

The pain had to come back. There was no way that I woke up last week and suddenly found a way to be cured. Could I suddenly not be revolted when someone put their hands on me? Would my skin not crawl and my stomach not churn now?

It didn't matter, though.

Because there was no way in hell I was going to find out.

EIGHT
DAISY

KYE HAD PULLED out of the party, and neither of us said a word.

Ever since he set me down, he looked pissed. His eyebrows were still furrowed as he pulled out another cigarette.

I hated smoking, and I almost wanted to ask him to not, but he was already mad. I couldn't make it worse.

It wasn't that I thought Kye would hurt me. From everything I'd seen from him, he didn't seem randomly violent, but I knew he could be.

I didn't know how far I wanted to push to find out what made him snap.

"How long will you be at your dad's place?" he asked, breaking the silence.

The question pulled me out of my thoughts and sent me right back to that moment when Dean got mad at me for this.

"I don't know. At least until a dorm room opens up, and hopefully not a day longer. My older sister moved out a few months ago, so it's not that bad staying there. But if I pull up in your car, he's going to freak out, so please park around the corner. I need to keep the peace while I live there."

I bit at my lip, debating if I should ask him about what just happened. He was moving on like nothing happened, and I was wondering if he wasn't as mad about the kiss as I thought.

I definitely wasn't mad about it.

Even kissing his neck made my whole body turn to flames.

Regardless of what I thought about Kye, my body seemed more than happy when I touched him.

"Why do you call me Daze?" I asked.

He smirked, the dash casting him in a warm, blue hue. He shifted the car again, the smooth movement catching my attention. He seemed to do it mindlessly, but I couldn't figure out how he knew when exactly to do it.

"Because your name is Daisy, and I like the shortened version. It seemed more fitting."

"Everyone just calls me Daisy."

"Daze-ee," he said, sounding it out. "Same thing?"

"But it's not."

"Does it bother you?"

I looked over every feature of his face. From the strong jaw to the straight nose, which itself was a little surprising considering I would have guessed he had broken it more than once in his life.

"It's never been my favorite, but it's growing on me." I looked around, realizing we were getting closer to my dad's house. "And you can just pull off here. I'll walk down the road to the house."

"Yeah, of course. Wouldn't want you to have to explain to

your dad why you're pulling up in a car he is usually chasing after."

"How many times have you been chased by my dad, exactly?"

"I don't know. We've raced a few times."

"He's the town sheriff, Kye, I don't think he would agree that it's racing."

"Maybe he's just mad he loses."

"Bye, Kye." I got out, laughing as I shut the door and headed towards the house.

I made it to the front door, shutting it quietly before I slumped against it.

I've kissed Kye twice now, and each time made me weak. I wanted to forget it, but it still played over and over in my mind.

"Hey, Dad," I said, walking past where he sat in the living room. He was watching TV, but I knew he had been sitting there waiting for me to get home.

"Hey, honey, how was your night?"

"Fine, I guess. The usual."

I heard him then. Kye's car out front. The rev of the engine and then tires locking up on pavement.

"Those damn guys are always coming around here. You would think they would know better than to go to the sheriff's house."

"Yeah," I said, almost feeling bad that I was just out with that same guy.

My dad grabbed his radio. "Can someone come around my house? Some kids are out here racing."

"I'm going to bed. Goodnight," I said, running to my room.

> **DAISY**
>
> You better go. He's already called the other cops to patrol the area.

He texted me back a few minutes later.

> **KYE**
>
> I'm no longer in the area lol but thanks for the heads up. I couldn't leave and not piss him off a little.

> **DAISY**
>
> You're trying to make this harder on me, aren't you?

> **KYE**
>
> Not at all

> Is this another perk? An in with the cops to know when they are onto me.

> **DAISY**
>
> Sometimes

An hour went by while I went to get ready and slid into bed. I thought Kye would be done for the night, but another text came through and my stomach flipped.

> **KYE**
>
> You free Tuesday? I was thinking about setting up a meeting with Holt.

> **DAISY**
>
> I'm free after two. I have some classes.

> **KYE**
>
> Alright. I'll set it up for later in the day.

> What are relationship things I should do to convince Holt this is real?

I smiled as I turned off the lights and snuggled back into the blankets, nearly giddy as I texted back.

DAISY

I mean, you will need to hold my hand or put your arm around me at least once or twice when he's there. Make comments about things we do together, make a picture of me as your screensaver, stuff like that.

KYE

I don't have a picture of you?

I rolled my eyes, scrolling through my photos, and getting more nervous as I did. I wanted something cute enough, but part of me wanted a photo that was a little sexier. I didn't think Kye had any feelings for me, but thinking I was hot and maybe wanting to kiss me once or twice more would be nice.

I finally came across a photo of me at the beach. I had on a see-through wrap over my bikini, but it was cute and a little sexy. I settled on that being the winner.

I waited as it sent, and then waited even longer, staring at my phone as nothing happened.

Finally, the phone chimed.

KYE

Well…

Came right off the line strong with that, didn't you?

DAISY

I just sent a picture. That's all.

KYE

Right. Little miss innocent.

DAISY

My turn.

KYE

You need one of me?

DAISY

Of course. I'll need to make you the
background on my phone then, too.

KYE

Oh. I don't get this. Does me looking at
your face every time I open my phone
means we're dating?

DAISY

Don't your friends do that with their
girlfriends?

KYE

Yeah and now I'm questioning their sanity
even more.

How does a man even compete with yours?

DAISY

Try.

A few minutes went by and then he sent one.

I clicked it open and could feel how high my eyebrows
jumped. It was a good picture. It wasn't even a joke, just a
great picture of him. He was smiling with sunglasses and a hat
on, standing next to his car. It was obvious that he had just
raced or something. Banners and flags were in the background. He just looked relaxed and happy. The hard edges of
him were still there, but a little softer.

I didn't know why, but I wasn't expecting a good picture. I
was expecting dark rooms and blurry photos for him to hide
himself in. Not a full face, smiling photo of himself in broad

daylight. I'd really got to know Kye all of two weeks, and suddenly every perspective I had of him kept changing.

DAISY

Wow.

I felt pathetic, not even knowing what to say to him. Not even knowing what I thought now. I mean, he had always been hot in an off-limits type of way, but every minute I spent with him seemed to make him even better.

It felt freeing knowing that this relationship was fake, and even if I did want to kiss and flirt with him a bit, there was no harm to it.

DAISY

That is definitely getting to be my phone screen. I think I would make that guy my screen even if I didn't know him. Is that what you look like when you don't have the murder scowl on your face?

KYE

I have been told often by my friends that I have resting bitch face.

DAISY

You do, but damn, that guy is just...

KYE

Just?

DAISY

Hot. That guy is really fucking hot.

KYE

Just a heads up - that guy is me.

DAISY

And I can barely believe it. Give me another one lol.

KYE

Hold on.

I waited as another photo came through and I almost threw my phone.

He had taken a photo in the mirror, nothing but a towel slung low on his hips, leaving little to the imagination. I could see tattoos scattered around, but he wasn't completely covered in them. Although, I would imagine one day he would be at this rate. He must have taken a shower because his damp blonde hair was a mess, but he was scowling in this one. The typical Kye scowl. The one that made people step out of his way and think twice about fighting with him.

And somehow I found it even hotter.

KYE

That was to hopefully pay you back for your photo.

DAISY

What is going on? Why are you so hot? How have you hidden this so well? I mean, I guess I knew you were hot, but this different. This is…how is this happening?

KYE

Hidden? I don't hide it. I also don't always walk around with my shirt off so that could change things.

DAISY

I mean it could help get more girls? They might feel better about the scowl if your shirt is off.

KYE

I don't want more girls. And just because you're scared of me, Daze, doesn't mean other girls are.

DAISY

I'm not scared of you.

KYE

Maybe not as much now, but you were. You picked me out because I could kick your dumb boyfriend's ass and wouldn't hesitate to, not because you thought I was cute and cuddly.

DAISY

Okay, that might be true.

I had used Kye that first night, nearly betting on how scary he could be to save me the embarrassment. Now, I realized I might had misjudged him. There was more to Kye than tattoos and scowls, and I was surprised to find how much I liked him.

I rolled over, still staring at my phone. I was about ninety percent sure Kye was flirting with me, or at least trying to, and I couldn't contain the excitement it gave me.

KYE

Goodnight Daze. Enjoy the photos.

My mouth dropped open, the little devil emoji making me smile.

I was expecting grumpy, crude, dangerous, partying Kye. I was expecting a guy that I wouldn't want to spend more than twenty minutes with, not this.

Maybe it was a fluke, a different side of Kye because we

were pretending to date. Maybe he just felt like it was safer and easier to flirt because of that, too.

I could only hope because I didn't know what would happen with this guy.

A secretly happy, cute, and kind Kye seemed more dangerous than the reckless one.

NINE
KYE

"I'M PRETTY sure I'm going to fuck this up." I grabbed my coat and threw it on, hoping covering my tattoos for the day would help give Holt the impression that I wasn't a complete fuckup.

I mean, along with having Daisy next to me.

"You are not," Carly said with a cocky grin as I looked in the mirror. "He's going to be surprised you have a date, though."

"Hopefully, it's a good enough surprise that he knows I'm trying."

"I think it will be plenty to show him that. Especially since you went out and got the town princess. How did you convince her to do this exactly?"

"She practically begged me to be her fake boyfriend. I didn't have to convince her. If anything, she had to convince me."

Carly rolled her eyes as she got up and headed into my small kitchen. Her dog, Riot, lounged on the couch, not even bothering to get up when he could watch her from there. My apartment was the smallest in the building, but I liked it that way. I didn't need much, and what I did need fit here or in the garages.

She grabbed her coffee off the counter before waving me over to the door with her. "Interesting that she chose you, of all people. *Very* interesting. Are you going to be okay with her having to hold your hand and everything?"

I cleared my throat, pushing away the thoughts of her touching me. I had started to worry that I actually *was* going to be okay with it, and the thought of that was already getting under my skin.

"I'll handle it."

"Just don't push yourself too far. It's not worth working for Holt if he only thinks you're trustworthy with some fancy woman on your arm."

"I know, but I want him to see I'm trying and I just need this to show that for now."

"I would also suggest stop getting arrested," she said as she waved Riot out of the apartment with us. "I don't know. It *might* help."

"Well," I said, smiling as I shut the door behind us. "I can't promise that, which is why I need the good girl sheriff's daughter to help my image. Lucky for me, she needs someone that her stupid ex-boyfriend is scared of."

She gave a snorting laugh as we made it to her and Jax's apartment one floor down. "The toss-up of you having to not get arrested, *or* deal with the girl you call prom queen because she's so perfect now having to touch you and be your girl-friend is hilarious. Who would have thought your love life drama was going to be our entertainment for the week? The crew is going to eat this up."

"They aren't because you aren't going to tell them yet."

Carly rolled her eyes but nodded. "*Fine*, but only because I want to see their faces when you tell them."

"What does it matter anyway? It's a fake relationship, so I get my dream job and she gets...some sort of popularity, I think? Either way, it's all fake."

"Real or fake, it's entertaining for me. Are you coming over for a movie later?"

"Unless you go running off to tell Jax all about this, yeah, I'll be there."

She waved me off and disappeared inside the apartment. I kept going, heading downstairs to the garage we had on the bottom floor of our building.

It was a fake relationship, and even if she touched me and it didn't hurt, it was fake and it would always be.

DAISY LOOKED THE PART IN A LIGHT BLUE SUNDRESS AND denim jacket. A perfect prom queen coming with me to meet Holt and convince him I'm worth hiring as a driver.

I wasn't one to get nervous, but by the time I pulled into Holt Racing, I was ready to call it quits.

"I don't know what I'm going to do if he doesn't buy this, so please, sell it."

"I will," she said, her shoulders back and a bright smile on her face.

"And please tell me how the hell I can sell it more."

"I will, Kye, relax. We got this," she said, laying a hand over mine before I quickly pulled away.

"Let's go get this over with."

Twenty minutes later, we were sitting on the other side of

Holt's desk, trying to explain to him how we met and how I've been acting perfect since.

Minus the getting arrested part.

We talked over the things I would be doing before Holt finally came to the things I needed to do still.

"This is pretty hard to believe, Kye," he said.

"I can imagine."

"You've expressed plenty of times around me that you don't want a relationship when I've hung around with you all. Why now? And why her?"

I looked at Daisy, who smiled at me. "I think Kye will still tell you he doesn't want a relationship," she said, laughing. "But you find someone you really like and things change."

"Things changed so drastically that he went out and is dating the town sheriff's daughter? And just like that, he's going to act right? Does your dad know about this?"

Daisy sighed and laid a hand on my arm. "Not yet. We still aren't sure how to tell him, and honestly, Holt, I just wanted to make sure this worked out before I gave my dad a heart attack with that."

Holt's face was calm before it broke into a wide smile as he tried not to laugh. "Yeah, yeah, I imagine this one might give him one."

"So, you won't go and tell him immediately?" I asked.

"No. That's on you two. I don't want to be the one to kill the man," he said, smiling still. "I have the party down at the track coming up and he will be there, though. Do you think you two will be together in three weeks to attend? Or would that be an issue?" He looked directly at me, and I met his eye. "I would like you to be there, Kye, do some driving for a few people who are attending. And obviously, seeing you two there together would be nice if you were planning on being together that long."

I was still frozen, hating every second of this. It wasn't the lying that bothered me, really, but the pretending to be a fake boyfriend part.

"Unless Kye manages to mess up completely in the next three weeks, I don't see why we couldn't be there," Daisy said. At least the girl who wanted to be my fake girlfriend was also the girl that was a pro at putting on a show for the world to make everyone think she was perfect.

After a lot of nodding along and agreeing, we were leaving. Daisy held my hand as we walked out of the building before I stepped away, forcing her to drop it.

"I'm glad that's fucking over," I said, slamming my car door shut. "That went to hell fast."

"What are you talking about? I thought it went fine."

"He barely believed me. And now we have to keep this up for three more weeks? How the fuck am I supposed to manage that?"

"Oh, come on. I'm not that bad," she said, grinning.

"No, I meant how the hell am I supposed to keep up this idea that *I* have a girlfriend?" I asked, already shaking my head. "Forget it. I just can't believe he was that skeptical. I know we agreed on two outings each, but what about now? Can you handle adding another one or two?"

She shrugged. "I don't see why not. It's working great for me, and being seen out again with you could really rile Dean up. Plus, the girls even invited me out for a day on the boat, which is basically an invitation back into the friend group. They want to know all your dirty secrets, or more like *our* dirty secrets."

I hid my eye roll. It wasn't that I didn't understand

wanting friends—I couldn't think of my life without mine—but what I didn't understand was the stupid games she had to play just for them to like her.

"Am I supposed to be going on this boat with you?"

"No, you weren't invited. I think they are still scared of you."

"Thank the damn world for that because being stuck on a boat for hours with those people and having to play nice sounds like my own personal hell."

"Don't worry. It will be the entire group of friends, and I don't think you're experienced enough in that type of group to play nice for that long."

"At least you recognize that," I said, laughing. "Do you want to go out for a drive before I bring you home?"

I didn't know what made me ask. I usually liked to go out alone, but the other day she came with me was...nice.

She was already agreeing, pulling on the harness and leaning her head back to look out the window as I idled out of the parking lot.

My mind that usually raced had been quiet, and as much as I liked to go out for late night drives, I was starting to think I liked going out on a drive with her more.

TEN

DAISY

THE CAR WAS quiet as he wove through town. He didn't even have the music on, instead choosing to let the rev of the engine drown out everything.

Not that I minded. Driving around with Kye like this was peaceful. Loud, but peaceful.

"I want a milkshake. Do you want anything from the diner?"

"The diner?"

His eyebrows shot up. "Yeah, the one right on the edge of town? Do you not go?"

"I mean, maybe? What's the name of it?"

"The diner," he said again. "That's what it's called. If it has another name, I don't know it."

I laughed. "Okay, then, yeah, I would also like one."

He nodded and hit the gas. The only problem with that was we were coming up to an intersection.

"What are you doing?" I yelled, grabbing onto the harness.

He laughed as he turned the wheel, the back of the car

breaking free as he went around the corner. The car moved sideways, drifting around the corner as I yelled.

I squeezed my eyes shut until I could feel the car straighten out again.

"When I said I wanted to go for a milkshake, I didn't mean get there as fast as possible."

"Oh," he said, laughing harder now. "Well, you are going to have to be more specific next time."

"How about I make a blanket rule of not doing...whatever *that* was around any corner."

"Are you serious? How am I supposed to get around turns?"

"The boring, old-fashioned way? By coming to a stop, putting on a turn signal, and slowly turning."

He pulled into what I assumed was the diner, but there really was no sign out front. He huffed, but shut the car off. "There is no way in hell that I will be agreeing to that," he said with a smirk. "What do you want?"

"I'll take one of whatever you are having."

With one sharp nod, he got out and headed inside.

I waited in the silence, the warmth of the car still wrapping around me. It was strange being out with Kye, but even more strange how normal it felt. The pressure to be anyone but myself was gone around him. It didn't matter because he seemed to have no expectations of me. I didn't have to be a good daughter, or girlfriend, or even friend with Kye. I could just be me.

Kye came to my side and ripped the door open, his face stone as he shoved the drinks at me.

"Here," he said, barely letting me grab them before he was standing back up straight. "Lock the doors and *do not* get out of this car for anything until I am back. And I mean anything, Daisy."

"What?" I said, panicking as I took the drinks. "What's wrong?" I finally noticed the two guys walking towards the car. They looked like Kye in some ways, the tattoos, the scowls, but I was suddenly worried they were nothing like them. "Who are those guys?"

He didn't answer, slamming the door and motioning for me to lock them.

I did, my eyes glued to them as they walked up and started talking. None of it looked friendly, but Kye still had that smirk on his face. I was starting to be convinced that it was there solely to piss people off.

The other guy yelled something, the muffled word lost to me, but then he swung, hitting Kye right in the face.

I screamed, but no one paid any attention to me. Instead, Kye went after him.

The glow of the lights from the diner was the only thing letting me keep track of what was happening now. As soon as Kye got close enough, the guy swung again, hitting Kye squarely in the nose, but somehow it didn't deter him.

With one swift swing of his arm, Kye's fist connected with the guy's jaw. The guy yelled in pain as he stumbled back, trying to regain his balance.

He didn't have a chance, though. Before he could see straight again, Kye was on him, swinging over and over.

It felt like hours, but the entire thing was over in less than a minute. Kye had kept punching, his fists landing on the guy's face, chest, stomach, and anywhere else he could connect. The guy stayed standing, his hands weakly trying to fight back, but Kye was ruthless, not giving him a chance.

Finally, the guy fell back, landing in the dirt behind him.

Kye watched for a few seconds before, apparently, deciding that it was officially over.

He got in, blood dripping from a large cut at the bridge of his nose. When he reached for his milkshake, I could see his red, bloody knuckles. Like it didn't even phase him, he took a sip.

"Fuck, these things are my favorite," he said. "Ready to go?"

I nodded, but I couldn't find any words.

For the first time since getting to know Kye, *really* getting to know Kye, I was terrified of him.

ELEVEN
DAISY

TWO DAYS HAD GONE by since I watched Kye beat a guy until he was bleeding and broken on the ground.

Knowing Kye was feral was one thing.

Seeing it in action was another.

He had punched and punched until the guy was on the ground, hitting him a few more times until he knew he wouldn't get up, and then walked away like nothing had happened.

His knuckles had been bleeding and his lips had split open from being hit, but he hadn't seemed fazed, and drove around with me in the car for another hour after.

Even now, the thought of how wild he went made me shudder.

I still didn't think he would ever hurt me, but how could someone be that brutal and not be expected to turn on me at some point?

The thought was stuck in my head as I waited outside for my friends. We were headed out to the boat today, and I needed to not be lost in thought about Kye. The car pulled up, three of the girls packed inside. I slid into the back seat and came face-to-face with Sydney.

"I didn't know you were coming today," I said, the polite edge to my tone not hiding the anger that rolled through me. This was the girl that was trying to sleep with my boyfriend before we even broke up and then succeeded immediately the second we did break up. What reason did I have to be nice?

But it didn't matter. I was going to play nice and not cause any issues, like always.

Jessica and Isabella turned around in the front seat, both giving me an apologetic smile. They felt bad for me.

I was the loser Dean dumped, and Sydney was his prize for that. The tight smiles were a harsh reminder that I was the pathetic one here, and they honestly pitied me for it.

Of course, they did this on purpose.

"Is that a problem?" she asked, wincing a little.

"No, not at all," I said, smiling and hiding any ounce of anger I had. "I just didn't know. Ready?" I asked, facing Jessica and Isabella. They smirked and turned back.

We pulled out of the driveway and headed for the beach. The conversation lulled into surface level topics. It was easy enough, but I could feel my anxiety bubbling underneath, making me watch every word that came out of my mouth. Anything I said would be ammunition if they turned on me again, and this time, I was going to be a lot more careful about what I said.

I GOT INTO THE BOAT, THE LAZY ROCKING ALREADY SETTING me on edge. The entire group consisted of us four girls and the three of the guys. Dean, Steven, and Michael were taking turns driving out farther into the lake, trying to get us far enough out that we wouldn't be bothered by anyone else.

I was too busy trying not to throw up the farther out we got. I had always gotten a little sick on boats, but their careless driving was making it get out of control.

The glint in Steven's eye since we got on the boat wasn't making me feel any better.

I didn't want to make a scene, though. I didn't want to ruin everyone's day or be called names for backing out.

This was fine. I was safe, and it was just my anxiety making my thoughts get out of hand.

The rest of the group teased and joked, poking fun of me for holding on so tight to the railing of the boat, but the deeper the water, the more anxious I got. Jessica and Isabella came to my side, and the knot in my chest grew.

"Soooo," Jessica started. "Tell us about Kye."

Isabella looked at Dean with a smirk, but she still talked to me. "Yeah, tell us all about the new boyfriend who is mysteriously not here today. I thought you would bring him."

"Yeah, he couldn't make it. Maybe next time."

Dean snorted. "Couldn't make it because he's not actually your boyfriend? Or because he already broke up with you?"

"Neither," I said as sweetly as I could. "He's just busy today."

"Right," Dean said, the cocky smile still on his face. "Maybe he just couldn't handle spending the day with me here."

"You think Kye would be bothered by *you*?"

"I think he might be annoyed about you wanting to spend your day falling all over me."

My eyes narrowed, and I looked him over. "I have literally not said a word to you until right now."

"Doesn't mean you haven't been eyeing me up the entire time," he said, laughing as he fist bumped with Steven.

My lip curled, and I looked at Jessica, who was trying to hide her laugh.

Isabella gave me a sad, apologetic look, and I wanted to hug her. I hadn't had a friend care in so long that even her one sympathetic look made me emotional.

Just as fast, though, her eyes went wide. By the time I felt hands on me, it was too late.

"Come on, Daisy, let's go for a swim."

I screamed, fighting back as Dean grabbed me while Steven and Michael grabbed Jessica and Sydney.

"Dean, put me down! You know I hate the deep water."

"You know how to swim. What's the problem?"

"Because I'm scared. Put me down!" I screamed, as he threw me into the water.

For one terrifying moment, I was engulfed in darkness, my frantic kicks and splashing doing little to bring me back up to the surface. The panic threatened to overwhelm me as I struggled against the fear. When I finally broke the surface, a hand was already outstretched, waiting to help me up.

Isabella.

The rest were laughing, the other two girls giggling as they made it back into the boat, but I was nearly screaming.

"Bring me back. Take me back to shore right now."

"Calm down," Dean said. "You know how to swim."

"And I told you I didn't want to be thrown in because I'm scared. Take me back right now or I'm going to call my dad and tell him that you're out here drinking."

Dean rolled his eyes and the other guys groaned.

"Damn, Daisy, you are such a loser. I don't know how I ever managed to date you."

"And you're such an asshole that I don't know how I managed to date *you*!" I yelled. "Take me to shore now."

TWENTY MISERABLE MINUTES LATER, I WAS BACK ON LAND, and the entire group was booing as they went back out. No one cared that I was upset, and no one cared I would be standing here alone without a ride until they were done.

No one cared because they never cared.

I had already known it, but having it thrown back into my face again felt worse than if they had slapped me.

I could already see Sydney sidling back up to Dean as they pulled away, and I was surprised at how little I cared about that even.

Maybe they didn't care, but apparently I didn't either.

I wrapped the towel tighter around myself and moved to hide by the tree. The trunk kept me hidden from all of my friends.

My ex-friends?

Did you break up with an entire group all at once?

I guess that's exactly what I was doing.

My hands were shaking as I pulled out my phone and hit his name. My dad would come get me in a heartbeat, but I knew there was no explaining this situation to him now. He knew all of my friends and their parents—he would have too hard of a time understanding what they did wrong. Plus, as much as I didn't want to care, part of me didn't want to actually be the loser that brought her sheriff dad to pick her up and rat out all her friends.

And as much as Kye freaked me out the other day, I was pretty sure I could count on him showing up.

At least, I hoped.

"Hey." Kye's voice came over the phone and the simple word made me sag against the tree.

"Hey, what are you up to?"

"At two o'clock on a Thursday? I'm working like all the peasants have to do. What's the prom queen doing? Ruling her kingdom from the throne? Getting her nails done?" The words that were supposed to be funny had an edge to them that only upset me more. Maybe he noticed I hadn't talked to him since the other night, or maybe he was just showing exactly how fake this relationship was, but either way, I wasn't in the mood.

"Wow, forget it. I'll talk to you later."

"No, wait. I was trying to make a joke, but my day's been shit. Why are you calling me? You said you were hanging out with Dean."

"I said I was hanging out with my friends. Dean just happens to be a part of that group. Unfortunately."

"Yeah, how unfortunate that you *choose* to go hang out with people who treat you like shit."

"Kye," I said, ready to say more but not even knowing how to deny it. It was true.

"Daisy."

"You seem to only call me that when you're mad."

"Yeah, well." I heard something drop and him swear before he said anything else. "Why are you calling me if you are with your friends and boyfriend?"

"You are supposed to be my boyfriend."

"No, I'm the fake one, remember? You've been with the real one. Or the 'maybe' real one? I don't know. This shit is hard to keep track of."

"Is that suddenly a problem?" I asked, trying to figure out why he was mad.

"No, but it is when you are bothering me when you are with him. I need to get back to work. What did you want?"

"Well, I needed a ride, but you're being an ass, so I will just call an Uber."

He was silent, probably deciding how much he didn't like me at this moment.

"Where are you?"

"In the main parking lot at the Emerald Bay beach."

He huffed loud. "And how did you get a ride there, but suddenly don't have one back?"

"Because I came with that friend group, and they decided it would be hilarious to throw me off of the boat even though I am scared of swimming in deep water, and when they pulled me back in the boat, they called me names for having a panic attack. So really, I thought getting back to shore and letting them go back out was a better idea than staying."

The line was quiet before he swore again. "Are you fucking kidding me? How the fuck is that funny?" He yelled something and someone else yelled back before I heard his car start up. "I'm coming to get you under one fucking condition. You are going to promise not to hang out with these people anymore, at least not alone. That isn't funny, Daisy. They are going to get you killed. Do you understand that isn't how friends work?"

"Yeah, that's kind of how it felt. And obviously I understand this isn't how friendships should work, but, besides Dean, these have been my friends for years. It's been hard to wrap my head around the idea that they really don't care about me."

"Well, wrap your head around it quick because I'm not

going to be picking you up every time they hurt you, or waiting for them to leave you in the middle of the fucking ocean next time. This isn't funny."

"I know."

"Alright, I'll come quick, but it will still be a while. Do you have somewhere you can wait without them bothering you?"

"Yeah, I'm okay."

"Fuck, Daze. They don't even care if you're upset or scared. Why is it even fun to hang out with them?"

"It's not."

"Then I don't get it."

"It was mainly Dean. He thought it would be funny. The girls tried to tell him to stop, but I think he's just mad at me and thought it would be some kind of revenge."

"The girls I know would kick my fucking ass if I did that to another girl. I wouldn't be walking. Get better friends, Daze."

"Maybe I just stop hanging out anytime he's around."

He huffed again but didn't argue more.

"I'll be there soon. Just stay out of sight of Dean."

KYE MADE IT FORTY-FIVE MINUTES LATER, HIS CAR REVVING loud as he pulled into a parking spot. He didn't see me at first, but he still got out and walked to the front of his car. He leaned back on his hood and pulled out his phone, calling me.

"I'm here," he said, still annoyed.

"I see that."

He looked around but still didn't see me. He looked good, even from this distance. His hat was turned backwards, his glasses hiding any hint of his blue eyes, and I still couldn't get over how hot I found him.

High school me would be laughing at myself that Kye Baker was the one making me lose my damn mind.

"So you called me out here to stalk me?" he asked. Finally, he broke into a small smile.

"Yeah, it's so much easier when the person you're stalking comes to you. It really beats having to track you down."

"Good choice. You couldn't keep up with me even if you tried to stalk me."

"Is that a challenge to try to stalk you? How do you know I couldn't keep up?"

"Because you watch me shift my car like it's another wonder of the world to you. I really doubt you could."

"I guess we will never know," I said, not able to stop the smile that had come over me.

He laughed, the deep sound reverberating through the phone, and I could see him sit back against the hood. "You think I can't get you set up in a car to race me to test that?"

"Like I said, I guess we will never know." I didn't hide my laugh, my entire life feeling so much lighter now.

He laughed again and looked around. "Are you coming out of hiding so we can go? I don't know if I feel like playing a game of hide-and-seek."

"Really? I would have thought you would like that type of thing."

"You think I like children's games?"

"No. You just seem so feral. I would have guessed the hunting someone down was some sort of fantasy or something."

Without missing a beat, his eyes flashed to mine, and I gasped that he found me so easily. "Interesting that you know about those types of fantasies. I wouldn't think a girl like you even knew that was a thing. Projecting your own fantasies onto me, maybe?" he asked.

I stepped out from behind the tree, in full view of him now. "Not projecting, just making educated guesses."

"Educated guesses based on what?" he asked, pushing off the car and facing me. There was easily a hundred feet between us, maybe more, but it felt like too much now.

The thought of Kye stalking over here to kiss me was all-consuming. The heat moved down my spine until my thighs clenched.

Somehow I had spent the day around Dean and the guys, but Kye was the one making me hot and bothered.

And I wasn't even near him yet.

"Guesses based on you being one step away from a wild animal."

"Is this because of the fight the other day?" he asked.

"Yes."

"And that's why we haven't talked at all? Because you think I'm wild."

"Yes."

"And you're scared of me?"

"A little."

"But you called me for a ride?"

"I didn't know of anyone else who would come out here to get me. Besides my dad, at least, but I wasn't about to tell him about this."

"So once again, you're scared of me, but you need my help. Seems like we've been here before."

"I'm sorry," I whispered.

"For what?"

"Being scared of you, but still asking for your help. Repeatedly, apparently."

I could see him grin from here, and I struggled not to smile back.

"Can't blame a girl for being smart. Get in the car, Daze."

"Are you sure?"

"Get your ass over here and get in the damn car, Daisy," he said, but it wasn't as angry as I would have expected. If anything, it was full of humor.

Maybe Kye could be vicious, and a little scary, but he came out here to get me. To make sure I was safe and got home tonight.

And as scary as he could be, I knew right then he wasn't going to hurt me.

TWELVE
KYE

IT WASN'T until she was safely in my passenger seat that I felt like I could take my first full breath of the day.

When she told me she was spending the day out with Dean, something had settled in my gut that made me want to puke.

I didn't like it.

There was no way a guy like him wanted to hang out with his ex, the girl he thought was currently dating me, unless he had a plan.

I thought he might hurt her feelings. I didn't think he would actually put her in physical danger.

If she was scared of deep water and panicked too much, she could have drowned.

"You aren't driving at death speeds. Why?" she asked.

"I assumed you've had enough of being an adrenaline junkie today."

"No. I've had enough of being thrown off boats today. Go ahead. I want to know what it's like to go your death speeds."

I knew my eyebrows were furrowing hard, and I avoided looking over at her. "Are you going to explain why?"

"Because I want to do it? I want to see what it's like in the car with you. Go fast. As fast as you can."

"I mean, less than an hour ago, you were telling me how scared you were of me," I said, laughing. She was apparently terrified of me, but now wanted to race? "It's dangerous."

"You do it all the time!"

"Not with you in the car."

"Come on. There's literally miles of no one. Look," she said, pointing to the road.

It really was an empty road and I could probably go for miles without another person. We were close to town, but this route rarely had people on it. It's one of the main reasons the crew and I would go this way often. I slowed, trying to decide. I knew I was reckless, but she wasn't.

But she should know what it feels like if she wanted to.

Before I could think about it more, four cars surrounded us. Circling the car and revving engines.

Daisy grabbed my arm. "What is happening?"

"We're being kidnapped, or maybe just robbed," I said with a laugh, my eyes glued on her hand grabbing my arm. I waited and waited, but nothing but warmth spread over me.

"Kye!"

"It's my friends, relax." I grabbed the radio, shaking her off. "I'm about to go as fast as I can down this road. Daisy would like to see what happens."

"Daisy?" Scout asked.

"What's fast for you, Kye? Like eighty?" Ash said.

"Are you driving?" I asked.

"Yep. Let's gooooooo."

"Shit," I said, already laughing.

"Sorry, she's all wound up tonight," Fox said. "She's going to kick your ass on the road or mine if we stay home, so please give her a real race."

Ash took their car, revving it up on the passenger side of mine.

"Hey, Daisy!" she said over the radio. "Are you coming over tonight?"

"If she's not scared to death of all of us, yes, she is," I said, not even asking her.

I didn't know what the hell was wrong with me, but I didn't even want to risk asking her if she wanted to. I just wanted her to, and I wasn't sure how to take that.

"Can we go, please?" Jax asked. "I am hungry."

I rolled my eyes and put the radio back, honking once to Ash before we both took off.

I pushed the car hard, hitting the shifter until I ran out of gears, hitting a hundred in seconds and still kept pushing. Ash stayed by my side, then hit her nitrous and pulled out ahead of me fast.

I kept up for another minute before slowing.

We made it back down to seventy before I grabbed the radio again. "That was cheating."

"I'm supposed to tell you there were no rules. But I agree with you," Fox said, whispering the last part.

I looked over at Daisy, whose knuckles were white as she gripped the harness. "You okay?"

She didn't say anything, staring out the windshield.

"Daze?" I reached for her hand, my stomach clenching as my fingers ran along hers before pulling away.

I slowed down a little more as everyone else caught up.

"Back to the garage," Ransom said, veering off at our exit, and we all followed.

"Daisy," I said again, and she finally looked over at me.

"You do *that* all the time?"

"Yeah, but it's hard to get that much open road. When we race at events, we might go faster in shorter times."

"Faster?"

"Yes."

"How are you alive?"

"Harnesses, roll cages, well-built cars, various other safety things. You okay?"

"Yeah, I'm fine. Shocked, but fine."

"I'm assuming you don't want to come over now?"

"What, no? I mean, I'm nervous about actually meeting your friends, but I wanted to hang out tonight. I'm surprised you wanted me to."

"I figured you would be over it after that."

"Over it? No. Like I said, I'm just shocked. That was... fun."

I almost hit the brakes. "Did you just say you had fun doing that? You liked something so dangerous and illegal?"

"Yeah, that was fun. With you driving, I don't feel unsafe, so it was just...fun."

"Shit, that was not what I was expecting. Can I go more? Not that fast, of course, but get back to the garage?"

"Yeah, I'm good. Go."

I did, weaving around the crew's cars and drifting corners until we were at the garage.

By the time I parked, she looked terrified again. I wasn't surprised, but I thought she would have grown a little used to it by the second round. Maybe it was something that she would never get used to.

Which would make sense, since she may never be in my car to do it again.

I pulled off my harness, and she still hadn't moved. The rest of the crew was already parked and heading around back.

"Daze?" I asked for what felt like the hundredth time. When she didn't respond, I could only huff and lean over, unclipping her harness and trying to pull it off. When she stayed frozen, I leaned in more, pulling it over her.

She turned, her face only an inch from mine now.

I sucked in a breath, not knowing what to do. I could smell her body wash again, feel her breath on my face and the heat rolling off of her. All it was making me want to do was lean in.

I didn't have to, though, because she did.

I froze as her lips pressed against mine. The soft kiss made every part of me burn, the heat moving through my veins and giving me that same high that it had before.

She hesitated for a second but didn't stop. Her tongue moved along my lips, and I parted them more. It wasn't that I didn't know how to kiss, I had some experience, but every intimate interaction was tangled in the blinding hate for people touching me, so I wasn't sure how to go about it when I liked it. I thought it would be that way with her again, but just like each time before, my body was in peaceful bliss.

I almost hated it more than the pain.

How could I suddenly like being touched? And was it just her or was I cured of this suddenly?

I pulled back, my eyes wide as the panic set in. "Do you want me to take you home?"

"What? No? You think I kiss you and that means I want to leave?" she asked, almost laughing.

"I don't really know what it means. A bit ago you said you were scared of me, then you're asking me to speed, then this."

Her hand came up, and I winced, trying to hide it as her fingers settled on my jaw and ran along it.

"Do you want me to leave?" she asked quietly.

I didn't say anything. My mind focused on her fingers moving down my face and then my neck until it finally fell away.

"No. No, I'm fine. Come on," I said through gritted teeth, already kicking the door open and taking a deep breath of cool fall air. The sun was setting now, the chill that came in at night already here, and it cooled my body that was on fire.

I had grown used to a few people over the years, like the crew, but it took time. Even Carly had been here two years and it wasn't until recently that I really settled into touching her here and there. I still avoided everyone whenever I could, but I knew it was inevitable with certain things.

This, though, it didn't feel real. My body somehow calmed and burned anytime Daisy touched me, and I could already feel the nagging in the pit of my stomach that I wanted to try it again.

I wanted her to kiss me again, but there was no way I could ask.

She had got out and walked around to me, the smile on her face making me want to smile back, but I forced myself not to.

"Wow," she said. "That was like a pure shot of adrenaline, but in a good way."

"One of the best highs you can get," I said, wishing my brain didn't want to add kissing her on that list.

"Are your friends going to be dicks to me?"

"If you're asking if they are going to throw you in front of a car or something, no, they are cool. They will be dicks to me, though."

"Why?"

"Because I'm showing up with you."

We were walking around the back of the shop when she stopped dead in her tracks.

"What? Why? Do they know we are just fake dating?"

"Yeah, they already know the main points of what's going on and why. At least, why for me, not for you."

Her chest rose and fell, the panic in her eyes clear.

"Calm down," I said, stepping a little closer. "Nothing bad is going to happen."

"What if they are all just hitting on me all night? What if they grab at me? Are you going to care to stop them? What if they say nasty things to me? And do you really think telling me to calm down works?"

"What the fuck?" I asked. "Who the fuck have you been hanging out with all the time? You think they are going to *grab* you?"

"I'm nervous! Dean's friends were assholes to me, and I just had to sit there and take it. He thought it was funny and would go along with it. I don't know what to expect. Based on you, your friends will be even more scary than his."

"I can guarantee that none of that will happen. I would give my damn car with that guarantee. Not only would I fight any of my friends that treated you anything like that, none of them would. Unfortunately for them, they seem to all have a thing for strong, demanding, stubborn women. Don't be fooled by any single one of us or our looks. We would lay down and let any one of you run us over before we thought we were in charge or hurt you." I laughed harder. "Some of these guys might let their girls do it for less. I don't know much about Dean, but I promise none of the guys think they could get away with any of that shit, and they don't want to."

"You're serious?"

"About as serious you can be about getting run over," I said. "You can run the world here, Daze, and no one is going to make you feel less than that."

She finally got quiet, but I knew it wouldn't last long.

I went around the fire, introducing her to everyone. I figured she already knew Ransom, Fox, Jax, and Scout from high school, but I still named them off, explaining that Ransom was with Quinn, Fox was dating Ash, Jax was with Carly, and Scout was now dating Chase.

"So, you all work together?"

They looked around at each other, but Quinn spoke up.

"Yes, in a very messy way. We all work at the garage in some capacity, but Ash's dad has a big racing empire that we all do things at, too. Ash, Scout, Fox and hopefully Kye all race with him. Carly is an amazing chef and not only feeds us all, but runs her social media cooking business stuff. Ransom and I run and organize most of the garage stuff now, since everyone else is so busy. Has Kye told you about his racing?"

Daisy looked at me, and then back at Quinn. "A little, but nothing more than wanting to race with Holt. I mean, we met with him, but they didn't talk about the racing part much, just the Kye messing up part."

"Quinn, can we not?" I asked, not needing Daisy to know more about me, and already knowing what Quinn was going to say. I guess I should have thought more about that when I brought her here, though.

"No, we absolutely can."

"We're the embarrassing family that wants to tell everyone how proud of our little Kye we are," Jax said.

"I'm going to kill you."

"Ha. You'll have to get through Carly first."

"Hiding behind your girlfriend again?"

"Always."

I groaned, but Quinn continued.

"We can't help that we're proud of you and want to tell her. He's amazing, Daisy. He's going to be one of the best racers in the country, and that's if he doesn't become a professional stunt driver," Quinn said, beaming at me.

"Is she serious?" Daisy asked, looking at me as her eyebrows jumped up.

"We can only hope," I said.

Quinn shook her head. "Fine, Kye. Since you are only going to talk less and less if we talk about you, I'll ask Daisy questions."

Daisy moved closer, her hand going down on the bench between us, and I realized it was because she wanted to touch me.

And fuck my life that I wanted her to.

I moved my hand the smallest amount closer until our pinkies were nearly touching. I ignored the way my heart rate picked up and tried to focus on the conversation again.

"Tell us about you, Daisy. What are you doing out with Kye tonight?" Carly asked, leaning back against Jax and looking at me with a smile.

"Oh, and what do you think of Kye and all of us now?" Scout asked.

Daisy let out a hard breath and leaned the smallest amount closer to me, her hand sliding across the bench until we were touching.

"Honestly, I just spent the day with my so-called friends and my ex-boyfriend, who threw me off a boat. And really, if you would have asked me a few weeks ago which group was more likely to try to get me killed, I would have said you guys without a doubt, but obviously I was wrong, so there is now zero judgment of you all from me. I literally went death warp speed a bit ago, and that still felt safer than being on a boat with my friends. At this point, I literally know nothing about how to read people, so even if you all sucked, I may not notice, but I don't think you do. And besides that, I was hanging out with Kye because he was the only one I thought I could call that would one, actually show up, and two, not judge me to no end for what happened."

They all stared at her, silent and mouths open, until Carly got up and walked to the cooler. "*Honestly,*" she said. "It sounds like you could use a drink."

"Or maybe ten," Scout added, her eyes wide as she looked at me.

Carly handed her a drink, and for the first time since picking her up, she relaxed, letting me relax right along with her.

In the mess of my doubts, I couldn't shake the feeling that bringing her tonight wasn't the smartest move. But deep down, I knew it was the one I wanted.

THIRTEEN

DAISY

KYE WAS SO close to me now that I could feel the heat rolling off of him. I still couldn't understand what was happening. We were fake dating, using each other for outings and meetings, but then here we were. He had invited me back here tonight and seemed content sitting by me.

He did not seem all that interested in making out, though. The guy had been a statue when I kissed him, and I almost died of embarrassment.

I kept throwing myself at him, and he kept kindly reminding me he wasn't interested.

But then he was asking me to hang out more and sitting as close as he could without touching me.

Although now his hand was up against mine, and I was trying to figure out if that was on purpose or not.

I thought Kye would be uninterested or way too interested. This strange middle ground was confusing.

"Having fun yet?" he asked before taking a swig of his drink. He seemed so relaxed and calm. It was such a difference to the guy I always saw stalking around school and parties.

"I really can't believe you are all so nice," I said quietly. "And you would fight your friends before letting them get away with being an ass to me?"

"Absolutely. Honestly, though, I would fight for a lot less," he said with a smirk.

"I don't believe it. The fighting friends part. Obviously you're happy to fight."

"Do you think none of us have ever got into a fistfight? These guys would kill me if I was honestly rude to the girls." He shook his head and looked around, his eyes falling on Ransom.

"Alright, honest question for you all. If I was mean to any one of the girls, would you hit me?" Kye asked.

A round of yes's echoed, but Chase spoke up.

"I don't think it's the guys you need to worry about hitting you, though. If you insult one of them, I'm pretty sure they all take it personally."

"All vipers," Fox said to me. "And they will go for the throat."

I looked at each of the girls, each one smiling and laughing. None of them looked particularly scary, but they weren't disagreeing.

"Obviously, her ex-boyfriend's friends were assholes. I'm just trying to prove my point that while we can be assholes, she is fine here."

"You're more than fine here," Ash said. "These guys love us. They aren't going to be mean to you in any way."

"Come on," Kye said, his arm moving to rest on the bench behind me. He still wasn't touching me, but it felt close enough. "Just relax. You don't have to keep up any appearances here."

I was supposed to relax with him this close? The guy who had both beat a guy up in front of me and drove nearly an hour to come pick me up when I needed him.

"Fake dating appearances or all appearances?" I asked.

"All the fake appearances. Including the *I'm a perfect prom queen* appearance you seem to think you have to do."

"You're one to talk. You are sitting awfully close for someone who doesn't need to keep up appearances on fake dating me."

He shrugged. "Maybe I just want to? If I want to sit close, I sit close. Do you need me to move?"

"No. Do you always just do whatever you want?"

"I mean, yeah, do you not?"

"No. Not at all. Not even a little. There are rules and expectations. Won't your friends think something else is going on?"

"I'm sure they are thinking a lot."

"And you don't care? They know this isn't real."

"I don't think you understand how little I care about what other people think. Call me self-centered, but I don't spend my days thinking about how other people see me. You shouldn't either. Obviously, I care about what my friends think to some extent, but what I do is none of their business. And when you leave with me tonight, that is none of their business, and when you spend the night at my place, that is still none of their business. I don't know why you think everything and anything needs to not only be on display, but talked about to everyone. That is not how I do things."

"I guess with Dean, it had to be. He told his friends every

detail, shared every intimate thing he could, and then it was just ammunition to use against me when they needed it." I looked at the fire, and then back at him, my eyebrows furrowing hard. "Did you say I'm staying at your apartment tonight?"

"Yeah? I wasn't planning on bringing you back to your dad's after you've been drinking. I assumed that was obvious."

"I mean, I would prefer not to because he's like a drug-sniffing dog if I have alcohol on my breath, but I didn't actually think you would want me to stay over."

"I don't really care. I have a couch to sleep on or a big enough bed," he said, the words a normal conversation for him, but it made my stomach flip.

It wasn't like I went to bed with a lot of people, but I didn't usually go to bed with guys who seemed so uninterested in me.

"If you want to leave now instead, I can take you home."

"No, I'm alright. I would rather stay."

"Whatever you want. I'm just saying be yourself and do whatever the fuck you want to do when you're with me. No judgment, no anger over it, nothing."

"Interesting. If that's the case, I would like another drink," I said with a smile. He laughed, the deep sound hitting me again and making a shiver run down my spine.

I went to stand, but he pulled me back down, his fingers clamped down on my wrist.

"Ransom, toss me a drink," he said.

Everyone froze, turning to us and looking at Kye's hand holding onto me and pulling me back down.

They didn't say a word, their eyes locked on us, until Kye finally dropped my wrist.

"The drink?" he asked, nodding to Ransom.

They all snapped out of it, going back to their conversations, but still glancing our way.

So much for doing what I wanted. If they thought Kye touching my wrist made them freak out like that, I was pretty sure crawling into his lap to kiss him again was off-limits.

THE RIDE TO HIS APARTMENT WASN'T FAR, AND I WAS surprised when we pulled up to a four-story brick building.

"Isn't this the old firehouse?" I asked.

"Yeah. It was a long time ago. We converted the entire place into apartments for all of us."

"Oh. How did I not know that?"

"I mean, it's not a secret, but I don't exactly go around telling people where we all live. I think you can imagine why after the other night."

"I guess that does make sense," I said, watching as a garage door opened and he pulled inside.

My stomach clenched, nervous about walking into Kye's apartment. I wasn't sure what to expect from what the place looked like, and I definitely wasn't sure what to expect from him still.

We got out, and I turned to the door.

"Not that one," he said, his hand moving to my lower back. His fingers pressed against me, turning me to the door on the left. I sucked in a breath, holding it until his hand fell away.

One touch on my lower back and I was ready to throw myself at him again.

We made it up the three flights to his apartment, and he

waved me inside, shutting the door and immediately started to throw his stuff on the counter.

"Do you want something to drink?"

"Yes, some water would be great. I don't drink a lot, so even those three cocktails have me preparing for a hangover."

He handed me a cup and headed to the bathroom as he pulled off his shoes and shirt.

"Get comfortable however you want. TV, remote, food, bed." He pointed out each item as though I couldn't find a TV or fridge in a studio apartment.

I sat back on the bed, looking around. It was all dark. The walls painted a deep blue and nothing bright laying anywhere, but it was comfortable. It was like a little cave, the dark, soft blankets only making it cozier.

"I like your apartment. Even if the only decorations seem to be trophies and pictures of car things."

I heard the shower turn on, surprised that the door was still partially open. He seemed to hesitate about everything sexual, and I wasn't sure if this was some sort of invitation from him.

"I don't really need to decorate more. What am I going to get? Those little signs with sayings on them, throw pillows? I don't need any of that stuff. I want my bed, a comfortable couch, a nice TV, and enough food to not go hungry," he said, walking out of the bathroom a few minutes later with a towel wrapped around his waist.

"Wow, I'm getting the picture come to life," I said. He flashed a smile and then it really was the picture come to life, down to the dimples that seemed to emerge when he was really smiling.

And it was so much better in person.

"Daze," he said, stopping me as I headed into the bathroom. "Here." He threw me a t-shirt. "It should cover everything for you."

"Oh, thanks." I went in, cleaning up and changing before coming out to a dark room, the TV on and lighting everything up enough to see.

Kye was already in bed, one arm stretched behind him as he clicked through what to watch.

"Are you naked?"

He jumped, seemingly not hearing me come out.

"Completely."

"Are you—"

"Kidding? Yes." He pulled back the covers, revealing shorts on but no shirt.

"Oh, okay."

"Glad to know the horror that you would think if I was, though," he said, still laughing.

"No, I just… Honestly, I'm not sure what to expect right now."

"Expect? Do you think I am planning a sneak attack or something? We are watching a movie and going to bed. You can sleep here or on the couch. Both are reasonably comfortable."

"But that's the only reason you invited me over? To sleep?"

"You keep saying these things and it's making me wonder if you want me to try to sleep with you. I told you, it was less awkward than dropping you off half drunk to your dad. Although, now that I say it that way, that would be a funnier plan. His face if me, of all people, brought you to the door drunk. What a missed opportunity."

"That would be the farthest thing from funny. Somehow, I would be grounded again, even if it is legal for me to drink," I said, as he landed on a scary movie. "No, no chance that I'm watching that. I'll be terrified."

"It's hardly a scary movie. It's one of the lesser scary movies, and you will have me here all night. I won't let any monsters get to you."

"If I get scared, I'm turning it off."

"Fine." He clicked play, putting us in darkness for seconds before opening right to a scary scene.

"Kye," I groaned, rolling into him, burying my head into the pillow.

"Daze," he said, mocking my tone.

"So we are literally watching a scary movie and going to sleep? You aren't making any move on me?"

"You seem to really think this is all me manipulating you to sleep together? I don't want to sleep with you, Daisy."

"Ouch," I said, shrinking back into the blankets.

He groaned. "I just mean that I wasn't trying to get you over here to fuck you. I just thought we would sleep. You don't have to feel like this is a game or trick or something."

I stayed snuggled back in the pillows, pulling the blanket higher up on my chest.

"Wow. You know, if you had told me two weeks ago that Kye likes to cuddle and sleep and not try to have sex with the half-naked girl in his bed, I would have bet everything that you were lying. This is the weirdest night of my life. You are the weirdest man I've ever met. "

"Funny enough, I have never cuddled and I rarely, if I ever at all, have half-naked girls in my bed, so two weeks ago, you would have been correct. And really, I gotta keep you on your toes."

"It's working. And what does all that mean? You don't have girls over?"

"Nothing. We can talk about it later."

We laid like that for another twenty minutes, Kye seeming very content with our position and the movie because he still hadn't made a move on me.

And it wasn't fair that it was turning me on more. The voice in my head screamed at him to touch me. My body felt like a magnet, a constant buzzing demanding that I touch him.

I finally couldn't hold it back.

"Are you really not going to touch me at all?"

"You...want me to?" He seemed so surprised, and I wasn't sure why. How was this not a standard night for him? I pictured him as a womanizer, and now here he was, acting like me wanting more was a surprise.

"I mean, yeah?"

He was laughing now. "Does this mean you're making a move on me?"

"No," I said. "I mean, I just wanted *you* to make a move on *me*."

"And you're entitled to get everything you want?"

"No, but that doesn't mean I don't want it still."

"We're not sleeping together."

"But does that mean everything is off the table, then?"

"I guess I didn't think that far ahead. I didn't think you would be expecting anything else."

"I honestly don't see what the issue is if we sleep together."

"The issue is that would make a bigger mess of this fake dating thing," he said, rolling to face me more.

"How? I can handle sleeping together and still fake date."

He rolled his eyes, but he still reached out, his hand only an inch from my arm now. "I can tell you that we sure as hell aren't making this decision when you've had alcohol and you're all horny."

I grabbed his hand, setting it on my hip, and closing my eyes. It was somehow everything I needed while making the need for him worse. He might be somewhat right because I was a little drunk and horny.

"No sex, Daze," he murmured.

"Fine," I growled, laying back. "Does that mean everything is completely off the table?"

"Are you trying to ask me nicely to get you off?" he asked, the confusion genuine.

"Yes, *please*," I begged. "I've been staring at you for days, wondering why you weren't ripping my clothes off and wanting to rip yours off. I'll take anything at this point."

His eyebrows furrowed as he looked me over. "What do you want me to do, exactly?" His hand moved from my hip, the light touch of his fingers moving over my stomach and thighs. I shivered, but the gentle movement wasn't enough.

"Keep going," I whispered. His hand hesitated, and I grabbed it, pulling it further between my thighs.

He took over, running down until he ran along my wetness, and I arched into him. He groaned, moving over me again.

"Do you want me to get you off?" I asked, trying to sound sweeter.

"No. I want you to lie here, not touch me, and you get off," he said. He was near me, but he wasn't against me, the few inches still between us feeling like we were still too far from each other. His hand pressed between my legs, his fingers pushing against me slightly.

He kicked back the blankets and moved over top of me. Two strong arms caged me in, the dark shadows casting over him, turning him back into the Kye that I didn't know. The one that was scary and dangerous and unpredictable.

I gasped again as he shifted his body and pushed his fingers into me with one hard thrust. "I like you over top of me. I feel like I have a wild animal over me, ready to do my bidding and make me cum," I said, smiling now.

"And you like that control? You want me on a leash?"

"Not a leash necessarily. More like cage you here on the bed so that I'm the only option you have to let out whatever this is. I like knowing someone like you would turn all that reckless energy onto me, onto pleasing me." I moaned. "I can only imagine what it would feel like if you let it all loose to fuck me. Every reckless thing you do, every wild, dangerous thing, I want to feel that on my body."

His head dropped, his teeth running along my neck. "You are filthy," he muttered. He pushed another finger into me harder now and my eyes flew open at the fullness.

"Maybe I do need a leash for you. I think I am suddenly the prey," I said.

"You need to stop talking like that before I lose my mind."

"Now that only makes me want to talk more." I ran my hands up his arms and down his chest to his stomach, reaching into his pants and wrapping my hands around his cock.

"Oh, wow," I said. "Now I'm not so sure I want you to go feral and fuck me. That is a little intimidating."

"*Stop* talking about me fucking you as you're touching my dick."

Watching Kye come undone with my touch was powerful. A power that I suddenly craved. Every part of his self control seemed to be unraveling and I couldn't let myself stop it.

I tightened my grip, sliding up the length of him.

"Daisy," he said, dropping his head with a groan.

With a growl, he pulled away, getting up onto his knees in between my legs. My mouth fell open at the sight and for a moment, I thought he was really going to break and actually have sex with me.

His fingers moved back, teasing slow circles around my clit. "I know you don't actually want that, and I know you don't want to ruin the facade you have. I will not be doing that and I'm sure as fuck not doing it after you've been drinking." His own hand wrapped around his cock, moving over the length as he pushed his fingers into me. "I'll still get you off, though."

His fingers sped up, pushing into me harder as his hand around his cock moved faster. I had never experienced anything like it.

"This might be the hottest thing I've ever seen," I said, moving my hand down to rub my clit as his fingers fucked me. "I thought I wanted all that power on me, but I like this, too. Did you have to do that because of me?" I asked, panting.

"Yes," he said through gritted teeth. "Fuck," he murmured, but I couldn't care what it was about. Every part of me tightened, the orgasm crashing over me. I knew I yelled out his name again, and he said something else, but I was lost. Everything went black for a few seconds before I could feel again. His fingers slowed and pulled out of me.

My chest heaved, the orgasm wracking my body until I couldn't move.

"Fuck, Daisy," he said, moving off the bed to go into the bathroom and coming back to clean me up.

"What?"

"You are more of a handful than I anticipated."

"I could say the same about you. My hand was definitely full," I said, laughing.

His mouth fell open with a smile. "Who would have thought my little Daisy flower was fucking dirtier and hornier than me? No one would have ever guessed." He grabbed another pair of shorts and climbed back into bed.

"I am not."

"You just begged me to fuck you and when I didn't, you got off to me, getting off to you. You're filthy. Just admit it."

"No."

He laid down a little closer this time, but didn't touch me more, and didn't seem to want me to touch him again.

"Come on, admit it to me. Admit that you like all those dirty thoughts you have about me and are dying to fuck me." He laughed, enjoying this way too much now.

"Fine. Fine, maybe I am. But it's ridiculous, you're right. After I wake up, my thoughts will be a lot more clear."

"Good girl. Get some sleep."

"Did you just praise me for saying that I *won't* want to sleep with you in the morning?"

"Yes." He leaned in, kissing my head. "I've always been expecting the perfect prom queen that wouldn't dream of touching someone as dangerous or dirty as me, so the fact that she is already coming back means you were just hot and bothered tonight and you'll keep yourself at a distance from me still. Go to sleep."

"Does that mean we can sleep together?"

"Yes, sleep."

"You know what I meant."

"No, that means that our plan is working out just fine as is and can end soon enough without a problem. Now, please. Go. To. Sleep."

I laid there awake longer, hearing Kye's breathing turn deeper, and I knew he was sleeping now.

He was right. The plan was working. Everyone thought we were dating. Sometimes I even felt like we were. He had been right. Keeping sex out of this really did make it easier.

The problem was, even without the sex, I was already craving his touch.

FOURTEEN
KYE

I WALKED into the garage the next morning unprepared for the crew. I honestly should have expected it, but I was still reeling from what happened last night.

"Hey, Lover Boy!" Carly yelled, and I immediately groaned. While I was close with everyone in the crew, Carly had quickly, and surprisingly, become my best friend. Somehow, our dislike for people made us like each other.

I should have known she was going to be the one to give me the most shit for Daisy coming yesterday. Riot ran up to me, immediately flipping onto his back for me to pet him.

Carly came up right behind him, smirking as she kicked at my leg. "I *said*, hey, Lover Boy."

"Oh, I heard, and I ignored it on purpose."

She laughed harder and followed me over to the car I had been working on. I had a rolling shop stool that she sat back on, and I rolled my eyes.

"I take it you aren't dropping this?" I asked.

"Dropping it? Not a damn chance. Not only am I in the group chat, but I share an apartment with Jax. I won't hear the end of this until one of us asks. What the fuck is going on? Because we all saw it, Kye."

"Saw what?" I asked, playing dumb as I turned back to start working on the car.

"Kye!" she yelled, throwing a rag at me. "We all saw you touching her. *Willingly.* And the general agreement is that you weren't touching all night, but you were sitting closer than we've ever seen you sit next to a woman."

"Yeah."

"Nope, it's going to take more than that."

"What's the group chat say?"

"Well, if you would read it, you would know, but the bullet point list ranges from you're head over heels in love, to you actually just hate all of us, to you've lost your fucking mind and we may never get you back. I might have added alien abduction as a possibility, but of course, everyone didn't want to get on board with that one."

That finally made me laugh. "I have no idea why they wouldn't go along with it. It honestly sounds like the most plausible reason."

"Agreed. You going to tell me which one it is?"

"None of the above? Somewhere in the middle of hate you all, and finding one person who doesn't make my whole body scream in pain when they are near me," I said, kicking the stool she was on until she was rolled a few feet farther from me.

Her eyes went wide, and she rolled closer. "Are you saying you are in love?"

"Hell, no. I'm saying that I might have found out that there are people in this world that I can touch without it killing me. No love needed, apparently."

"Hmmm," she said. "Sounds improbable."

"Says the girl who had bets on it being alien abduction."

"Exactly. Does this mean she will be coming around more?"

I shrugged. "Not sure. I guess it depends on how long she needs me around and how long Holt needs all this to believe me. Let's hope it only takes another week or so."

As though all of their drama alarm bells went off, the rest of the crew gathered around, but they weren't looking at me, they looked at Carly.

"Well," Jax said. "What's the verdict?"

She nodded, her face falling as though it was bad. "I was right, you guys. He was abducted." Their hopeful faces fell, shooting daggers at Carly before they glared at me.

"Come on, Kye," Fox said. "We left you alone last night. Tell us what's up."

"What's up is that Daisy had a shit day, and I thought it might be helpful for her to be around a group of friends that don't secretly hate each other."

"Yeah, that wasn't what we were talking about," Scout said, crossing her arms. I realized that all the girls were crossing their arms, and for the first time I realized it was because they were ganging up on me. Usually, it was one of the guys that they actually had to date.

"I already know how this goes, so everyone put away the claws. I have found out that there may be one or two people in this world that I can touch and not be disgusted by. No, none of you are on that list, but I promise I tolerate all of you. Daisy is apparently one of them. And before you go off like Carly did, no, I'm not suddenly in love, and yes, this will still be ending in the next week or two as long as we both accomplish what we need."

Eyes rolled, and a round of groans went through the crowd.

"Are you guys good now?" I asked, my phone going off and giving me a reason to look away from all of them.

DAISY
I'm having a party this weekend.

KYE
And?

DAISY
And you're invited?

The crew all leaned in, but only Carly managed to look at the screen. Her lips pursed together with a smile and she turned, walking away before I could yell at her.

The rest of the crew either cocked their eyebrows or narrowed their eyes, but followed after her to get the gossip, leaving me in peace.

KYE
Is this an invite like I can come if I want or is this fake boyfriend invite?

DAISY
......

KYE
Daisy.

DAISY
It's a fake boyfriend invite. A 'please show up because I decided to do this last minute to save face with the girls, and it would help if they see that we are still very much involved' type of invite.

KYE

I can make it.

She sent back a smiley face followed by a heart. My stomach flipped.

What the fuck did the heart mean?

Did that mean she was suddenly getting feelings?

Or was it just a thank you?

I looked down at the text again before looking up at the group of girls in front of me. If I asked them, there were going to be endless questions to get to the bottom of it.

And if I didn't ask them, I was going to be worrying about this constantly.

I looked back at the texts and immediately came up with a third option.

KYE

Okay, please tell me what the hell the heart means because I'm now wondering if you're going to profess your love for me or something tomorrow. I don't understand relationship things or this communication.

DAISY

Oh my god.

I forget you might not know these things.

But no. I'm totally not confessing my love or anything. It's just a thank you type of heart, not an I'm in love with you type of heart.

KYE

Honestly, the emojis make this a hundred times more confusing. When the girls send me those things I usually ignore it.

DAISY

Alright, you old man, I'll lay off the emojis.

KYE

Then I will come tomorrow.

I added a smile emoji. At least I knew what that one meant.

KYE

What are you doing tonight?

DAISY

On a Wednesday? Idk studying?

KYE

Want to come out for a drive with me?

DAISY

Absolutely yes.

I sent her back a ridiculous range of emojis and let her know what time I'd get there. Then I threw my phone aside, ignoring the wave of calm that came over me, knowing that I would see her in a few hours.

FIFTEEN
KYE

MY FAKE GIRLFRIEND was ruining my life.

I'd been thinking about her for three fucking days straight, to the point I was struggling to focus on anything else.

Now, I had agreed to come to her party that was, apparently, being held at a pool.

I walked around the back of the country club's building, already hating the entire day. There was something nagging me, though, making me know I couldn't miss this, even if I would rather just wait and take her out for a drive later tonight.

Years of hanging around the crew, driving it into my head, that I couldn't let her down over something so simple.

I didn't know when or why I cared so much, but for some reason, fate had brought Daisy into my life. I wasn't sure why, but it seemed inevitable now.

The worst part of all of it, though, I was desperate to see her.

I pulled my hat lower, trying to hide more of my face as I made it around back.

Then I saw her.

Her black bikini was covered in small little white daisy flowers, and her hair was up, clipped away and threatening to fall as she laughed.

Even looking right at her, I couldn't figure out what it was that made me feel...anything.

But fuck if I didn't feel things around her.

She looked my way, and the smile that spread over her face was real.

"Hey," she said, walking up to me. She moved to hug me, but she seemed to think better of it and froze. "For appearance's sake, could I hug you?"

It didn't matter if I could figure out why we were brought together. I just knew that for the first time in my life that I could remember, I *wanted* to touch her, and I did not deny myself what I wanted.

I moved first, pulling her in and hugging her. Her crowd of friends looked our way, but they made it less obvious than my friends about how hard they were staring.

She turned, pressing a small kiss to my lips, and I froze like always. It wasn't even that I didn't like it, but I kept waiting for the pleasure to disappear and the pain to come back.

"You taste like candy," I mumbled, leaning in further. I kissed her again, and she smiled against me. Her arms wrapped around my neck and lips parted so I could take more. And for a second, I did.

Until I realized how fast I was losing control.

I wanted her hand wrapped around my neck again, for her to kiss me like her next breath depended on it, and I was seconds from asking when I finally broke away.

I pushed back, putting space between us fast.

The fact that her smile grew only shocked me. Most people were mad when I denied them affection, not smiling and ready to spend more time with me.

"Come on, drinks and party over here."

She led me over, not reaching for my hand or hanging on me.

And I hated it.

She was doing exactly what I had told her I wanted, and now I was pissed.

What the fuck happened that I suddenly wanted affection, and what was it about Daisy that triggered it? Unless it wasn't just Daisy.

I looked around. The party was packed with girls, and I tried to look at each one as though my brain would suddenly light up and want their touch.

Nothing happened.

Maybe it was just that I hadn't been touched much in so long in an affectionate way that I had been cured and hadn't known it. Which meant I needed to find another girl that would touch me to test it.

Even the thought of it made my skin crawl, and I didn't think that was a good sign.

Daisy introduced me to a few people before I couldn't stand anymore. I needed a break from the small talk that she seemed happy to continue.

"I'm going to sit in the pool. Preferably away from everyone. Come get me if you need me for anything besides arm candy," I said, grinning.

She smiled but didn't say anything, just nodded in agreement.

I slid into the pool and pulled my hat down low. This way I was technically at the party, but I didn't have to socialize.

I could also see Daisy's every move from here.

If this was how people lived every day of their life with the opposite sex when they liked them, it really wasn't as much of a mystery to me now why the guys lost their minds trying to get their girl.

A girl swam up to me, coming way too close to only be friendly.

"Hey. Kye, right?"

"Yes," I said, not matching her friendliness at all. There was no reason to be so close to me, and I could already feel the creep of disgust moving over my skin.

"Wow, Daisy's mentioned a few things about you, but she never mentioned how hot you were. I like the whole, I'm dangerous, leave me alone thing you have going on."

"Okay," I said, sliding farther away from her. I had plenty of women come up and hang all over me, but none of them had ever been friends with my fake girlfriend, so I couldn't exactly handle it the way I always did. Which usually ranged from one of the girls in the crew stepping in or me turning and walking away immediately.

Here, I was trapped.

I moved down the wall of the pool, putting a few more feet between us, but she seemed intent on closing it again.

"Going somewhere?"

"I assume some space would be appropriate."

She looked back at Daisy, who was wrapped up in a conversation with someone, not noticing what was happening. "I don't agree. Do you not like pretty women near you?"

"No."

She laughed now, her hand resting on my arm. Bile rose in my throat and I ripped my arm away. I needed to keep my cool, but I was already so overwhelmed dealing with Daisy touching me and liking it, that I was struggling to keep control of my body's visceral reaction to this girl.

Apparently, the test of liking other people touching me had a clear outcome.

"Can you please get off of me?" I asked, taking a deep breath.

"Get you off?" Her confident hand reached down, sliding her hand along my stomach, heading towards my dick. "Are you saying that you don't find me attractive?" she asked, the purr of her voice making my skin crawl.

"That's exactly what I'm saying," I said, as her hand landed on me again.

I moved to grab it, intent on pushing her away as a body came down into the water next to me, stepping between us.

Daisy's body slid against mine, the soothing calm of her coursed through me. My arm snaked around her waist, pulling her hard against me. Every part of my body calmed, and I could finally take a breath.

"What are you doing, Sydney?" she asked.

"Just meeting your boyfriend," Sydney said with a smirk.

"Wait, this is Sydney? The girl Dean said he was going to sleep with after your breakup?" I should have known, but it didn't occur to me that Daisy would even think to invite her. "Now she's over here desperately trying to grab my dick."

"Are you serious?" Daisy asked, pushing back into me and shoving me harder into the side of the pool. Her back pushed against the front of me, and all I wanted to do was curl my body around hers.

"No, he's not serious. He was the one all over me, Daisy. Maybe keep better track of your boyfriends."

"Don't even try it, Sydney. Dean might have been a

cheater, but Kye wants nothing to do with you. Go away before you embarrass yourself anymore."

She scoffed and turned, swimming away without a word.

"Why is she here?" I asked, glad we were in the water. The touch of her washed away and was replaced with everything Daisy.

"I had a stupid idea that I could keep up appearances," she said, turning to face me. "I'm so sorry. I didn't realize she would be desperate enough to assault my boyfriend."

"Fake."

"That was implied."

"Is there somewhere I can go for a second?" I asked, taking a deep breath. "I just need a minute away from... people."

"Yeah, come on."

Her hand wrapped in mine and I held on, letting her lead me out and pull me along until she was shutting us in the pool house.

"I'm sorry about her. I really wasn't expecting that. I should have, though. It's not like it's the first time she's tried to take my boyfriend."

"It's fine. She just wanted to get under your skin."

"Yeah, it always worked with me on Dean. I would get so upset and storm off."

I leaned back, sitting on some barrels while Daisy hopped onto a few boxes across from me. "So, are you mad, then? But you didn't storm off?"

"Because I was always upset before, not mad. This time, I was pissed. Why would she think she could do that? You looked horrified. There's no reason to be mad when you're the one who was basically assaulted. Dean's face was always... lustful. He liked it."

"I *was* horrified. Not a big fan of friends who betray people or women who try to grab me so blatantly. The touching," I said, my body involuntarily shivering.

"It's funny. If you would have put you and Dean next to each other before all of this, I would have figured you would be the one to put me on edge and make me feel insecure."

"Why?" I asked, cocking an eyebrow.

"Don't even play that game. You know what you look like, what you act like," she said. "I'm not the only one who assumes it. And you know what it does to me, so I guess I should have assumed it would do it to other people, too."

"I didn't realize I was doing anything to you."

She reached out, moving to swat at my knee with a smile, but I flinched away.

Her eyebrows furrowed as she looked at me, but didn't ask more about it. "But I don't set *you* on edge like that? Or do you just hate me touching you in any way?" she asked.

I let out a hard breath, knowing it was time to come clean. I wasn't even sure how to tell her that I couldn't stand to be touched, but then to add on that out of everyone I'd ever met, I like *her* touching me. If I kept trying to hide it, though, this was only going to get messier.

But I knew I sounded out of my mind.

This was a fake relationship, and I worried telling her that would make it all too real.

"I need to tell you something," I said. I could hit and fight without a second thought, but telling someone new that I hated being touched made me want to gouge my eyes out.

It was going to be better to just jump right in and lay it all out. There were going to be questions, so I started from the beginning.

"So, I was beaten pretty much every day of my life. I

think every inch of me has been covered in bruises at some point, and I've had broken bones more than once from the beatings," I said.

Her eyes didn't leave mine, the horrified look in them almost painful. "Kye," she whispered, but I continued.

"Even after I moved in with the crew at the apartment building, I would have to go home a few times a week just to be beat. We were doing some pretty illegal things back then and my choices were not to not go back and have the cops all over us, or go back, take the beating, and get to go back to my life. I think the guys saw what was happening, what I was choosing between, and helped us not do those illegal things anymore. They always felt bad because I was younger, but I never cared. The minutes I spent outside that house were good, illegal activities or not. It wasn't until I was eighteen that I really had a chance to break free from it," I said, leaning back, my chest heaving now as I tried to find anything to calm myself.

"Come over here," I said, sounding way more angry than I felt. Her eyes went wide, but she jumped down. She took one careful step towards me and stopped. "Come here, Daisy."

She finally did, and I grabbed her hands, placing each one on my chest and letting my head fall back. A tingling warmth went through me, the world falling away as the calm warmth spread over me.

"I guess the damage was done, though, because I haven't been able to deal with people touching me since. I can deal with the crew now. Their hugs and stuff, but they try to avoid it for my sake. When I said I wasn't affectionate, it's because it's physically painful and disgusting. I don't kiss people. Sex is the worst. I have to make the other person realize that they can't touch me, like palms down flat on the bed and don't move, which doesn't go well for most girls. The times I've made it further than that, I've tried to get it over with as fast as I can. It's never felt good because I'm so worried about the touching. My brain is screaming the entire time. Rationally, I know that person isn't there to beat the shit out of me, but my body doesn't care. It's tense to the point that light touches actually hurt. Hands on me hurt, Daisy. Even Sydney doing that. As soon as she got close, every muscle tightened until it was painful, and I can't stop it. It takes so long for my body to uncoil that I feel like I've worked out for days, even if I've only been sitting there for a few minutes. I've never found anything to stop it. If it's not painful, it's horrifyingly gross. My stomach churns, and that feeling of disgust just washes over me."

Her hands jerked away, but I grabbed them, forcing them back onto my bare chest.

"Don't," I said. "It's helping."

"But you *just* said you hate being touched."

"I do. I fucking hate it so much. I've hit people for doing it. Even accidentally, I've hit them. I've yelled, and screamed, and fought against it."

"Then let me take my hands off of you, Kye. I didn't realize that's what you meant. You should have told me sooner. I've touched you so much. I've kissed you," she said, talking faster now. Her face fell, and she finally looked me in the eye. "Oh my god, Kye, I've made you kiss me repeatedly! I've literally jumped on top of you."

"Yeah, that was the shock of a fucking lifetime, because I felt none of that."

"So you like me touching you?" she asked quietly.

"Yes. I never want it to stop. This has never felt good to me until you."

I pulled off my hat and her soft hands moved up my neck until they pushed into my hair. My head dropped towards her and I could only groan at the sensation.

"Why?"

"I have no idea." Her hands moved back down, over my neck, my chest, my arms and then over my stomach, going over the same place Sydney had just been. "It erases it. You move your hands over me and it undoes it. Every muscle calms down until I can breathe again. It's warm and soft and soothing, and I have no idea why."

She stepped between my legs, getting closer. I held my breath as she reached up, placing a soft kiss on my lips.

"For the first time in my life," I said, "I can be touched, but I keep assuming that it's going to end. That suddenly, it will hurt again when you touch me."

"I hope it doesn't," she whispered against my lips. "You deserve to feel how good it is, to have it not hurt." Her hands hadn't stopped moving over my back and shoulders. "Do you want me to touch you more or keep our distance still?"

"No, I want you to touch me until it hurts again," I said, the painful tone to my voice making me want to die in embarrassment, but there was nothing I could do.

"Have you thought about the fact that you could just be getting better? Like it could be anyone touching you, and maybe it doesn't hurt anymore?"

"I did think that," I said, already knowing that wasn't what was happening. It would still hurt, except with her. "Sydney just proved that wrong."

I cut her off, kissing her again. I didn't want to think about this ending or about experimenting with my body with anyone else again right now. For once, I liked the calm, and I wanted to hold on to that.

I already knew it would still be different with other people. There was something about Daisy that was different, not me.

She leaned in harder for a second, swiping her tongue against my lips before moving against mine. It didn't take long before I was losing my mind.

Her hands moved down, resting over my hard cock as she kept kissing me. "Does this mean you are fine with me touching you here? Or should I stop?"

"No, it's okay. Keep going," I breathed. I tried to focus on every brush of her fingers and push of her palm against me, but my head started to spin.

"So have you had a blowjob before, then?"

"Yes."

"And? Did that at least feel good?"

"No."

"No?"

"I think I flinched more than anything and never got off." I tried to laugh it off, but my voice gave me away. I hated admitting to any of this. I knew the wild range of thoughts people had when I did tell them that I couldn't be touched, and I never actually admitted to anyone exactly how little sexual experience I had. It's not that I couldn't figure it all out. I had just never wanted to.

Until now, apparently.

Daisy's hand still moved over my cock and I pushed against her, wishing there was nothing between us now.

"Does that mean you might want to try it now?"

Her fingers moved along the seam of my shorts, and I didn't stop her. Instead, I nodded.

Her face lit up with a smile, and she moved to undo my shorts completely when someone started banging on the door.

"Daisy!" a girl yelled. "We're out of beer, and need you to find more."

"Can you give me a few minutes?" she yelled back.

"No! Get your ass out here and take care of us," the girl yelled, laughing as she banged on the door again.

"It's alright," I said. "Go take care of your party."

"Are you sure? I really don't mind staying in here to take care of you." Her eyebrows jumped as she smiled, but I shook my head.

"Maybe some other time. Come on." I jumped down, angling her towards the door and back out into the crowd of people.

I really didn't mind waiting. It was a lot to even learn that I liked touching Daisy, but it was another to find out how bad I wanted her to touch me, and having another day to take that in wasn't a problem for me.

Maybe by then, I would have a clear head and realize how bad of an idea this all was.

SIXTEEN

DAISY

A FEW DAYS LATER, I was sitting silently next to Kye as he drove us to Isabella's house.

He was already annoyed.

I guess it shouldn't have been a surprise based on his earlier texts telling me that he would be, but I wasn't sure what to do with him now. We were already on our way to Isabella's party, and this would be my first time seeing Dean since the whole boat incident. I had invited the girls to my party earlier in the week, but left him out. It had been enough, though, and Isabella had invited me to the party that the sorority house was throwing.

"And what party is this now?" he asked. His hand tapped the shifter as we sat in the car, looking at the huge house. He had been agitated since we got into the car, and I couldn't imagine this was helping.

"One Isabella is having at the sorority house."

"The sorority that you left because they were treating you so badly?"

I drummed my fingers against my thigh. "Yeah, but this is

for Isabella, not for the other girls. She's the only one that has been more of a friend to me still, and I want to show up for her."

"And of course you couldn't still be friends if you didn't make an appearance," he said in a mocking tone.

"Do you just want to go?" I snapped.

"No. I want to get this shit over with. Come on." He kicked the door open, getting out and heading to my side, but not bothering to open the door.

"I feel like you're going to start a fight tonight."

He stared down at me, the frown on his face deepening. "And? Isn't that what you like about me? That I'll punch the stupid ex-boyfriend or try to kill anyone who gets too close to us?"

"Kye," I said, reaching out and touching his arm. He pulled away, stepping back until he was out of reach.

"Listen, I've had a shit day, Daze. All I want to do is go be at the garage or go home, but I'm here playing fake fucking boyfriend, so don't even give me shit for not being happy about it."

"Wow," I said, slamming the door. "Sorry, I wanted these people to think I was fine without them after last weekend. And sorry that I wanted Dean to see you here, and maybe think twice about trying to basically kill me again. Maybe I'll act the same way next weekend when I have to go to the stupid party with you and Holt. Oh, and when I have to tell my dad that I'm dating you, and handle the fight from that. My dad, the sheriff, who you seem to love pissing off. Sorry it's too difficult to be my boyfriend, but I have to play nice and be your girlfriend. Just go home, Kye." I stomped towards the house, not bothering to look back, no matter how badly I wanted to.

Music and people spilled out onto the front patio, and I pushed through them, trying to make my way to the kitchen but winding up in the living room.

Isabella sat on a guy's lap on one couch, Sydney sitting on Dean's lap next to them.

Of course, I had to run into him first.

Fighting with Kye was stupid since he wasn't actually my boyfriend, but somehow I was upset about it, and seeing Dean after Kye leaving me here wasn't going to help me save face at all.

"Oh, hey, Daisy," Dean said, smiling.

"Daisy!" Isabella squealed. "I'm so happy you came!"

I leaned down, hugging her as she stayed on the guy's lap. "Of course, I came. I wouldn't miss it."

"Really?" Dean asked. "After last week, I assumed you wouldn't be coming around much." He looked past me and grinned. "And alone at that?"

I looked behind me, my heart falling more when I realized Kye had really left.

"Well, I didn't think there would be any more issues, so why wouldn't I?"

He smirked, looking around at the other guys before starting in on his game. "There is a pool outback. Maybe we could recreate our weekend?" The group broke out into laughter. Everyone besides Isabella. At least I still had one real friend left.

Dean's laughter died out as he looked at me. A hand wrapped around my wrist, spinning me until I was face-to-face with Kye.

"What the fuck, Daze?" he said.

"Kye, I thought you left," I said, hoping I was quiet enough they wouldn't hear.

"Why would I? You think you get to snap at me and not give me a chance to give a comeback?" His face was hard. The tight jaw and angry flash of his eyes made me want to step back.

"Yes," I breathed. "I get to do whatever I want."

He groaned and leaned down, wrapping his hands around my thighs until he was lifting me up.

"Yes, you fucking do," he said, before his lips found mine. For the first time, he wasn't frozen solid. I could hear someone gasp, but I was already losing myself to his mouth. He turned to walk out, but he stopped, pulling his lips from mine. "If you even attempt to throw her in that pool tonight. I will kill you, Dean."

He carried me out without another word, and I didn't waste a second before finding his lips again. His tongue moved against mine, and I moaned.

"I thought you didn't want to be here."

"I didn't want to be in there," he breathed. "I'm perfectly fine to be out here with you."

He leaned me back against something, but I kept my eyes closed, preferring to take in every second of him kissing me.

"Where's your car?"

"You're nearly on top of it."

"Perfect. Get in."

"With you attached to me?"

"Yes. Figure it out, Kye," I demanded before putting his attention back to my mouth. His tongue moving with a confidence he didn't have the first time we did this.

He got in, moving his seat back with me on top of him. My hands slipped under his shirt, pulling it up and off of him.

"I really keep hoping you're going to look worse with this off, but somehow it gets better every time."

I started pulling at his belt, but he grabbed my wrists, holding them tight in front of me.

"What are you doing?" I asked.

"Stopping you."

"Why?"

"Because I think that you think I'm about to have sex with you in the car, and I am not. We agreed that there would only be messing around. No sex."

"I thought that might have changed after the whole touching confession."

He shook his head. "You still want to do this fake dating thing. We aren't adding sex to that."

"Break the rules. You always do."

"Not this time."

I sat up straighter, trying not to look at him.

"Got it," I said, pulling myself off of him and sliding into the passenger seat. "Kye Baker is going to break every rule, except when it comes to me."

The way I fell kept my legs draped over him, and he grabbed my ankles before I could pull away completely.

"Let me go."

"No. You are getting all pissy with me because we aren't having sex."

"And?"

"And I literally just found someone who doesn't make me want to cut my own skin off when they touch me. Maybe give me a break. I've touched you more in a week than I touched some girls the entire time I've known them."

"Okay, fair, but I swear my feelings are going to get hurt every time you reject me," I said, trying to smile. "When was the last time you did…anything like this?"

"It's been a while. Years, maybe? I don't know. I don't think about it."

"*At all?*" I sounded horrified, but I couldn't remember the last person I met that wasn't worried about having sex in some way, or at some point.

"At all," he said. "Why would I purposely seek out something I don't like?"

"But how do you survive?"

"A few weeks ago, I would have said it was easy, but I am currently more curious than ever about what the fuss of all this fooling around is."

That wicked grin grew on his face as he moved to the back seat and slid me onto the console, before undoing the button of my shorts with one hand, pulling them down immediately.

"Kye!" I yelled. "What are you doing?"

"Exactly what I want to do?"

"I thought you said no sex?"

"And I said yes to fooling around. Is that fine with you?"

"I mean, yeah, but I–"

"Hey, look, there's Dean and his friends out front," he said before leaning down and running his tongue along my wetness.

I gasped, not expecting it. The pleasure rolled through me as he did it again. "Kye!"

"Say my name any louder and everyone really will know what's going on in here," he said, laughing.

I moaned as his tongue moved harder against me.

"Maybe I should. Maybe if he saw it happening, he would really leave me alone."

"Doubt it. You taste too good. Any man would be stupid not to keep chasing after you."

"But not you."

"No, not me."

"But you're going to do this?"

"Yes, apparently."

My body relaxed more, and he held me up, running his tongue over my wetness again.

"That feels good." I moaned again as he kept going, but it was only seconds before I started talking again. "I want you to take me right now, right here. I want to look at him while you make me cum better than he ever did. I want your hands on me, knowing that his will never be again."

"You know, the dirty talk is working way too well. I'm already losing my mind. Now you are just trying to kill me."

He pushed two fingers into me and clamped his mouth down on my clit. My hips bucked up, and I yelled his name.

He groaned in pleasure, and I pushed up against his mouth again as I came.

Seconds felt like hours as I came down off of my high. He had sat up, his eyes not leaving me as his chest heaved.

"That was perfect," I said. "It's hard to be mad at the no sex thing when you're so good at that. I mean, that's still not off the table for me. I like the idea of having all that feral attitude at my fingertips. Yeah," I said, nodding as I caught my breath, "sex definitely isn't off the table for me."

"You make it sound like if we have sex, I will be tamed for you," he said, laughing quietly as he slipped my shorts back on.

"Maybe you will. Maybe I can pretend you are," I said.

"And that's exactly why we aren't having sex. Because you think there's a lot more meaning behind it than just getting an orgasm."

I looked down at him with a scowl. "Let me have my fantasies."

"It's not happening, even if that face and your words are doing everything possible to break my will and make me give in." He shook his head. "I can't believe you talk to me like that."

"Sorry, is it too annoying?"

"Annoying?" he said, almost at a yell. "The only way it's annoying is because it's working. There's not a second that I won't enjoy it and dream of hearing more. But good girl Daisy has a fucking mouth on her, and I am beyond shocked. My little prom queen who likes everyone to see how perfect she is wants to be fucked in the back of my car and for everyone to hear it. Always tell me these thoughts because I wouldn't believe them otherwise."

"I've been told it's not exactly a mood setter because sometimes I just say dumb things. It's like some filter comes off and I can't hold back."

"I like you unfiltered."

"I like being able to say anything I want to you."

"Good, always speak your mind. Good, bad, dirty, I'll listen to it all."

I leaned down, pressing a quick kiss to his lips again. Then I moved down, kissing his neck once.

"Fuck, you have to stop doing that." I trailed my nails down to his chest, the blood red color standing out against him. "You need to change your nail color, too," he added.

"Why?"

"Because all I'm thinking about is you digging them in until they draw the same color of blood."

I laughed. "Is this some sort of horror movie fantasy, or is that really what you want?" My hand trailed back up his chest to his neck before raking down him a little harder now.

"Considering I want you to draw blood, I think it's safe to say I don't know what the fuck I want." He groaned, his hips pushing up. My hand wrapped around his neck and I squeezed harder now. His head tipped back, eyes closing as he pushed into me.

"Fuck, I like that. Do you like choking and scratching and all this? If you weren't as talkative with *other people,* were you like this?" he asked.

"No. The opposite, actually. I had to be all soft and perfect, but you don't seem to mind either way."

"You're right. Be whoever you want to be. Come on," he said. "Get me out of here so I can get dressed again. Are we staying or going?"

"Going," I said, pushing open the door. "Definitely going."

I could only hope that if we got out of here now, he might be more inclined to continue this.

SEVENTEEN

DAISY

KYE WAS STILL SHIRTLESS, and I couldn't stop staring at the full picture of him again. He had a bigger tattoo across one of his rib cages, smaller ones littering his chest and stomach. None of them seemed to have any connection, but they were all well done.

He smiled at me as he pulled a pack of cigarettes out of his pocket.

"You're really still smoking? That's disgusting."

"Not always, but you really have me stressed the fuck out these days."

"It's disgusting."

"I don't disagree."

"Are you going to stop?" I asked, trying not to sound demanding, and failing immediately.

He stepped closer until I could smell the smoke and see the smile in his eyes. "You going to make me?"

"No. I wouldn't dream that I could make you do anything. Probably won't want to make out anytime soon, though."

He started to laugh, but it died on his lips as he looked past me and groaned. I turned, surprised when I faced Dean.

His face was already turning red, his hands fisting at his sides. We had somehow managed to park next to him, his door still half open.

"Are you seriously still doing this?" he asked, waving between us.

"Still with Kye? Yeah, still doing that. Doing him." I said, eyebrows furrowing as I looked at Kye with the question. He grinned, hiding his laugh behind his cigarette.

"Come on Daisy. You're better than him. People are talking about you. They think you are just one of his sluts. You're a good girl, you don't hang around guys like him," Dean said. "Why are you stooping down to his level? Just to prove a point?"

The words only made my stomach churn because being with Kye didn't make me any less of a good person, but I knew that wasn't what he thought.

I heard Kye's quiet laugh behind me and felt his body step hard against mine, my back pressed against his front. His hand wrapped around my neck, his fingers digging in as he pulled me harder against him.

"Is that true, Daze? Are you a good girl?"

I nodded as he brought his cigarette up to my lips, his other still tight around my neck. "Well, then, show me. Do as you're told and suck."

He moved it closer, and I took it between my lips before sucking in a breath. I let it out before it burned my throat, not ready to cough my lungs out in front of either of them.

His lips pressed against my neck, his mouth trailing up it. "Look at that, Dean, you were right. She is a good girl. Should we see what else you do when you're told?"

His hand stayed around my neck, squeezing lightly. "Yes," I breathed, so turned on my legs were threatening to give out. I had just had an orgasm and somehow he was already making me need another.

I knew it was all for show. I knew Kye had literally just told me we wouldn't be sleeping together, but my imagination still ran wild.

"Yeah? Or maybe right now, you would rather show Dean that he can't talk to you like that? That he can't call you names and think he's better than you for no reason. Isn't he the one fucking your friends faster than you can count? Tell me, Daze. Be that good girl and tell me what you want."

He wanted me to say it. To hear that I didn't want Dean around me anymore. I couldn't believe how easy of a decision it was for me.

"I want him to leave me alone, us alone. I don't want him to talk to me like that or think he can call me names."

"Perfect. Done," Kye said, kissing the side of my neck and pulling away. He dropped the cigarette, stomping it out before heading towards Dean.

The calm of his walk was an act. His body coiled and his arm swung, his fist connecting with Dean's face before he even knew what was happening.

Dean dropped, falling back against his car before hitting the ground. Kye was already grabbing him by the shirt and dragging him back up, only to swing again. Blood sprayed from Dean's nose, but Kye held him up.

"I'm not really sure what you don't understand about not bothering Daisy anymore, but it really gives me a great excuse to beat the shit out of you."

He let him go, and Dean dropped back again.

Kye spun, heading back to his car, and I thought it was

over until I saw him pull a long piece of metal out from behind his seat.

"Oh my god, Kye!" I yelled. "You can't kill him."

He glanced back at me. His face twisted into a smile as he brought the piece of metal up, stabbing it into Dean's grill until it popped through the radiator.

"You're honestly fucking pathetic," he spat, putting his boot on Dean's leg. "Don't fucking talk to her again unless she asks you to."

Dean staggered back, the shock and hatred on his face almost laughable. "She will. She will be back once she realizes you're a piece of trash. I've heard plenty about you, Kye. I know you've always been trash. Not worth a fucking minute of her time, and she's going to realize that soon enough. This charity case shit is going to end and she will be back, begging for me."

Kye stepped aside, waving his hands, showing Dean that I had all the chances to go with him. I reached out, sliding my hand into Kye's.

"Keep telling yourself she will be back. I would kill you before that happened."

We went to move away, and I tried to steady my shaking body.

"Are you serious, Daisy?" Dean yelled, trying to catch up to us. "This kind of behavior is fine with you?"

Kye turned, swinging again and hitting Dean in the stomach this time.

"That's probably enough," Kye said. "Let's get out of here before his friends come out. I don't want you in the middle of anything."

"Aren't I right in the middle of this?"

"I meant a physical fight. I'm not going to fight him and all his friends if I'm worried about them grabbing you, too."

"Oh," I said, as he opened my car door, shutting me inside and going around to slide into the driver's seat. "I thought you were going to kill him with that thing."

"Honestly?" he asked, already pulling out and grinning over at me.

"Yeah. I don't know, you just looked…"

"Looked?"

"Like you could have killed him."

"Not like I didn't want to when he talks about you like that."

He made it a few miles down the road before ripping the car to the side.

"He's not wrong, Daze. You know I've been trash growing up. You know I'm not worth a damn compared to him and what his life will be. You can't think I'm going to be good for your image long term, and if you want to head back to him right now, I wouldn't blame you. I will only kill him if you go back to him unwillingly. If this fake thing needs to be done on your end, it's okay. I'm hoping you would still come to the thing with Holt, though."

I was quiet as I took in each word. Surprised that Dean had got to him. He never seemed fazed when people said anything, but then again, I'd never been with him after they said it.

He looked so torn, angry and broken in the same breath that I could barely figure out where to start to help.

I pulled off the harness and crawled over, settling myself in his lap. His hands found me, roaming over my sides and hips in a lazy, comforting way, and I realized how much more he was reaching out to touch me now.

"You weren't trash growing up. You were handed a very bad start to life. I really don't want to go back to him. The thought of him touching me again, and you never touching me, makes me want to cry. And there is no guarantee for any of us in life. You might end up on top of the world and his life goes to hell. I wouldn't want to be with anyone for what their life *could* be. Do you know how good you have to be to end up like you after what crap you had to deal with? After what they did to you? Dean could never have done that. There's no way to compare you both, but if someone honestly could, it's me, and I think you win every single time."

"Damn, Daze. I've never had anyone say something like that to me. I don't know what I'm supposed to say back."

"Nothing. You don't have to say anything." The car roared to life, and he shifted into gear to peel out. I yelled, trying to move back to my seat, but he had me caged in. "What are you doing?"

"Taking you home."

"Let me back in my seat!"

He laughed, grabbing my hand and putting it back on his chest as he idled down the road. "We are literally around the corner. Kiss me until I get there."

"That's dangerous."

"Then I'll keep my eyes on the road," he said, tilting his head and giving me full access to his neck. "And you kiss me."

I pursed my lips, trying to keep my thoughts to myself on how cute it was that he wanted to be kissed. Instead, I leaned in, letting my lips linger as I kissed up his neck and back down once before running my teeth along the soft skin. He groaned and wrapped one strong arm around me to pull me harder against him. I ground down, feeling how hard he had grown under me, and moaned, my lips still against his neck.

"Daze," he breathed, the car coming to a stop. I didn't stop, not caring where we were now when he was enjoying this so much. "Daze," he said again, pulling back as much as he could. "We are here."

"I know."

"I...I need to stop, Daisy." He stumbled over his words and I sat up fast.

"Too much?"

"Just for tonight, yeah." I was already pushing the door open, nearly falling out as he tried to help me. "Don't be mad."

The words were a plea, and my chest tightened. I turned back, grabbing my bag and meeting his eye. "I told you I won't like being rejected, but I understand why you need to take it slow."

"I told you it has nothing to do with you and everything to do with me."

I shook my head, but I smiled. "Goodnight, Kye. I'll talk to you later."

The door to Kye's car shut as I turned onto my dad's road. I could already hear the idle of his car, and was surprised when he turned onto my dad's road behind me.

My phone buzzed, and I read it as I walked inside.

KYE

Goodnight, Daze.

EIGHTEEN
KYE

MY BODY BUZZED as I pulled up, Daisy already waiting at the curb for me.

"You came," she said, slipping into the passenger seat.

"I said I would be here."

"Yeah, but I didn't know after how you left things."

"Left things? What does that mean?" I asked, pulling into the street and spinning the car back around to head to the races.

"It means you told me to kiss you and then begged me to stop. I'm not sure what I'm supposed to follow that up with."

"Do you have to follow it up with anything? We're not actually dating, right? And I've said a hundred times I'm not good at the touching stuff. You wanted to go out tonight, and I have an open seat. There's nothing to follow it up with."

"Oh," she said. "Okay, then. I guess that's an easy way to solve that problem, then."

I shifted again, pushing the car faster as we got further from town. I glanced over, surprised to see her calm. She had her blonde hair pulled back into a messy bun at her shoulders, and it was just messy enough to make me wonder if she tried to make it look like that. I had told her not to wear one of her dresses tonight and was glad to see she listened. The hoodie and jeans were better for the races anyway, and better for me not having to wonder what every other guy would be thinking about her.

I didn't know what happened. One minute, I had my perfectly normal life, and the next, I was obsessing over other guys, thinking they had a chance at my fake girlfriend.

If I wasn't thinking about that, I was thinking about her.

Just her.

When I looked back at her again, she smiled, but it quickly faded when she glanced at the dash and back to me.

"Kye, the road!"

"What about it?"

"Look at it, not me. You're speeding."

"The road isn't going to disappear."

"But we will if you launch us into the forest!"

"I can do it with my eyes closed, Daze."

"Don't you dare."

I laughed, looking back at the road but not slowing down. "Fine, but I'm going to try it out next time I'm by myself."

"That is the dumbest thing you could try to do."

"I promise it isn't the dumbest thing I could do. I could think of at least ten other things I could try that would be dumber."

I turned into the lot of the races, and couldn't help but glance over to watch as she took in the sight.

Race night was always hit or miss on the turnout, but tonight was busy. There were at least fifty other cars already pulled up next to the makeshift track, and I angled us through the crowd to find the rest of the crew.

"Wow," she said, pulling off the harness as she looked over the crowd and cars. "This is what you do every week?"

"Close to it, yeah. We go out looking for races instead sometimes. Just depends on our mood, or how much money we need."

"What am I supposed to do here?" she asked as I parked.

"What do you mean?"

"Am I supposed to do something? Should I just be around you all night?"

"Whatever you want. I would say stay with someone in the crew. The girls are there," I said, pointing to Quinn, Ash, Scout, and Carly, who were leaning back on Ash's car. "You can hang out with them or me."

"Oh, okay."

"What's wrong? Do you not like them?"

"No! They are great."

"But?"

"But what if they don't like me hanging around? I don't want to bother them or anything."

"You're overthinking this. They already like you."

She suddenly looked on the verge of tears, and I wasn't sure why.

"What is wrong? Are you really that upset at being here?" I didn't know why, but her being so upset she wanted to cry at seeing part of my life hit hard.

"I'm here because we are pretending to be together, not because you actually like hanging out with me, and I know they are just being nice because of that. But then I don't want to be bothering you all night, and following you around if you want to hang out with the guys."

"You really need to think that through. Why would I have invited you tonight to pretend to be your boyfriend? Holt isn't here. I'm going to take a big leap here, but I doubt Dean or your friends are."

"I guess that's true."

"I invited you because I like you around, and the girls demanded you come. They were excited when you agreed. They aren't like your friends, and I'm not like Dean. Glue yourself to my side all night for all I care."

"Won't that interrupt?"

"Interrupt...what, exactly?"

"I don't know. All the things you guys talk about."

"Unless you are going to start fighting with one of them on why one car is better than another, no, I don't think there's anything to interrupt. Although, please start fighting with them on that. It would be hilarious."

"I'm being serious!"

"So am I? What do you think we are talking about that you can't hear? We talk about cars, Daze. The girls talk about shit they want to do, and I don't know, whatever else they want."

"They are just a little intimidating as a group. All of you are."

"Yet you were comfortable enough to jump me. Come on. You are already here. Just stay by me until you feel more comfortable."

"I don't want to—"

"If the next word out of your mouth is bother, I'm going to tell you to shut up."

"That's rude."

"So is assuming I invited you here because I secretly hate being around you. I get the concern based on other people you hang around, but I promise I don't ask women to hang out with me, especially if I find them annoying."

I got out, already heading around to her side. I was pretty sure I was going to be prying her from the car, but she really couldn't think this place was that bad.

The door pushed open, and she glanced up at me. My legs almost gave out. The look of her with her eyes wide, looking up at me, her lips parted and hair a mess, was making me understand why blowjobs could be a good thing.

"Touch me," I said, throwing my arm over her shoulder to pull her closer.

"What?"

I leaned down to her ear, my lips against it. "Please put your hands on me and don't drop them until I say so."

"A little demanding, but I'll take it," she said. "You should understand, though, when you say *touch me,* I'm thinking you mean something much dirtier than me putting my arm around your waist."

"Oh. Do you want me to say something else, then?"

"No. Not at all, but don't be mad at me if I get confused about what I'm supposed to be touching," she said, fighting back laughter.

"Some of us are innocent minds that aren't perpetually horny," I said.

"I am not!" she yelled, and I smiled as the crew all looked at her. "Sorry," she said, sinking further against me.

The girls quickly took over, ripping her away from me to talk, and I almost got mad about it until I realized she still looked relaxed.

Twenty minutes later, I moved to her side. She had set up on the back of my car with Quinn next to her. Ash, Carly, and Scout were on Ash's car next to them.

"Hey, a friend of ours is having some trouble with his car.

We're heading over there. Want to go or stay with them?" I asked.

Her smile grew. "I'll wait here."

"Then I'll be back soon."

I HAD ALMOST EXPECTED DAISY TO START TEXTING ME TO come back, but I didn't hear a word from her. Finally, we got the car running again and I could head back to her.

When I finally broke through the crowd, though, my blood started to boil immediately.

Daisy was still sitting there on the back of my car, but instead of the girls around her, one guy sat next to her instead.

I couldn't tell from here who he was, but it didn't matter. He shouldn't be there.

I stalked over immediately, grabbing his head and slamming it down onto the trunk of the car with a satisfying thud.

"Get off my car, and get off my girl," I said, pushing him hard until he slid onto the ground.

"Kye!" Daisy yelled. "What are you doing?"

I moved to the spot he had been next to her. "I thought that was pretty clear?"

"You can't just hit people!"

I looked around at the crowd and back at her. "Where the fuck do you think you are? I can punch someone if I want to here, and fake or not, I am not letting another guy hit on you while sitting on my car."

The guy finally stood up, and I realized I knew him.

"What the fuck, Kye?"

"I could say the same to you. You don't go hitting on other guys' girlfriends."

"I didn't know she was your girlfriend," he yelled back.

"She's on my fucking car waiting for me. What part confused you?"

"The part where I've met you, *asshole*," he said, grabbing his head. "You've never had girlfriends here. I thought she was another one of your friends."

"My friends are off-limits, too. Get the fuck out of here and don't come around her or my car again."

He flipped me off but disappeared.

Daisy still watched me, her eyes wide and lips pressed together. "You can't just go around giving people concussions."

"Again, why? I just did, and I don't see anyone coming for me. Do you think anyone here is calling your dad to come to arrest me? This entire place is illegal, Daisy. You don't get to act like Miss Prissy here, and you sure as fuck don't flirt with other guys when you're here with me."

"I wasn't flirting!"

"He thought you were."

"Does it matter? Like you said earlier, we aren't actually together. I could flirt with someone if I wanted to."

"Do you want me going to your stupid parties and flirting with your friends?" I asked, already knowing the answer.

"Well, no, but I really wasn't flirting. And I would hate it because I care what people think of me and don't want to be embarrassed again by a boyfriend who can't stay loyal. What's your excuse?"

I leaned back, the roar of engines from the next race giving me a few seconds to find my answer.

"Do you want the truth?" I asked.

"Obviously."

"I like kissing you, touching you, you touching me. I like

it and don't know why, or really how to handle it, but until I do figure all that out, I want to be selfish and not let anyone else have you," I said, leaning in closer. Her breath hitched and chest rose. "If you're going to be the only person who doesn't make me want to rip my own skin off, I want to keep you all to myself until it's over."

"Until we are done with the fake relationship?"

"I think my feelings on the touching will change sooner than the downfall of this relationship."

"You think you're going to wake up one of these days and not like me touching you?"

"Yes."

"Is that how that works?"

"I don't fucking know, but I can't imagine this feeling is going to last."

A different group of guys pushed through the crowd, looking around, before their eyes landed on me.

"Shit," I said, already sliding off the car and picking her up to set her on the ground. "Go get the crew."

"For what?"

"Me. Hurry up."

I knew they weren't far, but I didn't want her around if these guys were going to start a fight. Which, based on our last interactions, would be happening.

The three of them were already at me no. Two of them were ones I got in a fight with outside the diner. The other was the guy I had raced and, according to him, lost to.

"What do you want?" I asked, still relaxed. There wasn't much they could do now—fight me or leave—but I could handle either option.

"I want the car you owe me."

"I don't owe you a car. I won the race. You don't get to lie, make your friends lie, and then think you get my car."

"I won. It's as simple as that, and you can't run around here racing more when you've backed out of the deal we had. We raced, I won, I get your car, so hand over the keys."

"We raced, I won, and you and your friends lied."

The crew stepped next to my car now. The tightness in my chest eased at their presence. I didn't want Daisy anywhere near a fight, and the other night at the diner had been close enough. I had never fought so hard, purely from the fear that they would break into the car to steal it and take her with them. I knew the crew would have my back, and the chances of these guys starting a fight against all of us were slim.

"Instead of you two getting into fights every time you see each other, why don't you just race again?" Ransom said. "Plenty of witnesses, no confusion, and whoever loses can give up their car. If you really won, there should be no trouble doing it again."

Ransom was goading him into another race, and even though that was clear enough to us, I knew he would fall for it.

"I'm fine with that," I said.

He thought it over, and I wondered if he would need to run and talk to his friends, but he squared his shoulders. "Fine. I can kick your ass again. Let's go. Right now."

"I'll be at the line in five minutes," I said, already stepping back towards my car.

"Kye!" Daisy yelled, running past the crew to my side.

"I'll be fine, Daze. Come on, I need to get up there."

"No, we have to go. Right now," she panted. The crew gathered around my car as we made it over to them.

"Everyone, now!" she hissed, looking around. "I have a

police scanner on my phone. I'm paranoid. My dad and the other sheriffs are headed here. It sounds like they might block everyone in, but I don't know for sure."

"Shit," I said. "Alright, we should go just in case they do."

"Your race?" Ransom asked.

"No one can race if we are all in jail."

He smiled, sliding behind the wheel of his car before it roared to life. If anyone wondered why we were all leaving, they didn't ask.

Daisy had already buckled herself in by the time I got in. "Hurry," she said, her legs bouncing wildly. "I don't know how long until they are here."

"It's alright. We already have the heads up, thanks to you. We will get out without an issue."

"Are you sure, Kye? I really don't want my dad to find out about us hanging out like this."

"I feel like that's a little dig at me, but I am sure," I said, grinning. "He won't find out like this."

"It's not a dig at you. If this is how he finds out, and you and the crew are doing something illegal, he will do whatever he can to charge you on it, simply for having me here with you."

"Oh, so you don't want to be seen with me to protect me?"

"Yes, actually."

We all headed down the side street before turning out onto the main road. Daisy sucked in a hard breath, and I immediately saw why. Six sheriffs cars headed down the road at us, their lights and sirens off as they passed. They were going to sneak up on everyone, ticketing who they could and arresting anyone who fought it. We'd been there for it before and it sucked. You could be there for hours as they blocked off streets and handcuffed whoever they wanted.

"Thanks for the heads up, Daze. None of us felt like dealing with that tonight."

The sheriff's cars all turned down the side road we had just come from and disappeared.

"They aren't going to come after us," I said. "We technically aren't doing anything wrong right now, and they can go catch plenty of people who are. Relax, we're good now."

Silence surrounded us as she sat there, not saying a word. I really didn't know how to soothe someone who was panicking, but I had watched Fox do it plenty of times for Ash. I grabbed for her hand, resting it on mine and setting them both onto the shifter.

"You want to drive for a little longer?" I asked, not ready to drop her off. She shifted in her seat, and I realized it was only to get more comfortable.

"Yeah, I'd like that."

I turned right, heading towards the winding, quiet roads as she turned up the radio.

NINETEEN

KYE

MY HEAD POUNDED as I pushed the car into the next gear. I could feel blood trickle down my neck, but I tried to ignore it.

Two days went by since I had seen Daisy. I had gone out to street race for a few hours, trying to drive off every ounce of need I felt for her. I had fought every waking second to not reach out to her, hoping I could cut some of the contact between us to ease the need that built in my chest. Tonight, though, I went to race and wound up running right back into the guy who thought I owed him a car, and this time, I had been alone. They started hitting me and somehow ended up getting one too many punches in. Now I was a mess and needed the one thing that seemed to calm me down.

I pulled out my phone and hit her name. It rang a few times before it connected.

"Hello?"

"Daze," I said, finally taking a deep breath.

"What's going on? What's wrong?"

"Are you home?" I asked, knowing she only had one more day at her dad's house before she moved into her new dorm room which was, apparently, a good thing since her sister was planning on moving back in, and Daisy wanted out before that happened.

"Yeah? Where else would I be?"

"Can I come over?"

"Right now? I mean, yeah, but what's wrong?"

"Nothing. I just need to see you."

"Oh. Okay. Yeah, of course," she said, the panic in her voice getting worse. "How long until you're here?"

"Five minutes. I'll park around the corner."

"Okay," she said, as I ended the call. I didn't need more questions.

I needed her.

Exactly five minutes later, I made it to her window and crawled in. She had been sitting on her bed, but she hurried to come over to me. I was ready for her to wrap herself around me, but she stopped in her tracks, eyes wide as she looked up at me.

"You got in a fight," she stated. "Your eye is already turning purple."

"Yeah."

"What are you doing here now?" She didn't sound mad or upset. If anything, just confused. Worst of all, she still wasn't touching me.

Then I remembered her face after the last fight I had got in. Not the one that she wanted when I hit Dean, but the one at the diner with the same guys.

"You're scared of me."

She was already shaking her head and reached out. Her

hand ran along my chest and unfurled the pain that I had been holding there."No. I'm just not sure what's going on. You've had me freaked out since you called, and then you show up like this. What's going on?"

"I got in a fight," I said, stepping closer to her. She didn't move, letting me press up against her. "And then all I could think about was you." I grabbed her hands, forcing them up to my neck as I stepped forward. My hands slid under her legs, and I picked her up just to throw her back onto the bed to come down over her.

"Everywhere, Daze. Touch me everywhere," I said, before I slammed my lips onto hers. If she was freaked out or worried now, she didn't show it. Her legs wrapped around my waist, her hands moving over every inch they could reach as she kissed me. Each movement of her lips pressed into me harder, her tongue demanding that I open up for her.

I still barely touched her, my hands pressed into the mattress to hold myself up, and for the first time in my life, I wasn't worried about not being in control.

She pushed at me, flipping me over so she could straddle herself over my lap.

My already hard cock pressed against her, straining against my jeans where I could already feel the warmth of her. I'd always let my body control me. The way I would fight or pull away; the screaming agony that controlled how I acted around people who wanted to touch me. It was always in control, and now was no different, but for the first time, my body wanted more.

I reached down, running my hand along the seam of the ridiculously small pajama shorts she had on. My fingers pushed against her entrance, surprised that she was already wet. I slid two fingers into her, watching as her eyes went wide and her mouth dropped open.

My hand flew over her mouth before she made a sound, and she bit down. Her body squirmed against my hand before I moved it back to her hip.

My other hand was still between her teeth.

"You're about to draw blood."

"Well, I wasn't exactly expecting the man who doesn't want to touch to go right to my pussy. I'll be more careful."

"No need. Bite down, dig your nails into me, draw blood. I don't care what you do to me, but especially not that."

"You want me to draw blood? What? Do you like pain?" she asked with a laugh.

"I, apparently, like anything done by your hands. Pain or not."

"Why are you here, Kye? Sex or just this?"

It was a fair question. I think any guy that came in through a girl's window would generally be looking for sex, but it hadn't crossed my mind yet. I was so wrapped up in all of this being new that I hadn't even thought about having sex.

My chest caved in with the worry that this pleasure of her touch would be gone the second I forced myself to take it further.

"You."

"That doesn't answer my question."

"It does. I'm here for you. For your fucking hands that seem to erase every goddamn ounce of pain that my body goes through. It erases everything until I'm fucking high on it. I wasn't coming for sex, just this."

"Okay," she said, leaning back down to kiss me. "Why don't I finish what we started in the pool house, then?"

She gave me one wicked smile before sliding down my body.

Before she could even get my jeans unbuttoned, though, another fucking knock came from the door.

"Daisy?"

Her eyes went wide and she jumped up.

"Yeah?"

"You okay?" her dad asked from the other side of the door.

I couldn't stop my laugh, my lips tight together to keep silent. "I'm so happy," I whispered. "Best day of my life."

"Shut. Up. Get in the closet," she hissed. "Before he comes in here and sees this."

"You're twenty-one years old. I think you are allowed to have boys in your room."

"Maybe, but you definitely aren't on that list of approved boys." She pulled me up, trying to make me actually get in the closet, but there wasn't a chance that was going to happen.

"No? He won't love knowing you're in here with me? That you snuck me into your room because you want to fuck me so bad," I said, still laughing against her ear. I lifted her up, stepping across the room to push her quietly against the door just in case he really opened it.

Her eyes went wider, and she smacked at my shoulder, but I leaned in, kissing up her neck.

"I'm good. Why?" she finally asked.

"Just heard some noises."

"All good in here. Going to bed, actually."

"Okay," he said. The long pause made me wonder if he really would open the door. "Goodnight, then."

"Goodnight!" she yelled, her voice a little too high-pitched. Seconds passed before she smacked at me again, but when I put a little space between our chests, she quickly leaned back in, kissing me hard. "Honestly, at this rate, you may never get a blowjob."

"That's fine."

"No, it's not. Put me down."

I dropped her legs immediately and stayed glued against the door. She was already undoing my jeans, reaching in and wrapping her hand around my cock. I fell harder against the door, the pleasure rippling through me so fast I nearly fell over.

My head fell back, taking in every second, wondering if I would ever feel it again.

"Kye," she whispered. I looked down just in time to see her tongue dart out, running along my length. My mouth dropped open, watching as she did it again. Her mouth slipped over the head, and before I even had a chance to take another breath, she was taking all of it.

I groaned, the warmth of her mouth sliding over me again and again.

"Daze," I whispered, plunging a hand into her hair. I didn't know anything could feel this good.

She kept moving, her hands running over my stomach and back down to wrap her hand around my length. When I looked down again, she was looking back up at me, her eyes wide and my cock buried in her throat.

I fell apart, my body shaking hard as I came. It took everything in me to stay upright, and as much as I tried to say anything to her, I couldn't find words.

She pulled back, and I quickly fixed my jeans so I could slide down to the floor. She stayed down on her knees, smiling as I sunk down to eye level. As soon as I made it to the ground, she crawled on top of me.

"How was that?" she asked.

I could only stare at her lips, the ones that just got me off, and wondered who she was that she could do this to me.

"Perfect," I finally said. "Fucking perfect."

She sat there in silence, and I welcomed the peace sitting there for a few minutes. I finally got up, taking her up with me, until she was back on her feet.

"So, that was a no strings attached blowjob, of course, but I feel like this might be a good time to ask, and since you're my fake boyfriend and all, how would you feel about helping me move into my new dorm tomorrow?"

I smirked. "I feel like that falls under real boyfriend responsibilities."

She huffed and nodded. "Okay, that's true. Fair enough. I don't have that much stuff anyway."

"I'm kidding, Daze. I can help. Not a big deal."

"Are you sure?"

"Yeah, but I don't know how you're getting all this shit into my car without your dad noticing."

"Can you come during the day? We can get the majority of it in a trip or two, and he works until five."

I thought it over. I was busy with the garage, and needed to get to Holt's to practice on the track more, but this wouldn't take too much time out of my day.

"I'll be here around three."

Her smile grew, and she threw her arms around me. "Perfect. Thank you."

"See you tomorrow?"

"See you tomorrow," she repeated, watching me get back out the window with a smirk.

I didn't look back as I headed to my car, wondering the

entire time how the fuck I wanted to stay the night with her instead of going home alone.

I never knew what was wrong with me, but now it felt worse. The problem I had lived with my entire life was gone, or at least glitching, when I was with her.

I couldn't go home and face this all now.

So, I didn't. I went out, spending the entire night winding through curved roads and dead-end streets until I could head home with my mind having no other thought but sleep.

TWENTY
DAISY

KYE GRABBED ANOTHER PILLOW, shoving it behind his head. He spread out on my bed with his shirt off, the view still a shock to me. Every muscle and tattoo felt so familiar now, but there was still some sort of distance between us I wanted gone.

I had spent the last two hours watching him carry every heavy item I owned from the house to the car, and then the car to the dorm room, and had enjoyed every single second. Even with liking every second I was spending with Kye, something about moving back to campus was getting under my skin.

It's not that I wanted to stay with my dad. With my sister Willow moving back in with him for now, I knew I would quickly be unwelcome there, even if my dad didn't say it outright. My sister was a lot to handle, and being at my dad's house was hard enough without her there adding to it.

"This is really where you have to live? I always thought dorms were cool, but this is basically prison. Concrete walls, shared bathrooms, locked doors. What else is there? Curfews?"

"No curfews, but there are quiet times. Although, I think the majority of the student body ignores that. And are you insinuating that you have been in prison and can accurately make that comparison?"

He shrugged. "Jail, prison, whatever."

"Wow. You know you make yourself sound a lot worse than you are?"

"You show the world you're perfect. I show the world I'm dangerous. We do what we have to, to survive in the lives we were given. I'm trying to tell you the truth. It's not my fault if I wave a red flag and you get turned on."

"I am not turned on that you may or may not have been to jail!"

His smile grew. "Are you turned on by anything else, then? Turned on *again*?"

"Not currently," I lied. "Why? Trying to exchange help with moving for sex?" I huffed, the edge to my voice more serious than I meant it. I was so out of sorts after last weekend, I didn't know what to think. Part of me was waiting for him to suggest it, to make a new rule that we had to sleep together to continue, but so far he hadn't said a word. And besides his light flirting, I had no indication that he wanted anything else, but here I was, ready to rip his clothes off.

Now today, he had come over to help me move my stuff in without so much as one annoyed groan. He seemed fine being here, even smiling throughout the drive and carrying my stuff in. He even kissed me when he got here. And now he was happy to lie there on my bed, shirt off, flirting, while I unpacked. I didn't know what to do with it.

We'd fooled around. I watched him get off, gave him a blowjob that seemed to make him fall to the ground, and yet he didn't want sex. Specifically with me, since we were fake dating and that would make it messy. My brain was screaming that it might mean he had found someone else to sleep with, and that made me more upset than I liked. I knew he said that he didn't like to be touched, but that was far from the experience I'd been having with him.

All at once, his smile faded and eyebrows furrowed.

"No? Didn't we already make the rule that we aren't sleeping together? Aren't *you* the one continually trying to break that rule? Glad I make one joke and suddenly, I'm the asshole."

"Haven't you told me more than once that you *are* an asshole?" I said, but the words came out with another bite that I didn't mean.

"Wow. Well, then. I guess I'll see you around. Call me if you want anything else since I seem to only be around for your needs. Fuck what I think or want, right? Just a burnout mechanic who couldn't possibly be nice without getting laid," he said, obviously mad, but he grabbed my hand, kissing it once with a bow. "I'm sure you can find some other sucker with a car that will do your bidding. Forgive me for helping you move your shit, *prom queen*."

"Kye, wait. I didn't mean it like that," I said, running out into the hallway after him.

He threw his hand up in a wave, his shirt still tucked in his back pocket, and I hated the wave of wanting that rolled through me at the sight. "Bye, Daze."

My new roommate walked past him, taking a few extra seconds to look him over."Wow, who is that?"

"That's Kye. My—" My what? Could I really call him my boyfriend when it was fake? I guessed with a school this size, though, I would need to keep up the facade, even with her. "My boyfriend."

"Ugh, he's hot. Like, *hot*, hot. Don't really find that type on campus, do you?"

She walked past me into the room, throwing an armful of bags down.

Amber was nice. A little more…dark than I was, but after getting to know Kye and the crew, I realized that made me instantly like her more. So far, I had been right not to judge her because she was nice, honest, and blunt enough to be exactly who I wanted to share a room with.

"No. No, you don't," I finally replied.

I went back in, unpacking a few more things as I scolded myself. Kye had been nothing but nice and sweet and there for me. Every time I reached out to him, he responded, but somehow I was still treating him like he was less than.

It wasn't on purpose, but even with everything he confessed to me, it was hard to believe. He was so good at kissing me, touching me, and even giving me orgasms, that it felt stupid of me to believe he was as inexperienced as he said.

But it wasn't like he had ever done anything to make me think he was lying. And even besides playing fake boyfriend, he had come to get me after the boat incident, took me out with his friends, and now helped me move. None of that was in our agreement.

I really was the asshole.

DAISY

I'm sorry. I really didn't mean it like that.

I waited two hours, clicking my phone on but seeing no new notifications. It was the first time that he hadn't responded to me, and each minute that passed was more upsetting.

"Trouble in bad boy paradise?" Amber asked.

"Yeah, I think so. I said something and I think it pissed him off. No, wait, I know that it pissed him off, and for good reason."

"Well, you know guys like that. They get all hotheaded and probably just need to go burn it off."

"What does that mean? Like, go for a run? I couldn't really picture him putting on running shoes just because he was mad at me. Driving at horrific speeds around town maybe, but running? No," I said with a laugh.

"*Ompf,* my naïve little roommate. Is this your first guy like that?"

"Like what?" Her eyebrows went even higher. "Can you just spit this all out? Because I am already upset."

"Like, not a popular athlete? A guy that looks like that goes into bad boy categories and those types of guys burn off their frustrations in non-athletic ways. I mean, I guess the jocks do, too, so I'm not sure where your confusion comes in."

I shook my hands, needing her to explain more and faster.

"Oh, wow. Um, Daisy, I hate to be the bearer of bad news, but guys like that don't usually do the exclusive thing. I've had my fair share of them and even as boyfriends, they usually are with other girls. I mean, girls throw themselves at that type, knowing they are getting sex with no strings. You can't really believe he walks around on this campus and doesn't get ten phone numbers from here to his car, do you?"

"No, why would I think that? We are dating!" I nearly yelled. Even if it was a lie, he wouldn't really be coming here to collect numbers, would he? Looking back, I could see Dean doing that, but Kye? Somehow my views of him changed, and it didn't cross my mind he would do anything like that. Then again, I might have said that about Dean before.

"Listen, if you hadn't been standing there and telling me he was with you, I would have been all over that. Literally. If he didn't have my number by the end of the conversation, it would be because we were behind the building doing other things. I am not the only woman here with those thoughts either. We are all here to have a good time. I did not realize you were this…new to this."

I groaned. "Things in the sorority are different. Everything is conniving, personal. The girls didn't hit on my boyfriends outright. They were planned attacks and sabotage. I was never thinking that someone would just go up to him and hit on him."

"I mean, you saw people hit on Dean, though," she said. "Those athletes can be the same way."

"Well, Dean did cheat on me, so I can't say that you are wrong. I don't know what to think now."

"I would double check with your boy what exclusivity means to him and don't get your hopes up for much. Most of the guys I know like that have a girlfriend, so they don't have to be alone if the side chicks don't pick up. I'm not saying your guy is like that for sure, but like I said, at least ten numbers each time."

"Dammit. *Dammit*," I said, changing into a lighter dress. I had no right to care, no right to go talk to him, but I suddenly wanted to know exactly what was happening.

We weren't sleeping together, so I had to assume he was sleeping with other people, but he said he didn't sleep with anyone. Would a guy really go months to years without sex? I knew that he didn't like the touch, but he never said if that had changed with other people now because it definitely wasn't the case with me. There was no reason that I was special enough to him to be able to touch him and other people wouldn't be able to. Maybe it had changed for all women and he liked it now.

I pulled out my phone, ordering an Uber and waiting impatiently for it to get closer.

"Just don't get your heart broken," Amber said. "Guys like that aren't usually worth the mess."

I nodded. "Thank you. Seriously, thank you for making me think this through."

"Of course. What are friends for?"

I waved, heading down, and waited quietly as the car brought me up to his building. The towering brick building looked more ominous than it had before. I remembered Kye ran into the side door, so that's where I went. I didn't see any buzzer, and the door was locked.

Great, now I was out in the dark and would have to wait for another car unless someone showed up.

I knocked, wondering if there was anyone that could hear, but nothing happened.

"Can I help you?" a girl's voice came from the speaker on the door, making me jump. I grabbed my chest, trying to slow my breathing.

"Um, I was trying to find Kye?"

"Daisy?"

"Yeah," I said back. It sounded like Ash, but I wasn't sure, and the thought of a random girl being here was making my stomach churn. "He didn't know I was coming, but I need to talk to him."

I could hear laughing now. "Amazing. Come on up."

The door clicked, and I pulled it open, stepping into the well-lit hallway with stairs right in front of me.

"Come on," she said, waving. "Hurry up."

I walked up the first flight of stairs, coming face-to-face with Ash.

"Hey," she said with a smirk.

I tried to smile back, but I was still too nervous. "Hey. Thanks."

"Oh, anytime. Do you have your phone?"

I held it up, and she grabbed it, typing in a number before calling it.

"That's my number. If you need anything, of course call me, but please—I mean a huge *please*—text me tomorrow and tell me everything. Or you know, just come down here for coffee," she said, winking as I laughed and nodded.

"I'll see what I can do. Let's just hope I even make it into the apartment."

"Ehh. Kye's tough but a big softy for people he likes. You got this. Good luck."

I nodded, taking a deep breath. "Thank you."

"Sometimes we need a pep talk with guys like this."

I waved, forcing myself up two more flights of steps and coming face-to-face with his dark blue door.

Why was I so nervous? I had talked to Kye plenty of times. This didn't need to be any different. I was just clearing up the terms of our agreements, apologizing for my attitude. Nothing serious. I took another deep breath, repeating that sentence a hundred more times.

I finally pulled my hand up and knocked.

"What the fuck?" I heard him say from the other side, followed by footsteps that grew louder. "Why are you knocking?" he asked, pulling open the door.

He froze as he saw me. I did, too. Taking in every relaxed inch of him, from the messy damp hair to the sweatpants that hung off his hips. The tattoos that littered his chest and stomach and muscled arms. Every part of me heated at the sight.

I managed to miss him in the four hours we had been apart.

"Daisy. What are you doing here?" He almost sounded angry, and that was when reality crashed in again.

I took a step back. "I'm sorry. I tried texting, but you didn't respond."

"Yes, usually that's because the person doesn't want to talk at that moment."

"I'm so sorry. I should have told you I was coming. Are you not alone? Of course you're not. I was coming over to ask, and now I realize how stupid that sounds."

"Not alone?" he asked with a shake of his head. "You came over here to see if I wasn't alone?"

"Well, I didn't know. You didn't respond."

"And I owe you a response every damn time you text?"

"I mean, no, of course not, but then Amber made a comment about how hot you were and that you might not be texting because you weren't alone, and I just...I don't know, I thought I would come see if that's what we were doing. Like, are we faking being together to people in my life, but maybe you're trying to sleep with other people?" I pinched my nose. "And now, hearing this part out loud, I hear what I sound like. I'm so sorry, Kye. I'll leave now. You can get back to whoever. I'm sorry for interrupting."

He leaned against the door with raised eyebrows, seemingly as shocked at my ridiculousness as I was now. I turned, ready to run.

"Daisy," he said, the word so commanding that I stopped and faced him.

"Yes?"

"I am alone. I was only surprised because everyone in this damn building has come to an agreement that unless the door is locked, we don't need to knock. I thought you were one of my friends, and I was going to give you shit because I wasn't in the mood."

"Mood for what?"

"Company."

"Because of me?"

"Yes," he said, the word so matter-of-fact that I felt even worse.

"Does that mean you aren't having someone over to sleep with tonight?"

"No, I wasn't planning on it. But you already knew that because I told you I don't do that. I am also not experimenting with other people to see if I'm cured because we already know that I am not."

"Have you had anyone over to sleep with since our fake dating has started?"

"No, I haven't. Embarrassingly enough, you already know the problems I have, so I'm not even sure why the concern would cross your mind."

I didn't say it out loud, but I knew exactly why it had crossed my mind. I didn't want him with anyone else, and it felt so strange to me that he really wouldn't be.

"Oh." A thousand options of what I could do next flickered through my mind. I looked back over at him, my mouth nearly watering. It had become impossible to not want to touch him every time he was close.

"Do you get phone numbers given to you when you walk through campus?"

He shrugged. "I guess they try, but I ignore it. I really don't have time for more than one perfect little prom queen in my life. The one I have now is more needy than I planned for."

"I'm not perfect."

"Oh, I know it. You like to make everyone think you are, though. Interesting that's the only word you picked up on."

"Is that why you ignore them, though? It's not like they are all like me. Even Amber commented that she would give you her number if we weren't together. Well, fake together, but she doesn't know that."

"It was a joke. I ignore them because I don't care about any of them or about making you the brunt of any jokes. I don't think your pretend boyfriend sleeping with other girls on campus would take long to get out. I quite honestly have no interest in sleeping with anyone, even though you seem to not believe it. And I know they're vicious, Daze. I wouldn't do that to you. I won't try sleeping with anyone else until this charade is up for you."

"You would do that?"

It was stupid of me to ask, knowing that he didn't like anyone else touching him, but the thought of that being true still felt strange. How could he truly only like me touching him? As if there was something special about me.

He nodded his head. "I would."

And like the naive girl I was, it took this long for the pieces to finally click into place.

I wasn't just there to check if our fake dating was exclusive.

I mean, I was, but now that I knew it was exclusive, everything else I wanted was obvious.

I took three determined steps towards him before grabbing his head and pulling it down to mine.

I didn't come here just to check on our agreement.

I came here to sleep with my fake boyfriend.

TWENTY-ONE
KYE

ONE MINUTE, I was reminding her that I was already not sleeping with anyone, and the next she was kissing me like her life depended on it.

"Kye, do not question this anymore and please, *please,* just let this happen."

I wasn't going to question it. I didn't know if I could anymore. Walking out of the dorm room earlier was torture—pulling my teeth out would have been more pleasant. I *did* want to sleep with her, and I wasn't sure how to say it. It wasn't why I agreed to help her move, but the wanting was still there.

Not sleeping with her had taken over every second of my day, and I didn't think I could keep this up. I needed her. I needed her touch. I needed a break from the constant burning ache in my chest.

I didn't say anything, but I picked her up, urging her legs around me as I shut, and *locked*, the door.

I had made my apartment a studio, the open space less

suffocating to a boy who had lived in what should be considered a closet most of his life.

Now it made it easy to navigate, carrying her to my bed and laying her down as I crawled over top of her.

"So this is why you came here?" I asked, noticing the way her eyes went heavy as she looked up at me.

"I guess so. I didn't know that until you said no one else was here."

I leaned down, kissing her. "And now you want to sleep with me?"

"Yes. A thousand times, yes. I need to. Please, just let me sleep with my fake boyfriend," she said with a laugh. "If you want to, obviously. If the touching is okay."

"It's still okay. Are you sure that's what you really want to do?"

"Are you forgetting that I have been the one asking for this over and over? You're the one that said no sex, so do *you* want to do this?"

"Mmm," I groaned, and moved down her body, pulling her dress up. "Damn, Daze, you can say that you didn't plan this, but you didn't even wear underwear."

"I really didn't—" Her words died with a gasp as I covered her pussy with my mouth.

"Kye!"

Tasting her was like a drug. My mind lost as I pushed my tongue inside her.

She gasped again, and I pulled away.

"I will do that all night if you need, but right now, I need you."

"Yes," she said, the word short between hard breaths.

She was already pulling off clothes, and I sat up.

"Problem?" she asked.

I rubbed the back of my neck, realizing how unprepared I was. "About the not sleeping with anyone... That also means I don't have condoms."

She started laughing and moved to the edge of the bed. "Okay, I have to ask, how many people have you slept with exactly?"

"Two."

"And how long has it been since you last slept with someone?"

"Three years."

Her mouth fell open as she stopped digging in her bag. "Three years? How did you even manage that? Aren't you, like, losing your mind or something? The guys I know around our age can barely make it three days before they are doing the dumbest things to sleep with literally anyone."

"Taking care of things on my own is one, a lot easier logistically, and two, feels better than trying to grit my teeth and touch someone. Also, if you tell someone not to touch you during sex, they get weirded out and usually don't listen."

She threw her bag to the side, smirking as she held up a condom before pulling her dress off. She was half under the blankets but completely naked now, her hair off to the side, and smiling at me. "Do you want me to not touch you until you say you're ready?"

I was already shaking my head before she finished her sentence. There had been small instances of liking someone, even finding them pretty, but it was nothing compared to the bone-deep need that she gave me.

Every fucking part of her was beautiful, and every part of her seemed to spark something inside of me until I was blindingly turned on.

"No. Just be you. Do what you want to do." I crawled

back over her, kicking off my sweatpants as I went. "I like when you seem to lose rational thought and touch me or say what's on your mind."

Her cheeks turned red, but she laughed. "I'll be me, and you tell me if you need to stop."

I nodded and I leaned down to kiss her neck, that same scent of lavender and mint already making me high.

My hands shook as I held myself over her. I didn't want it to end. The idea of this being ruined was eating away at any mental stability I had left, but it didn't matter. I was doing this, even if it was the last fucking time I ever did.

I put on the condom and positioned myself at her entrance, pushing against her. In one motion, I filled her. It wasn't sweet, and it wasn't slow, but I didn't have a coherent enough thought to make this better. She gasped, clinging to me harder. I thought I should wait, but her hips moved, urging me to do it again. I pulled away and slammed into her again. The heat of her wrapped around me was everything I had hoped for, everything I never knew that sex could be.

The sigh that escaped her made a shot of ecstasy run down my spine. Everything was a blur of movement, and I knew I should slow down, make whatever was happening more special somehow, but some part of my brain was shutting off as the other part of it screamed for her. Her back arched as I buried myself deeper, and she let out a small moan. She didn't seem to mind the pace, moving her hips and keeping pace with me.

I pushed deeper again, my body tightening until I broke. I came hard, not stopping as my entire body shook from the orgasm.

I kept going until she screamed, her body tightening

around me as her nails dug into my shoulders. I leaned down, kissing her neck as she started shaking along with me.

Finally, I slowed, but I stayed buried in her. When I finally pulled back, I knew I was screwed.

Her big eyes looked up at me, and there was nothing in the world I cared about more.

There was nothing in the entire world that I wanted to look at again.

"Kye? Are you okay?" she whispered, running her hands through my hair and down over my shoulders, holding onto my arms for a moment before repeating the movement. "Is it bad? Are you hurting?"

I was definitely not okay, but not for the reason she was asking about.

Sex shouldn't feel like this.

It should be horrible and painful, and I should be counting down the seconds until it was over.

It shouldn't feel this good just being with her.

It shouldn't feel any different from any other girl I had slept with.

But it was.

It was my heart shattering into a thousand pieces and coming back together.

A lump caught in my throat, and I had to set my head down next to hers just to take another deep breath, careful not to crush her with my weight.

"Kye, what's wrong? We can be done, it's okay," she said, almost sounding scared, but I couldn't say anything, knowing the sound of my own voice would betray me right now, so I only shook my head no.

She shuddered underneath me as I moved finally, lazily

sliding back into her. Her eyes closed and lips parted, whispering my name this time.

She wanted to be here with me. It wasn't someone else she was hoping for or thinking about. She moved underneath me, picking up the pace as she whispered my name again.

How did she manage to know what I needed? Every part of me was falling apart, and she was only ready to give me more of herself.

"What do you need?" I whispered, my throat so tight it hurt.

"You. This. Whatever second orgasm that is teasing me."

I laughed. She was fucking perfect. I already knew she wanted to be perfect, but I wasn't expecting her to be perfect to me.

For me.

I lifted her hips and moved faster again, loving every small moan and mumble of my name. I already came, but that wasn't stopping me from doing this again and again.

I leaned back, bringing her hips up with me until I was nearly holding her up in the air.

"Yes," she said. "Please, Kye, yes."

I didn't stop or ease up, needing every second of this. Her moans got higher until her hands wound into my sheets and her body broke free, shaking and pulsing around me harder this time.

I finally let myself go, slamming harder into her as her pussy clenched around me. By the time I stopped, I could barely breathe, her heavy panting matching mine. I knew this was the point I was supposed to pull away and clean us up, but I couldn't move, staying buried in her.

"I've never had an orgasm like that," she said, panting.

"Me either," I said, regretting the words immediately.

She pulled away, my cock moving out of her as she did, so I followed, slamming back into her as she gasped.

"What are you doing?"

"I don't want to be done yet," I said, the words more threatening than sweet, but I had lost all control.

She laughed, wrapping her arms around my neck and pulling me down, kissing me. "Then why don't we clean up, take a minute to breathe, and do all of that again?"

"You're staying?"

"I don't know if I can make it home without collapsing. I don't even know if I can make it to the shower without falling over."

If I was going to get a night with her, I was going to take in every second. I would fuck up a lot of things in my life, but tonight wouldn't be one of them. I finally pulled away and picked her up to carry her into the bathroom.

"Then prepare not to sleep because I don't know how long it's going to take for me to be finished with you," I said, hoping that the answer was one night.

I was now praying to the universe that had never cared about me that this feeling would be over in one fucking night.

TWENTY-TWO

DAISY

I ROLLED over to find myself face-to-face with a sleeping Kye.

I slept with Kye.

Like, I *slept* with Kye.

I reached out, running a hand down his arm, and he turned over more. His hand ran across the sheets until his finger hooked in mine as he smiled, eyes still closed. My entire chest tightened. Kye was happy to punch someone without a second thought, yet here he was, wrapping a finger around mine.

I ran my other hand down his stomach, tracing over each tattoo.

"I'm worried if you keep doing that, I'm going to redo what I did last night," he said, the deep rumble of his voice making me sigh.

"I would have zero complaints about that."

"Except we have Holt's track day party today. I have to be there soon."

I rolled closer to him. "Are you sure we don't have any time?"

His arms wrapped around me, and he was about to agree until there was a thud at the door.

"Ouch. What the hell?" a girl said. "It's locked."

Then it was just laughter.

"Kye," she yelled. "I don't know what you are doing, but you better stop doing it and get out here. Being late to this is not going to help win any points with my dad."

Kye groaned and sat up, dragging me into his arms until I was against his chest.

"I'm getting ready," he yelled back.

"Yeah? Then why is the door locked?"

"Ashton."

"Kye."

"Daisy," she added, not hiding her laughter.

"How does she know you are here?" he asked me.

"Because she's the one who let me in the building last night, and I'm assuming she kept an eye on if I left."

"Give us ten minutes," Kye yelled, shaking his head. "Come on. Time to start an entire day quizzing me, not only about cars, but about you."

"No one is going to be quizzing you about me today."

He got up, pulling me along with him, but he stopped, leaning down to kiss me hard as his hands moved down my sides.

"You just spent another night at my place. Do you know how many questions I had last time you did? The crew isn't going to shut up."

I shrugged. "You'll figure it out. In the meantime, I'll be spending the day as the supportive girlfriend, eating some delicious food, and hanging out."

"And I'll be dodging questions, racing around the track to

show off my skills, and trying to give one more chance to getting my dream career."

I smiled, grabbing clothes and getting ready. "So we both have a hard day." He glared down at me. "Kidding. I'll be there all day. Just tell me what you need me to do to help, and I'll be there."

OF COURSE, THE FIRST THING KYE NEEDED TO DO BEFORE heading to the track was stop at the diner for a strawberry milkshake.

"I think you are addicted to these things," I said, grabbing it from him to take a sip.

"And? They are fucking delicious."

"And I'm just saying you are addicted. We are running late, but you still had to stop for it," I said, laughing now.

He looked over, smiling as he reached to take it back.

Before he could grab it, a car pulled out on the winding road, making me scream as he looked out the windshield.

He slammed the brakes, the tires locking up as he jerked the car to the left. We finally came to a screeching stop, missing the other car by inches.

"Kye!" I yelled. I had still been holding his milkshake, the contents of which were now covering everything from my chin down.

His eyes went wide when he looked at me, until he started laughing. He kept laughing as he pulled off to the side of the road.

"I'm sorry, Daze. He shouldn't have pulled out. I had to stop."

"That's fine, but can you please get this off of me?"

He pulled off the harness and leaned over, carefully trying to pull mine off.

"My milkshake," he said with a small laugh.

"You can get another one. Just clean me off."

"Oh. If you insist..." He leaned over, licking at my chest. "Mmm, still delicious."

Then he crawled over, hitting the release for my seat until I was laying flat, and he came over me. His tongue roamed, running over my neck, to my shoulders, to my chest, where he stopped to pull down the top of my dress.

"Did you always taste this good?"

I laughed. "Kye, your seat. It's everywhere."

"I don't care."

"You don't care...about your car?"

"Wreck my car. Burn it. I'll buy new seats. I don't care. I'm not stopping what I'm doing right this second."

He pulled off his shirt and flipped us until I was on top of him. His hands moved so fast that I couldn't keep up. His eyes almost glazed over, the feral look back as he pulled at my underwear.

I didn't think I would ever get over that look. The world could be falling apart around us, and all Kye's unwavering attention would be on me.

"Are you trying to fuck me?" I asked, my voice low as he still worked on moving clothes out of the way.

"Yes. Move these damn things. Get them off before I rip them off," he said, pulling at my underwear. I moved until I could slide them down and came back over him.

His jeans were still on, and I ground my hips down before he could unbutton them.

The groan that came from him was worth the wait. I kept moving, grinding against him harder.

"Could you fuck me hard?" I asked.

"Daisy," he growled, trying to push me up so he could free his cock.

"I want it how you like it. All teeth and nails and bruising force. I want to feel you buried in me, losing your mind."

I shrieked as he kicked open the door, lifting me up with him as he got out.

"Kye, what are you doing? I'm half naked," I yelled.

"Fuck if I care. There's no one else out here now," he said, throwing his hoodie onto the hood of the car and putting me on top of it. His hands wrapped around my thighs, pulling me to him, and in seconds, he was filling me. "They can see. I spent years with my pain on display to the world and they didn't care. Why can't I show my pleasure?"

A wave of pleasure rolled through me and I moaned. There was no time to take it in, though, as Kye pulled, holding my hips and legs up until he was thrusting into me. His hands moved to my hips, fingers digging in, and he moved me.

It was desperate and wild, and I loved every second. Every part of me loved it, my body climbing higher and higher as I got closer. I looked up at him, his hair a mess and eyes still trained on me. His fingers moved over my clit, sending me over the edge so fast I yelled, my body clenching around him.

He kept moving until he groaned and pulled me tight against him.

"That somehow gets better each time," he said, breathing hard.

"Yeah. Yeah, it does."

I ADJUSTED MY DRESS, GETTING IT STRAIGHTENED JUST AS A car came over the hill behind us.

"Perfect timing," Kye said, turning the car on and getting ready to pull out.

Before he could, the red and blue lights flashed behind us.

"Or not," he said, slowing back down.

"Dammit," I said, making sure my clothes were straight and searching for the jacket I had brought with me. "What if it's my dad?"

"What if it's someone else?"

"What if it's him and this is how he finds out?"

Kye started laughing and leaned back, obviously too relaxed about this. "That would be pretty hilarious."

"No, Kye. No, it would not." I took a deep breath and said something I never thought I would have. "Go."

"What?"

"Go! You run from him all the time, do it now. Go!" I yelled.

He was already putting the car in gear, but he shook his head. "You know that isn't going to work, right?"

"Because you can't outrun him?"

"Because he is going to be at the track today and see us together."

"That's a lot better than finding us on the side of the road after we just had sex. Go! Now!"

"For you? Of course. Put the harness on," he said, laughing as he took off. I squeezed my eyes shut, trying not to look at anything as he sped through the winding road.

Before long, I couldn't see the lights behind us. I knew it would catch up to me. I knew my dad was about to find out what was going on, and he wouldn't know none of it was real, but it wasn't going to happen like that.

Ten minutes later, he pulled into Holt Racing's track, and we got out.

"I can't believe my perfect little prom queen just told me to run from the cops," he said, wrapping his hand in mine. I stared down at our intertwined fingers, noticing how right it felt.

I knew there was no escaping the truth now. I would be facing my dad, and he would be facing Holt. My friends were back, at least the ones I wanted, and I was happily living on campus again.

A sudden wave of nausea hit me as I realized this was it.

After today, there would be no reason to keep dating Kye.

TWENTY-THREE

DAISY

HIS HAND STAYED WRAPPED in mine the entire walk, and he didn't seem to mind. He even tightened his grip as the crowd thickened.

We made it to the pit area where they let us by and Kye continued on, heading towards the only building on this side. The entire wall facing the track was glass, giving anyone inside the perfect view of everything happening below.

"We need to go up and find Holt first, then we can come back down and hang out before I do a few laps."

"A few laps doing what, exactly?"

"Showing Holt that I will be the best damn driver on his racing team. I would do any type of racing if he wanted me to. Rally, drift, stunt. I want to do it all."

"Those all sound...dangerous," I said, my hand tightening.

"It is, but I'm good at it, so no worries."

"No worries? I have *all* the worries, *all* the time. This will just add to my endless pile of worries," I said, talking faster now.

"Why would you worry about me?"

I thought it over, but couldn't respond. How could I tell him that I would worry because I actually cared about him? Not in a pretending fake boyfriend way, but in a very real, very scary way.

We made it to the room overlooking the track. Holt was sitting at a bar top area with Ash and Fox next to him. Scout, Chase, Jax, and Carly were lounging on some of the chairs in front of the glass windows. Ransom and Quinn cut us off immediately.

"You're late," Ransom said.

"By, like, five minutes."

"Well, Holt noticed," Quinn said. "You better have a reasonable excuse because he is watching you like a damn hawk today, and already asked if you were going to flake."

Kye huffed and pulled me along with him towards Holt.

Honestly, I'd known Holt most of my life. He was always nice to me. I knew that he and my dad were close enough that we went to a lot of his parties and events, but my dad always tried to stay away from the bigger ones. The track party was one that Holt threw every year, though, and my dad never missed it. Fast cars, food, all the new announcements of racers, cars, events, and anything else outlandish that Holt could tell people. It had always been fun when I came with my dad, but I never imagined I would be here with someone who was going to be racing for him. I couldn't help the pride that grew in my chest when I looked over at Kye.

My life was beginning to feel surreal, and it was strange how much I liked it all.

I liked waking up with Kye, hanging out, and driving here. I was even excited to watch him race, even if it made me worried. I liked every second with Kye.

I slid my hand around until it rested on his lower back. He seemed confused when he looked down at me, but he threw his arm over my shoulders and started talking to Holt.

"You made it," Holt said, shaking his hand.

"You know I wasn't going to miss it."

Holt shrugged. "Never know with guys like you."

"I forgot something at home. I had to make a stop," I said, the anger in my chest flaring. I hated the way people talked to Kye, as if anything was wrong with him. As if he hadn't been doing everything to show Holt he could handle this career.

Ash beamed at me. "Better stop asking interrogating questions about what Daisy needed to turn back for now, Dad, or you might have a full meltdown like you did when you found out I actually have to go out and buy tampons sometimes."

"Oh, come on, Ashton, I wasn't going to ask more," Holt said, his face immediately turning red.

"Well, you were interrogating Kye. Just wanted to remind you that you don't need to interrogate Daisy, too."

The heat crept up my neck, but I knew Ash was helping.

"I wasn't going to ask her, Ashton. You are a menace to me," Holt said, laughing as she smiled at him. "Let me intimidate Kye in peace, so he knows how serious this is."

The tightness in my chest eased as I realized Holt wasn't going to be more of a dick to Kye.

"No intimidating necessary," Kye said. "I'm already taking this seriously."

Holt made a huffing noise as the door slammed open, an old man stepping inside looking very pissed off.

"Did no one tell you to install a damn elevator in this building, Holt? Do you not care about the elderly?"

Carly got up, running over to the door and grabbing the

guy's arm. "What are you doing, Grandpa? I told you that we would meet you downstairs."

"And then they told me that you have food and air conditioning up here, so I didn't want to wait."

Carly walked him over to us as he looked me over. "Daisy, this is my grandpa. Grandpa, this is Daisy, Kye's...girlfriend," she said, her lips pursing together to stifle a laugh.

"Oh, no," Kye said, stepping a little closer to me.

"Girlfriend?" Grandpa asked, his eyes going wide and a frown deepening on his face. Everyone had yelled hello to him, but I wasn't sure why. He didn't look friendly at all."You mean to tell me this guy *finally* found a girlfriend?"

"I did," Kye said. "But there is no finally, Grandpa, I wasn't looking."

He frowned harder at Kye before turning back to me. Shock reverberated through me when he grinned, the wide smile softening his face. "None of us ever are," he said. "You beauties just seem to find us, and what's a man supposed to do other than fall in love?"

I laughed as Carly pointed him at the table of food next to Holt.

They immediately started bickering over the elevator situation, with Holt accusing Grandpa of being blind because the elevator was right outside the door and in full operation. Grandpa continued the argument back and forth until Holt was the one apologizing.

The rest of the crew was gathered around talking about cars and the races today. Scout, Kye, and Ash would be doing some form of racing today with Ransom, Quinn, Fox, and Chase helping them. Jax and Carly apparently helped run a charity side of Holt's business, and they would be doing different demonstrations and games for younger races.

No one seemed to mind that I would be lingering around, and Quinn even told me a few things I could do to help Kye before his race. It was all simple things—getting helmets, and running things back and forth—but they didn't hesitate to include me, even if I knew nothing about cars.

It was easy, fun, and more relaxing than I anticipated.

My chest ached. The never-ending reminder that none of this was real was like a knife in my heart.

Kye leaned into me until his lips were at my ear. "Ready to go watch some races?"

Heat ran down my spine until my thighs clenched. "No. I'm ready to go do other things, though."

He grinned, but pulled me up with him as he stood. "Maybe later. For now, I have some work to do."

Later.

The word echoed in my mind because I wasn't sure what later meant for us now.

I LEANED AGAINST THE CAR KYE WOULD BE DRIVING AND watched as he checked over things under the hood.

"It's so weird that I am the first girlfriend you brought around. I'm so used to Dean's mom, who would constantly tell me how perfect his girlfriend before me was. They were friends from childhood and the family still loved her. Looking back now, though, I don't think I ever stood a chance for them to like me when they were still so obsessed with her."

"That's weird. I mean, I guess if any of the crew broke up, we would be screwed because we're all so close. I don't know how anyone new could make it in without us at least mentioning the ex. Lucky for you, you're the first girlfriend, and I think with what I have learned about relationships, you will be the last girlfriend I introduce, too."

I sucked in a breath, warmth spreading over me at the small sliver of hope that I would be the last because he couldn't want anyone else, but that died when I realized I was talking to Kye. The man who could go years without sex, and could probably make it another decade without a girlfriend, and not bat an eye. It had nothing to do with me and everything to do with his own preferences.

"Yeah," I echoed. "Lucky me."

"Ready to watch your fake boyfriend go those death speeds around a track?"

"No, not even a little."

He leaned down, kissing me hard, and I wrapped my arms around him. He lifted me up, my legs automatically wrapping around him.

"What are you doing? There is a crowd of people here."

"And?"

"And we don't have to fake date for them."

He gave an annoyed grunt before setting me down. "Holt is very much watching us from up there in his perch, right now. And I don't know a lot of things, but I do know that I would be kissing my girlfriend before I race. I've seen the guys do it a hundred times."

He hadn't let me go, so I leaned back in. "I guess that is true," I said, smiling as I kissed him again.

We stayed like that for a minute, his arms wrapped around me and expert lips kissing me. I was letting myself get caught up in the fantasy of this being real when the sound of my name cut through the noise of the crowd.

"Daisy?" my dad said. I could hear the disbelief in his voice. His face was white when I turned to him, his mouth still hanging open. I jumped back, but Kye grabbed my hand before I got too far.

"Daisy. What the hell are you doing?"

"Umm." I couldn't think of a single word as blood rushed to my ears, drowning out every sound besides my fast beating heart.

"Just a little luck before I go race," he said with a wide grin. "Great to see you, Sheriff."

"See me *again*," my dad said. "You know I have you running from me earlier."

"That was you? Wow, I was just getting a little practice in. Honestly, you are a great opponent. Maybe you should get out on the track with me today."

"Kye," I hissed. He wasn't helping any of this.

"What the hell are you doing with my daughter?"

"Dating her?" Kye said, the pleased grin on his face making my dad's turn red.

"Daisy," my dad said, almost screaming now.

"Well, I have to go race. I'll talk to you later...*sweetheart*," Kye said, smiling as he leaned down to me. He liked this too much, taking every opening he could to mess with my dad more.

Before my dad had any chance to respond, Kye was getting in the car, waving as he pulled away.

"Daisy," my dad said, stomping over as Kye peeled out to line up.

"Whatever lecture you have for me, can you not?"

"You just kissed Kye Baker. The guy I have arrested more times than I can count. The guy who just outran me when I was trying to pull him over." He ran a hand down his face and sighed. "Dammit, you were in the car, weren't you?"

"I'm the one who told him to go. I didn't want to deal with you. With this," I hissed.

"Maybe think about going out with a guy who wouldn't run from the police. One who doesn't love getting arrested and fucking up his life. Maybe one you are proud to date, not one you *want* to hide from me."

I met his eyes, my hands on my hips. "I was hiding it because of you, not because of him."

"I doubt that. You know, if he was a good guy, I would be fine with you two together."

"Then are you going to believe me if I tell you that he is a good guy?"

"There isn't a chance in hell I'm going to believe you. And based on what he just did and said, I'm going to tell you that he's using you and you need to break it off."

"And if I refuse?"

"You and I are going to have issues. *A lot* of issues."

"I don't live at home anymore. Why are you acting like I have to follow your rules?"

"Because I still pay for where you do live. And it isn't cheap. Have your grades gone down? Are you even still in school?"

"No, Dad, I started dating Kye and thought it would be better to drop out," I mocked. "Of course, I'm still in school. Stop being ridiculous."

"Ridiculous? That's the farthest thing from ridiculous. That's exactly what happens with guys like him. You need someone more mature, someone who has their life on track."

"I swear, if you tell me again that I should go on a date with your sheriff friend's son, I'm going to scream. I do not need to be set up on a blind date."

"It would make me pretty happy to see you give it a shot,

at least. Maybe see the difference between boys like him compared to Kye. Maybe you would even be happy with what you learn."

I turned back to the track, watching as Kye lined up and then was off. His car veered around the track, sliding around the corners. My fist clenched into my dress at each curve, worry gnawing at me that he was about to run into a wall, but he didn't. He would make it around each curve with ease until he hit a straighter part of the track and would take off again. It looked like he was going full speed at a wall each time, and each second was making me realize how dangerous this career would be.

And how much I loved sitting here watching him.

He was amazing. I didn't know anything about racing, and it was clear that he was good at this. I couldn't imagine why Holt wouldn't be signing him on as a driver immediately. He moved past the other cars with ease and drifted around the last corner. It was apparently only one of a few race events that would be happening today, and Kye would be doing more of these drifting events along with one on a dirt track that Holt had. All of it was to show off, and Kye was doing amazing at showing off his skills. I thought back to the picture Kye sent me. The one that was currently the lock screen on my phone, and I nearly laughed. It was so dumb that we made each other's photos our lock screens like anyone would notice, but I noticed every time I opened my phone.

And I loved it.

I wanted to go down there and see him smile like that in person after winning a race.

But I could feel my dad's glare on me, and my heart sank more.

Between knowing this relationship was always fake, to my dad never letting it be real, I knew it was over.

TWENTY-FOUR

KYE

THE THOUGHT of Daisy meeting me at the end of the race spurred me faster toward the finish line.

I was fucked, honestly.

There was no part of me that wasn't looking forward to kissing her after this.

I passed over the finish line, knowing I won but not caring.

Today was for Holt to see I was serious and to show off that I could be a good driver for him. Whether I won or not barely mattered to me.

Getting back to Daisy to find out what was happening with her dad was a lot more interesting right this second.

By the time I pulled around and parked, Daisy was standing alone by Jax and Carly's blacked-out Charger.

She definitely looked more pissed off than when I left her.

"What happened?" I asked.

"My dad is pissed. Thanks so much for helping with that, by the way. So, I guess it's time for our public breakup."

"Why? Because of your dad?"

"Because it's over? What reason do we have to keep the facade up? You're good with Holt now, and I came to the realization that I have friends that I like, and I don't need to keep up this stupid show."

The words hit me harder than I expected, my chest nearly caving in. It wasn't like I ever thought it was a real relationship, but I still liked spending time with her.

I gave a harsh laugh, my chest tightening, turning it all into anger. "So, you're just going from pleasing your friends to pleasing your dad? I'm useful when your friends need something to gossip about, and now that he's pissed about this, I'm useless again."

"No, Kye. That's not it at all."

"No?"

Her face fell, and she stepped closer, but I stepped back. "I mean, we agreed to fake the whole relationship for two things. Now we have those things, so wouldn't this be done?"

The entire rest of the day I had planned for dropped out from under me. The week, the month, everything I had wanted to do with her vanished.

A sheriff's car crept down the side of the track towards us. I knew her dad would be out driving around, meeting with people, and apparently ruining my life some more.

"Fine. I think that's your ride," I said, nodding towards it.

"I rode with you."

"Like I said, I think that's your ride." I pulled out my keys again. I still had more races to get to, but there was no reason to drag this out. I wasn't sure if I would even find the words to drag this out more. I was about eighty percent sure we just broke up, which meant I had no obligation to take her home.

I had no obligation to do anything.

I could feel my heartbeat picking up with each step. I

would lose myself to racing today. I would get so lost in going faster that I would forget about her.

I turned the car over, not looking back as I pulled on the small marked road, passing Sheriff Wells and flipping him off as I went.

It had been six days since Daisy decided to tell me it was all still fake for her.

Six nights that I had barely slept. Six days, I had barely gotten through without texting her. And each day that passed was pissing me off more. I threw the wrench I had been using on a bolt that was refusing to come off, not caring as it bounced off the tire of the car Fox was working on.

"What the fuck, Kye? Knock it off."

"It slipped."

"And nearly hit me. Don't come around me starting shit because you're mad at the sheriff, or maybe it's Holt. Who fucking knows because you won't tell us anything."

"Maybe I don't want to tell you anything because all you like to do is run your fucking mouth and gossip about shit."

He turned back to me now. If he was shocked, he barely showed it. "You think I'm running my mouth? It's not like I'm talking and gossiping just to be a dick. Unlike you, I care about what's happening in my friends' lives."

"Oh, you can fuck off with that," I said. "You think I don't care because I don't want to hear all of you whining over your fucking girlfriends? They whine less than you guys do." He stepped up to me now. Fox was a few inches taller than me, but I didn't care. I also didn't care that he was one of my best friends.

I was about to hit him.

"Just because you're mad that *you* want to whine over a girl now because she ended the stupid charade you had going on doesn't mean you can come around and start shit with me."

I charged forward, slamming my shoulder into him, but Fox knew me and swung up, hitting my jaw hard.

It only spurred me on, and I pushed harder until he fell back against the car.

Before I could hit him, I was being pulled back.

"Alright, children," Jax said, grabbing my shirt and ripping me back until I was tripping over my own feet. "Kye, go the fuck home."

"I don't want to go home. How the fuck am I supposed to go there and sit around thinking about her being there? What the fuck do I do when she won't even respond to me?"

"You wait," Jax said.

"For what?"

"For her to respond? Or maybe you tell her that it isn't a charade anymore? Have you even said that you want to date her for real?"

"Of course, I haven't said that. That's ridiculous."

"Ridiculous because you haven't said that, or ridiculous that you want to actually date her."

I shook my head, more confused than before. "Both? Why would I want to date her? I don't know how to be in a relationship. I don't know what I'm supposed to do with a girlfriend."

"You've been doing it for months now," Fox said, calm now. "There's not much more to it than what you've been doing. Don't be a dick and care about her."

"And then what?" I asked.

"What do you mean?" Jax asked, eyebrows furrowed.

"I mean, I go tell her all this and that I do want to date her, and then what happens?"

They looked at each other and then at me. "You date?" Jax asked. "That's what comes next."

"Just endless dating? Endless time together?"

"Isn't that the goal?" Fox asked. "Aren't you upset right now because you feel like you've lost her?"

He was right. That's exactly what the problem was, and I hated it. I wanted her back around. I wanted her texting me, bothering me, and touching me constantly. Anger swelled in my chest that she cut off our relationship without even talking to me. She didn't even have one conversation to ask what I wanted or even tell me what she wanted. She had been too worried about what everyone else wanted to not even bother about what we wanted.

"You got this, Kye. Just tell her you want a real relationship and then take it one day at a time. You're already better at it than a lot of people," Jax said.

I stared at them both before stalking out to my car to leave. I didn't want to be here today. I didn't want to work on cars; I didn't want to go out for a drive; I didn't want to do anything but find Daisy and fuck her until all she could say was my name.

A FEW HOURS LATER, CARLY BARGED INTO MY APARTMENT, Riot right behind her.

"Hey, I heard you're being an asshole today. Very on brand," she said, smirking as she grabbed my candy bar off the counter and tore into it.

"That was mine."

She nodded, taking a bite. "Kinda figured. Going to fight me now, too?"

"No. I don't feel like getting my ass kicked."

"At least you haven't lost your mind completely," she said, smirking as she took a bite.

"How can I be sure of that?" I asked, feeling like I had lost any sanity I had left.

"Oh, I would for sure be the first to let you know."

"Did you need something? Or just came to steal my candy?"

"Mainly the candy, but I also figured you forgot that we all made plans tonight to go to the haunted acres and do all the haunted houses."

I hadn't forgotten. I'd almost been looking forward to it, but now I felt so on edge that I wasn't sure if I wanted to go anywhere.

"I'm not going now."

"Come on, Kye," she groaned. "Let's just go out. You love the haunted house, and I heard this year is the best one they have ever had."

Fake blood, the sounds of screams and chainsaws, scary clowns. It did sound like a good way to get my mind off the girl who hated all of that. There was nothing there that would remind me of her, and maybe that's what I needed.

I could barely sleep in my bed without thinking of her there with me.

"Fine. I'll go. It's better than this."

Carly rolled her eyes. "Moping around isn't as fun as you hoped?"

"Not at all."

She waved me out of the apartment and downstairs to all our cars.

Everyone avoided me when I went downstairs, choosing to tiptoe around me and the questions I knew they had for me.

"I'll meet you guys there," I said, wanting to drive myself and avoid more of their awkwardness.

It was short-lived, though, because when I finally made it into the haunted acres and met them by the first haunted house, they did not look happy.

"What now?" I groaned.

Jax pushed Carly forward, and she glared back at him. "Nice," she said. "Literally throwing me to the wolves."

"You're the one that wanted to be best friends with him. So go on, be a good friend."

She rolled her eyes and pointed to something behind me.

When I looked back, my chest sank. The pit of my stomach churned until I felt sick. There was Daisy, dressed up in what appeared to be an attempt at a scary costume and a guy next to her. His hand moved to her lower back, pointing her towards a food cart. Red blurred my vision, and I wanted to scream.

The only girl that could touch me, the only one I wanted to touch, and now another guy's hands were on her.

I stepped forward, heading their way, when Carly grabbed my shirt and pulled me back.

"What are you doing?" she asked, her hand fisting to hold me in place.

I twisted, slipping out of my shirt and stalking away.

"Kye, what are you doing? You can't just go hit him."

"I'm not."

"Then what are you doing?" Scout yelled.

"Following them."

"You can't stalk her," Carly said.

"Like fuck I can't."

They headed towards the biggest haunted house, and I could only laugh. She hated scary things, but came here with him? And there he was, hoping she was going to cling to him because of it.

I grabbed a cheap mask off of one of the vendor tables, throwing a twenty down without stopping.

There was no chance in hell that she was going to be clinging to him. Daisy wasn't even going to make it through the entire haunted house with him.

Before she even had a chance, I was going to take her.

TWENTY-FIVE
DAISY

I WAS ABOUT five seconds from having a full-on meltdown.

The screaming, the chainsaws, the strobing lights. Every second was pushing me closer to breaking down and hiding in a corner.

I moved to the wall, clenching my fists as Mark got lost in the crowd, not seeming to notice I wasn't with him anymore.

I was frozen, my fear taking over, just like this place was designed to do.

Then it got worse. Arms wrapped around me, ripping me back into the dark.

I screamed, but there was no use in this place. The sound blended in perfectly.

"You're not supposed to touch me!" I screamed in panic as a door shut, sealing us into a back room.

"I'm the *only* one that's supposed to be touching you," he whispered into my ear, the heat of his breath making a ripple of pleasure move through me.

I took a deep breath as I sagged against him. "Kye. What are you doing? We shouldn't be back here," I said as he pulled me further into the dark. The music was muffled now, but I could still hear everything, the sounds of fake chainsaws and screams making me shudder.

He turned me around and pushed me up against the wall. I didn't come face-to-face with Kye, though, I came face-to-face with another terrifying mask.

"Why are you wearing that?" I yelled.

"So they didn't bother me sneaking around to grab you." He ripped it off, throwing it into a dark corner of the room.

I stopped shaking the moment I saw his face. The twisted pain and anger made me wish I could take a step back, but I was trapped, caged in by the man hunting me, apparently.

"You're here on a date with another guy?"

"Yes."

"I thought we were supposed to be dating."

"I told you the lie can be over, Kye. It's been long enough. I will be fine. We got into that fight and haven't talked all week. It's already been over."

He leaned down, whispering in my ear. "I wasn't done."

His teeth found my neck, biting and licking his way to my mouth before taking it, kissing it like it was his.

"I don't like *my* girlfriend on a date with another guy. It is making me want to commit acts of violence towards a guy who probably doesn't even know he's here with my girlfriend."

"I'm not your—"

"You are."

I let out a deep breath, trying to find words when his lips were back on my neck.

"I was on a date to forget about you and move on, not to piss you off, and not to get you in a back room for this."

"And did it work? Did you think about me at all?"

He pushed against me now, his cock hard against my leg. The crude position in a back room should feel just like that, crude, but Kye never made me feel like anything we did was wrong.

"I thought about you all night," I said, softer now.

"Tell me."

I didn't say anything, quietly trying to decide what I was going to do. He bit hard at my neck, making me wince.

"*Now*, Daisy," he yelled. "Tell me everything."

I closed my eyes and leaned my head back. "I thought about the way he drove and how it was so careful compared to you. And the way he's nice but doesn't cross the line like you try to. I wondered why he kept ignoring me and talking to everyone until I realized I had become so used to the way you whisper to me all the time, like you only want to talk to me, even when there's a hundred people around. I thought about how you wouldn't have made me come into the haunted house because you would already know that I would hate it. That you would burn it down if I asked. Or that you would carry me through and just fight anyone who bothered me." I was laughing now, but I opened my eyes. "I wondered if I was never with you again, would I ever find someone who touches me like they need it to breathe? It's like you can't get enough of me."

He didn't say anything, but he watched me, so I continued.

"I thought about the way you kiss right behind my ear every chance you get and the way I think I'm the one who needs you to breathe. Mark is so sweet, and careful. He's levelheaded, he is always saying all the right things, and my dad already loves him. And he doesn't just throw me up against walls. I mean, he asks to hold my hand. He *asks.*"

Kye's lips twitched, but he didn't smile completely.

"But it doesn't matter. None of it matters because I love you and your chaos. You don't always say the right thing and you scare me with your reckless attitude, but I can't get enough. And then all I can think is that I don't know if I'm just young and stupid, or if I will spend the rest of my life comparing guys to you."

He leaned forward, his forehead against mine. "I don't care if I am young and stupid. I don't have to compare anyone to you. I don't know that I ever will. There will never be any competition. What is this costume?" he asked, moving the skirt around.

I smiled. "I'm a prom queen. Duh?"

"You are the sluttiest prom queen I have ever seen. Did you really dress up like this for him?" Realization dawned as his eyes went wider. "No, you wore this for me."

"Obviously. I don't think anyone else is going around calling me that to get the joke. Although, I thought you would like the more murderous version."

"I do. My perfect daisy flower looks as murderous as I feel. How did you know I would come?"

"I didn't, but I might have hoped that you would show up."

"Why were you on a date, then, if you were just hoping for me to be here?"

"We haven't talked all week, and I thought you would at least say something. And then I was told that I had to go on this date with him and didn't want to disappoint my dad."

"What about disappointing me?"

"Yeah. I'm realizing now that I hate that more than anything else."

There was a breath of silence between us, until he broke loose.

He moved fast now, pulling out his cock and pushing my underwear aside. His fingers swiped, and I knew he could feel how wet I already was.

"What about this? Is this for me or him?"

"I don't know what you're talking about."

"Are you so wet for me? Or *him*?" he asked again, the edge to his voice deadly.

"Kye, I don't—"

"Answer me," he said.

"You."

"Good. You're mine."

"It was fake, Kye. None of it was real."

"All of it was real," he said, hiking up my leg and putting his cock at my entrance. "Every minute I spent with you was real. What about now? Is this not real?"

"Sex doesn't mean real, no."

"I would have taken you out tonight, but you didn't give me a chance, so this is the only real we get."With that, he thrust into me, making me cry out at the sudden fullness. "Scream my name. Tell them all that you're mine."

I didn't say it, my mind to focused on wanting him to move, to fuck me hard against the wall. I was a terrible person. I was supposed to be here with Mark.

"I want to hear how much you enjoy fucking me, and then I'll let you get back to your date." He started moving hard, moving against me with a blinding rage.

I couldn't stop it. No part of me wanted to either, so I let myself enjoy it.

"Kye," I yelled, getting so close to an orgasm I couldn't think of anything but him.

"I can't believe you thought we were done for good. That I wasn't yours anymore, and you weren't mine. Is that really what you wanted?" he asked, the angry edge to his tone matching his frantic pace now.

"No," I mumbled, losing myself to him.

"Good. I'll send you back to him with my cum running down your legs. Then there's no mistake that you're mine."

He pushed into me again, thrusting his hips up and into me.

"Do you know what it was like to find out you went out with another guy? That I already thought about killing him if I had to see him touching you?"

He pushed me closer and closer to the edge until I fell, the orgasm tearing through me. Stars burst in my eyes as I looked up to the dark ceiling, wishing I could hold on to this feeling longer.

He thrust one more time, burying himself deep in me as his forehead fell against mine.

"I would have taken you out and then fucked you like that all night. You could have come with me if you didn't go out with him."

"Can you stop reminding me that I am on a date? That I'm the slut fucking you in the back room of a haunted house while he is probably outside looking for me." I dropped my legs to the floor and pushed him back, but he stepped right back against me.

"Don't even think that about yourself when I'm the only one you're doing it for or with."

"What if I want to be with someone else? What if I was planning on sleeping with Mark?"

His face fell further. "Then I hope me fucking you messed that up or I will go outside and beat the hell out of him for taking my girlfriend on a date. He should know better. *You* should know better. You don't go out on dates when you are dating someone!" He was almost yelling now, but I didn't get it. I thought we were over. I thought he would be relieved this entire fake relationship was done.

"You didn't call me or text me or anything. I'm not your girlfriend."

"Pretty sure you have been for months now."

"I thought it was over. You told me as much and didn't talk anymore about it. I thought the agreement was done."

"It was never over. At least not for me. Do you want to get back to your date now?"

I adjusted my outfit and nodded. "Yes."

"Fuck," he said, kissing me again. "Say no."

"I at least need to tell him I'm leaving. I did agree to come."

His arms wrapped around me from behind, walking to the door with his lips against my ear. "You should remember that you're mine. You're covered in me. He better not touch you now."

I paused at the door. He couldn't see my smile, but I was having too much fun with Kye like this that I wanted to prod him a little more. "What if I want him, too?"

His hand snaked around my neck, pulling me harder back against him. "Then you're going to stay in here and fuck me until you can't even stand to think of him touching you. Until I cover every inch of your skin in me."

I leaned back, falling against him, loving the way he adjusted to hold me there.

His lips came to my neck where he bit down, hard enough to let me know there would be a mark. "I will bite and suck at your perfect skin until my name is etched in it."

"Why?"

"Because you belong with me. I belong with you. We were made for each other, and because I want to kill any other guy touching you," he said, kissing me lightly. "It is also possible that I might be a little possessive of the first, and only, person in my life that I want to touch, and taste, and be with."

I was silent, taking in every word.

"And if I want to go home with you?"

He sucked in a hard breath. "I will bring you to my car and take you home, without another word about you so clearly cheating on me," he said, but I heard the smile on his lips. "We can eat or watch a movie, or both. I can hold you all night or we can have sex all night. Anything you want if you're staying with me."

I thought it over, knowing what I wanted to do and what I had to do were two opposite things.

I pushed off of him, opening the door as the screams and music overtook us again.

A shudder went through me. I was ready to make a grand exit, except I forgot why I was happy to come in here in the first place. It wasn't just Kye making me want to hide in the closet, it was the anxiety that came with the haunted house.

I hated them. It was like my body went into fight or flight, my heart racing and hands shaking from the rush of anxiety.

"Daisy?" Kye said, coming up behind me. I could feel him right there, the heat of his body covering my back, but he didn't touch me again.

"Just the haunted house. I hate scary things, remember?"

He gave a small laugh. "Why did you come, then?"

"Because Mark brought me here and I don't know how to say no."

I was shaking now, my heart ready to burst from racing so fast.

"You should work on that. You look like you're going to pass out."

"Wow, thanks for the advice. Completely needed right now."

He grabbed my shoulders, turning me around to face him, "Come on. We'll get you out of here."

"No, I'm fine."

"What a bad time to start practicing standing up to people," he mumbled. "Come on. Take a breath and try to not pay attention to anyone else."

His hands wrapped around the back of my thighs and he lifted until my legs wrapped around him. He pulled open the door and stepped out, the loud music pulsing around us along with screams and chainsaws. The noise was deafening, but Kye leaned forward.

"If your anxiety is this bad, how did you make it this far in here?"

"I barely did. I was clinging to everyone like a madwoman."

"I only want you clinging to me. Damn, I already want to fuck you again."

"This is turning you on?"

"Yes. Your body so tight against mine in this stupidly short skirt is doing it. Sex with you is a drug. A high I can't find anywhere else, with anyone else. Come home with me."

I leaned in, kissing his neck as he carried me. Something jumped out at us, screaming to scare us, but Kye only held on tighter, his steps steady.

"We are at the end," he said and I looked back, seeing the exit.

"Okay, let me get off of you."

"We could walk out this way. What a fun way to tell your date that it's over."

"You're trying to start a fight."

"Maybe. He did take my girlfriend on a date."

"I'm not your —"

"Finish that sentence and I'm not setting you down. I'll walk you out of this place with my tongue in your mouth."

"You would do it, too," I mumbled, pulling myself off of him.

"Of course I would. Do you want to stay with him or go home with me?"

"That's a trick question."

"How?"

"If I say him, then you're going to be angry and stomp away, and then I'll feel guilty and go with you anyway."

He took a deep breath. "That's a fair assessment. How about this? If you want to stay here, I will leave, not angry, and call you later, as long as you agree not to sleep with him or fuck around doing anything else, even kiss him, for tonight at least. If you want to come home with me, I will wait in my car for you to go make up whatever excuse you need to."

My eyebrows jumped. "How mature."

"I am trying to be fair because I do not want you to be a people pleaser to me, and I thought that us being together was clear."

"It wasn't."

"I can assure you, it will be after tonight."

"What does that mean?"

"It means that whether you stay here on your date or come

with me, I will be in a bed with you tonight, not him, and I will be making sure there is no confusion about where our relationship stands."

"You would still come to bed with me to show me that even if I stayed on a date?"

"You could drag me behind my car right now and I would still do that tonight."

"I think you have some issues."

"I do. I'm currently trying to work on them but it is a very long list and I can only do one thing at a time."

I smiled at the realization of how hard he really was working to make himself better. I could politely back out of my date with Mark, go home with Kye, and no one else would know. I could find an excuse for my dad and tell him that I tried to go on the date so he would be happy, too.

It felt like a win-win.

"Give me ten minutes."

Kye's mouth dropped open with a smile, but he nodded.

"I won't interfere, but if you're more than twenty, I'm coming back to find you."

"Okay. Give me ten. I have to find him first."

He kissed my cheek.

"Don't give in to your people pleasing ways when he tries to beg you to stay. Because any man would beg you to stay. Do what *you* want, Daisy. Text me if coming with me ends up not being what you want."

Ten minutes later, I ran over to Kye's car, pulling open the driver's side door and crawling over top of him. My mouth found his immediately. If he was surprised, he didn't show it. Instead, he wrapped his arms around me and slammed my body against his harder.

This was everything I had been wanting, and everything that I knew I technically shouldn't be doing.

But it didn't matter. Tonight, I was doing exactly what I wanted to do, not what someone else told me to do.

TWENTY-SIX
DAISY

I HOPPED up on the car next to the one Kye was working on and leaned back on the hood. It had been one week since the night at the haunted house, and one week of me wondering what was going on between us but being too scared to ask.

We'd spend some part of every day together doing all the things we had come to normally do. The diner, a late night drive, watching movies at his place, and even spending Thursday at the races before hanging out with the crew all night.

Every night together, half the days, and I still was choosing to work on some of my classwork here at the garage instead of anywhere else.

My head rolled to the side to watch as he grabbed a different wrench and got back to work. Each push of the wrench made his arm flex. A sheen of sweat coating him, and I couldn't take my eyes off him. I didn't know how he managed to focus on anything else, because I was entirely wrapped up in him, and there was no chance of me actually taking in what I was reading.

"Are you almost done?"

He smirked, but kept working. "Have somewhere to be?"

"I do, in fact. I need to be in your bed," I said.

He grabbed a rag and set the wrench down, smiling as he headed over to me. "We could probably get a head start on things before we make it to bed."

"Considering half of your friends are in the office right behind us, I think we will be making it to the bed before anything gets started."

He made an annoyed groan, but he turned back to the car, throwing tools and parts into a pile on his toolbox before reaching out to help me down.

"Don't you need to finish that?"

"No. I have more important things to work on. Come on, hurry up," he said with a grin as I packed up my bag. "You said I had to get you all the way to my bed before anything happens. Don't slow down now."

"Geez, two minutes ago you were focused on the car. Now you are rushing me out the door."

"Two minutes ago, I thought you were being a good girl and doing your work. I didn't realize you were over here with all your dirty thoughts."

"Hey! I never said anything dirty."

"No, but I know all about those filthy things in your head, and I know you're thinking them now."

I rolled my eyes, but didn't deny it. Instead, I followed him out to his car, where he was already waiting with my door open.

"Have somewhere to be?" I asked, mimicking his earlier words.

"Yeah, my bed," he said with a smile. "And I'm about to

get there faster than you ever thought possible, so I would get that harness on."

I listened, clicking it into place as he got in, shooting us out of the parking lot and down the road before I could blink.

Before we made it fully into the apartment, Kye was grabbing me. His lips found mine in the dark as he lifted me up and headed to the bed.

"Okay, prom queen, we're all alone and in bed. Can I finally get you naked?"

"Hmmm, no. Actually, can we go back to the garage? I think I changed my mind."

His chest rumbled, and he threw me back onto the bed before coming down over me.

I wrapped my hand around his neck, letting the tips of my nails dig into his skin. He leaned into it, pushing harder against my hand and making my nails dig in even more.

"I have never wanted to die at someone's touch, but that's exactly what you make me feel."

"That sounds a little messed up."

He looked me over, eyebrows high. "I hate affection, don't like being touched, don't like sex normally, and love when you're rough with me. At what point was it not obvious that I'm more than a little messed up? I said it before and I will say it a thousand more times. I wave the reg flag and you're immediately wet."

"That is not true."

He crawled over me, and I knew right away I was screwed. Whatever he was up to, it was going to prove me wrong.

"Nails down my back."

"What?"

"Run those murder nails down my back," he repeated, the commanding whisper making a shiver run through me.

"I'll hurt you."

"That's partially the point. Do it."

I did, starting near his shoulders, my nails digging in as I dragged them down. His back arched, and he groaned. His eyes closed and head fell to the side.

"Fuck," he said. "Now my neck. Dig them in and bite me."

I listened again, forcing his neck to the side and biting down.

"Back again," he panted. I started lower this time, trying to make sure I didn't actually hurt him. His hand went down my side, slipping under my shorts before he dipped his fingers into me.

"Based on how wet you are, I would say I'm right. I tell you I want you to be rough, that I don't like fucking anyone, that I would happily *die* at your hands, and you're so wet your shorts are soaked."

"Maybe I would be like that no matter what you said. Maybe I'm just attracted to you."

He fell to my side, his hands tracing small circles on my arm.

"I think I'd like to have sex now," he said in a monotone voice, playing innocent. "It could be fun. Don't hurt me, though. No teeth, no nails. Don't go too fast or hard. Just carefully get it done and over with."

"Done and over with? How sexy," I said with a laugh.

"Yeah, and if we could keep touching to a minimum, that would be great."

"You're very good at proving your point. Is that the speech you give all the girls?"

"Just the last part," he said with a shameless smirk. "Now, which version do you want?"

I pushed at him and he rolled back over top of me. "You know exactly what I want," I said.

"You want me obsessed with you, drowning in you, clawing at my own skin to get you closer, and I am. Can we do something?" he asked, nuzzling into my neck.

"Something like sex or something like going out for a drive?"

He flipped, rolling me with him until I was on top of him.

"The sex part. For now, at least. I want you on top, riding me."

"Oh. Why wouldn't we do that?"

"I never have," he said, running his hands up my side and pulling my shirt off.

"Excuse me? You've never had someone on top for sex?"

"Okay. Technically, I did try it once for maybe five seconds, and I couldn't stand it, so it was short-lived and hasn't happened since."

"Why couldn't you stand it?" I asked, moving to pull off my shorts.

"There is a level of control with sex that I like to have. A level that I could always stop when I needed to if I was in control of the situation."

"Did you stop during sex all the time?"

"All the time? You make it sound like I've tried this more than twice. But yes, I wasn't exactly smooth about things and stopped more than once each time. When I kept the control, it was easier to push through the pain of touching."

"Then why have me be rough with you? Wouldn't that make it worse?"

"Apparently not. I trust you, Daze. I don't think you would actually hurt me and giving you that control makes me somehow feel in control. I can control when you're rough with me, and I know if I tell you to stop, you will. My body isn't in control. I am. I've never had that, and no one has ever made me feel like you do enough to give them any control. I had to force myself through it, and now I want your filthy mouth telling me everything you are going to do to me. I want you clawing for me, tearing me apart to get off."

"With the way you have always been fine with me touching you, it's still hard to believe." I crawled back over him, grabbing his cock and positioning it at my entrance.

"You are different."

"I don't know how," I said.

"A thousand ways."

"But you want this?"

"More than anything," he breathed.

I sank down, moaning as he filled me. Somehow, the sensation got better each time. I stilled, making sure he was fine, before starting to run my nails lightly over him.

Down his jaw, to his neck, to his chest and down his stomach before going back up.

"Do you feel out of control?"

"Yes," he said, pushing his hips up, taking me with them. "The good kind. Keep going."

He closed his eyes, his hands on my hips as I moved. I kept a slow pace, needing him to be okay and not rush through it.

"Wait, stop," he said, his chest rising and falling faster.

I froze, my heart stopping as I realized he could be stopping this. I didn't know if I could handle the rejection of him stopping midway through something so deeply close and passionate.

"Are you okay?"

"More than okay," he said through deep breaths.

I splayed my hands out over his chest. "Does that mean I don't have to stop?"

"No, don't. Please, don't." His hips pushed up again. "Okay. Keep going."

"No, tell me what you're thinking first," I said, worried now.

"You're the talker here."

"Start," I demanded.

"I think that every time we have sex feels like the first time I ever have. This included, because for the first time, both my head and body are here. I'm not thinking about anything other than your body on mine and I fucking love it. Drugs and drinking make me think more and only make me more reckless, so I fuck my life up. Racing is as close as I have ever come to shutting out the world. This, though, is consuming every part of me."

It was enough explanation for me, so I moved, pushing up onto my knees and riding him.

I kept moving until I could feel my own orgasm growing as Kye said my name. He grabbed my hips, holding me in place as he pushed up into me over and over, not stopping until I yelled out.

We stayed wrapped together until Kye pulled me up and carried me to the shower. He moved slowly, taking care of every step, from making sure the water was warm to taking his time washing my entire body.

Every movement was soft, careful...and so loving. Tears

pricked my eyes as he helped me out and wrapped me in a big towel with a soft kiss.

"Back to bed?" I asked, wrapping my arms around him.

"Nowhere else I would rather be," he said, pulling me back into the room and under the covers. He moved close until we were entwined, every part of him pressed against me.

I couldn't think of anywhere else I would rather be either.

TWENTY-SEVEN

DAISY

TWO DAYS LATER, Kye was dropping me off at my dorm again. We had gone out with the crew for a few hours to drive around and race, but I had to stay on campus tonight. There was no way I could keep staying at his place without completely failing out of college and knew I needed to come back for a few days to catch up and get to my classes. The crew had followed us over, and even now they were out doing donuts in the empty parking lot on the other side of the road.

In a matter of months, I had gone from a mess of my life to feeling completely content.

The confusion was quickly dissipating in my mind, and Kye seemed quick to call me his girlfriend now. No *fake* attached to it. Even the crew seemed welcoming of me being his girlfriend, the girls telling me that I would now be forced to go to their girls' nights. And as nervous as I felt about that, I was excited.

The world felt surreal, the entire relationship somehow both months old and brand new. The life I had been leaving behind felt so distant, even Dean didn't cross my mind at all.

He had been calling and texting constantly, but I sent them to voicemail and deleted the texts. I had nothing to say to him.

There was nothing I wanted from Dean when I had Kye.

I walked down the dark, dimly lit path that went from the parking lot to the dorms. It twisted and turned through gardens of beautiful flowers until it branched out to each dorm building.

I heard the footsteps behind me, but it was rare to be out here alone. I still sped up, never liking being out here this late. It wasn't far from my dorm, but far enough to make me uneasy. The footsteps behind me picked up their pace and my heartbeat picked up along with it. I fumbled for my phone, hitting Kye's name and walking even faster down the path.

"Please let this be a call that you changed your mind and want to come home with me."

"No," I hissed. "I think someone is following me."

"What? I *just* dropped you off. Where are you now?"

"On the sidewalk, still heading to my dorm."

"Hold on. I'm turning around. Keep walking, I will catch up."

"This is freaking me out." I heard tires squeal, the echo through the phone adding to the echo behind me.

"I'm coming, Daze. I'm already back in the parking lot."

"Okay. I can see my dorm building now. Maybe I'm just making a bigger deal out of this than necessary."

"I'm still coming, and now I'm staying the night."

"I told you Amber won't—"

"Amber will be fine. I'll talk to her. Are you inside yet?"

"No," I said, fumbling for the keycard to open the first door. I pushed it open, and arms wrapped around me as I stepped inside.

I screamed, pushing back and dropping all my stuff.

"Stop it," Dean said, pushing me inside more. I tried to elbow him. "Knock it off, Daisy."

"Let. Me. Go." I elbowed him again, hitting him in the sternum hard enough that his arms dropped from me.

I took off, heading for the stairs to make it to my dorm. Kye wouldn't be far, but he wouldn't get into the building without someone opening the front door. My dorm was only one floor up, but Dean was quick, grabbing me right before I made it to my door.

His fingers dug into my arms, forcing me to face him. One hand held onto me, the other grabbing my jaw hard.

"Let me go, Dean!" I screamed, hoping anyone in their room would open the door. He forced me back until I was up against my own dorm room door, but it didn't help. I knew it would be locked.

Dean still gripped my face, holding it so tight that I knew it was going to bruise.

"Stop, Dean. You have to stop."

"No, you have to stop fucking around behind my back."

"Kye is—"

"Kye is trash."

"You are the trash."

"You've been going behind my back to fuck him and now you're not calling me back? You're back in the dorm, and we are supposed to be together again."

"You didn't honestly think that would happen, did you?"

I pulled against his grip, trying to break free. One of his hands held my arm while his large body pressed my other shoulder into the door, his arm pinned between us and holding my face. I knew someone had to have peeked out into the hallway by now, and it pissed me off even further that they weren't stepping out to help. Kye should be here, but the door to the building would slow him down.

"Kye is right behind me. He's going to see this."

"I don't care."

The sound of glass shattering echoed around us, and I cried out as Dean tightened his hand on my face again. I knew it was Kye, and the idea that he just broke the door instead of waiting for someone to open it calmed me more.

It would be seconds before he was here.

Panic rose faster as Dean yelled something in my face. He stepped back, his hands moving down until he was squeezing my arms.

"Dean, let me go!" I yelled.

"No!" he screamed and slapped me, the force making my head turn and stinging pain radiate through my skull.

I opened my eyes, looking down the hall as Dean gripped my face harder.

"Kye," I breathed in relief, but the relief changed to fear as I saw Kye's face.

He had watched what had just happened.

Dean's head snapped to him, loosening his grip on me immediately.

"What the fuck are you doing here?" Dean asked.

"Get your hands off of her," Kye said, the quiet tone not matching the deadly look to him. I had come to know so many sides of Kye, even the reckless ones, but this wasn't any of them I was familiar with. He didn't even look at me, his eyes not straying from Dean.

"Dean, you better fucking run, and you better be faster than me," Kye said, his words so calm and even that I shuddered. "You better run faster, drive faster, and disappear faster because I'm *going* to kill you."

"This is none of your fucking business, we—"

"There is no we for you and her now." Kye started walking forward. Each step looked calm, but I could see they were anything but that. He was coiled up, ready to strike the moment he got close enough, and I wasn't going to doubt that he was about to kill Dean or at least try.

Dean took a step back, letting me go before he turned and ran.

It didn't matter, though.

I could see on Kye's face that it didn't matter how fast Dean was.

Kye was going to be faster.

TWENTY-EIGHT

DAISY

MY HEART RACED as I watched them disappear out the back door to the dorms. Dean knew the place well, but it would take them longer to get to the parking lot that way.

Since the entire college wasn't that big, Dean's car would be parked relatively close to Kye's, so I took off, running the same way I came in.

I reached the broken glass of the door and saw my phone in the mess. My hand sliced on the glass as I picked it up and searched for any of the crew's numbers. I finally hit Ash's, connecting the call as fast as I could while I ran towards the parking lot.

"Hello?"

"Is Kye at his car?"

"No?" she said. "He told us to wait a second because he was checking on you."

"Well, now he is out here running after my ex-boyfriend, who was just attacking me, and I'm pretty sure Kye is either about to kill him or already killing him."

The line was silent before I heard slamming car doors and Ash yelling to the others what I said.

I was still running towards them, hoping he would be at his car before seriously hurting Dean.

I made it to Fox's car first, panting as they circled around me.

"Where is he?" Fox asked, but I only shook my head.

Before I could say anything, the sound of Kye's engine filled the air. Dean's tires squealed as he peeled out, his car so quiet I didn't hear his turn on first. Kye wasn't far behind, though, and I stood frozen, watching them go.

Scout grabbed me, pushing me into her small back seat as everyone got in their cars. Chase got into the passenger seat and reached for a radio that was bolted to the floor between them.

Apparently, they all could talk to each other because a round of yelling at Kye went over the radio before Ransom's voice cut through.

"I think he turned it off. Just keep on top of him."

"Faster! Go faster!" I yelled as Scout shifted again. The car jumped forward, moving faster.

"Jax is right behind us," I said. "Where are the rest of them?"

"Ransom and Quinn took another route. He wanted to see if he could cut him off somewhere. Fox and Ash did, too. Anything to not lose him. One of us has to be able to keep up. He's not *that* good of a racer," Scout said.

"No, but he's better at these winding roads than any of you," Chase said.

"Can we please stop talking and go? He's going to kill him!"

"No, we won't let him. He's not throwing his life away

because of one idiot," Scout said. They all seemed so unbothered, but they were racing after him.

I was already a mess. Tears threatened my eyes, and I wanted to rip my hair out, anything to feel something other than blinding fear. "He is. You didn't see him. He's going to do it."

We rounded the corner as it happened. Kye's car slammed into Dean's, the front end clipping the back of Dean's car enough that it spun out of control, coming to a stop next to an old, run-down gas station.

We were still too far. Kye's car stopped, and he got out, stalking over to Dean's as we pulled up.

"Out! Get out." I kicked Chase's seat.

"I'm going, come on." He reached back, dragging me over the middle console and out of the car with him.

Ransom's and Jax's cars pulled up with Fox only a second behind them. My eyes were fixed on Kye as he dragged Dean out, throwing him hard against the building. He swung his elbow out, connecting with Dean's face. I watched the blood spurt from his nose, and for one second, I thought that it might be done, but Kye swung.

His fist connected with Dean's face, hitting him over and over as Dean yelled and tried to fight back. His yells only seemed to encourage Kye, who started saying something back, but I couldn't make it out.

Kye's hair fell over his forehead, the longer strands covering his face until he pushed it back with one bloodied hand. I didn't know if it was his blood from punching or Dean's, but the sight of so much of it still made me gasp.

Dean was falling down now, losing his balance and trying to hold himself up against the car when Kye finally stopped. It wasn't the end, though, a knife glinting in the headlights as Kye pulled it out and held it to Dean's throat.

"Kye, stop!" I yelled, running closer finally. "Just stop. You can't hurt him. They will come after you for everything. You'll go to jail."

"I don't care."

"Kye, you can't. He means everything to that school, to those people. You will never see me again."

That caught his attention, his eyes jumping to mine for a second. Dean took the opportunity, punching Kye in the face, but it didn't seem to faze him as Kye swung his elbow up, hitting Dean in the jaw.

Sirens wailed around us as the night was bathed in red and blue lights.

I groaned, knowing that Dean had to have called as soon as he got in the car. Now, my dad was about to be involved and this was only going to get worse.

Kye only pressed the blade harder against his neck, pushing until I thought I could see blood seeping out. I ran closer, stopping a few feet behind Kye's back. He punched Dean again, more blood spurted from his nose before the knife went back to his neck.

"Kye, stop. Please. I don't want to never see you again."

"Put the knife down, Kye. Daisy, step back." It was my dad's voice. He was standing by his sheriff's car. Three officers stood along with him, each one resting a hand on their guns.

"Don't you dare!" I yelled at him. My dad nodded and moved his hand, but the other officers kept theirs on their guns. "Kye, please. I need you. Please, stop. Stop because I'm the one asking you to."

"Fine. Because you're asking," he said before turning his attention back to Dean. He spun, turning to Dean until they both faced me. Dean went to move, but Kye's boot came up, kicking Dean in the back so hard that he fell to his knees with a cry.

"I hope you understand that you are only still alive because of her. I would push this knife so hard into your fucking neck you wouldn't even stand a chance to breathe her air again, so apologize to the woman who just saved your life."

Dean's eyes went wide, and I could see tears brimming. There was no wavering in Kye's tone, and I think we both realized that he had truly meant to kill him.

The hard realization hit me that Kye didn't care about the consequences, he cared about me.

"I'm sorry, Daisy. I'm so sorry," Dean said, his voice cracking.

"For what?" Kye said, the deadly tone keeping me frozen. "Tell everyone why her face is red."

"I'm sorry for hitting you. I'm sorry for hurting you."

Kye nodded, apparently satisfied with the admission, but when he leaned down, only the three of us could hear him.

"If you ever so much as put a fucking finger on her again, I *will* kill you, and she won't be able to save you twice." His words were calm, a harsh contrast to the chaos around us, and I knew he meant every word of it.

"Fuck you," Dean said.

Kye stepped back and Dean took his chance, running off, leaving me by Kye as chaos erupted behind me.

He was only looking at me, though. Red streaked his blonde hair and there was already a red spot on his cheek that I knew would bruise.

"Daze," he said, snapping my attention back to his eyes. I held my breath, too scared to breathe. "I love you."

I didn't know how it was possible, but my already racing heartbeat picked up.

"What?" I could hear him, but I couldn't comprehend the words, never expecting them from Kye.

He reached up, running his fingers down my face. "I said, I love you. I love you like I've never loved anyone, and I don't know if I ever could."

I stared, his face flashing blue and red, as I reached out, sliding my hands into his bloody ones.

"I love you, too."

He leaned down, kissing me once. "I'm going to go talk to your dad now."

"Okay."

"I love you," he said again. "I love you with every fucking part of me. Every stupid, broken part is yours."

"I love you, too." I said the words again, but my tears came harder now. A terrifying feeling sank into my gut.

I turned back, and someone wrapped their arms around me. Quinn, maybe, but I couldn't see through my blur of tears.

I was desperately in love with Kye and somehow it felt like I just lost him.

TWENTY-NINE

KYE

"HE WAS HITTING HER. I had to stop it," I said as her dad pushed me into the police car.

"Just shut up for one damn second." He shut the door, and I could only lean my head back and close my eyes.

It was worth being here.

Ash slid into the passenger seat, and Daisy's dad got behind the wheel. The car was quiet, the silence a harsh contrast to my heartbeat roaring in my ears.

"Where did he hit her?" he asked quietly.

"Her face, mainly. I think he choked her. I don't know how bad it was before I got there, but what I saw was bad enough that I wanted to kill him. I dropped her off, and she called me that someone was following her. I headed back, and by the time I got there, he was outside her dorm room door, trying to force her inside and hitting her. I chased him down and that's how we ended up here."

"Dammit," he mumbled. "You know who he is, right? You know no one is going to believe he was the problem here."

"I know."

"Kye was doing the right thing," Ash said. "Even if he maybe took it a step too far. You know you would have wanted to do the same thing. Please, you can't arrest him."

"I can and I will. He chased him down and tried to kill the guy. A guy that I need to remind you is very loved by this college and will stand behind him. I mean, dammit, Kye, I knew you were no good when you came into my daughter's life, but this?"

I laughed. "Sorry. Should I leave Dean to beat her up a little more next time? Or maybe just walk away completely?"

"Kye," Ash hissed. "We all know that Kye did the right thing. Can you please help him? Come on, you've known me my whole life, you know my dad. You know I wouldn't be hanging around Kye if he wasn't a good person. He was doing the right thing by Daisy. Dean was *hitting* her, Sheriff. Won't this be dropped if she presses charges against Dean?"

"That's if she does. She dated Dean for years. She might not want to," he said.

I wanted to snap at him, but Ash jumped in for me.

"I know this may be hard for you to understand, but I truly believe Daisy will do anything for Kye. She will press any charges possible against Dean if it keeps Kye safe. You cannot underestimate what she will do for him. I promise she is not out there crying for Dean. She's crying with worry over Kye."

"Ash, I can't just pretend this didn't happen. And even if it was justified at first, hunting him down and trying to kill him is not."

"Would a bribe help? We can get you new cars, fast ones that can keep up with our cars. Maybe then you will be able to catch one of these guys." She smiled, trying to lighten his mood, but it wasn't working.

"I can't take a bribe."

"No, you take donations, and I know for a fact that you have let Dean off the hook for a long list of things. Don't forget that I know what goes on behind the closed doors around here. Kye kept your *daughter* safe. Doesn't that count for something?"

"My daughter has been getting into more and more trouble since he has been around."

Ash looked back at me as though I could add something, but I couldn't. He wasn't wrong.

He ran a hand down his face and stared out the windshield. "How about this? I will try to convince Dean to not pursue this based on his own career and history with police run-ins," he said as he turned to look at me. "And in return, you will never talk to Daisy again."

My eyes met his, and I knew that second how serious he was. I knew because I had basically just told Dean the same damn thing. I knew with every single part of me that I meant I would rather die than have him get close to her again.

I was pretty sure that her dad was telling me the exact same thing.

"I can't promise that."

"Then I cannot promise to help you. I can't promise that all of your friends won't be involved in this now because they were here. I can't help you. Any of you, unless you let Daisy have a better life. Let her not be standing with her *supposed* boyfriend at 1 a.m., getting arrested by her father, for almost killing another guy she dated. She deserves a lot better than that."

"She does."

"Then we have a deal?"

I looked at Ash, and for the first time that night, my chest tightened, the all too familiar feeling of my heart dying coming over me. Even if I went about it wrong, I was trying to do what was right, and I would keep trying.

"Yeah, we have a deal. Can I go for now?"

"Yes, but I can't make any promises about what is going to happen."

"Then neither can I."

"Fine, go now, and leave Daisy here. I'll drive her home."

I got out and turned to Ash. "Should I tell her?"

"Are you able to tell her without going back on your promise? If you talk to her right now, are you just going to want more?"

"Yes."

"Then go. I'll give her the best explanation I can."

I nodded and headed to my car, the guys surrounding me immediately.

"I'm going to go for a week or two," I said, surprised that tears were threatening me now. "Unless I get a call to come back. I might just hang out for a few days. Okay?"

"Alright," Fox said. "We understand."

"It's going to be okay, Kye. It will all work out fine," Jax said.

Ransom knocked my arm. "Just let everyone cool down."

"I think it's worse than just cooling down now. If Dean or the Sheriff press charges, Daisy and all of you could get dragged into this mess. I don't want that for any of you. I'll see you guys soon."

"Just be safe."

I nodded and got in the car, heading to the apartment to grab a few things and then back out. Leaving the apartment, leaving town, leaving the state. The overwhelming pounding of my heart filled my ears. I loved her and I couldn't risk ruining her life.

Even for a day, I needed to be as far away as physically possible from Daisy.

THIRTY

DAISY

THERE WERE NO TEXTS.

No calls.

His name didn't come up again on my phone.

Mine didn't come up on his anymore.

And even if it did, I knew he wouldn't respond. I had tried, but they never went through.

I was told that every day gets easier until one day I will wake up and it won't hurt.

But when you make a million mistakes, that doesn't happen.

It was always what-if. A thousand what-ifs that made me lie down each night and wonder: if I had done one thing different, would that mean I would be at his apartment tonight instead of my dorm?

If I would be spending every night with him.

I knew I loved Kye, but each day that passed without him, I was only loving him more.

That wasn't what was supposed to happen.

It was supposed to get better, but every day got worse. A

pain that kept burrowing deeper into my bones until it took over. Until all I could feel was the pain of being ripped apart.

And just like the hundred other nights before tonight, I grabbed his shirt I wore the first night I stayed with him.

And I lay down.

And I cried until I was forced to sleep.

Until my body had no other choice but to give up for the day.

And I knew tomorrow would be the same.

And every night after that.

6 Years Later

THIRTY-ONE

KYE

I FIDGETED with the ring on my middle finger as the plane touched down before hitting my phone off airplane mode. I was already bracing myself for the onslaught of texts from the group chat.

SCOUT

I swear, Kye, if you aren't here, I'm missing my own wedding to hunt you down.

FOX

Could you catch him?

JAX

Only if he goes in a straight line, she can't make those corners for anything.

QUINN

Could one of you please come down to the garage and help me load my car?

RANSOM

I literally just texted Jax to help you. Why aren't you helping my wife?

CARLY

Because he was driving his own wife and the first seventeen bags of groceries to the diner. Prepping a dinner for 150 people isn't going to happen overnight. Why aren't you helping her?

RANSOM

Because I'm at the garage trying to make sure all these cars are going to get done while we are all busy this week. Have you ever tried to deal with four young guys who think they are the best thing to walk the fucking planet?

QUINN

Actually, I have. I had to deal with a garage full of guys and one little redhead. Good luck, babe. It's taken me ten years and I still haven't been able to keep you guys in line.

ASH

Ohh Carly, can you bring me a sandwich from the diner? Fox hasn't fed me all day.

FOX

I fed you two hours ago.

ASH

And??

SCOUT

KYE

FOX

He's on the plane, Scout, relax.

I had my phone off for five hours and they acted like they would never hear from me again. I rolled my eyes, deciding it was better to respond now than to let it continue.

KYE

I literally just touched down. I will be there in an hour.

SCOUT

An hour? We have the dinner reservation in an hour.

KYE

So what's the issue? I will be there on time.

SCOUT

BARELY

KYE

I will be there. Promise.

JAX

cough Bridezilla *cough

QUINN

Oh no...

CARLY

Jax!

KYE

I will see you guys in an hour.

I pushed the phone back into my pocket and grabbed my bag. I had only been gone for a week this time, so I didn't have much with me. This week, I had gone to Georgia for a race event with Holt, but ended up staying a few extra days for a drift event. Usually, it wouldn't be an issue, but it meant I was cutting it a little close getting back today.

Now I had a week off for Scout's wedding, another week of being home, and then a few races and events planned after that. It was non-stop, and exactly the way I liked it.

My life was racing and events. From plane to car, and

back to the plane, just to go to a new place with a new car. Holt used me in every area of his business that he could, and I never took it for granted. He gave me everything I wanted for my career, and in return I worked my ass off to be the head of all his drift and stunt areas of his company, while trying to add anything else I could manage.

I pushed my hat back on and found my car in the parking lot. Home was another hour's drive, but I was heading right to the restaurant, which would add a few more minutes. Hopefully, Scout wouldn't hate me forever if I made it by the hour mark.

The car flew down the highway as I got lost in thought. I came home pretty often. Sometimes I would be gone for months, sometimes days, but it never mattered.

Every time I crossed the sign letting me know I was back in town, I always thought of one thing.

Daisy.

THIRTY-TWO

DAISY

MY PHONE RANG for the fifth time in a row, and I finally picked up.

"What, Dad? If you couldn't tell, I'm busy. Hence the not picking up," I said, my tone already annoyed. Not that I didn't like my dad, but he always went overboard on everything, and I knew this wouldn't be any different.

"You're busy, but it's my day to see Bailey and you're ignoring me."

"Because I told you I have the get together today with my friend for her wedding next weekend."

"And you can drop Bailey off with me while you go."

"No, Bailey is friends with all of their kids and wants to go. Which is why I'm even attempting to get her ready to go out. She wants to go, and I like her getting to hang out with kids close in age."

Between Liam, Fox and Ash's kid, who was five, and Lily, Jax and Carly's four-year-old daughter, there was a pack of kids that were quickly becoming inseparable when we got together. It was one of the biggest reasons I started hanging out with the crew again. Now, though, I was best friends with the girls and ended up spending most of my free time with one of them, if not all of them.

My dad was still going on about seeing Bailey. "She's *my* granddaughter, Daisy. You know your sister would want me to have more time with her."

"My *sister* would understand that her daughter has more of a life than I do and would like her to have friends."

"Exactly. She's Willow's daughter, not yours, and you need to stop acting like you get to make all the decisions for her."

Red hot anger sliced through me anytime he tried to say Bailey wasn't mine. "Bailey became my daughter the minute Willow passed, and someone had to take custody of her. I took *full custody* and as sheriff, I think you understand that means I get to make all the decisions for her."

"Daisy, you need to bring her here. I—"

"*I* will bring her to your house tomorrow. For now, I'm going to my friend's dinner. Goodbye."

Bailey ran past me, yelling out the same line of a song over and over with her dress already twisted and halfway off. I grabbed the backup clothes I had for her and shoved them in my bag before grabbing her.

"Come on, Bee, we have to go."

She screeched, and I continued out the door.

Mark pulled into the driveway. The window to his cruiser was down, and I waved as he stopped next to me.

"Thank you so much for the ride," I said, and he nodded, getting out to help me. "My car will be back from the garage tomorrow, hopefully."

"Come on, Bailey," I said as she hesitated. "You get to go

see Liam and Lily." Her head fell to the side, and she gave me a sweet smile.

"Okay, let's go," she said, sliding down my side to get into the car. Mark was already putting the car seat in the back and Bailey jumped into it.

Her little crush on Liam was already paying off for me, and she happily got into her car seat and buckled herself in. I tried to tell myself that every month, and every year, was only getting easier. Bailey was becoming more self-suffi-cient, which I thought would be a relief, but it somehow became a nightmare with how smart she was getting. It didn't help that she had a wild streak in her I couldn't contain.

Bailey would never be the girl following her friends jumping off the proverbial bridge. She would be the leader, and I never realized how scary it was for the parent of the leader.

"Really, Mark. I appreciate the ride."

He smiled, reaching over to pat my hand as he drove. "Anytime. I don't mind getting to see you two for a few minutes."

While we'd gone on a couple dates, and while I consid-ered us dating, I still couldn't bring myself to call Mark my boyfriend. He was sweet, and likable. My dad loved him, and I really had nothing to complain about, but I still hesitated to push the relationship along any faster.

"You work all day?"

"Till ten. Yeah. I would offer to see you after, but I'm guessing you'll be sleeping by then after a day with this one." He pointed back at Bailey and gave me an apologetic smile. He knew how much it took for me to keep up with her. Between my anxiety and her antics, I was either running after her or panicking about her safety. It was endless and exhausting.

And while Mark didn't mind helping me with things like a ride or bringing over some food for us to hang out, he wasn't sure what to do with Bailey. Not that I blamed him exactly, but it felt strange that the guy I was dating couldn't understand what to do with her. He wanted his own kids, at least that's what he'd told me, but the look of fear that came over him anytime Bailey needed anything more than a snack made me think he wasn't quite ready for them yet.

He kept the conversation going, telling me about work and things going on in town. He was an officer now, working under my dad, but was currently running to take over for my dad. He wanted to be the sheriff, and I was helping with it. Dating the current sheriff's daughter looked great to the town, and he was using every opportunity to show us off together. He went on about it all, my mind wandering the moment he started about the logistics of everything. I'd heard so much about the sheriff's life growing up with my dad, that listening to it now was like white noise. It wasn't Mark's fault, but no part of me could tune into the ramblings.

By the time we made it to the country club for the dinner, Bailey was humming in excitement. I jumped out to help her out and was already five seconds behind her flurry of excited movements.

"Thanks again," I said, leaning down and pressing a quick kiss to his cheek. I liked Mark.

Mark was fine, and fine was the exact reason we hadn't made it past a quick kiss here and there.

He seemed fine with it, and I definitely would not be the one pushing for more. I knew he liked me. The constant reaching out and taking me out was obvious. He had made it clear he would respect me and let me make the first move towards anything more physical, which was nice, but it meant we had been dating for months with nothing past a make-out session.

I should have known Bailey was going to bolt, but part of me was too preoccupied thinking about everything I had to do this week, and everything about Mark.

"Bailey!" I yelled, already running after her as I waved back at Mark. She made it inside seconds before I did. "Bailey!" I yelled, running down the hallway. I knew the crew would be in the banquet hall, looking over the place Scout was holding the wedding, and I knew Bailey knew the entire place well enough, but I still needed to catch her.

I turned the corner, slamming hard into someone's chest.

THIRTY-THREE

DAISY

ARMS REACHED OUT, steadying me.

I didn't know it was possible to happen twice in my life.

That moment when you look at someone and the world around you shatters. This time, though, it was memories flooding back in. Like a movie playing so fast, I couldn't get the entire story, but felt each scene with the same heightened emotion I felt when it happened in real time.

Every kiss. Every fight. When I said I loved him, when he said it to me, and the feeling of my heart breaking under the weight of the words.

The first night at the party that I kissed him.

Anger and heartbreak rushed in, ready to knock me over.

It was like a day had gone by since the last night I saw him, not six years.

"Kye?" I asked, not quite believing he was standing in front of me, touching me. I knew he had been back in town plenty of times, but we had managed not to run into each other. I had avoided the crew when he was around and he managed to not come around the diner when I was there.

"Daisy," he said, sounding as surprised as I was.

Another wave of heartbreak washed over me at the sound of my name, my eyes already threatening tears.

He stepped back fast, shoving his hands into his pockets, but not taking his eyes off of me. He looked different. We had both grown up, but unlike me, he had gained plenty more tattoos, from what I could tell. His mess of blonde hair hadn't changed, though, still as unruly as the look in his eyes. Every part of him had filled out, muscles more defined, jaw sharper, every deadly part of him harsher now.

He hadn't seemed to have lost any edge to him. Something about him was still feral.

I had wondered if that would ever die. If the wild part of him would ever be quiet enough to live a normal life, but I could tell it hadn't.

I guessed that should be expected when you raced cars and cheated death for a living.

"I wasn't expecting you here so soon," I said, breathless.

"You thought I would miss my sister's wedding?"

"No, but I assumed it would be a last-minute stop on the way to your next race. I didn't think we would see much of you this week."

He smirked. "Not this time. I haven't heard the end of it for cutting it so close to Fox and Ash's wedding. I've become a lot better at planning over the years."

"I see that. A week early? I'm almost impressed."

"Would it get you all the way impressed if I say that I am helping plan and set up everything for the wedding?"

"It would make me say that I know your friends' hectic lives and I assume you got as guilted into it as I did."

"Ahh, they are good at that. You look good," he said, looking me over, but his eyes didn't linger. It should have been a kind thing, the gentleman's thing to do, but I smoothed out my dress, wondering if I looked as chaotic as I felt. "How are you?"

"I'm good. Busy, but good. You?" I asked, hating each word. The small talk was not anywhere near what I wanted to say. Then again, anything I had to say was a conversation I didn't know if I was ready to have. He had left, and I still struggled to accept it. Worse than that, I was struggling with the feeling that jumping into his arms seemed like the most natural thing to do. I had never spent over twenty minutes with Kye without touching him, and apparently muscle memory would not let me forget that.

It had been six years.

Six years without a word.

I had to hear about him a lot. Ever since I became closer to the crew, I heard the updates about him constantly. How well his races were going, how ridiculous his stunts were, how good he was doing. I stayed away when he was home, though. He was a superstar and his friends were proud of him, so I tried to never ask them to stay quiet. I had become used to the updates, but seeing him now was something different.

"Busy, but slowing down finally."

"Wow, never thought I would hear that from your mouth." At the word mouth, he looked at mine, and I was too aware of how badly I wanted to run my tongue over my lips. As soon as I thought about it, it was a battle to stop.

There was no way I could already have these thoughts about him.

I should be pissed, heartbroken, and angry at him, but my heart was thundering in my chest, forgetting every second of the pain.

Maybe it was because I had barely let Mark anywhere

near getting in my pants, even though we had been going on dates for months.

Months of dating and the man had barely made a move to do anything more than kiss me, and I hadn't asked for more.

Maybe I was just to horny, and standing in front of the man who gave me the best orgasms of my life. That fact still held up to this day.

"I never thought I would, but with how much is changing around here, I think I'll be around more. I'm still traveling a lot for work, but I'll spend more time here when I can."

"So, I might have to see more of you, then?" I asked.

"Considering you seem to be best friends with the crew now, I would say yes. You don't sound pleased about that, though," he said with a smirk.

"No, of course, it's fine. I'm just surprised. And yeah, they've been great to me. They somehow came back into my life the moment I needed them."

"They have that effect on people, always knowing when to be there and how to be there."

Bailey rounded the corner, running full force. "Hey," she said, grabbing my hand with a pant, her tone was so serious for a four-year-old. "Hey, we are going outside."

"You are still in trouble for running off without me, so you are going to wait. I'm talking." That's when she looked up at Kye, her eyes going wide. I didn't think she was scared, having become used to all the guys on the crew, their scowls, and their tattoos, but more curious than anything.

Her eyebrow cocked. "Who are you?" she asked, stepping closer.

I looked at Kye, his eyes wide. I knew he loved his niece and nephew, but I didn't know how he felt about other kids.

One look at him wouldn't have anyone screaming 'good with kids,' but then again, most of the crew looked like that.

He knelt down, reaching out a hand. "I'm Kye, and you are?"

"Bailey," she said, shaking his hand with her hard little stare, sizing him up.

"Unless something has changed in the last four months since being home, I do not believe I have any nieces that are named Bailey."

"No," she sang out, but I didn't think she actually knew what she was answering.

I laughed. "She's mine."

His eyes flew to mine, fear frozen in them. "I did not know you had a kid."

"Well, that's complicated. Hey, Bailey, will you go grab Quinn or Scout so we can go outside?"

She was still looking at Kye, though.

"Why do you have her name on your hands?" she asked, staring at the hands he shoved back into his pockets.

"What?" I asked, looking at her.

"D-A-Z-E," she read out slowly. "That's how she taught me to write her name when I write it for fun." She jerked a thumb at me. This little girl's attitude could fill a room, and I tried to get it under control, but it never seemed to work.

"The attitude, Bailey," I scolded, knowing her accusing tone was going to come again.

"Like Daisy, but without *eeee*," she said, sounding it out.

"I think I'm going to need some clarification now," Kye said, looking at me.

"Yeah, me, too. Bailey, please go get Quinn or Scout or Carly. Literally, anyone. I need a minute to talk to Kye."

"Fine," she said, crossing her little arms. "But I want to see it again later."

Kye gave a serious nod. "We can absolutely do that."

She nodded back and took off, running full force towards the lobby area.

"Slow down!" I yelled.

"I really don't think you are slowing that one down," he said, standing back up with a laugh.

"No, I struggle every day with it. That, and the attitude that is bigger than this whole town. I think the crew has rubbed off on her."

He shook his head. "Why did I not know that you have a child? Way to give a man a heart attack. She looks enough like me I had to do some quick math. Please tell me this isn't what I think it is?"

"She isn't mine. Or ours," I added fast, the words causing a flutter of butterflies through my stomach. "Not how you are thinking. Bailey is four. She's my sister's. *Was* my sister's. Willow passed away a little over three years ago. It was an accident. My dad was getting too old to keep up with a kid and having some health problems at the time, and I don't have much more family. I decided to take her."

"Shit, Daze, I'm sorry. I didn't know. The crew doesn't really tell me about you."

Daze. The nickname I hadn't heard in years. The one I never wanted anyone else to call me. I had told Bailey about it when she started trying to spell my name, but she really just called me Mom now.

"Yeah, I asked them not to."

"What? Why?"

I shrugged. "I don't know. It seemed easier. One more way to keep our lives separate."

He nodded. "I see."

"Come on. Tell me she's wrong. Let me see," I said, holding out my hands for his, needing to know if what Bailey said was true.

"See what?" he asked, looking past me to the doors.

I wasn't going to wait or play this game. I grabbed his wrists, hiding the shot of excitement that went through me from touching him. I pulled his hands out of his pockets, bringing them up until his knuckles touched. The moment my skin met his, I sucked in a hard breath. All I wanted to do was thread my fingers in his.

Bailey had been right.

Clear as day. The letters on one hand read D-A-Z-E and on the other hand read E-E with one little daisy on the pinky finger.

I dropped his hand, stepping back like it hurt. Touching him *did* hurt, but seeing that was like a knife twisting in my gut.

I could feel how wide my eyes were, how hard my heart was beating, but he only stared, his face stone.

"When did you get that?"

"I've had it for a while." His tone was hard and angry, like I was the one who had done something wrong.

"How long is a while?"

"I don't know, Daisy, a couple years? Does it matter?" he asked, his face hardening into indifference.

"Yes, it matters. When?"

"Maybe four years ago."

Even around four years ago meant he got it tattooed two years *after* he left.

"Why did you get it?"

He shrugged. It was like he was trying to act like we

weren't talking about anything of importance, but tattooing someone's name on you definitely felt important.

"I don't know. I guess I had too much to drink one night and missed you. A stupid, impulsive, permanent mistake."

My mouth fell open. The words twisted like a knife, but it didn't matter. My name was on his hands.

I didn't have any tattoos, never being able to decide on one thing that I would want on my body for the rest of my life, but he seemed like it wasn't a big deal to have my name on his hands.

He was branded with my name and acting like this was normal.

Not only that, but a place where everyone would see it.

"Kye!" I said, stepping back again.

Bailey walked around the corner. "I found one!" she yelled.

Carly followed, letting out a screech as she saw Kye.

"You're here," she cried, coming over to him, Jax trailing behind her. "Why didn't you come see us first?" she said, tears actually falling now.

"I told you he was meeting us here," Jax said.

"I just got in. I was going to be late if I didn't come straight here," Kye added.

She was nearly sobbing, Kye's arms wrapped tight around her.

"Glad you made it," Jax said. "If you haven't heard, we have hit the point in pregnancy where everything makes her cry. *Everything*. So watch yourself."

"I can't help it. I haven't seen him in two months and I missed him."

Kye just shook his head at Jax. "At least someone missed me."

"We all missed you," Jax said, shaking his head. "Carly, why don't you go sit with the girls outside by the pool? The water will feel great on your feet."

Carly looked down. "My swollen, ugly feet that I can't even see. You know I can't make them look any better," she cried.

"No, sweetie," I said, stepping in with raised brows at Jax. "He meant you deserve a rest. Come on." I grabbed Lily's hand, still holding Bailey's, who then grabbed Carly. "The girls are waiting for us, anyway. Remember?"

"No. I don't remember anything. Ugh, this is it, Jax. No more kids. We're done."

We headed to the door, and I couldn't stop myself from looking back at Kye. He was talking with Jax now, but his eyes still found mine.

He gave a tight smile, one that shattered my heart like he had done years ago.

I had stayed away from Kye for six years, thinking that my heart couldn't take being close to him, that I would never be strong enough to be around him again.

And I was right.

THIRTY-FOUR

KYE

"ARE YOU OKAY?" Jax asked, making me look away from Daisy to him.

"What? Yeah, I'm fine. Just tired from the trip."

"That's not what I was talking about."

He was talking about Daisy running into me after six years of not seeing her. Six years of avoiding everything about her from the crew talking about her to seeing her when I was in town. I couldn't bring myself to face anything having to do with her. The cruel twist of fate that took her away from me and now it would put her here in front of me without a chance of getting closer. It was an unbearable torment.

I wondered if she ever thought of me, if she ever missed me the way I missed her. It was an easy thing to wonder, but now she was close enough to ask and I wished I could.

"Daisy? Yeah, we are good. We even just had a polite conversation. One where I got ratted out about the tattoo on my hands that I had been doing well at hiding."

He laughed. "Bailey?"

"Yes, pointed it out immediately."

"Yeah, she's observant. And tough. She's a great kid, though. That's the one I tell you is best friends with Liam and Lily. Daisy's done well with her."

"You told me about their friends, but failed to mention whose kid she was. Why didn't anyone tell me?" The anger and regret were coming over me, and I could feel my temper flaring. I had gotten it under more control as I got older, but any one of them could have told me what Daisy was going through. It wasn't like they never talked about her, but they failed to mention one of the biggest things in her life.

"She asked us not to. Ash said she seemed sad anytime we brought you up, so we tried to not do that too much around her either. It just seemed like it would help you two keep your lives separate. You looked fucking miserable anytime something about her was mentioned, so we just got the hint and stopped mentioning everything."

"I could have come back, though."

"To what? Take care of her? Take care of Bailey? We've obviously done what we could to make sure they are both okay. She doesn't take help easily, though."

"I don't know. I could have at least come back to help through the funeral."

"She was dating someone, anyway. Not that it lasted after Bailey came around. That guy ran for the hills and Daisy was too busy to care."

"Is she with someone now?"

"Yeah, but I don't actually know how serious it is. He seems...fine."

"Fine?"

"Yeah, like a good guy, a simple guy. He's a cop, so I'm assuming her dad likes him, and he seems to want to be a family guy, so he likes Bailey enough. I don't know if it's serious yet." He smirked. "She makes sure not to bring him around us much, so that's about what I know."

"Why? How long have they been dating?"

"Maybe four months? The gossip is that he tried for a long time to get her to go out on a date and finally she caved one day. He's been trying to move for more, but she's taking it slow. The girls don't like him much, but I don't know why."

"The gossip, Jax? Really?"

"I have a pregnant wife whose friends pile into the apartment to tell her all about the outside world anytime they can. I overhear stuff."

"Damn, we need to get you out more."

"I currently can't be more than ten minutes from my wife and child, so maybe we can do that after the baby comes."

"Fine, fine. We will wait. Or just load everyone up and go to the track."

"*That* we can do."

"I'm serious. We should do that this week."

"And I'm a hundred percent in. Ask Scout, it's her week. Well, hers and Chase's, but I'm assuming Scout would be there faster than any of us. She wants the wedding, but she hates everything leading up to it."

I rolled my eyes. He wasn't wrong. Scout would always take a chance to be at the track. Even on her wedding day, I bet we could get her there.

I looked at Daisy as we went outside. She was dating someone. A cop, at that. I guess it made sense. I'm surprised she wasn't already married or something. She had only grown more beautiful and still kept her head up high, the prom queen that would never let anyone see her trip. I admired it, though. She was always trying her best, and no one could claim otherwise.

We made it through the doors just in time to watch Bailey jump into the pool, fully clothed, with a yelp of joy.

"Bailey, no," Daisy yelled, running to the edge. Her face fell, and I could see the exhaustion now.

"Can she swim?" I asked, running to the other side, ready to jump in.

"She's a great swimmer, and that's the problem. She will not get out now. Bailey, come on."

She only laughed, splashing back and forth from each side. She was a good swimmer and knew to stay out of Daisy's reach.

"I should not have bought swimming lessons for you," she groaned. "Bailey, come out, now. You are going to go dry yourself off before dinner."

I couldn't help smiling as she spun around in the water, grinning.

"You think this is funny?" Daisy said, staring daggers at me.

"I mean, yeah, a bit," I said.

Suddenly, the entire crew was laughing behind her.

"You guys," she said. "Stop laughing. I can't even control her."

"We aren't laughing *at* you, Daisy. We are laughing *with* you," Quinn said. "No one here is expecting you to control her. She is uncontrollable, and unfortunately for you, it's adorable."

Bailey spun again, smiling up at me.

"Are you going to get out like she told you?" I asked.

She shook her head no, her smile bigger than ever.

I kicked off my shoes, and pulled off my shirt. Luckily, I was still in my shorts from the plane and, unlike everyone else, had a change of clothes in the car.

"What are you doing?" Daisy asked, and I didn't miss the panic in her voice. I looked up, and her mouth dropped open, staring at me.

"Getting your daughter."

I sat on the edge and slid in. The water was a perfect temperature that I could hardly blame Bailey for not getting out.

As soon as she saw me in the pool with her, she screamed in joy, paddling the opposite way.

"Oh, man. This is the exact type of shit we would have done. I can catch you, Bailey. You better swim faster."

"Kye, language."

"Oh, shit." I shook my head. "Sorry!"

"Ohhh, shit," Bailey repeated, her lips sounding out the O, and I knew I was in trouble.

"Kye!" Daisy yelled.

"I'm sorry! I forgot," I said, grabbing for Bailey, who thought she was faster. "You don't stand a chance outrunning me."

I picked her up, pulling her back to the shallow end.

"Oh, shit," she said again.

"Listen, if we don't stop saying that, we are both going to be in trouble," I whispered to her.

"I'm in trouble for going into the pool," she whispered, sucking in a breath between each word like that was going to keep the words quieter. "So more trouble is fine."

I lifted her onto the edge, sitting her down so her feet were still in the water. My body shook with quiet laughter before I doubled over. My forehead rested on the cold concrete next to her as I tried to hide it, not able to stop as Bailey patted the back of my head as she laughed.

"Kye, what's wrong?" Daisy said. My back was to her, so she couldn't see the tears forming from laughing so hard.

I finally turned, calming myself. "I hate to tell you this, but at four years old, your child has the same plan for getting out of trouble that I did when I was a teenager."

"Which is?" she asked, arms crossed and clear worry across her face.

"If you're already in trouble, just do all the fun things at once, so you're only in trouble once. She said you're already mad at her for getting in the pool, why not cuss, too? Ahh, damn, Daze, good luck raising her because you're going to need it."

At my words, Daisy's mouth dropped open, and Bailey jumped over my head and back into the pool. I grabbed for her, but I was surprised when she resurfaced, her nose plugged as she blinked water from her eyes.

"Do all four-year-olds swim like this or is she just a daredevil?"

"No, not at all. She just thinks she's invincible."

"Me too, Bailey. Me, too."

I grabbed her, playing in the water for another few minutes before we really had to get out and change.

By the time I dried off, changed, and headed back inside, everyone was waiting for me, including Daisy and Bailey.

"How did you beat me getting ready when you have this unruly child?" I asked.

"Because she takes punishment well enough when she knows what she did and she hustled getting cleaned up. At least I have something under control."

"I think you are doing just fine. She's clean, healthy, obviously happy. Not much else you have to worry about."

"There's a thousand things to worry about."

I shrugged, knocking against Bailey, who was trying to get Liam's attention.

"Want to go eat?" I asked them.

"Yes," they both said together.

"Me, too. I had to eat dry crackers on the plane."

Daisy almost looked upset that I was helping, and I wondered if it was her old habit of appearances. If she was worried, she didn't look like a good enough parent with so many people around. I grabbed Bailey, picking her up and heading over to the table.

Everyone sat and ate, Liam next to me, with Bailey next to him, and Daisy on her right. Everything went fine enough, the crew catching me up on some things I missed, and Chase catching all of us up on the wedding plans for the week.

It was another hour later before I needed air. The room feeling crowded, and my eyes kept wandering to Daisy.

"I'll be back," I said to the table before getting up, and walking out to the back porch. The place had little fires going in two of the pits and I sat by one.

Daisy was here. Back in my life without any notice, and she had a kid.

I had never slowed down enough to think about her life. Sometimes, I wanted to believe she was married and happy. Sometimes, I wanted to think that she thought about me as much as I thought about her.

Most days, I wanted to not think about her at all.

It happened. I made it through days and weeks without her on my mind, but the moment I felt lonely, she flooded my memories until I couldn't think of anything but her.

The door opened, and the girl that took over my dreams and nightmares stepped out. Her dress blew in the wind, but she didn't seem to care as her head tipped back and eyes closed. A moment of peace, before her eyes opened and met mine.

She froze like she might go back inside, and I laughed.

"I already saw you, Daze. Might as well come sit down."

"I didn't know if you wanted to be alone," she said, heading my way.

"Is that why you are out here? To be alone?"

"I just get a little overwhelmed sometimes."

"I get it. I'm good with company. I won't be long out here if you need to be alone, though."

"No," she said, sitting down and smoothing her dress again. Another sign that she was still the girl I knew, not wanting anything out of place. The green of the dress brought out the greens and brown hues in her eyes, and showed off plenty of her long legs. "It's fine."

We sat in silence for a minute. For everything I ever thought about asking Daisy, I couldn't bring myself to ask one fucking question.

"So why are you still single?" she asked, and I could see how hard she was focusing on the fire, not daring to look at me.

I smiled because I only wanted to ask her why she wasn't. "Well, between traveling a lot and having this small issue that I still don't like people getting all touchy with me, dating isn't easy. I'm still the same. I never needed to date or worry about it. You did, though. What about you?"

"Aside from the dating pool going down to what feels like zero, I have been kind of seeing someone."

"Oh, yeah? Would I know him?"

She looked at me and bit at her lip. For a second, I thought she wasn't going to tell me, and my stomach sank.

"Fuck, I know him, don't I?" I asked with a scowl. "If you

say Dean, I might have to leave. Even years of therapy can't erase the hatred I have for that man."

"No!" she said fast. "Not Dean, but you do know him."

"Thank fuck all my friends are with someone. Who is it?"

She chewed on her lip more, and I could only think of all the times that lip was between my teeth.

"Mark," she finally said, snapping me out of my thoughts.

The words took a minute to process, trying to think through all the people I knew in town, before I remembered how I knew the name.

My mouth dropped open before I broke out in laughter. "Mark? As in Mark you went on a date with while we were dating? Mark, who took you to the haunted house?"

"Hey! In my defense, I did not know we were dating for real."

"How long have you been seeing him?"

"We've just gone on a couple of dates. It's only been a few months."

I was still laughing, and it was making her laugh now.

"And here I am again. Showing up right in time to piss him off. I don't care how much I grow up, that will continue to be hilarious to me."

The moment I said it, I realized what I was implying. The image of everything we did in that haunted house came back all at once, along with a hard wave of wanting. A feeling that had died in me so many years ago, hitting me like it never went away. No one had ever made me want them like Daisy. All she had to do was look at me, and I was ready to do anything for one more second with her.

Her eyebrows jumped up and lips parted. "You really have impeccable timing."

"Does he know what happened that night?"

"He knows that I left with you, yeah."

"You told him?"

"I guess indirectly. I told my dad that I had left with you that night, and he ended up telling Mark."

"So basically, I'm getting arrested this week by Mark, no matter what I do?"

"What? No! He wouldn't do that. I think we've grown up more than that, Kye."

"Maybe you have, but I guarantee that guy hates me now. He will not be happy to learn I'm going to be around you all week."

"Why are you going to be around me all week?"

My eyebrows furrowed. "The wedding? All of us have plenty to do for it this week. I just assume I'll see you."

"Oh, right. Yeah, and I have to work and help Mark with his stuff." She leaned her head back, exposing more of her neck.

Six years of thinking of her was already threatening to come out. Six years of no one else because the only thing that could turn me on was thoughts of Daisy. The only person who didn't make me want to scream when she touched me was now five feet away, and I couldn't touch her.

"Where do you work?"

Now she looked confused. "I work at Carly's diner? I assumed you knew that."

I was already shaking my head. "No. Definitely didn't."

"Now that you say it, I've never seen you there."

"I've stopped by when I'm in town. I've never seen you there, and Carly never told me." I made a mental note to talk to Carly, because that was something they could have clued me in on. "Apparently, they took a lot of precautions to make sure I knew nothing about you or see you."

"Why?"

I stood up, reaching out to help her up when she moved to stand with me. I couldn't be out here alone with her any longer.

She slipped her hand into mine and I pulled until she was staring up at me. I didn't pull it away, my thumb running over hers once before I dropped it.

"I think we both know why."

"I don't think I do." Her words were breathless, and I stepped closer. My hands twitched to reach out and grab her, but I held them in place.

The back door opened and Scout stepped out, her hands on her hips. "I swear, Kye, you need to be tied to one of us or you run off."

Daisy gave a sad laugh. "She might not be the only one who thinks that."

"Come on. I'm sure Bailey's looking for you, too."

She nodded and walked past me, that all too familiar scent of lavender and mint hitting me like it had the night I met her. The night she had jumped into my arms and begged me for a kiss.

The night that changed my life forever.

Because it didn't matter how far away I was or how long we had been apart, I was still completely in love with Daisy.

THIRTY-FIVE

DAISY

BAILEY RAN AHEAD of me up the stairs toward Fox and Ash's apartment. She already knew the place inside and out for how much we came over, except for one place.

One apartment that I hadn't even been in front of, let alone inside, in six years.

I looked up the last flight of stairs that led to Kye's apartment and wondered if he was up there now. The first time I came over to see the girls, I blocked it out until I was back in my car and then cried the entire night. After that, I never came over when Kye would be around, and when I had come over, I made it a point to not look up there.

Now, it was impossible because I knew he was there. How was I supposed to not want to see him after his big show at dinner the other night? He had taken his shirt off, and I couldn't remember my name, let alone why I shouldn't be talking to him.

I pushed open the apartment door, trying to grab Bailey, but she was already running to launch herself over the back of the couch. A loud grunt came before Bailey was lifted up in the air, Kye sitting up with her above him.

"You Wells woman are really always trying to jump me," he said, laughing and setting her on the ground. "Liam's in his room."

Bailey laughed, too, and took off. Disappearing into the bedroom, they added on for Liam.

"Sorry," I said, apologizing for what felt like the hundredth time for Bailey's antics. He was already up, smiling at me as he went towards the kitchen.

"It will never be something you have to apologize for," he said. I sucked in a hard breath, remembering every second of the night I had jumped him. I wondered what it would be like now. If he would still be stiff and awkward at first or if he would melt against me.

"Are you staying here to watch the kids?" I asked, trying to stop myself from following him more.

"Yep. Apparently, the girls had to watch the kids last time, so tonight's guy's night consists of us and three unruly children," he said, smirking.

"I'm sorry," I said again, already hearing the kids yelling in the room.

He grabbed his drink and walked back towards me, his eyebrows furrowed. "For what this time?"

"Ruining your guy's night."

He was already shaking his head. "I see your people-pleasing tendencies haven't changed."

I looked down, seeing the pink hue of the drink he had. "And your choice of beverages hasn't changed either."

"I guess some things will never be different," he said, shrugging. His face hardened as he looked towards the room and back at me. The sudden seriousness on his face made me chew my bottom lip.

"You might want to stop apologizing for Bailey. She's going to hear you doing it and think she's a problem. I'm choosing to be here. There's nothing to be sorry for."

He waited a second before walking back to the couch to sit back next to Ash. I stayed frozen, feeling like I had just been slapped. I was never trying to make it sound like Bailey was an issue, but I knew she was a lot for some people to be around. She had literally just launched herself on top of him. I couldn't expect everyone to be fine with that.

Kye's words were still echoing in my mind when the girls waved me out the door with them. I wondered if he knew from firsthand experience or really just thought I was a bad parent. From the day I took Bailey, I had worried constantly about what I was doing wrong. If I was ruining her life a little more each day, or was I raising a strong girl who would grow up to do great things?

But what if Kye thought I was messing it all up? Somehow, his opinion carried a heavy weight to it, and the thought that he could already be disappointed in me was sickening.

We made it to the restaurant, and the girls kept me moving until I sat at the table.

"Daisy?" Quinn asked. "Are you getting a drink?"

"I'm the driver," Carly said, her frown deepening. "Obviously."

"Oh yeah, sorry. I'll take a Long Island," I said, immediately dropping back into thought about Kye's words.

A few more minutes passed by before Scout got my attention.

"What is going on? Are you okay tonight?"

"Yeah, I'm fine. It's just such a busy week. I'm a little out of it."

"You're telling me," she said. "I thought planning a would be all fun and games, but apparently, making sure 150 eat and have a good time is anything but that. How the hell do I even *know* 150 people?"

"You could always do what we did. Hurry and get married in Vegas. Boom, done," Quinn said with a grin.

"As fun as your wedding was, I'm already committed to this thing. Oh, by the way, Daisy," Scout said, getting my attention again. "Is Bailey all set for flower girl duties?"

"As long as you're okay with her antics, she's more than ready. It was so nice of you to have her do it. She's already excited."

"I love her and will be looking forward to antics, so don't even worry."

"She's walking down the aisle with Liam. The girl is going to be so love-struck she might do nothing but smile."

I groaned. "Let's hope. She's so much sometimes, and I worry I'm ruining all of it."

Ash laughed and patted my shoulder. "You're doing great, babe. Stop worrying so much. I think you've made her too smart for her own good. She's perfect."

"I try to remember that, but this single-parent thing is a lot."

The server set my drink in front of me, shooting me a cute smile as he did. A round of laughter went around the table as he walked off.

"Bet you could get his number," Quinn said.

"For what? I have a…guy in my life, remember?" I asked, still not bringing myself to call him my boyfriend. The word felt so final that we were together and somehow it didn't feel right for us.

"Honestly?" Ash asked, her nose scrunching. "Not really. I forget the man exists with how little you talk about him, and I rarely see him with you."

I gave a halfhearted shrug. "He's busy. I'm busy. I already know he would drive you all crazy, so I don't bring him around."

They all glanced at each other before each of them broke into a smile.

"Wow, please tone down the passion, Daisy. We're in public," Carly said, mocking my bored tone and laughing when I finally smiled along with them.

"There's nothing wrong with Mark. I just feel so obligated to Bailey. It's hard to add another obligation like that."

The table went quiet, and I did, too. Maybe it was wrong to call Mark an obligation, but it felt like it. The only reason I agreed to a first date again with him was because my dad asked. With Mark running for sheriff, my dad thought it would help his chances dating me. I had agreed to one date, but Mark had been so nice. We kept going on dates until suddenly, we were dating. At least, I think we are. He really doesn't call me a girlfriend, and we are both busy, so spending time together doesn't happen much. Especially not time without Bailey. It didn't bother me either way. I could go out to dinner when I needed out of the house, and he didn't seem to care if I went days without responding to him.

The girls kept talking. From the wedding to Carly's pregnancy, the conversation moved with ease, but Kye's words still bothered me.

"Could I have Kye's number? I want to check on Bailey,"

I asked all of them, hoping no one would interrogate me. I should have known better. The girls would have a thousand questions, but they were all apparently going to wait. Carly was silent as she opened her phone and slid it over with Kye's number already up.

DAISY

Do you really think I'm a bad parent or something?

KYE

Daze?

DAISY

Yes

KYE

Why would you think I think that?

DAISY

Because of what you said about me calling her a problem, I don't think she's a burden, but I just want people to know she's a lot.

KYE

I do not think you are a bad parent. Not at all.

DAISY

Then why say that?

KYE

Because I was always told that. Constantly. The words are so burned in my brain and no, I'm not comparing you to my parents, but the words sound the same to a kid.

I get why you say it, but she might not hear it how you mean it.

Tears threatened me at the words. He was right. She

wouldn't know what I meant, and I never want her to think badly about herself.

But the kind, caring words from Kye made my heart break. Not only for him now but for the boy he had been. The one who thought he was the problem, the root of all the bad things in his life. Did he really spend days thinking he deserved what happened to him?

DAISY

Thank you

KYE

You're fucking killing it as a parent.

Bailey is amazing.

My heart jumped, but I tried not to show it to the girls.

DAISY

I hope that means she being good.

KYE

Currently racing Liam and winning

DAISY

I don't even know if I want to ask what type of racing. I'm almost worried she's driving your car.

KYE

...can she reach the pedals?

DAISY

NO, KYE IT'S A JOKE

KYE

Right, yeah, of course. Maybe in a year or two?

Forget it. Fox is making some sort of car
setup for Liam, so we will just make a
second one.

My heart squeezed at the thought. Kye, being in my life,
our lives, for another year or two sounded way too appealing.
He would be gone again soon, back to his life that had him
traveling endlessly and never home. He would leave, and I
would be right here.

Not that I hated where I was. I was proud of it, but that
didn't mean I didn't think about the what-ifs. Six years later, I
still think about him constantly. I had too many nights laying
in bed, staring up at my ceiling, wondering what life would be
like with Kye there with me. I knew I had to keep my
distance. I couldn't risk Bailey getting close to him just to
have him go again, but I wanted to. I wanted to go right back
to the apartments and drag him upstairs to bed.

I took a deep, clarifying breath. I couldn't, and I wouldn't.

We wrapped up dinner. Carly going on about the diner,
Ash debated on having another kid, Scout about her wedding,
and Quinn about the garage, but I tried to stay quiet. Most
weeks, I was relieved to be here with them, but tonight, all I
could think about was getting home and trying to make it
through the week without crying.

I knew I would have to spend a lot of time with Kye, and I
already knew the mess I was going to be at the end of it. It
was Scout's wedding, though, and I would not bother any of
them about this. I knew they would listen and probably even
play buffer between Kye and I this week, but I wouldn't make
them.

I pulled my shoulders back and smiled as Carly joked

about something. I could spend one week with Kye and then get back to my life.

But I knew it wasn't just a week—it was a reminder of everything I couldn't have. I knew this week would test my resolve, and by the end, I would be left picking up the pieces of my heart again.

One week with Kye, I repeated in my head. I could handle one hundred and sixty-eight hours with Kye before going back to my life.

THIRTY-SIX

KYE

I MADE it to Holt's track late the next day. Everyone turned to watch me pull in with a small shake of their head.

"I should've known you wouldn't be here on time," Scout said.

"Listen, I overslept. Give me a break because I just got in yesterday."

She only shook her head, the oversized sunglasses most likely hiding an eye roll.

"Miss the wedding by one second and I'm going to ruin your life."

"Who says you aren't already?"

She lunged, grabbing my arm as I stepped away. She only used it for leverage, though, punching me hard in the stomach.

I bent over with a grunt. The problem with Scout was she was small but knew exactly where to hit to knock the breath out of a grown man.

"Wow, I leave for fifteen minutes and you two are already fighting like children," Carly said, but I didn't look up, still catching my breath. "I swear, if my own kids are this bad together, I'm making you two babysit all the time."

I finally stood up, but it wasn't Carly who met my eyes. It was Daisy. She stood next to Carly, her eyes wide as she looked at me. Her hand adjusted nervously in Bailey's, but she didn't say a word.

"I didn't know you two were coming today," I said. She looked beautiful in another light sundress that showed off every curve of her body. I could feel the heat creeping down my spine, and I tried to ignore it.

Her chin tilted up to me, her shoulders pulled back, and I gave a soft smile, loving that some things didn't change.

I still knew Daisy. Maybe I didn't know everything about her life, but I knew *her,* and I knew she was putting on her proud face.

"Is that a problem?"

"Not even a little. I just wasn't expecting you."

"I am friends with everyone," she said, the words tight but proud.

"Then you should absolutely be here."

Without a word, Bailey took off, running to where Liam and Lily were playing off to the side.

"Alright, Scout," Fox said, breaking the weird tension. "It's your week. What are we doing today?"

"Everything," she said.

"Seriously," Ransom said. "Are we just drag racing or the circle track or dirt, what?"

"Everything," she said with a grin. "We haven't been here together in months and it will be a few more months until we are again. Carly ordered tons of food from the diner that Daisy and her already set upstairs. Kye brought drinks. We are set for the rest of the day."

"And," Chase added, grabbing her hand to pull her around the back of the nearest garage. "I have a surprise for you."

We followed, and I was surprised to see a bunch of over-sized chairs facing the garage wall.

"You got me...outdoor seating?" she asked, her eyebrows furrowed hard.

He rolled his eyes. "I mean, kind of, but I thought you might like a movie night out here with everyone instead of all of us trying to pack into an apartment tonight. I have a projector we can set up later."

Her bottom lip pouted out as she smiled at him. "I thought I was marrying you for your money, but here you go, being all sweet again."

They both laughed, lost to their own world with their own jokes. It was something Scout always joked about, only to remember that Chase literally gave up everything to be with her. He worked hard now, running half the business side of Carly's diner, and being Scout's manager basically, which only made her career take off even more.

I was lost in thought and didn't notice Daisy heading my way until she was right in front of me.

"If me being here is a problem, we can go," Daisy said. I looked down over the dress again, the slit up the side showing off all of one leg, and I struggled to look away.

"Why would it be a problem?"

"Because you keep giving me that look and I'm assuming you don't want me hanging around your friends when you are home."

My hand twitched, wanting so badly to reach up and run her hair through my fingers. "The look is probably my resting bitch face problem. I'm glad you're here. A little surprised you want to be within five feet of me, but glad. And they are your friends, too."

"But you get first dibs on hanging out with them."

My smile grew and I stepped a little closer. "Is this split custody? Do I get weekends or weekdays?"

She fought the smile that was threatening to take over, but looked at me with those bright hazel eyes. She didn't step back, and I wanted to pretend that was a good thing, but I was pretty sure it had less to do with me and more her need to always stand strong.

"Well, I'm pretty busy during the week, so weekends are better for me, but that would mean I have to leave because it is Tuesday."

"I'm kidding, Daze. Stay. *Please* stay."

"Are you sure? I–"

"Want to go for a ride?" I asked, interrupting her. She wasn't going to stop trying to people please, so cutting her off seemed like the quickest way.

"With you?"

"Yeah. Just around the track. Unless you'd rather ride with someone else."

"Should I want to ride with anyone? I was planning on sitting here with Carly the entire time."

"You're about to spend your entire day at a racetrack with professional drivers. You have a herd of people to watch Bailey, and I know for a fact you have been fine riding with me before. Why not go for one ride?"

"I'm sure you can only go faster now."

"Maybe, but I'm also about ten times better of a driver, so my skill matches my speed."

"And I won't get hurt?"

"I wouldn't ask you if I thought there was any chance of that."

"Then fine. Take me for a ride, Kye." It wasn't like it was anything different. It was my name, one I had heard a thousand times, but it never sounded the same as when she said it.

I headed back to the cars, grabbing two helmets and beckoning for her to follow me to one of the cars set up for this track. It was beat up. Any logos or markings had long been painted over or broken off, but it still ran great. It didn't really matter what they looked like when they were built to do this.

She looked as skeptical as I would have guessed her to be, but she grabbed the helmet and got in.

"What am I supposed to do?"

It took me a second to take it all in. Daisy was sitting in my passenger seat, her long blonde hair pulled over her shoulder as she looked over the helmet. The fear and memories kept slamming back into me, each one hitting me harder, and now was one of the worst. It was like a day had gone by, like she was still mine and I could lean over and pull her close, like I could kiss her until I couldn't breathe.

I tried to shake it off, waiting until she had her helmet on before peeling out and onto the track. I didn't check on her at first, didn't look over as I hit the first three turns. The car ran flawlessly, the back letting go the second I wanted it to so the car could drift around the curve.

The back end swung, drifting around the last one as she yelled out something. She grabbed my arm, holding onto me tight.

"Do not do that again," she said, her fingers digging into my forearm.

I adjusted my hand on the shifter and slowed more, motioning that she could take off the helmet.

"You okay?"

She pulled the helmet off with a gasp and looked over at me with wide eyes. "I can't believe you do this all the time."

I laughed, leaning back into the seat as the car rumbled around us. "The most fun I can have doing something legal."

She shot me a look, and for one beat of my heart, I thought I knew what she was thinking. Daisy had always been thinking something dirty, and right now, I was pretty sure there was something like that on her mind.

There was on mine, at least. Because no matter what type of fun I could have, I could always have even more fun with her. I would give up any car or race for the rest of my life to have a fraction of the fun I could have with her.

Her eyes wandered down to my hand, looking at her name so clearly stamped on my fingers.

I never regretted it. I had wanted to, plenty of days I had wished I did regret it, but it kept me sane. If I had to go back, I would only get it tattooed there sooner.

Her hand slid along my forearm, her fingers trailing down until she reached my hand, where she stopped to trace the letters.

A shiver of need came over me, wishing I could have more. I wanted to take more, but she pulled back.

"Sorry," she said, panting now. "I'm sorry. I just still can't believe you did that."

"There's nothing to be sorry about. It's your name, I would think you're allowed to touch it."

"But I know you hate being touched. I just–I wasn't thinking. Sorry."

"You know I don't mind you touching me."

"Still?"

I could only nod, wishing she would do it again. I held my

hand out, and finally took a breath when she grabbed it, inspecting the tattoo closer.

As if she could hear my thoughts, she looked up at me. "Do you regret it?"

"No," I said, surprised at myself. I was about to lie, to tell her I did, but the truth slipped out. "There's nothing about you that I regret. Besides leaving."

Her eyes met mine, and I wanted to stick a knife in my chest at the pain I saw there. I knew she had to hate me to some extent, but there was only hurt there now.

"Can we go back?" she asked, her eyes not leaving mine. "To the crew, I mean."

"Yeah, of course." She hadn't dropped my hand, but I set it back on the shifter. Hers lingered on mine for a few more seconds before she pulled it off.

I parked back at the garage area and spent the rest of the day trying to ignore the burning in my chest. We raced and hung out, eating nearly everything Carly brought, until night fell and we headed over to watch the movie. Scout was ecstatic as we sat back, and I tried again to ignore my own problems.

Then Daisy sat down in the chair next to mine, Bailey on her lap as they snuggled back under a blanket with a smile.

I looked around. The rest of the crew piled up with their person. Ash and Fox with Liam sprawled out next to them on his own little chair. Jax and Carly with Lily, and Ransom and Quinn wrapped up together next to them.

I looked back at Daisy and Bailey. I guessed I could be thankful that Mark wasn't there to make me witness whatever sickeningly cute shit they did together, but it barely eased the tension.

That could be me. I could be sitting over there with Daisy,

Bailey on top of us. If I wouldn't have left, that could have been my life.

There was never anyone else for me. She was it, and I realized I needed to do anything I could to make her see that I was it for her.

She looked over, her eyes catching mine, and I didn't hide the fact that I had been looking at them. I could see her cheeks turn red, and I smiled, making her turn back to the movie.

That was the life I wanted, but I didn't think there was a chance left for me to have it.

THIRTY-SEVEN

DAISY

I WAS HALFWAY through another day of work, and I was already exhausted. I had stayed up too late, lying awake thinking about Kye. The way he looked so happy driving, the way he smiled at me during the movie, the way he held his hand out for me to touch him more.

I spent most of the night thinking about him a little *too* much. My cheeks flamed at the thought, but I reached the counter and tried to calm my thoughts down. I needed to take orders, not worry about how good Kye still looked without a shirt on. I also needed to stop concerning myself with what he would look like without shorts on, too.

Somehow, I grew up and my thoughts only grew dirtier.

I reached the counter and nearly tripped over my own feet as Kye walked in. If he noticed me flustered, he didn't react. He only smiled and turned back to the line, waiting to order like this was a normal, everyday occurrence.

"Daisy!" Mark yelled as he opened the to-go box. "The fries are everywhere now. My burger fell apart."

"Oh dammit. I'm sorry."

He huffed, heading to the counter and fixing the food. He glanced at me over his shoulder with a tight smile. "You know what? It's okay, just be more careful, please."

"Yeah, yeah, of course. I have to get back...The line," I mumbled, walking back up as Kye waited.

"Hey," he said, looking me over. His eyes raked along my body, and I tried not to shudder. I didn't know how he could still look at me like he was currently fucking me, but he was doing a great job of it.

"Hey, are you here to order?"

"Yes, I'm starving. I unfortunately can't expect Carly's cooking when she's pregnant, and being dragged to every wedding prep event possible, so I'm resorting to this."

"No, I guess not, and I'm sorry in advance, while this is her restaurant, I swear somehow it's not even close to her food still."

He groaned. "I assumed, but I am running out of energy, so please, a burger and fries."

Mark had stepped up behind him, not seeming to notice who it was yet, as he clicked at his phone.

I took a second to look Kye over, from his t-shirt, to his backwards hat, his tattoos to his smiling face, and the dimples that came out when he really smiled. The look of him made me melt. He looked so good that it was ruining my focus.

"And a strawberry milkshake?"

His face lit up more. "Yes, actually. Thank you for remembering."

"Hard to forget when you've been covered in it."

He let out a bark of laughter. "The most fun I've ever had cleaning my car."

He looked at my chest, seeming to remember every part of me he licked that day just as well as I was, and I hated that it made me turned on just standing there.

Mark gave a scowl at Kye's laugh. "Hey, I'm in a hurry. Could we get this rung up?"

As fast as Kye's face had turned happy before it twisted into a frown now. "You should be nicer to people who prepare and serve your food," he said gently, only turning his head slightly, and then looking back at me. "Thanks, Daze."

He walked to a table, his legs kicking out as he sat back, his eyes still focused on me. I knew he saw Mark, and I knew he was following his every move, but his eyes didn't leave mine.

"Kye?"

"Hey, Mark."

"What are you doing here?"

"Getting food? Obviously."

"I meant in town."

"Aside from living here? I'm in town for a wedding."

"Right, of course, the one she's in."

"She?"

"Daisy," he said, getting more and more angry at Kye's presence.

"Oh, I wasn't sure if you knew her name."

"Of course I—"

"Here, Mark, all taken care of."

Mark leaned over the counter more. "Do you want me to wait until he leaves? I don't want you to have any trouble."

"I'll be fine, Mark. This is a diner, and he is getting food. No trouble."

I wasn't going to add that, historically, any day Kye made trouble was probably a good day for me.

Amber walked over, giving a small sneer at Mark and letting out a little shriek when she saw Kye.

She raced around the counter to him. "Kye?"

He jumped up, a big smile back as he pulled her into a hug without hesitation, not seeming to mind touching her. "Hey, Amber. What are you doing here?"

"Working," she groaned.

"You work here, too?"

"I really do have to go, Daisy," Mark said, catching my attention again. "Are you sure you don't want me to send someone over to check on you soon?"

"No, I would like you to stop suggesting it and let me work."

"Okay, okay, be careful. I will call you later," he whispered, but I was already back to listening to Amber and Kye. He leaned over, kissing my cheek, and I knew they turned red immediately. Kye had watched the entire thing and somehow, Mark's lips on me felt wrong in front of him.

I shook my head again. No. I was dating Mark. I mean, kind of dating him. Kye being here didn't change that, and nothing was going on between us. I couldn't expect there to ever be anything between us again. He left. He drove away and didn't talk to me for six years. That wasn't the type of guy I could have a stable life with, right?

"No, not lately," Amber said, but I hadn't caught the question Kye had asked.

"Well, call me if you need to or call me if you need help with the boys," Kye said.

Amber nodded with a bright smile, but I wanted to know what she would be calling him about her needs. What *needs* could she possibly have that Kye would help with?

She walked back over to me, and I was already glaring at her. "I can't believe Kye was back, and you didn't tell me."

"Daze has been too busy running around for a wedding and probably trying to avoid me. It's basically a full-time job," Kye said.

"I'm not avoiding you."

"I said you were trying to, not that you were succeeding." He was smiling now, those two ridiculously cute dimples coming out.

"Here's your milkshake. The food will be out in a second. I have to go help a table."

"I will be waiting. Is it just you two working?"

"Aside from the cook today, yes."

"And where's Bailey?"

"Preschool for another hour, and then she'll be here with me until I'm done."

"What? You bring the wild child to work?"

I huffed. "Well, it isn't easy, but yes, I have to. I would spend more on a babysitter than I made working half the time. Thanks for the judgment, though."

"No, I didn't mean it like that. Why don't I get her? Can you call and let them know I will pick her up?"

"I mean, I can, but you don't have to. You know she's a handful."

"And she shouldn't be sitting still for hours before bed. I'll run laps around the house with her or something. Trust me, I can keep up. Come on, Daze, you know I can handle her just fine, and it would help you both. Plus, it would give me a really great reason to be at your house waiting for you when you get home because the only other reasons I can think of range from stalker to weirdo."

"Seriously?"

"About the stalker part? I mean, yeah, I couldn't think of a way to show up that wouldn't sound weird."

"No, about the Bailey part," I said with a laugh. "But we can circle back to that."

"Oh, of course. I've seen her energy, and I know what I'm signing up for. I have nothing to do tonight, so at least I'll have someone fun to hang out with."

"And if you get overwhelmed or annoyed, you will bring her here?"

"I'll stop by before we head home and yes, I will, but I will not be overwhelmed and bring her here. I can handle one child, Daze."

"If you're sure, then okay, that would be great. She hates sitting here."

"I do not blame her. Sitting for hours with nothing to do is also my own form of torture." Amber handed him his food. "I'm eating this here now and heading over to get her. Wait, can she ride a bike?"

"Kind of. She's getting better, but her bike is at my house."

"No, that's fine. I'll go buy us both one. And a helmet. Does she have boots? You know what, I'll get them because I've met her."

"Kye, take a breath. You don't have to go buy that stuff. We have it at home." He was talking faster, apparently getting more excited, and it was only making me melt.

"No, it's fine. You don't have to worry about it. I'm going to eat quick."

I walked away, needing to help other tables and maybe distance myself from the scary-looking racer that was currently falling apart for my kid.

Ten minutes later, he jumped up and came back to the counter. "Did you call?"

"Yeah, you're good to go."

"Perfect, I have to go—" He looked me over and narrowed his eyes. "Run an errand before I get her."

"You're going to the bike shop, aren't you?" I asked with a smile.

"Maybe." He pulled out his wallet as Amber walked around to my side.

"Best waitresses in the world," he said loudly. "I've never had this level of service."

"Kye," I hissed with a laugh. "Quiet."

"I can't help it. Everything about this was perfect." He shoved money into the tip jar. Lots of money, like multiple hundred dollar bills. "I will definitely be back."

"Yes," I hissed more. "In, like, twenty minutes with Bailey. Stop that!" I said, slapping his hand as he put another one in.

"I will if you won't be mad when we show up with new bikes," he said with a laugh.

"You don't need to—"

He shoved two more in.

"Fine! I won't be mad. Just take all that back out if you're buying her a bike."

He smiled. "No. See you soon." He nearly ran out the front as Amber looked at the tip jar. She had become my best friend when we lived together in college. She was the one person who helped me every step after Kye left, and was possibly the only reason I ever graduated. Even now, she was still my best friend, but I was currently fuming at her sudden closeness with Kye. She seemed more comfortable with him now than I felt.

"Shit," she said, looking into the tip jar. "He's sneaky."

"What does that mean? He did it right in front of our faces."

"I just told him I needed to make extra money for my boys' sports equipment," she said. "I think I said, like, four hundred dollars and look, four hundred dollars. I magically have enough to get their equipment."

"He didn't."

"Pretty sure he did. I'm not surprised, though. After Lane left, Kye stopped over a few months later and helped me with a ton of stuff. Including getting the boys' beds bought and built. There was so much to do and I just couldn't manage."

"You never told me that. I would have helped you!"

"I didn't think you'd want to know about Kye, I mean, and I really didn't want you to think I was sleeping with him or something. I know how possessive you've always been of him." I went to protest, but she stopped me. "Babe, I don't blame you, I'm just saying. It was nice to have someone that helped without wanting anything or telling me sorry that Lane walked out on you a million times. He came, helped, and I haven't seen him since. Now, though, he basically hands me the money I need. I wish you didn't already have your claws in him because damn, he's still hot, too. And god, that bit of edge he has still? Like you know that man is good in bed."

I rolled my eyes, not wanting to say how much I agreed. "You have apparently talked to him more in the past six years than me. How do I have my claws in him?"

"Pretty sure you've had those claws in him since you met him. And I'm also pretty sure he's not trying to remove them. Plus, he just went to pick up your kid, so we get to see how that plays out now."

She moved to hand me half of the money, but I shook my head. "No thanks, that was for you. I'm good right now."

Another hour went by and I started to worry.

I had looked out the window every minute for the past fifteen. He should already have picked her up, and if they were biking here, they should make it here any minute now. Then again, she wasn't great on a bike, so he might end up carrying both of them.

I looked up again, and this time I saw them. Kye was on a dirtbike, riding with his front tire off the ground next to Bailey as she rode on a smaller one with two little training wheels, and she was laughing hysterically. Then he got off, pulling her and her front wheel up and holding it to let her ride around in a wheelie as she yelled in joy.

Amber came over, looking out with me.

"Well, I take back what I said. I'm starting to not care if you have your claws in him. I might just shoot my shot."

"*Amber,*" I said, glaring at her.

"Almost kidding. Go talk to your new babysitter before that group of women over there starts lining up to have his babies."

I looked at the group, who were smiling and whispering to each other as they watched Kye out the window.

I walked out, worried about how bad I wanted to be at the front of that line suddenly.

"You said bikes, Kye, not dirtbikes!" I yelled as he shut his off. My heart was racing, and I wasn't sure if it was from the anxiety of Bailey on a little dirt bike or the fact that I wanted to jump Kye and kiss him for being so sweet.

"I didn't clarify? My bad," he said, giving me that smile. The one showing that he knew he was in trouble, but thought he was sweet enough to get out of it.

And he was right.

"You seriously bought her new everything?"

"Yes, and she loves it, so you better not yell at me in front of her."

"I didn't doubt that she would love it, but you didn't have to do that."

"Obviously. Consider it an early Christmas present."

"It's June."

"Then consider it an early, or late, birthday present. When is her birthday?"

"Next month. The 23rd."

"There you go. Happy early birthday to her."

I only shook my head and watched as she drove in little circles. "As much as I would like to hang out, I still have to work, and I suggest you two move along home because the women inside are deciding who gets to be in line first to have your babies."

His eyebrows shot up, looking around me to the diner. I didn't even need to turn back to know that the group of women was still looking out here.

"Where does the line start?" he asked.

"I'm assuming they would have to trip over each other to line up in front of you wherever, but I'm not sure of the rules."

He rolled over on the dirtbike until he was right in front of me.

"Well, look at that, Daze. Looks like you're first," he said, smiling up at the women with a wave.

They waved back, and I turned to him.

"Funny."

"Do you come home with me now to get that done? Or just go behind the building? I can try to make it romantic either way, or go get a milkshake if you feel like getting wild." His eyebrows jumped, and he smiled.

Well, damn.

Younger Kye was hot. All the reckless, unruly energy he had, the way he had been so obsessed with me.

Grown Kye was worse, though. That same recklessness was there, but now he was a little more free somehow. Funnier, sweeter, caring. Calmer in a dangerous way.

And I suddenly knew that he meant every word. I was worried that if I asked, Kye would figure out how to do exactly that.

I really wanted to ask.

"Stop talking. *Please*, stop talking," I said, needing to get away from him before I took him up on that offer. I hadn't stopped wondering if Kye could affect me the way he used to. So far, even him being close to me was turning me on, but I knew that every time I had touched him was worse.

It made me wonder if he felt the same or if the wild way he liked touching me had disappeared like he had thought it would.

"Go ride your bikes and try not to get worn out before she does."

Instead of dwelling on those thoughts more, I kissed Bailey and told her to behave.

"You, too, Kye. Behave."

"I always try to behave."

"Right, *try* being the keyword there. You both *try* to behave. I'll be home in a few hours. Please let there still be a house when I get there."

He nodded, and they took off, Bailey hitting the gas and the little bike speeding up the slightest bit. It couldn't be going any faster than a peddle bike, but she had to feel like it was flying. Kye moved alongside her, popping the front of his bike up onto one wheel again and watching as Bailey tried to do the same, but never making it more than an inch off the ground.

I realized that all I had done with letting Kye babysit was give my Evil Knieval daughter a teacher.

THIRTY-EIGHT

DAISY

I WALKED IN, already hearing the sounds of laughter coming from the living room.

"Bailey, no, that part tickles," Kye said, prompting Bailey to laugh harder and continue with what she was doing.

I didn't think any part of me was ready to see what was happening, though, and when I turned the corner, my feet stopped moving, frozen as I watched.

Neither of them seemed to have heard me and continued on with their game.

Their game being Bailey with a pile of markers, washable thankfully, and Kye on his back, letting her draw all over him.

He laughed again, his stomach shaking, and Bailey threw down a hand.

"Hold still!" she shrieked. "You are going to mess up my drawing!"

His lips pressed together as he tried to stop it, but as Bailey scribbled, it got out of control again.

I had never thought much about having my own children,

and by the time I had taken over care of Bailey at twenty-three, I never really had much time to think about having any of my own after that, my hands too full with her as a single parent. And with her big personality, it hadn't grown any easier in the past months.

Now, though, I could only think about walking into a house filled with this type of laughter forever.

"What are you two doing?" I finally asked.

"Tattoos!" Bailey yelled, turning back to Kye, who didn't seem to mind staying put on the floor.

"Bailey saw some of my tattoos and decided I needed more. Then I showed her the black and white ones and asked for some color. She's just helping me out. Really saving me time and money, too. Who would have thought I could have just had my tattoos done on your living room floor by a very talented four-year-old?"

"Look," she yelled, waving me over and holding up Kyes' hands. She had colored in the letters of my name on his fingers, each one either green, yellow, or red. "I colored them like the flowers."

"Wow, how creative." I said.

"What about you, Daze? Need some tattoos?"

"Not today. Right now, I just need some food."

"In the fridge," he said, his smiling face watching me.

"You cooked?"

"Not a chance," he said. "We ordered pizza and luckily, me and Bailey here like it the same way, so I ordered one for us and a different one for you."

My brows furrowed. "And you remember what type of pizza I like?"

"Cheese and olives is not exactly a hard order to remember. Go on, go get your food. We're not quite done yet, anyway."

He laid his head back, closing his eyes and letting Bailey keep working. She seemed pleased to keep going, switching out markers and focusing. It was hard to get her to stay quiet, so that alone was surprising, but that Kye seemed fine with it was equally surprising.

I warmed up my pizza and brought it back to the living room, finally sitting down after working all day on my feet. I didn't mind my job, but mainly only kept it for the paycheck. I needed something to sustain my life with Bailey, and not many jobs made enough to support a single person with a kid and a house while offering flexible hours.

When I sat back, Kye looked over, his eyes bright. "How was work?"

"Long, busy, exhausting."

"Do you like your job?"

"Like it? No. Need it? Yes," I said with a laugh as I took another bite.

"Just good money?"

"Yeah, enough to get us by fine, and it helps me be able to work when she's at school or sleeping."

"I can't believe what you have done for her. You should be proud, Daze. Really fucking proud."

"Language, Kye."

"I think I should be let off the hook this time, considering she's asleep and drooling on me."

He was right. I thought she was still coloring, but the marker was in her limp hand, her head down, and she was asleep on his stomach.

I groaned, about to get up, when he held up a hand.

"I got it, just eat." He grabbed for the marker, sliding the cap back on and carefully lifting her as he got up. She shifted, wrapping around him as he carried her towards the rooms.

He appeared again but grabbed a washcloth from the kitchen.

"Marker all over her face and arms," he said, disappearing again.

Mark had tried to help me, coming over to cook and play with Bailey, but each time it had been a little awkward. Like he wasn't quite comfortable in my little house, and his discomfort only made Bailey and me uncomfortable.

Plus, Bailey was too much for him. No matter how kind he was, I could see it in his eyes that all her energy and tricks really wore him down. Now, he politely avoided it when he could. I think in his mind, she would grow out of it soon and we could have more time together.

Kye, though, seemed right at home.

He walked out and went around the couch, grabbing his shirt from the ground before giving me a look of her artwork.

"Honestly, this one she freehanded is pretty great. I think it's a narwal? Maybe a horse? Either way, it's growing on me."

I looked at it, but I was quickly distracted, looking over every tattoo and hard plane of his body. Six years of growing up had been very, very kind to him. Every muscle was more pronounced, each new tattoo a part of him that I wanted to know.

"Please, stop looking at me like that."

"Like what?" I finally met his eye, and I wished I hadn't.

"Like you like what you see."

"I was just admiring the artwork."

His face hardened, and I could see his chest rise and fall with one deep breath. "I have to go home and wash some marker off my body."

I bit my lip, holding back every word I wanted to say. I had a perfectly good shower and could definitely help wash that all off.

"Don't you dare say what you're thinking, Daisy," he said, the words somewhere between a joke and a command.

He finally pulled a shirt on, letting me have some brain cells back.

I followed him as he grabbed his things and headed to the door.

"Have a good night. I'll talk to you soon."

I nodded, but grabbed his hand, pulling him to a stop. "Kye, wait."

He spun, backing me up against the wall in one step. His body pressed against mine.

"Please just let me leave before I don't."

For all the years that had gone by, my body still reacted the same way. The burning want, the feeling that there was nothing else in this world but him and the need for him to take over every part of me. My hips pushed forward, already wanting more than I should even be thinking about.

"I just wanted to say thank you for everything tonight," I said, trying to calm my breathing. "And that I don't want you to leave."

"I don't want to leave."

"Then stay. Didn't you want to talk?"

He pulled me in, burying his head into my neck. "I can't seem to remember anything I was going to *talk* about right this second, so I am going to do the right thing and leave."

He stepped back, my hands trailing over every inch I could before we parted.

"I'll see you later, Daze. Call me if you need anything." He leaned down, pressing a long kiss to my cheek before walking out. He got on the dirtbike and took off, disappearing into the night without so much as a glance back.

"YOU HAVE A SICK SENSE OF HUMOR," I said to Carly as we walked into the back door of the diner. Luckily, Daisy wasn't working. Unluckily, it was because she was downtown, being paraded around on Mark's arm for his upcoming run for sheriff, and that's exactly where we were headed.

"Hey, you already agreed. I assumed you knew you would be running into her."

"Yeah, I did, but I figured it would be at the diner. I wasn't expecting to watch her walk around town all over Mark."

She huffed and handed me a bag. "I honestly forgot about that part. Blame the pregnancy brain. If you really can't handle it, I'll call Jax and make him come help."

I was already shaking my head, knowing that Jax had a long to-do list today, and I did actually want to hang out with Carly. "No, it's fine. I'll handle it. What are we doing, anyway?"

"The diner is getting a new menu, and I figured this would be a good time to let people know."

"I swear if you take those milkshakes off the menu, I will riot."

At his name, Riot came over to sit in front of me, patiently waiting for a treat or to be pet. I leaned down, rubbing his head as Carly grabbed a few more things out of the office. He was getting old now, but would perk up at any chance to be pet. The entire town was having events downtown today, from food, to Mark's campaign, to the carnival that came every year. It was a big deal, and Carly was smart for using it to get the word out more about the diner.

We headed out, packing into my car to make a five minute drive, but there was no way I was going to ask the pregnant lady to walk downtown with an arm full of things she wanted to hand out.

"Sorry, Kye," she said, and I was surprised when I looked over to see tears in her eyes. I couldn't actually remember a time I saw Carly cry, and the immediate panic nearly made me puke.

"For what? What's wrong?" I pulled hard into a parking spot.

"I didn't think about Daisy being here with Mark. I mean, I knew you were still in love with her and all, but I didn't think about it. I would probably commit murder if I were in your position. We shouldn't go. If you get upset, then I'll get upset. Then Jax will get upset because I'm upset, and it will be a whole mess."

I laughed and reached over to grab the bag she brought. "I will not be causing any of that drama, and won't be upset. I know what I'm getting into, and I'm here to help you. I'm the one who fucked up any chance I had with Daisy, not you. If I have to see her with Mark, that's also my fault."

"But it isn't fair," she said, still near tears. "I would go insane if I had to see Jax with anyone else like that."

"Maybe not, but it will be okay. Come on, let's go get this done."

She got out, Riot next to her, and I grabbed his leash before we headed into the crowd. Carly immediately got to work, stopping to talk to people and hand out her flyers. An hour went by before she stopped and groaned.

"I'm too pregnant for this."

"Then I'm texting Jax to come get you."

"No, we still have more to do."

I grabbed the stack of flyers left in her hand, already sending off a text to Jax to come get her. "And I'm going to finish."

She groaned again. "I'm really glad I chose you as a best friend. You don't touch me, you watch my scary movies with me, and you do my job when I don't feel like it."

I grinned, and checked my phone, already knowing Jax would be on his way. "He's coming to get you. He asked that you wait by the library corner because he has to get back to the track for work stuff."

"The library? The man had to choose the other side of town?"

"It's two blocks, Carly."

She huffed again and took off. "You walk two blocks with a human inside you that won't stop kicking your organs. Thanks, Kye. I owe you one."

She walked off, and I turned, suddenly determined to find Daisy.

I saw her before she saw me. Her blonde hair was pulled back and her fake prom queen smile was plastered on her face.

I circled around, coming up behind her and stepping by her side so she wouldn't see me right away.

"Having fun?" I asked, leaning down next to her.

She jumped, glancing over once as her fake smile fell before her eyes went back to the crowd. "You know what, Kye? I'm going to be honest with you because I can't seem to be with anyone else. No, I'm absolutely not having fun. This is stupid."

"Then why are you here?"

"I agreed to help Mark."

"By doing…what, exactly?"

"I don't know. Showing the town he has my dad's support?"

I laughed, knocking against her a little. "Do you want to know what would really show that your dad supports him?"

"What?"

"Your dad being here. Not you."

She finally spun, looking at me with a blank stare.

"I'm just saying. I don't get why you have to be the middle woman when he could be here."

"He was working."

"And he couldn't take off?"

She only stared more, her eyebrows furrowing the slightest amount. "Stop," she finally said.

"Stop what?"

"Making things sound more simple than they are. I agreed to help Mark show the town that he's capable of taking over the position and he…agreed."

It felt like the floor dropped out beneath me for a moment, and my brain tried to speed up enough to understand what she was implying.

"How exactly did you agree to help Mark do that?"

"I don't know. My dad asked me to just be seen with him, talk him up, or tell people how much my dad supported him being sheriff."

I forced my mouth not to drop open. "I have a very specific question, and I am going to need a *very* specific answer, Daisy."

"Don't call me Daisy," she said, throwing her shoulders back. It was so defiant. Every time she tried to straighten up and look perfect, it was all a show to look more capable, and as strong as I knew she was, I always thought the show of it was cute.

"I thought that was your name."

"It is, but you only call me Daisy when you're mad or upset. I feel like I'm getting scolded when you call me that."

"Is there something that you think I would be scolding you about?"

She didn't answer, and I was starting to worry I already knew the answer to my question.

"Daisy," I said again. "Are you pretending to date Mark to make him look good for all of this?"

"No. I mean, we are dating, I guess, and it does help his image, but it's not like we agreed to pretend to date."

"Why did you start dating him, then?"

"I don't know. My dad asked me to go on another date with him, you know, since you ruined the last one, and I agreed. He was nice enough, so I went on another, and then another, and I guess then it turned into us dating. Why are you bothering me about all of this?"

"I'm not sure if I should be mad or start laughing. Are you saying you only started dating Mark because you wanted to make your dad happy and then you kept dating him to make him happy?"

"Kye," she warned.

"Tell me right this second I have it all wrong, that none of what I said is true at all, and you are actually crazy about him. Tell me, and I won't bring it up again."

She spun back towards the crowd, her arms crossed over her chest, as her frown deepened. "You are the worst. No one asked for your opinion."

"It wasn't an opinion. It's, apparently, a fact because you aren't giving me an answer."

"Because I don't know what the answer is."

It felt like as good of a time as any to test my chances. Maybe it was wrong, maybe she would instantly hate me, but I had to know.

I stepped closer, angling myself at her back. She wore another dress today, this one pulled down on her arms so her shoulders were exposed, leaving me with thoughts of wanting to lean down and kiss along the bare skin. It would be so easy, from her shoulder to her neck to her lips.

"It can be pretty simple," I said, quieter now. "Is Mark happy with you two together?"

"I think so. He hasn't said otherwise."

"Is your dad happy that you two are together?"

"Happier than I've ever seen him when I've dated someone."

I moved a little closer, her back pressed against me now. "And what about you? Is the perfect prom queen as happy as she's trying to look?"

She stepped away, turning back to me with wide eyes and nostrils flaring. "I don't think that's any of your business anymore, is it? And don't call me that again. It's been ten years since I was any sort of prom queen, and I don't like you calling me that. I need to go. I have to go find Mark and my dad. He has Bailey with him, and I'm sure they are both ready for a break."

She was already trying to walk away, but I followed after her.

"Daisy," I said, hating how much I loved the way she stopped and immediately turned.

"What?"

"I just want you to be happy, and it looks like you're doing what you always do and trying to please other people instead of making sure you are happy."

"You don't know what is going to make me happy."

"No, but is being paraded around by Mark and your dad really what you want? Does he know you're pretending?"

She shrunk back. "Maybe I'm not–"

"Does he know? Is this like what we did? You pretend to date and each gets something out of it. Is that what this is?"

"No," she said, taking a deep, shaky breath and looking away. "No, it's not like that."

"Then what's it like?"

"I don't know. We are dating, Kye. He takes me out, I go along, he wins his Sheriff stuff, and then…"

"Then? You ride off into the sunset together? You get married? Have a family? Then, what?" I asked. I could hear my temper rising in my voice and feel it in my chest. I wasn't trying to get upset. When I walked over here, I thought I was going to keep my cool, but now I was learning that she wasn't actually interested in the guy she was dating.

"Does he know?" I asked.

She gave a half-hearted shrug with one shake of her head.

"Daisy." This time it really did sound like I was scolding her.

"Kye!" she said, matching my tone. "You have no room to

judge my life. You walked out of it. You don't get to throw your judgment at me the moment you walk back into it. I have to go."

I took three steps until I was only inches from her. "You are amazing, Daze. Perfect exactly the way you are, and you do not need to be paraded around for other people's benefits like that just so they think you are a good girl and staying out of trouble."

"Isn't that what we did? Didn't you like that I was seen as a good girl, and you used it to your benefit?"

I smirked. "Didn't you like that I was seen as trash who would fight anything that moved, and you used that to your benefit?"

"I never saw you that way."

"I know that's a lie, but I'll let it slide. Do you want to know the difference between what happened with us compared to what's happening with you and Mark?"

"What?"

"First, we were both in on it. And second." I reached out, running my fingers down her arm and wishing I could do more. "I think I fell in love with you the moment you kissed me, and I'm pretty sure you fell in love with me. We can say different, but I don't think much of what happened between us was fake from that night."

A speaker sounded behind her, and I could hear Mark's voice.

"I have to go," she said again, but moved closer.

"Alright. I'm texting you later."

"You are?"

"I can call you if that's better?"

"No. Texting is fine," she said, but I could see the confusion.

Part of me did feel bad that her relationship didn't seem to be everything she hoped for, but the other part of me was hopeful.

There might still be a chance that Daisy could love me again.

FORTY

DAISY

IT WAS ten o'clock that night before I got home, tucked Bailey in, and got into my bed. There was already a text waiting for me when I turned over and clicked open my phone.

KYE
You two get home, okay?

DAISY
Home and in bed.

My cheeks immediately flamed, and I felt so stupid. I would think I was enough of an adult to tell him that I was in bed without it having some alternative meaning. Even if it did make me a *little* hopeful that he would be picturing it.

KYE
Did you both have fun?

DAISY
Enough, yeah, but exhausted.

KYE

That might be good for you. Get a break for the night. You get a lot of help with her?

DAISY

Some. The crew, of course. My dad, but that's hit or miss if I want him to.

KYE

Shocked that he hasn't pulled me over yet.

DAISY

Give it another day or two.

KYE

You looked great today

I liked the blue dress

So, besides parading around town with Mark, chasing after the bee, and hanging out with the crew, what else do you do for fun?

DAISY

Fun? That's all the fun I have.

KYE

No seriously, what do you do for fun?

DAISY

Nothing? My free time is spent with the crew and I have no other free time.

KYE

None?

DAISY

Not really.

KYE

Okay, if you did have free time. What are you doing?

DAISY

I like to read when I can and love writing. If I had anymore free time, I would write more.

KYE

Interesting. Like what?

DAISY

If you make it a joke I'm blocking your number

KYE

Promise.

DAISY

I like reading and writing romance

KYE

So you and Jax are best friends then?

DAISY

What? No? Why?

KYE

Oh damn. Have you told anyone you read those books? Because Jax does. I mean, Carly does by association now, too.

DAISY

Okay, now I'm the one laughing. JAX? I can't. I'm bothering him about this all day tomorrow.

KYE

I'm here with alllll the dirty little secrets

DAISY

Then tell me one of yours.

KYE

What if I don't have any?

DAISY

I'm sure you have one thing you've never told someone.

KYE

How dirty are we talking exactly?

DAISY

Anything from PG to extremely x-rated

KYE

Oh, that's right. How could I forget that sweet little Daisy has a filthy mind? Bet those books are extremely x-rated, too.

DAISY

Probably even more than you're imagining.

KYE

Does that mean you are going to tell me a dirty secret?

DAISY

I think it depends on how good yours is

KYE

Fine. Since we are talking about your filthy mind, those things you would always say to me still get me off to this day

DAISY

Hold on I'm fanning myself so I don't pass out.

KYE

Better not because it's your turn.

DAISY

I can't

KYE

That means you have something in mind. Tell me.

DAISY

It's a lot

KYE

More than admitting that my ex-girlfriend's words from six years ago is still one of the main things that gets me off?? How?

DAISY

Maybe

And maybe it's just wrong to tell you

KYE

That's my favorite kind.

Tell me.

DAISY

Every time I was with someone else, I just closed my eyes and thought of you

KYE

Fuck.

I think I love the dirty little secrets game.

I WOKE UP GROGGY THE NEXT DAY AS BAILEY RAN SCREAMING through the house. It was too early, and I had stayed up too late texting Kye. It was the day before the wedding and I was already exhausted for the weekend.

KYE

Come outside.

DAISY

Why?

KYE

Because I'm almost there.

DAISY

Okay. Why?

KYE

Get your ass outside, Daze.

DAISY

Bossy.

I stepped outside just as his car rolled to the curb at my house, and my stomach flipped when he rolled down his window and smiled.

There wasn't much more I loved than when Kye smiled at me.

"What are you doing here?" I asked, reaching the car.

"I'm the delivery boy today. I have Bailey's dress for the wedding tomorrow."

"Oh, I thought Scout wanted me to pick it up later?"

"And I offered to drop it off sooner so you didn't have to."

"That was nice. Really nice. Thank you."

He got out and reached in the back, pulling out a small dress bag to hand to me.

"I'll still be in town after the wedding," he said. "Can you just let me know when you need something? I don't care if it's errands or whatever. I won't be working, obviously, so just... let me help when you need help."

It wasn't what I was expecting him to say, but from the day I met Kye, he was always ready to help me. I guess a lot of things didn't change. "Why would you offer that?"

"Because I have time, and you don't. Plus, I never mind seeing you or her. I've also heard that you're stubborn about the crew helping you."

"It's not their responsibility to help me."

"No, but they still like to."

"It's also not your responsibility."

"No, but I want to." He stepped closer now, handing me the bag and holding on to my hand as he did. "I've missed you," he whispered.

A sheriff's car pulled up behind his, parking along the curb and leaving me no chance to tell him how much I've missed him, too.

"Dad or Mark?" he asked.

I stepped back, knowing that it didn't matter who it was, neither of them would like how close we were standing.

"Dad," I said, the tightness in my chest giving me no relief.

"Daisy. Kye. What are you doing here?"

Kye only smiled and rolled his eyes. "Delivery for the wedding."

"Yeah? Along with bothering Daisy?"

"He's not bothering me. Would you knock it off?" I asked.

"She's dating Mark now, you know?"

My mouth dropped open, but Kye laughed. "Oh, I know it. I've heard all about it. Don't worry, Sheriff. I'm just dropping off a dress for the little Bee."

"The little Bee?" my dad asked, the edge of anger not hidden.

"Bailey," I said.

"Oh, I got that, but I wanted to know why he suddenly knows Bailey enough to have nicknames."

"Because he's watched her for me."

My dad's eyebrows shot up, and I could see the angry red color coating his face.

Kye leaned down, whispering to me like he always used to. "Do you want me to stay or go?"

"I think going would save you a lot of trouble," I said. "It's alright. I've dealt with him enough. I'll see you tomorrow?"

"Yeah, I'll see you then. Like I said, Daze, text me if you need anything. And I mean *anything.*"

I smiled as he waved to my dad. I was pretty sure Kye really meant anything. From burying bodies to giving me orgasms. I couldn't think of one thing that Kye would deny me.

"Why the hell are you letting that boy look after my granddaughter?"

"That boy is very much not a boy anymore, Dad."

"Daisy!" he scolded.

"I mean, he's a capable adult who helped me the other day instead of having Daisy sit with me at the diner. He had already watched her when Fox had Liam and her for the night. Relax. Bailey loves him."

"I don't care who Bailey loves. She would love a stranger if they gave her a bar of candy. It's your job to keep her safe and only let the right people watch her."

"And Kye did amazing!" I yelled. "She's completely happy, healthy, and safe. I'm doing my job, and I would like you to stop insinuating I'm not."

I didn't stand up to my dad much. Not that he was violent or anything, but it usually just didn't feel like it was worth the effort. Falling in line and avoiding conflict was always easier, but I really couldn't take this today. I still had work today and need to get ready for the wedding tomorrow. I was a brides-maid, which meant I was getting up as early as possible to be there for Scout. The girls had welcomed me with open arms to their group when I needed them. Even now, they were always there for me. I wouldn't let her down by missing a second of her day.

"I told that boy to leave you alone, and he said he would. Why the hell is he here to ruin your life again right as you're on track?" he said, looking down the road at where Kye's car had disappeared.

"You've seen Kye lately?"

"No. Mark told me he was back, but I thought we were in agreement of him leaving you alone to live your life. He's trouble, Daisy. He's going to bring trouble around and try to ruin your life all over again."

In the pit of my stomach, I already knew what he was saying, but the words took longer to register.

"When did you tell Kye to stay away from me?"

"You already know when. Back when he tried to kill your boyfriend."

"Dean was my ex-boyfriend at the time. *Kye* was my boyfriend. Is that why Kye left that night? You told him to leave me?"

"I told him staying would ruin not only his life, but yours and his friends'. I wasn't lying, Daisy. Dean could have gone after him, and you, and his friends. I was protecting you from a life living with that mess of a boy. And I told him that. He was no good for you, and he needed to realize that. I thought he had, but he looked more than comfortable there with you now."

"Who I'm comfortable with is none of your business. I can't believe you did that. I can't believe you thought you could make decisions for me like that. For him!"

"I did what I thought was right as your father."

"Get out," I said through gritted teeth.

"I came to see Bailey."

"You are not welcome here right now. Leave."

"You can't keep her from me."

"I'm her mother. I can do whatever the fuck I want. Leave!"

"You aren't her mother, Daisy, you are her aunt, and you need to stop acting like you aren't."

"I have raised her since she was a baby. I can call myself her mother while telling her about Willow. Would you rather her have no mother?"

"No, that's not what I meant."

"Go now or I'm calling you in for trespassing."

He laughed but shook his head. "No one would arrest me for that, Daisy."

"Are you saying your department is corrupt? That they wouldn't protect me because of who you are? That seems illegal. I should call about that, then."

"Don't do that," he said, the small panic in his tone making me more angry.

"Then leave."

His face was red with anger again, but he stepped back towards his car. "Fine. I'll give you time to get over this hissy fit, but don't you think I will be kept from Bailey forever?"

"Why not? Maybe it's not good for her to be around someone so angry. You thought you could make decisions for me as my father. According to you, I can make whatever choices I think are best for Bailey."

"Daisy, I—"

"Need to leave. Or you will be forced to."

He shook his head, slamming the car door as he got in and peeled away from the curb.

I made it back to the front porch before I couldn't go any further.

I knew Kye left so he wouldn't get in trouble, but I didn't realize my dad told him to leave *me*. I didn't know why it hadn't occurred to me. Why didn't I think my dad would have played a bigger part than I expected?

I knew he would have told Kye to leave, but to leave me? To tell Kye that he would ruin my life if he stayed?

I couldn't stop the wave of hatred for my dad — the way he thought he could run my life—but Kye was right. I was always the one going along with it.

But what now? I had built a life for myself. I had Bailey, my house, my job, and technically, I had Mark in some way. I was sure he told people we were together, and if I wanted, I was sure I could make that official.

As if he could hear me, a text came through.

Mark: Would you like to go out tonight?

Daisy: I don't think I can. I'm exhausted and have the wedding to prep for tomorrow.

Mark: Of course. I could still take off if you needed a date?

Daisy: It's alright. Between being a bridesmaid and Bailey, I will be pretty busy all day.

Mark: Alright. Text me when you're free then.

I threw my phone aside, getting to my long to-do list and trying to block out every problem that seemed to be coming to light in my life.

FORTY-ONE
KYE

SO FAR, the entire day of the wedding had gone perfectly.

I had endured walking Daisy down the aisle. I assumed it was planned by the crew on purpose, but I didn't know if it was because of the touching thing or the Daisy thing.

Either way, I was happy that, at the very least, I hadn't had to watch her walk down the aisle with anyone else.

Now, Scout and Chase were married, the bright smile on Scout's face making my chest hurt. Fox, Ransom, and Jax had all danced with her now, which meant it was my turn.

I stepped up behind her as she kissed Chase, who sighed. "Looks like I have to share you one more time," he said. "Who would have thought the girl of my dreams came with four other men?" he joked. He loved to mess with her about the other men in her life, but there was no confusion that Chase was the love of her life.

We were her brothers. Family, and best friends.

She turned to me, the broad smile still plastered on her face. "Ahh, the last brother. My twin. I wondered if I'd get a dance with you."

"This is one I wouldn't miss."

"Good," she said as I pulled her closer and started dancing with me.

"Although, I really re-thought my position when you chose Fox to walk you down the aisle."

She smacked my arm. "Don't even start. You know why I chose Fox. He appointed himself that role years ago. The man is worse than a father sometimes. Forever stuck between father figure, brother, and best friend. I don't call you twin because you want to be a dad figure in my life."

"No? What do I want to be, then?"

"My annoying twin. The exact opposite of me, the same age, and somehow exactly like me."

"I don't think we are anything alike, Scout. And you're a short little redhead. I don't think we look close enough to be twins."

"I think we are alike in all the other ways. In heart, you know? And god, have you annoyed me all my life like a twin brother would," she said with a grin, but my heart cracked.

Scout did always annoy me like a sister, and I loved her like one, too. "Well, no annoying you tonight. I'm here to celebrate you finding Chase and somehow convincing him to marry you."

She smacked me again. "Rude. I didn't have to convince him of anything. What about you?"

"What about me?"

"Finding the woman of your dreams anytime soon?"

"No, I don't think I will be."

"Because you already found her," she said, the words clearly a statement and not a question.

"Maybe."

"And you aren't doing anything about it?"

"What's there to do? She is with someone, and why would she give the guy that left her a second chance?"

"Because you left for a good reason. And you didn't want to. She should understand that."

"I think she does. Maybe, she does, but that doesn't mean she has to want me in her life. Plus, with Bailey now, she would have to be more careful who she lets in. I'm sure Mark is safe, and not a flight risk."

Scout gagged and rolled her eyes. "And *boring*. The man has zero hobbies besides running after her dad and being a cop. Like *zero*. He doesn't even like Bailey."

That made my eyebrows jump. I hadn't realized Daisy would be with anyone who wouldn't. "What? Why?"

"From what Daisy has said, she's too much for him. He likes quiet, organized fun, not wild child Bailey fun."

"Interesting," I said, trying not to ask a thousand more questions. "I wouldn't have guessed that."

"I don't know. Maybe he's just one of those people who doesn't like kids."

I shrugged, but wanted to change the subject, not needing to dwell on Mark or Daisy's love life when it was Scout's wedding.

"What about you? Planning out your life for kids now?"

She shrugged. "I'm not sure. I haven't decided yet, and Chase seems to be happy with whatever I decide. I have some time."

"Chase is a good guy," I said. "I'm glad you found him." She looked back at him, both of them smiling like idiots at each other. "Alright, come on, back to the husband before I gag at your happiness."

I dropped my hands, gesturing for her to go, but she threw her arms around me instead. "Thanks. Love you."

"Love you, too."

"You deserve her, Kye. You deserve them both, and if you want them, you should get them."

I nodded, but gave her a shove towards Chase. "This is your day. We can talk about my drama later."

"Oh, I will hold you to that," she said, and ran to jump into Chase's arms.

I turned, running right into the blonde-haired woman that had haunted me every day since she jumped into *my* arms and kissed me.

"I noticed you haven't danced with anyone but Scout," Daisy said. "Could you make an exception for me?"

I grabbed her hand and set my other one on her waist, taking every ounce of control I had to not pull her against me.

"You are always the exception, Daze. At least for me. I was kind of expecting you to be glaring at me across the room, not asking me to dance with you."

"It was a good assumption, but I'm not in the mood to glare."

She moved with me, quiet as she stared up at me.

"You okay?" I asked.

"I need to talk to you," she said.

"Alright. I'm listening."

She looked around and shook her head. "Maybe we can head outside later? I'd prefer a little more privacy, and people are looking at us."

"Isn't Mark with you tonight?"

"He had work tonight, so no."

"And couldn't call off?"

"No. He's very dedicated to his job."

I nodded, trying not to insult the man for everything he did. "Me, too," I said. "You look beautiful."

She was wrapped up in some green silky bridesmaid dress that hugged every curve of her, and I was struggling not to run my hands over her hips again and again.

"Thanks," she said. "I about died and ran back home when I saw you."

"Is that a good or bad thing?"

"For you? Good. For me? Bad. You look so hot in a suit, I don't even know what to do with myself."

Any comments about what she might be thinking about me had been all about the past. This was one of the clearest she had made about how she might feel now. I pulled her closer, her body flush against mine.

"You still think about me like that?"

She scoffed as I spun her around. "Like I want to pull you into a closet and see if you still lose your mind to fuck me? Yeah, I do," she said, nearly rolling her eyes. My cock jumped, the image of her dress pulled up to her waist and legs wrapped around me making me instantly hard. Her hand pulled from mine and flew to cover her mouth. "Oh my god, Kye, I'm so sorry."

I was already trying to hide my laughter as she looked at me in horror.

"I cannot believe I just said that out loud. And *here,* of all places? I am so sorry."

I leaned down, my lips brushing against her ear. "Don't be. Under different circumstances, that's exactly what I would be doing right now. And I promise, I still would."

She sucked in a hard breath and wrapped her arms around my neck until I couldn't look at her anymore.

Her head rested against my chest, and for a few more seconds, I felt like my life was perfect. This was what I wanted.

Her. I wanted her.

The song ended, and she pulled back. "I better go check on Bailey. Thanks for the dance."

"Still want to talk?"

"Yeah, I'll find you in a little bit."

She spun on her heel, taking off in the opposite direction. I took a hard right, leaving the dance floor before anyone else came up to me.

I didn't stop until I was outside, sucking in cool, fresh air as I tried to calm myself down. I grabbed a smoke from someone on the steps and kept going, heading out to my car before pulling out my phone.

KYE

If you still want to talk. I'll be at my car.

I hit send and threw the phone down. If she really wanted to talk, she would come find me, and if she didn't, I could leave and think about putting that distance between us again.

The wedding was basically over. I could leave the second I wanted to.

Fate could decide for me now.

I STEPPED OUTSIDE and could see Kye immediately. He leaned against his car, his head all the way back to look up at the dark sky. A puff of smoke blew through his lips, and my nose scrunched.

"Still smoking?" I asked, hands on hips.

He didn't move, not even lifting his head to look at me.

"Would you believe it if I said this was the first cigarette I've had in over six years? The last one I ever had, I shared with you."

The memory of being pressed against his body, his hand around my neck and lips on my skin, burned through me. I was already so worked up from dancing together that even the thought of his hands on me again turned me on.

"Why are you breaking and having one now?"

"Because I need something, *anything*, to occupy my hands before I lose my self-control and put them on you."

"Have you ever had self-control?"

He laughed, stepping closer. "I like to think it's gotten

better with age. I tend to think before I act now. At least sometimes."

"Really? I kind of liked it when you lost all control with me."

He came closer, but I stepped around him, moving until we traded places and my back was against his driver's door.

I smiled as he turned back to me.

"I want to ask what game you are playing, but I'm worried if I know I will want to play along," he said.

"And you can't?"

"I have to keep reminding myself that you have a boyfriend, and I do not play games with other guys' girl-friends."

"And if I didn't have one?"

He took a long drag of the smoke and threw it down to stomp it out.

In one step he was nearly against me, the heat of him rolling over me like a blanket.

"I would put your hands on me first. I miss the sheer ecstasy that comes over me when your hands are on me. I miss your body on mine," he said, the quiet rasp of his voice making my legs weak.

"Just my body? Not me?"

"Missing you is a given. I've missed you every fucking day, but missing your body is different. I've never missed anyone's hands on me," he said, leaning in, his eyes heavy as he looked over my face. "Or the way your body wraps around mine, how you say my name, how you get me off. I miss the slutty things you tell me when you come undone," he added with a smirk.

"Slutty?"

"Yes, and I loved every second of it. Even the thought of ever getting to hear those words on your lips again turns me on."

I looked down, my thighs clenching as I saw the outline of his hard cock.

"Kye," I said, breathless as my heart rate picked up. His hand reached to my chin, his thumb moving over my lower lip. I only closed my eyes, trying to memorize the feeling.

"Do you talk like that for Mark? Do you tell every guy how bad you want fucked? How you like it so hard, it hurts? How you want others to watch you get licked and fucked until they are burning with jealousy?"

My chest heaved, and my wetness soaked through my underwear. I was falling apart and didn't want to stop it. The type of inner thoughts I hadn't told anyone since him.

"No," I finally said. "I don't tell anyone else those thoughts. Have you been able to sleep with other women?"

He stepped against me now, his thumb still moving over my bottom lip.

"No. These lips were the last ones wrapped around my cock. Your body is the last one I sunk into. I've tried. I've tried so fucking hard, but even if I've gotten better about being touched, yours are still the only hands I *want* on me."

My heart somehow broke and leapt at the same time. I ran a hand down his side, brushing over his cock, and tried not to linger, even when I wanted to. He pressed against me with a groan, the pants the only thing between us.

"Please stop," he said, his throat tight.

"I thought you said you wanted my hands on you," I whispered, moving over his length again.

He grabbed my wrists, holding them tight as he pulled them up.

"I did. I *do,* but you are still with Mark, and I can't expect you to forgive me."

"Why? Are you just trying to sleep with me so you can leave for another six years?"

He didn't move, barely took a breath as he stared at me. "Do you really think I wanted to leave?"

"I did, but then yesterday, I talked to my dad. Well, I fought with him. He told me that he told you to leave or else you and the crew would face charges from Dean. I would have done something, Kye. I would have told them what Dean did."

"It didn't matter. I wasn't only defending you at that point, Daze. I was hunting him down to kill him. I followed him. Your dad was right. Even if you pressed charges, mine would be a lot worse. And worse than that, you were there. They could have grouped you in and you would have been kicked out of school. The crew could have faced charges. It would have been a mess."

"But why did you stay away?" I asked, the tears already threatening to fall. "You could have come back after a little while. Come back to me, at least."

"Because I was the problem. Not you. Me. And I couldn't ruin your life more."

"That's not true."

"At the time, it was for me. I grew up believing I was the problem and terrible things followed me everywhere. Then I find you, and you have this perfect life, and in a matter of months, I'm ruining it. Every time something bad happened, I was there. It was hard not to see a way that it wasn't my fault."

"But now you realize that's bullshit? That it was Dean's fault and not yours? Because you seem to have made sure I didn't do that to Bailey, so when did you realize you aren't the problem in all of this?"

"I've been to a lot of therapy, and I would love to say that fixed me. That I've been living in bliss of not being a problem, but none of that fixed my brain."

"Then how are you recognizing it now?"

"Because of Bailey. There's not one fucking thing wrong with her, but she's going to be told there is. She's going to be told she's too much to handle and deal with. I'm sure it isn't going to go away as she gets older. Honestly, it might get a hell of a lot worse."

"Are you saying you *just* realized this?"

"Honestly, yes. I wish I could say I figured it out on my own, but I didn't. There's nothing wrong with her, she just doesn't fit into the world we want her to. I thrive in the world that people say is wrong, but I didn't see how true that is until now. She's smart, and strong, and if the world doesn't try to take that away, she will probably grow up to have an amazing life."

Everything he was saying was coming together and I was nearly speechless. "But the world tried to take it from you. You were never told you were smart, or strong, or full of amazing things."

"No. I was told I was a problem, too much to handle, that there was something wrong with me that couldn't be fixed. That more people would be happy to see me dead than alive if it meant they didn't have to deal with me. Every problem in my house was my fault, and they didn't let me forget that. I didn't realize how goddamn unfair that was until I saw her. How the fuck could you tell a kid like that, that they are the problem? That they are so different from other people that it's terrifying. That because she isn't scared of the world at four years old means we should be scared of her. Maybe there was a time I was like that, but I never had a chance to know."

"Which is why you scolded me when I said she was a lot."

"I wasn't trying to scold you, Daze. I just realized when I heard it that she wasn't going to hear it the same way as you were. She was going to start telling it to herself until she believed it. It's not like you were doing anything bad, and maybe Bailey would never think that, but why risk it?"

"No, I was wrong. I was doing something bad, and I actually appreciate it. It's hard doing this whole thing alone, and it's nice to have someone there who might tell me if I'm messing something up. I don't want to ruin her life."

He smiled and moved the smallest amount closer. "You're not. I promise she will turn out ten times better than I did."

"There's nothing wrong with how you turned out. Back then or now. Why does it seem like we can never have things on track with us for more than a week or two? Maybe you're not the one messing this up all the time. Maybe it's me," I said, trying to force a smile. I wanted to lighten the mood, but everything felt so heavy that it didn't come out the way I hoped.

"It's not your fault, Daze. Maybe it's not either of our faults, exactly. We can blame fate. It was reckless giving me you."

"Why?" I asked, my words breathless as he stepped closer. Just the nearness of him was going to my head, making me want to fall forward into his arms.

"Because why would the world give me something so perfect and delicate to love? I would have ruined your life. That's why I stayed away."

"You shouldn't have."

"Maybe. And I am sorry, but I was trying to do what I

could to not ruin your life because I do love you. I didn't leave because I didn't."

My entire body screamed as I heard the words. Love. Not *loved*. Love.

"Come on. I'm sure Bailey is looking for you."

I rolled my eyes, but pushed off the car to follow him. "Yeah, right. I'm old news. She's probably looking for you. I really need to get my other shoes out of the car because it's officially reception time and I'm done with heels."

He laughed but changed direction, heading to my car that, of course, had to be on the other side of the parking lot.

I groaned as my feet screamed in pain from the heels while we walked across the parking lot. Being on my feet all day at work was somehow making heels ten times worse, and I'd been in them for nearly six hours.

"Alright, I'm not listening to that the entire way to your car," he said, leaning down and pulling my legs out from under me. I yelped as he lifted me up, carrying me bridal style towards my car.

My body jumped, immediately taking note of everywhere our bodies were touching. His arm under my legs and back, his chest against my arm.

"You're…touching a lot of me."

"Yeah."

"I never understood why you were fine with me."

"I guess we all get a soulmate, right?"

My heart flipped, trying to take in the words, but when I looked over at my car, I was already scrambling out of his arms.

"What the hell?" he asked, first at me and then at my car. The two tires we could see were flat, and we walked around the other side to see the other two flat as well.

"That can't be a coincidence, right?" I asked.

He was already shaking his head, pulling open my door to inspect inside. "No. I highly doubt that's a coincidence."

"Someone slashed my tires?" It was the obvious answer, but it felt surreal. "Who would slash all of my tires? And why?"

"Piss anyone off lately?" he asked, popping the hood open and inspecting that next.

"Not that I know of. And who would be so mad to come find me at the wedding just to slash my tires?"

"I don't know, but I'm not having you out here to see if we can find out." He grabbed my shoes and the car seat for Bailey out of the back.

"What are you doing?"

His eyebrows furrowed as he waited for me to change shoes. "I assumed you weren't driving this so I will be taking you two home."

My breath hitched, but I stood back up to face him. "With you?"

The grin on his face when I met his eye made my chest tighten. For one beat of my heart, I really thought I was going to get to go home with him, but then he shook his head.

"I was meaning I would take you to *your* home. And as much as I would love for you to come to mine, that's still off-limits. Come on. We need to find Bailey and unfortunately, I think you need to call Mark or your dad about this."

"Maybe it was an accident."

"It wasn't."

"I really don't want to call him."

"I think you have to this time."

I met his eyes, stepping closer, and wishing I could close

the space between us again. "Can we be gone by the time they get here?"

"You don't want to see either of them?"

I was already shaking my head. "No. They can do their job and take care of it. We'll hang out inside a little longer. You will give us a ride home after?" I asked.

"Always Daze, always."

OF COURSE, it had to be on the windiest day that I wore the shortest sundress. One I've had for a few years now, six and a half years, to be exact.

One that I was luckily able to wash the strawberry milk-shake stain out of without too much of an issue.

"Hey, Jax," I said, seeing him looking over a car. "Is my car or Kye here by chance?"

"Hey, Daisy. Both are around back. Dressed like that for any particular reason?" he asked, grinning hard.

"I don't know what you mean," I said, smoothing out the dress again.

"Uh-huh, sure you don't. Just don't break the man's heart too bad, please."

I smiled. "I couldn't even if I tried."

"Right. Like his heart isn't going to break the moment he sees you in that. Good luck."

I headed around the back of the garage, my car coming into view with Kye bent over the hood. New tires had already been installed, but he seemed lost to working on something else on it.

"Hey, Kye," I said, coming up behind him.

"Hey, Daze," he said, still leaning over the engine.

When he turned, I met his eyes, watching as he looked me over.

Like his legs couldn't hold him up any longer, he fell back against the car.

I could see him swallow hard, his eyes going over me again and again.

"What are you doing in that dress?"

"What's wrong with it?"

"Nothing. I'm only surprised there is no stain on the front."

He remembered.

He seemed to remember everything, but I was surprised by this one. I didn't realize he ever looked that much at what I was wearing.

"It came out luckily. I didn't think you would recognize it."

"I would never forget it."

He reached out the moment I stepped closer, running the hem of the dress through his fingers.

"Why are you wearing this?"

"I wanted to see if you'd remember."

"But why?"

"I don't know."

His hand ran down my hip and back up. His mouth dropped open, and his eyes went heavy. "I think I know exactly why, and you already know it's wrong."

"I really don't know what you are talking about," I

breathed as his thumb started moving in mind-numbing circles on my hip.

He leaned down, his hand pressing harder into me. "You are not wearing anything underneath this, and I know what that means."

"That I forgot to do laundry?"

"Mhm, little miss innocent again?"

"Always."

He pulled away, stepping back against my car and sitting on the front of it again. "Always trying to make me lose my mind. The part I find interesting is you did this with the intention that I would find out you aren't wearing any underwear under that dress. You already knew I wouldn't be able to not touch you, and you used that against me."

"Maybe, but it's not like I had a problem with it. Are you sure I'm wearing nothing under this? You should probably check again," I said, grinning as he scowled.

"Daisy. You are trouble. You think I'm bad? You're trying to seduce me, and it's about to work."

I didn't answer, watching as he picked up another tool and turned away from me.

Was I seducing him? I knew Kye wouldn't do anything with me while Mark was still around, but I also didn't know what Kye wanted. If he just wanted to sleep together and move on. Or if there were any deeper feelings still there. It had to be hard to only want to sleep with one person, and I guess I couldn't blame him if he was looking to sleep together before he left.

I leaned against the car next to him, watching him focus on the engine without even a glance in my direction.

"What are you doing to my car?"

"Fixing it."

"I thought everything was fine besides the tires. I just brought it to the shop the other week."

"Well, don't bring it to any shop but this one ever again," he said, the words scolding me. "They didn't even fill the oil, and there's no point trusting anyone else when you have a garage full of people that will take better care of your car than anyone else."

"And what if I do bring it somewhere else?"

He looked over at me, his blue eyes narrowing. "Instead of taunting me, can you hand me that wrench?"

I looked at the pile of wrenches he was pointing to. "Which one?"

"The half-inch."

"There are three of them that say half-inch, so again, which one?"

He huffed, leaning over and grabbing one of them. "If you take this car anywhere else again, I'll be forcing you to learn how to fix your own car, and you will not love the crash course I give you."

"I probably would."

It seemed to make him snap enough. He grabbed my waist, setting me on the car with a growl.

"What the fuck are you doing here, Daze? It's not to worry about your car, and I doubt you're here to tell me you broke up with Mark and want me right now, so why?"

"I do want you right now."

"Then tell me you actually broke up with Mark, and I'll run to your bed like a good little mutt."

"A mutt?"

"I'm sure as fuck not a purebred. Tell me, Daze. Tell me, and I will."

"I didn't."

"Then stop coming around trying to make me your newest dirty little secret while you run around town with your perfect boyfriend."

"It's not that, I just—"

"Just what? Don't know if you want me for sure? Want to see if you still like fucking me? Or are you worried if I'll still like fucking you?"

"No. I mean…maybe. What if we don't end up feeling the same way as we used to?"

He scoffed, but his hands covered mine, forcing them to drag down my thighs to my knees. He pushed, making my legs spread until they were open for him. My dress hung between my thighs, covering everything still, but I really wasn't wearing anything under this. I moved to close them, but he stepped between my legs, forcing me to keep them open.

"What are you doing?" I asked. I was already wet. Just his nearness turned me on now. Maybe I wasn't super worried about our chemistry, but it was scary to not know if it could ever be the same.

Kye kept his eyes on me, bringing my hand up.

"Two fingers," he murmured, pushing my own fingers to my lips. "Suck."

I listened, sucking two fingers into my mouth as he watched.

"Good," he said, still holding my wrist as he pulled. The painful ache between my legs worsened as he trailed my hand down, moving it under my dress until those two fingers were at my entrance.

"Kye, I want—"

My words were cut off as he pushed my wrist forward, my own fingers slipping into my already wet pussy.

My eyes went wide, but I didn't look away from him. He chose the pace. His hand was around my wrist, controlling everything, and the only thing I tried to control was not yelling out.

"Kye," I whispered. "What are you doing?"

"Holding your wrist. What are *you* doing?"

My mouth dropped open with a silent scream as he pushed hard, making my fingers push deeper. The next moan escaped me.

"What do you think? Does it feel the same, Daze? Would you do anything to have me sink into you right now because I would? Does it feel like it used to feel for you?"

My orgasm was building, my legs clenching as Kye pushed my wrist more, speeding up my pace, and I was ready to fall apart.

"No," I breathed. "It doesn't because you aren't even the one fucking me technically, and I still haven't felt this way since you. I think it's worse than before. I need you, please, right now. I need you."

He leaned in, his cheek against mine as one arm held me and the other still held my wrist. "Let me hear how much you still want me," he whispered. "Let me hear you struggle to stay quiet as you cum."

His hand pushed against me, forcing the palm of my hand against my clit. I clamped my mouth shut as I moaned, my body clenching as I came. He held me tighter as my body shook, my eyes squeezed shut against his neck.

I pulled my hand away, and he grabbed it, bringing it up to his lips before sucking two fingers into his mouth.

I couldn't look away as he sucked and licked them clean, staring at me the entire time. And as if I hadn't just had an orgasm, my body was already screaming for him.

His hand cupped my jaw as he stared down at me. "I'm still so fucking obsessed with you, Daze. No one else in this world compares to you, and years apart doesn't erase that. You can give yourself any excuse you want to not be with me, but questioning how bad either one of us want each other will not be one of them. Okay?"

I nodded, lost for words, as he helped me out of the car.

"You should go, Daze," he said. "I don't think staying right now is going to be good for either of us."

"Okay," I said, sounding as spaced out of the conversation as I felt. I said goodbye, already heading around to the front of the garage, but stopped when I saw the crew there. Not that they were looking at me.

Ransom grabbed Quinn, laughing as he kissed her. They had been together for ten years, and you wouldn't know it based on the giddy way they were always looking at each other.

Ten years and they still felt that way and I had barely been dating Mark for ten *weeks* and never felt like that. Not with him.

But I was pretty sure the chance of feeling that way with Kye was pretty high.

Would he love me like that in ten more years?

I guess the more pressing question was if he would love me like that now. I spun, took a deep breath, and headed right back to Kye.

He heard me coming, turning with a cocked eyebrow as I got closer.

"Miss me already?"

"Yes," I said.

I needed to know. We both did. I think we deserved to.

"I was kidding. What's up?"

"I wasn't," I said, my arms wrapped around his neck, forcing him to bend down to me as my lips fell against his.

Without hesitation, his arms snaked around me, pulling me into him and swiping his tongue into my mouth. I opened up with a moan.

A lump formed in my throat, and the tears already threatened me. Kissing him was no different than it was six years ago.

Every part of me melted as his hands moved down my sides, touching every place he could. He took everything, pulling me closer and giving me the full force of his lips.

I didn't realize until he was moving what he was doing. He finally set me down at the corner of the garage.

"That's a dangerous game, Daisy," he said, and I could see the same wild man I fell in love with before in front of me. The raging eyes, the scowl, the way his chest heaved wildly. He looked like he could kill, and I knew he would if he was pushed. He almost did it for me once. I also knew the way he would take me to bed when he was like this. How raging and angry it was, but it always made me feel so much love that I could cry.

"I'm sorry. I just wanted to see. I wanted to know for sure if we would feel the same way."

"And did you find out?"

"Yes."

"Then *never* do that again when you aren't mine."

FORTY-FOUR
DAISY

I TRIED to focus on work, but every few minutes, my mind would wander back to Kye and kissing him.

I walked around the counter, and Amber bumped into me.

"You good?" she asked, laughing as I leaned against the counter.

"Not really," I said, quieting down as Mia, the other waitress that worked here, came around the counter.

She was sweet, a little younger than us, and hated the job with a passion. She was also a town gossip, and I think she could last all of five seconds before running to someone to spill any secrets. When Mark and I started dating, she basically ran store to store telling anyone that would listen that we were dating. The sheriff's daughter dating the guy running for sheriff next? It was hot gossip, and she knew it. It played right into my dad's plans, though, and by the end of that day, Mark had multiple businesses calling to say they supported him in his campaign. So whether Mia was sweet or not, she was not about to hear the confession I was going to tell Amber.

Once she went back out to the tables, I pulled Amber closer.

"I kissed Kye," I said. Her eyes went wide, and she smiled, nearly jumping up and down in excitement.

"Yes, yes, yes. Finally! How did you last that long? It's almost been two weeks. I wouldn't have lasted two hours."

"Amber," I hissed. "It's not a good thing. Technically, I think I'm still dating Mark."

She rolled her eyes. "And shouldn't be? You should have dumped that man even before Kye came around. You don't even *like* him, Daisy. Do you even want to kiss him? Let alone get your hands on any other body parts? You've been avoiding sleeping with the man. Now Kye is back, obviously still ridiculously hot and in love with you. Why wouldn't you dump Mark and go with Kye?"

"Because Kye is leaving in a week or two, and then what? I'm left heartbroken again?"

She was shaking her head. "Have you even talked to Kye about that? Yeah, maybe he had plans to leave, but he also told me he was only here for the week and look at that, it's been nearly two. He didn't come to town thinking you would be back in his life."

"And how would you know any of this?"

She gave a cute smile, which, for a heavily tattooed and pierced dark-haired girl, somehow looked menacing. "Because I've wormed my way into your friend group. Did you really think my best friend was going to go out and get new best friends without me? I met Carly, and we got along, then she added me to a group chat with Kye because we like all the scary stuff. And don't even worry, Kye is off-limits and I don't want him," she said, sticking out her tongue.

I only shook my head. "And you say I'm crazy."

"I think you are crazy! You're choosing good old Mark who doesn't make your panties wet, instead of hot as sin Kye, who is so fucking in love with you, the man would rather die before loving someone else. Do you know what I would do to have that in my life? I don't get that chance. Kye is back, drop what you're doing and get him, Daisy."

"I'm sorry," I said, knowing how unfair it was that Lane had walked out on her with the kids. She did amazing with them, but it didn't seem fair.

"Don't be. I'm alright, but damn, open your eyes and see what you're risking losing."

"I already wanted to break up with Mark. I am now, but Kye left for six years. I'm scared it will happen again."

"Don't let it scare you. You said he left because of your dad. Stand the fuck up to that guy and protect Kye this time. He protected you, now protect your relationship. Not everyone is going to be happy if you're in love and that will be true no matter who you love. Kye left, and you let him."

My mouth dropped open. "I didn't *let* him."

"Then why didn't you find out why he left until this week? Because you never went looking. It's not your fault, and it's not his. Don't be a dick because you *both* fucked up."

"You're really direct today, aren't you?"

She gave me another sweet smile. "Always, babe. Oh, look, speak of the bore. You make your own choices, and I love you, but like...don't be a dumb bitch."

She smiled at Mark and turned to shoot me a glare.

"Hey, Mark," I said.

"Hey, honey," he said, leaning down to kiss my cheek. I tried to stop it, but my skin crawled. I didn't want his hands on me after Kyes were. I didn't want him to kiss me or call me *honey.*

If I had any doubts before, there were zero now. It was crystal clear that I needed to break up with Mark. Amber was right, I should have done it days ago, but Kye coming back into my life, and still loving me, seemed too good to be true.

"Can we talk outside for a second?"

He nodded, and followed after me. The buzz of the diner went silent as the door closed behind us. He was still doing that half smile, and it was making it harder to meet his eye.

Breaking up with anyone, even someone I wanted to break up with, was hard as a top tier people pleaser. I didn't want anyone mad at me. I didn't want him hurt or upset in general, but especially not at me.

I thought back to texting Kye the other night. Him walking home with Bailey. The way I truly felt like he thought I was perfect.

The thought made me want to smile, and I almost did before I finally looked up at Mark.

"What is it?" he asked.

There was no dancing around it. There truly wasn't enough to reflect on to tell him about our good times, and there was no lying to say how I needed to focus on my life and not a relationship because there would be no hiding from him if I did start dating Kye.

Was I about to start dating Kye?

It felt like that was an option, but now that I was standing here facing Mark, I realized I never asked for a clear answer.

My mind kept drifting to Kye and it had to stop.

"I just…We need to break up. Or end our dates?"

His eyebrows furrowed and he stepped closer to me, reaching out for my arm. "What? Why? I thought we were having a good time."

"We were, but things have changed for me, and I'm just not sure I can keep doing this."

His face hardened and eyes narrowed. "Does this have anything to do with Kye being back in town?"

The question caught me off guard and it shouldn't have. Mark knew.

He knew that Kye meant something to me, and the timing was no coincidence.

"It might have a little to do with him, yeah, but this is something I had been thinking about before he got here. We kind of just started going on dates and kept going. It wasn't like we actually agreed to start dating."

"Yeah, Daisy, because this isn't high school. I don't write a little note to see if you are going to be my girlfriend or not."

"No, I know. I meant that it never quite felt like we were actually together."

"Well, then I guess I'm the fool here, but I have been under the impression we were."

"I'm sorry, Mark. I really am, but it doesn't matter if we were dating or going on dates. It has to be over." My heart was pounding in my chest, the awful churn of my stomach making me want to take it all back and forget it happened.

I hated how upset he looked, knowing it was my fault.

"This isn't okay, Daisy. None of this is okay, and you know that no one is going to be happy about this."

That made me freeze, the empathy ending right there, because I knew what he was implying.

My *dad* wouldn't be happy with this, not random people on the street. He was going to run right to my dad and tell him what happened.

"Why does it matter if they are happy if I'm not?"

"And you think Kye is going to make you happy? The guy

who can't stay in town long enough to even pick up his mail is going to take care of you and Bailey? What are you thinking, Daisy? What has he said to fill your head with this even being a possibility?"

There were so many things I backed down for these days, things I would let people get away with and not complain, but telling me I was stupid and potentially a bad mother were not going to be one of them.

"I'm done, Mark. What happens now in my life is none of your business. I think it's best if you leave."

"Oh, it's going to be my business. I'm going to go talk to your dad and make damn sure it's my business." His nostrils flared, and the pure hatred in his eyes made me take a step back. I really didn't think Mark loved me. At least, he had given no indication that he did, which made me wonder if this was all because of the campaign.

He was backing up now, heading towards the side gate that led back to the parking lot.

"We *will* talk soon, Daisy."

I didn't say another word, waiting for him to close the gate behind him before heading towards the back door of the diner again. Mia stood watching us, the door propped open just enough that she probably heard it all.

I groaned. Now the entire town would know by morning, including my dad.

I grabbed my phone off the back counter, hiding in the back a little longer. It didn't matter what people said or if my dad was upset. Amber was right. Not everyone would be happy, but that didn't mean I couldn't be.

DAISY

Could you come over tonight?

KYE

I can't. I have plans.

The happy fluttering in my stomach died out, and the anxiety went crazy.

DAISY

Because you have a date?

KYE

Something like that.

DAISY

Oh.

KYE

I love how you think you can be mad about that.

DAISY

I'm not mad.

KYE

Are too.

DAISY

All I said was 'oh'. How does that mean I'm mad?

KYE

The equivalent of 'I'm fine'

DAISY

I AM fine.

KYE

Bet that pretty little brain of yours is already running a mile a minute wondering who I'm going out with.

DAISY

....

Are you going to tell me?

KYE

No.

DAISY

Why?

KYE

You're so jealous and I like it. Now think of how I feel thinking about Mark in your bed every night.

DAISY

Mark has never been in my bed.

KYE

Interesting.

Why do you want me at your house?

DAISY

I need to talk to you

KYE

Every time you need to talk to me, you make a move on me. I can't be near you for the sake of my own self-control.

DAISY

I don't want to not be near you.

KYE

I am sorry, Daisy. Have I told you that? I'm sorry I left.

I hit the FaceTime call, needing to see his face, actually hear his voice, if he wasn't coming over.

He didn't pick up, and my heart broke.

KYE

I'm out, Daze.

I went to type out the words that I broke up with Mark and needed him, but it felt so pathetic now. I wanted to see him, tell him in person. So instead of hitting send, I headed back out for my last two hours of work, leaving my phone in the back and not checking it, even when his name came back up.

FORTY-FIVE
DAISY

THE HOUSE WAS ALREADY DARK when I walked in after grabbing groceries and picking Bailey up. She had asked to see my dad, so I broke down and let him watch her for a few hours.

I held her hand harder, trying to keep her next to me as I fumbled my way into the house.

A crash came from the kitchen, the shattering glass echoing throughout the quiet house.

I dropped the groceries and grabbed Bailey, running back outside and racing to the car. My hands shook as I grabbed my phone, trying hard to focus as Bailey cried.

"It's okay, honey, we're okay," I said, as the call connected.

"What do you mean, we're okay? What's wrong?" Kye asked.

"You're not at my house, right?"

"No, I'm at mine. Why?"

"Because I think someone is inside mine."

"Are you two inside?"

"No, I ran back to the car."

"Okay, lock the doors. Did you already call the police?"

"No, I figured you could get here faster than them." I already heard keys jingling and doors slamming.

"That's not a lie. I'm already in the car. Did they hear you come in?"

"I'm not sure. Bailey was talking, and I did drop our stuff. I think I still see a light moving around."

"Okay, just don't leave the car. Lock the doors." I hit the button and waited. Bailey was still crying hard in the back seat.

"Hand her the phone," he said, and I did. In seconds, she was sucking in hard breaths, the crying calming down.

"Can I talk to him?" I asked, hitting the speakerphone when she held the phone out. "Are you almost here?"

"You should hear me any second now. Just don't get out."

He pulled up, jumping out and looking at the car with a calm smile and wave before stalking inside.

"Kye!" Bailey yelled.

"Yeah, he's checking on the house for us, and then you can see him."

Another five minutes later, he was back out, waving that I could get out of the car.

Bailey was already out, nearly giggling as she ran to him.

"What happened?" he asked.

"I went to walk in and heard glass shatter, so I turned and ran right back out. Was someone inside?"

"Yeah, I think so, but I'm not sure what they were doing. There's a vase of flowers on the ground in the kitchen, but I don't see anything else wrong. Did you call your dad?"

I chewed at my lip and looked at Bailey, who was sitting happily in his arms.

"Yeah, he should be here any second now," I said, chewing on my lip. "Would you mind staying?"

"I wasn't going anywhere, Daze, and you're staying at the apartments tonight. I'll text the crew and see where you two can sleep."

Relief flooded me as I watched Bailey in Kye's arms, talking to him like nothing was going on, and he didn't give any indication there was. I leaned back against my car, taking a deep breath and trying not to cry because, for the first time in a long time, I didn't have to handle it all on my own.

TWENTY MINUTES LATER, MY DAD, MARK, AND TWO OTHER officers were flooding the yard and house. They checked everything over before my dad came over, grabbing Bailey immediately.

He asked me a few questions, general things, before turning an angry glare on Kye.

"Where were you?"

"My apartment."

"And how did you get here before us?"

"I may not be a lot of things, but I promise I'm a better driver than all of you."

"And I called him first," I said, taking an obvious step closer.

"Why didn't you call Mark or me first?"

"I knew Kye could get here faster, and I was alone with Bailey. I'm going to make the decision to not be alone here with someone breaking into my house, regardless of who it is."

"Maybe he got here so fast because it was him," my dad said.

"It was him?" Mark asked, only hearing the last of the sentence. He came over, the anger twisting on his face like I had never seen. I didn't even know Mark could get angry.

"You come back into town and suddenly Daisy is having all these issues, but yet, you're always there to help, aren't you? These things weren't happening before you came."

"And I think that if you are going to demand hanging around him, then you can give me custody of Bailey until these things stop."

"Hold on, you want to take her kid because someone is after her? Like its her fault?"

"Oh, I don't think it's her fault. I think it's yours, but she seems to think she should be hanging around you, calling you over, letting you watch Bailey."

"You think you can tell me who I should hang out with still? And you think I would listen?" I asked. I didn't know how I could have a kid, a job, a house, and the thousand other things that went along with just being an adult, and he still thought he could tell me what to do or who to be around.

"I think you're being stupid if you throw away anything with Mark just to be with this guy. A guy that can't offer you more than a shit apartment that he has to share with his friends, and maybe comes home once a month. You think that's good for Bailey? For you?"

The adrenaline was already wearing off, my shoulders sagging, but anger still burned. I remembered what Amber said, and this was what she meant. I needed to protect Kye against my dad.

Bailey ran to Kye who, even with them all ready to haul him away, still picked her up with a smile.

Because he was going to do whatever he needed to protect *her* from thinking there was a problem.

Mark took off, heading towards Kye like he was either going to punch him or grab Bailey, both of which I wasn't going to let happen. I stepped between them, Mark running into me, but quickly steadying both of us.

I shook his hands off and stepped back into Kye. His hand rested on my waist, steadying me and making me more sure of myself.

"You can think you are going to use this to take Bailey, but you are going to have to do that the legal way. Fight me in court, Dad, that's fine. If that's what you think is best for Bailey, you can do it, but I promise you will not win. Kye, please put Bailey in your car."

"Daisy, you don't have to—"

"Now, please." I kept my voice calm, but I didn't move from between them. "I need to go inside and get Bailey a few things. Are you going to let me or make me go buy new things so you don't call me an unfit mother?"

"Are you going to his place?"

"Yes," I said, already knowing nothing was stopping me from staying with Kye tonight.

"Then go ahead and show me how great of a mother you are. You can't go back in the house. It's a crime scene."

I smiled, already walking towards Kye's car. "Great. Thanks so much, *Dad.*"

He caught up to me, grabbing my arm as Kye shut the car door, watching us.

"I heard you broke up with Mark, and now this? Daisy, I am worried about you and Bailey. This is your safety, *her* safety. Please, I'm trying to help."

"Well, stop it. I know I've gone along and done whatever

you wanted, but I'm not anymore. I want my own life and I get to choose who is in it. If you want to keep us safe, figure out who is slashing my tires and breaking into my house."

"And if it is Kye?"

"You better have undeniable proof before you think I will ever believe you."

He nodded, and I went to get in the car.

"Thanks," I said. "And now I'm exhausted, so let's go."

Kye didn't say anything, but he pulled out, taking me home. I could already feel the calm relief flooding me, and I leaned back into the seat, enjoying every quiet second.

FORTY-SIX

KYE

BY THE TIME we made it into Ransom and Quinn's place, Bailey was already passed out as I laid her on their couch. They only smiled, more than happy to have them over for the night.

Before Daisy could say anything, I was already heading out the door. I heard every word from her dad. I didn't realize she was risking anything for just talking to me, but apparently, this wasn't a new threat from him.

And Mark. Her fucking boyfriend who, instead of taking care of her and Bailey, wanted to blame me for breaking into her house. Who didn't even ask if they were okay, but instead wanted to hit me.

It didn't matter if I had grown up. I was still happy to fight, but there wasn't a chance I was going to do it in front of Bailey.

"Can you guys watch her?" Daisy asked as I pulled open the door. I gritted my teeth, already knowing she was coming after me, and already knowing I couldn't handle it.

The door shut behind us, and I kept stomping up the stairs with no intention of stopping.

"Kye?"

One word and I immediately turned, ready to do whatever she wanted.

"What?"

She looked up at me, her hazel eyes wide. Her blonde hair was up in a messy bun that was falling to the side now.

My chest tightened, every part of my heart shattering.

"I was wondering if I could come up and stay with you tonight," she said, the uncertainty in her tone only breaking me more. I really couldn't do this. I couldn't keep turning down the only person I wanted.

"Why?"

"Because I...need you?"

"Need me or need to not be alone? Why didn't you go with Mark? The man you're *dating*. The guy that is so much better than I am, and won't threaten your damn child being in your life. You've been with him the entire time I've been here, Daze. Don't ask to come to my fucking bed when you are with him."

The softness of her face turned until she was frowning, eyebrows furrowed.

"You left *me*, Kye. Did you think I should drop my entire life the moment you came back? The night you left killed me. I laid in bed for weeks. It took me months to realize you really weren't coming back. Should I have seen you step back into town and just assume you had any feelings? Should I even assume that now? Maybe you are just looking to sleep together to get you through another six years."

"That's bullshit. I would never just want you for sex and you know it. Every part of me died that night. *I* wanted to die that night," I said. "Do you somehow think it was easier for me?"

"You're the one who left! I was here. I never left. You did! Maybe it was easier."

I could only shake my head, already knowing where this was heading. I would never be what Daisy needed. It didn't matter how much I wanted to be, there would always be something, or someone, standing in our way.

"I left because I had to. Because your life was going to be fucked if I stayed. Please give me a damn break. What your dad says proves it. I will never be what you need. I am not the perfect one. I am not the guy that is always charming and safe and comfortable. Please, just go to Mark and stop with this, with us, because what I have to offer you is never going to be enough. Not for you, for your dad, for your life. I could cut my heart out and give it to you, and somehow everyone would think I'm trouble because I got blood on the floor. I could love you a thousand times better than anyone in this entire fucking world, but it's not the right kind of love apparently," I said, each word lifting the stress and fear off my chest. "And please, give me a fucking break. You know, Daisy. You fucking know I'm still in love with you and you are *killing me*." I took a ragged breath, trying to stop myself from getting more enraged. "I will not take anything else away from you. I thought it could be better this time, but I heard everything your dad said. I know what he's threatening this time, and you can't lose Bailey because of me. I'll die, Daisy. I would fucking die. Please don't ask me to come to my bed because I cannot say no again."

Cutting out my heart really would feel better because at least I would know the pain wouldn't last for more than a few minutes, not the rest of my life. I wanted Daisy. I wanted

Bailey. I wanted to give them everything, but there would always be someone taking something from her if she chose me, and there was nothing in the world I could give her to make up for that.

I spun back, heading up the next flight of steps. I made it to my apartment door when I heard her footsteps behind me.

"Kye, no, wait," she said, grabbing my hand. "You aren't going to give me a chance to say anything?"

"I've waited, Daze. I have waited six fucking years and it's still not enough. I have been here for weeks now and you haven't said a thing."

"I've wanted to, but I didn't know what to say. You left. For all I knew, it was because you didn't love me anymore. I didn't know until recently the real reason. And you know what, I did try to talk to you. Earlier tonight, I asked to talk, and you blew me off. So you know what, you lied," she said, a tight smile breaking across her face.

"I've never lied to you."

"But you did. You said that if I broke up with Mark, you would run to my bed like a good mutt. Yet here we are."

She reached up, her arms sliding around my neck as she pulled me down closer to her. Nothing soothed me more than her touching me, and I really couldn't deny her any longer.

I ran a finger over her lips and up her jaw. "It's hard to think when you are touching me."

"Then don't think, and kiss me."

"I can't."

Her lips met mine, and I gave up fighting it. There was nothing I could do except fall victim to her and her kiss. The warmth that spread over me still never happened with anyone else, the wanting in the pit of my stomach, the need to have her wrapped around me. It was all there, even stronger than before.

She pulled back, taking a breath and leaning her forehead against mine.

"My dad and Mark are mad because I broke up with Mark earlier. And while I didn't say it exactly, everyone knows it's because of you. I'm sure the rumors range from I'm already pregnant with your kid to I'm running away with you this time. My dad is saying nasty things because of all that. I won't let him take Bailey, but I also don't want to let him take you again. I want everything you've offered of yourself, every single imperfect and perfect part. There was never anything wrong with you, it was always me. I have always been the problem. I have never stood up to people for what I want. I do what they want so I look good in their eyes. But I should have protected you, protected us, back then, and I didn't, but that won't happen again."

"You broke up with him?"

Her lips turned up, and she nodded. "Yeah, earlier today."

"And it was because you want me?"

"Yes," she said, her smile widening.

That was all the permission I needed. I leaned down, grabbing her thighs and lifting her up.

"I hope you're prepared for six years of endless need to be let loose on you because I don't think I have an ounce of control left in me."

"Good," she said, wrapping a hand around my throat as I carried her inside. "Show me exactly how much you have missed me."

FORTY-SEVEN
DAISY

THE DOOR to the apartment slammed shut behind us as Kye carried me inside. He threw me back on the bed, already pulling at my shoes before I even laid back.

He stood up, rolling his shoulders as he pulled off his shirt.

I would never get over this view of Kye. Tall, tattooed, and smiling down at me. My thighs clenched as he pulled me up and reached for one strap of my dress. He flicked it down, but I stayed covered. His fingers trailed over my collarbone and up my neck, leaving a trail of burning-hot skin. I thought it would be all frantic hands and teeth, but Kye slowed, the soft look in his eyes making me worry.

"Are you okay?"

"I'm very okay. More than okay. I just can't believe you are here. And all mine," he murmured. His fingers trailed down my chest, pulling the other strap of my dress down as he went. "Hours to kiss, and lick, and touch every inch of you."

"Or you can hurry up and get me out of this."

He leaned down, his mouth covering a nipple. I arched

into him, the warmth seeping through the fabric until it was wet.

"Kye," I gasped. "Dress off. Now."

His tongue moved up my chest, nipping at my neck as he went. "I'm in no rush. You've been teasing me endlessly since I got here. What's another hour or two?"

"Kye, if you don't get this off of me right now, I'm going to scream."

"That's okay. I like it when you scream."

"Kye!"

"I like it even more when you say my name," he said with a groan.

"*Please.*"

"Little dirty Daisy flower is going to be all calm and sweet now? What happened to tearing me apart to get what you wanted? I recall one time when you literally grabbed my hair, put my head between your legs, and demanded I get you off."

"I did not," I said, almost horrified, but I couldn't help but laugh.

"Did, too."

"If you really need me to start making you do things to me, I will, but I assumed you knew what you were doing now."

"To you? Always." His head dipped again, licking and biting at my other nipple through the fabric. His fingers trailed down, running over my underwear. "I know exactly what you like. I remember every second of what you like, what made you scream, what made you writhe under me."

"Please, Kye, please hurry. I can't take waiting any longer."

"You are sure in a rush for someone staying the entire night with me."

"I'm not in a rush, but I have been waiting years, *years,* to be with you again. I do not need to waste any time."

"Does that mean you've missed me?"

"More than I will ever admit," I breathed.

"No, admit it. Tell me. Please tell me I wasn't alone in missing you every fucking day of my life. Tell me I'm not so fucking crazy that I had to tattoo your name on my hands, so at least when I thought of you, I had it as an excuse. I couldn't blame myself for thinking of you every fucking day when I had the tattoo."

"No, you weren't alone. Not at all."

He sat down on the bed, pulling me with him until I straddled over his lap.

"The first night we were together. Way back then," he said, laying me back on the bed as his hand ran down my side, pulling my underwear along with it. "I was praying to the entire world that one night would be enough with you. That I could have that one night and get you out of my system and never have to feel that way again. What a fucking joke that was. I will never have enough of you."

"I thought that was just because you suddenly liked sex," I said with a laugh.

"With *you*, Daze. Because my heart was fucking exploding. I was already in love with you and trying like hell to ignore it. That's pretty hard when you are sleeping with the love of your life for the first time."

"You did not think I was the love of your life at that point."

He laughed. "No, that was the moment that I found out. It was the moment that I knew that my heart was like one of those damn fucking necklaces. There are two pieces, and I need yours to make me feel like I actually have one. Every time I see one of those things, I think of you, wondering why I couldn't have been given my own damn heart; I had to share it with someone else."

He pulled me closer, kissing me hard.

"You are the most romantic person, but somehow make every part sound painful," I said.

"Six years, Daisy, six fucking years without you. It has been painful. Every moment has been painful."

"I can think of one thing to ease the pain," I said, lifting enough to undo his belt. He fell back with a satisfied groan.

"I won't deny you a fucking thing, Daisy. You want to skip the foreplay and sink onto my cock, done. If you want hours of my mouth tasting and teasing you, done. Anything you want, Daze. I'll give you fucking anything."

"Right now, I want the first option. Maybe after we can clean up and get right to the hours of teasing me."

He grinned as I undid his jeans. "You wouldn't last ten minutes of being teased before you were demanding to get off again."

I stood up, pulling his jeans and boxers off and taking in the sight. "That's true." I climbed back over him, my dress falling in the way. He sat back up, pulling it up and over my head until I was naked on top of him. My heart burst as I looked at him. "I can't resist anything about you, Kye."

He flipped, taking me with him until I was laid out underneath him.

"I was prepared for slutty, raunchy words. I didn't realize it would be sweet things that would break my heart."

I smiled as he leaned down to kiss my neck and jaw. "Why? Miss all the slutty things I say to you?"

"Every day."

My hands slid into his hair, and I used it to roll us again

until I was back on top. "I've thought about you so much. So many nights I would lie in my bed," I said, reaching down and wrapping my hand around his cock, "and think of you. Think of this. Of you buried deep in me, making me come so hard I couldn't see straight."

"And what did you do when you thought about that?"

My hand slid down between us until I was rubbing my clit, but he grabbed my wrist. "You will not be getting yourself off without me tonight."

"I was just showing you what I did when I thought about you," I said with a grin.

"And I will expect a full demonstration later, but right now, I get to make you come."

He flipped me again before coming down over me. "I missed you," I whispered, running my hands over every inch of him I could.

He nuzzled into my neck, kissing me once before finding my lips. "I missed you, too. I've spent six years wondering if this would ever happen again."

"And you really went six years without anyone else?"

"There is no one else. I don't look at anyone else and want them. I don't think about them like this. I decided I would rather go the rest of my life alone than deal with the agony of someone else."

I nearly blurted out how much I loved him but stayed quiet, not able to bring myself to say the words when I still felt like I could lose him again. I knew he didn't want to go anywhere now, and neither did I, but the pain at him leaving the first time only felt like it would be tripled if we were separated again.

I didn't know if I was ready to face that possibility.

He positioned himself at my entrance, but I stopped him.

"I don't have any condoms, and it's been so long since I slept with anyone that I'm not on birth control."

He groaned, dropping his head against me. "Why is that only turning me on more?"

I laughed as I grabbed his hips and pulled him harder against me. His cock threatened to sink into me, and for one second, I reveled in the feeling. "Wow, who would have thought you have a bit of breeding kink?"

"I don't even know what that is," he said through gritted teeth.

"It means I am going to have so much fun learning all your kinks that you don't even know about."

He pushed into me hard, filling me with one stroke and staying there. I let out a soft gasp, my nails digging into his back as I adjusted to his size. He trailed kisses along my jawline and down my neck.

"I don't care what you want to do when because that sounds like you are staying with me, and that's all I care about."

His words sent shivers down my spine, and I wrapped my legs around his waist, pulling him closer. He moved slowly, each deep and deliberate thrust making me ache with want. I clung to him, an overwhelming surge of satisfaction washing over me. This was what I'd been longing for all these years - his touch, his embrace, his love.

It was everything I had been craving and not finding for six damn years.

"Fuck," he hissed. "I can't believe how good you feel."

He seemed to slow again, but I arched into him. "More, Kye. Stop holding back. I need more."

His hands ran over my thighs, gripping me tightly as he angled himself deeper. With one sudden thrust, he plunged into me, making me cry out. I felt alive again, my body already climbing higher. His hips moved in a steady rhythm, and I matched it.

Every inch of him was familiar, and yet, everything felt brand new. The way his muscles tensed with each movement, the way his breath hitched in his throat as he pushed deeper into me, the way his eyes locked onto mine as he came. It was all so perfect, so intoxicating, that I knew I never wanted this moment with anyone else.

My body tightened, begging for release, and he gave it, pulling my hips up and moving faster. I grabbed onto him, trying not to scream as white stars burst in my eyes and pure ecstasy flowed through every part of me.

There would never be a better feeling.

There would never be anyone else for me.

"AS MUCH AS you want her to go everywhere with you, I am not putting Bailey in your death trap car every time," Daisy said as she threw more clothes into a bag.

"You're going to have to give me more than twelve hours to childproof my life, Daze," I said, lying back in her bed as she packed. After the break-in and us being together, she agreed to stay with me for the rest of the week at least, but I would be working to convince her to stay longer. "I'll get a new car. It's still going to have to be fast, but it will be safer. Promise."

She rolled her eyes and headed back out, not waiting for me to follow.

"You don't have to childproof your life," she said, grabbing the bags she packed for Bailey and heading out. I grabbed the bags from her, still trying to keep up. "I can't expect you to buy a new car."

"No? Want me to steal one from Holt today instead?"

"You aren't stealing anything, Kye."

I laughed, dropping the bags and grabbing her from

behind. I walked us to the car and spun her around, lifting her up onto the back.

"What's actually wrong, Daze?"

"Nothing. Nothing, I'm happy, but…"

"But?"

"But someone is still after me and I don't know why. What if they hurt Bailey? Or you?"

"Or you," I added.

"Sure. Yeah, that, too."

"It will be okay, Daze. Bailey will always be with one of the guys or me for now, and I will always be with you."

She gave a small smile. "What about when I'm at work?"

"I can set myself up there if you promise endless strawberry milkshakes."

"You can talk to Carly about that."

"Well, that's going to be a no, then. I was hoping I could seduce you for milkshakes." I pressed a soft kiss to her lips, but she held on. Her hands fisted into my hair and held me close. I groaned, the sting of her pulling on my hair already turning me on. I loved how she grabbed me and held on. I would have always thought I would need soft hands, but I needed hers. I like the demanding touch, and the strange way I felt in control and out-of-control at the same time.

I could feel her smile against my lips. "I forgot you liked all that."

"All what?" I said, already forgetting what we had been talking about, as I searched for her lips again.

"All the teeth and nails, and apparently, hair pulling."

I leaned in harder, my hands grabbing her hips to hold her against me. I was nearly crawling over her onto the car when her hands pushed against my chest as she started laughing.

"Down, boy. We have somewhere to be," she said,

laughing as she wrapped her arms around me and slid down off the car.

I dropped to my knees, already grabbing her legs to lift her back onto the car.

"Kye!" she yelled, laughing as she grabbed onto me again. "What are you doing?"

"You said down. I assume you meant to go down on you?"

"I absolutely did not. I have neighbors! And you can't miss all this at Holt today, so you better go get in the car so we can go get ready."

"Fine," I groaned, but I grabbed the bags, following her to my car. She laughed more, getting into *my* car, to go to *my* apartment, to then come with me to *my* work event.

It felt like Daisy really might be mine this time.

There was never a point in my life I thought I would get to be this happy.

———

Two hours later, I was standing on the track, watching as Jax, Quinn and Chase pulled up, lining their cars up next to mine. The sea of cars was nearly endless today, Holt's yearly track party only growing each year, and I figured this was going to be one of the biggest yet.

The entire place felt like home to me, since the track was one of the places I came the most when I was in town.

Daisy got out of Quinn's car, choosing to ride with her since I had to be here a little earlier. Bailey was right behind her, both of them smiling as they headed my way. My smile fell when I looked down at the thin, short dress Daisy had on.

I immediately looked at Chase, who gave me a sly smile

and grabbed Bailey, taking her off to the side with Quinn and Jax.

"Get over here," I said, pulling Daisy around the cars until we were partially blocked from everyone else.

"What's wrong?"

"What the hell is this dress?"

"What's wrong with it?"

"It's the hottest outfit I've ever seen. And the thing is so thin, I can make out every inch of your body through the fabric. Did you do it to kill me?"

"No, I did it because it's hot."

I leaned down and kissed her hard. "I think it's torture, and I'm dying to know what you have on under this."

"I bet you can guess."

"Daisy," I groaned.

"Kye." She basically purred my name and ran a hand over my chest.

"You're making it hard to think about racing."

She grinned, taking a step back. "Hopefully that's not the only thing I'm making hard."

My mouth dropped. Somehow, her bold words always shocked me, but I loved them every time.

"Where are you going after that comment?" I yelled as she headed back towards the crew and Bailey.

"To watch you race."

I jogged to catch up to her, glad my sunglasses could hide the way I was staring the entire time.

"Before I raced, I was going to see if you would be fine if I took Bailey for a ride."

"In that thing?" she asked, looking back at the car I had today.

"That is one of the nicest ones we have here."

"It looks like it might fall apart."

I laughed, pulling her under my arm. "I wouldn't ask to put Bailey in it if that was a possibility."

"Why do you want to take her?"

"I think she would like it, and you know I won't let her get hurt."

"Kye…"

"Is that a reluctant yes? She'll be well buckled in, and I bought her a helmet."

"You bought her a helmet for this, too? When?"

"The other night. We measured her head."

Her mouth dropped open. "You *what*? You two planned this?"

"Well, kind of. I told her I don't know if she can ride yet, though."

"I can't…You can't… You two are really going to be the death of me. I can already feel it."

"I hope that's a yes?"

"Yes, but I swear, Kye, if she gets hurt, I'm going to kill you."

"And I would let you." I leaned down to kiss her, surprised at how easy it was to be with her.

Daisy always was and always would be a magnet for me. I couldn't stop touching and kissing her if she was close.

"Sorry," I mumbled, pulling away and trying to focus back on the car and Bailey.

I waved her over, getting her helmet on and her buckled into the car seat. She was beaming the entire time.

"Now you do realize I go fast, right?"

"Yes."

"And you know that I spin the car in circles fast like I showed you."

"Yes!" she cheered.

Hell, she was adorable. Not an ounce of fear in her happy little face. If Daisy had told me she was my kid, I wouldn't have questioned it for a second.

"And what word do you say if you want me to stop?"

"Panda!"

"Alright. Let's go."

I had bought a small microphone, attaching it into Baileys helmet and connecting it to a headphone I could slip in my ear in case she did want to stop. I handed the other to Daisy.

"Here. Listen."

Her eyebrows furrowed, but she slipped it into her ear anyway.

I slid behind the wheel and looked back. For this one time, her seat faced me, and I could see the awe on her face as she looked around the car. It wasn't the same as my other cars I raced. This one wasn't gutted down to one seat, so there was still plenty of back seat for her to be strapped in, and that also meant it was slower, but that was fine for this.

I loved my nephew and niece. I couldn't wait for more in my life, but Bailey was different. She was like me. Even now, I could see it, and I wanted to help her use that to her advantage and not let everyone tell her it was wrong.

I had never let myself imagine having kids. It wasn't something that seemed possible with all the problems I had, but that was different now, too. Bailey didn't bother me. I could carry her and hug her. Daisy didn't bother me. The crew was fine with their hugs and affection. Even Liam and Lily didn't bother me.

I looked back at Bailey one more time.

I knew I was improving, but I didn't realize how far I had come. And now I had Daisy.

My chest squeezed, but I started up the car, revving it once before taking off.

I started off with a few laps around the small track, listening to her yells of happiness. Slowing down, I turned the car, forcing it to spin in circles, and loving the faint sound of giggling in my ear.

We parked as Daisy ran over, pulling open the door and checking over every inch of her, while Bailey recounted every second.

The crew gathered around, everyone listening to Bailey talk about us driving, and somehow I felt proud.

Fox stepped closer to me. "Looks like you have a kid."

"I think so. I mean, I hope so."

"You're good with it?"

"More than good. I don't know what you guys are complaining about. It's like a built-in best friend. Where is the problem?"

Fox's smile grew. "Oh, man, remember that when you have a baby to take care of."

I waved him off, trying to ignore that feeling in my chest again.

"Kye!" Ash yelled, heading around the cars to me. "Come on! Scout and my dad are already inside waiting."

"For what?"

She rolled her eyes, already grabbing me to drag me along. "The speeches, and all that boring stuff. Come on. All of you."

FORTY-NINE

DAISY

"I'M ABOUT TO MURDER SOMEONE," Kye said two hours later.

"For what now?"

"Making me stand here instead of being somewhere alone with you. I forgot how annoying everything was when I could be doing you."

I smacked his stomach lightly, leaning into him a little more.

"We could always find a closet," I said, knowing that my cheeks were about to turn red.

He grinned. "No closet here is prepared for me fucking you. Unless it is somehow padded and soundproof. I thought being apart was torture. It's even worse when we are right next to each other and I have to keep myself under control."

I looked down, grabbing his hands and bringing them together until my name was lined up.

I knew he said that he didn't regret it, that he even liked it, but it felt strange to see.

"If it helps," I said, "as someone who doesn't have the

struggles you do, I still think everyone is dull in comparison to you."

He leaned down, pressing his lips to my forehead with a groan.

"Does this mean you are considering letting me take you home right now?"

"I said it earlier and I'll say it again. *Down, boy.*"

"Tell me down, boy again and I'm going to drop to my knees right in front of everyone and show you exactly what that means to me."

My mouth dropped open as the heat moved down my spine. I liked the suggestion, and part of me wished he would follow through with it.

Instead, he pushed my hair off my shoulder, leaning down to whisper in my ear.

"This dress is making me want to fill you with cum until it's dripping down your pretty legs all day."

My breath hitched as I turned to him, wrapping my arms around his neck.

"Kye, am I finally going to get dirty talk from you all the time now?"

"Since I'm being driven to the brink of insanity, yes, constantly."

"Well, sorry about the insanity, but I like the outcome. I'm already wet."

He groaned. "Come on, tell me down, boy. Let me clean up the mess I've made."

"Or," I said, slipping my hand in his and pulling him towards a side door. I waited until it shut behind us before continuing. "We go with the first plan and you fuck me in one of these offices."

I could barely see straight, every part of me on fire with

want. He lifted me up, starting down the hallway of offices like he already knew where we were going.

"You're filthy," he said, my eyes focused on him. I pouted my bottom lip and he grabbed it between his teeth. "Poor Daisy flower has been pent up, haven't you? Not telling anyone those slutty little thoughts you have. The way you want to get on your knees and choke on my cock. The way part of you really wanted me to drop to my knees and get you off in a room full of people. The only woman I'm ever going to touch and fuck, and you love owning me."

Heat pooled between my thighs. He only wanted me.

It's not that I questioned it a lot, but hearing it again still gave me butterflies.

"The only woman? Are you sure about that?"

"Considering I haven't been with anyone else since you, yes, I'm sure."

He pulled me into one of the offices. Not that it helped—the walls to the hallway were glass, and so were the ones overlooking the track—but it was enough for me.

His arms wrapped around me as he leaned back against the desk, before kissing me hard.

My hands were already fighting with his belt and the button of his jeans. His hands moving up my sides until they were cupping my breasts.

My heart flipped, and my hands worked faster, pulling out his cock as I dropped to my knees. My tongue flicked out, running once along his length before I took the head into my mouth.

He grinned down at me. "Do you like hearing that, Daze? Do you like that your lips are the only ones that have been wrapped around my cock?" he asked, pressing deeper into my mouth. "That since the day I've met you, no other woman has touched my cock, let alone sucked it."

I pulled back. "How? How have you not been with anyone else?"

His hands hooked under my arms and he dragged me up, turning me to face the windows overlooking the track as we walked to them. "Because it's not about the sex. It never was." He pushed me forward until my head was resting against the window as he pulled my dress up, gathering it at my hips. "It's not the sex I need, it's *you*."

In one swift motion, he was filling me. My hands pressed flat against the window as my head dropped, pleasure rolling through me.

"Look out there," he whispered, his pace already picking up, growing more frantic as the desperation grew. "You love being perfect for them. Let them all see how perfect you are like this, too. How you moan and scream and beg to be filled and fucked like an animal."

My face pressed harder against the glass as he kept moving, sinking deep into me over and over again. My body tightened, every nerve in me feeling like it was exploding as white stars clouded my vision.

I glanced back as I tried to catch my breath. I was expecting to look out past Kye into an empty hall, but a figure stood there, watching us. The lights pooled at his back, leaving only a dark outline of a man. I yelled, my hands grabbing for Kye to pull him closer.

"What the hell?" Kye asked, crushing me against him.

"There's someone in the hall," I hissed.

He shielded me as I yanked the sides of my dress, but by the time we both looked over, the figure was gone.

Kye was silent, both of us frozen, until he started laughing. His body shook against mine, but he didn't loosen his grip.

"Kye, this isn't funny! Someone was literally standing there watching us have sex. We don't even know who it was!"

"I mean, you have mentioned that you would like an audience," he said, against my ear. "It was probably someone looking for a bathroom or a way out of here. It's alright, they left already."

My breathing finally slowed, and he pulled away to fix his jeans before wrapping his arms around me again.

"I'm staying with you tonight, right? That was already established?"

He ran a hand down my jaw, smiling. "Of course you are still staying with me tonight. And hopefully, all the nights after that."

"Good, because that goes on the list of scary things, and going anywhere alone tonight sounds like I'm setting myself up to be the dumb girl in the horror movie."

He laughed, making sure my dress was straight before we headed back out.

"I want to say that's not true, but with how often I think about sneaking away to have sex with you, I'm pretty sure I would be right there with you. Come on, let's get the rest of this over with because I am already excited to get to bed with you tonight."

FIFTY

DAISY

FOR THE THIRD day in a row, I woke up next to Kye. His arm draped over me as he slept, and the look of him there almost made me cry.

There was never anyone else for me. I didn't know that there was ever a question for me if he was the one, but at twenty-one, I had given my choices away to others, letting them tell me what was right and wrong, and the war I created between us was too much for him. Too much for both of us, and it was always my fault.

His eyes cracked open. "Are you watching me sleep?"

I smiled, moving his arm higher over me so I could get closer to kiss him.

"Yes."

"I'm surprised. I thought I would be the weirdo creeping at you. Who would have thought that Daisy Wells would be obsessed with me?"

"I've always been obsessed with you."

"My younger broken heart would beg to differ."

"Actually, that's what I was thinking about. I'm still sorry you were ever told to leave."

He rolled onto his back, dragging me up against him as he looked up at the ceiling. "It's okay now, and it was back then. You weren't doing anything wrong. Not when you consider the circumstances. You were perfect, Daze. A good life and good prospects for life. I was a burnout mechanic who was getting into any trouble I could find. Fuck, the last night I saw you, I was about to kill your boyfriend. You were right to think there were red flags, even if you did love me." He pulled me in, kissing my forehead. "Don't be sorry for being smart," he said with a laugh. "And I'm still sorry I stayed away for so long. I always thought it was the right thing to do for you."

"And now?"

"I have tried extremely hard to grow up, and if you feel like I am no longer a walking red flag, then I hope you will stay with me. If there's any part of you doubting it, then I guess we just won't."

"Depends. Are you still trying to get in trouble constantly?"

He flashed a wicked grin. "Of course, just a different type of trouble now."

"Interesting. And I don't have to worry about other women in your life?"

"Yeah, about that... There's one other one."

"What?" My heart dropped. He hadn't mentioned a girl-friend, so I had assumed there wasn't one, but I should have at least asked for sure. He had apparently gone out the other night, but I figured that was really just with Carly or something.

"Yeah, I'm sorry. I love her, though. Speaking of which, I

should go get her before she tears Quinn and Ransoms' apartment to pieces."

"You are terrible," I yelled, flopping back onto the bed.

"You're the one jumping to the worst possible conclusions."

"You're the one setting me up to freak out."

He laughed. "I thought it was funny. Not that you would immediately think I had a secret wife or something. Are we hanging out for the day?"

I rolled back onto my pillow. "You know what? Just for that, I'll let you know when you get back."

He threw on a pair of shorts and headed out with a laugh.

I got up, dressed, and just made it to the kitchen when they burst back in. Bailey was climbing all over Kye as he laughed.

"Bailey, you're not a monkey, stop climbing on him."

"It's okay, Daze. I told her she could. She also said she makes good pancakes. I think she's lying."

I looked at Bailey, who smiled as she crawled up onto his shoulders. She really did move like a monkey, climbing on him and swinging around his neck with a laugh as he caught her.

"How are you fine with her using you as a playground?"

"Have to get the energy out somehow."

I shook my head. "Come on. Pancakes it is."

We cooked and sat down. As Bailey ate, Kye walked back over to me, pulling me in and kissing me.

"Can we go ride bikes?" Bailey asked, looking at Kye.

"Sure. How about we bike to town later and get ice cream?" She pumped her fist with a yes, something that Scout taught her that she refused to stop doing. Kye must have noticed, because he laughed. "I'm pretty sure there's a specific noise that goes with that, Bailey."

She did it again, letting out a whoop with it.

"I can't go. I have to work at two today."

"Damn. Are you going to tell them you're quitting?"

"Quitting? Why would I quit?"

His eyebrows furrowed. "Why wouldn't you? Don't you hate your job?"

"Yes, but I need money, so it doesn't matter if I hate it or not. That's kind of how things work in life."

"Daisy," he said, the tone suddenly serious. "I leave in two weeks for a race in Colorado, and then back here before leaving again for a few events. I have four of them in different cities. Not big ones exactly, but I can't miss them. I have events booked throughout the year. I guess I shouldn't have, but I assumed you would know that and you two would come with me?"

I almost dropped my coffee. "You're leaving again? Why didn't you say that before?"

"Like I said, I guess I assumed you knew that I still had to work. I just like to take off for long periods to be home before heading out again, and with the wedding, I was happy to hang around longer. But then I just guessed you two would come with me when I go. Bailey won't be in school again until next year. Why wouldn't you?"

"Because I have a job, a kid, a house, responsibilities?"

"A house that you don't even want to sleep in. You hate your job, and I know damn well you would rather write, and the kid you have would come, too, and most likely have a blast. There are plenty of guys who bring their families, and she would have other kids around to play with at most stops. It's hard to be bored at these things."

"Hey, it's not my fault someone broke in. I figured I would sleep there again at some point. I can't just quit my job and write because that isn't going to pay my bills. I will give you the last one because that daredevil of a child would probably love watching you race all the time."

"There would be no bills to pay if you get rid of that house, so it doesn't matter if what you do makes you money."

"There are always bills to pay. Electricity, food, traveling, hotels, clothes. I can keep going. Do you know how expensive it is to raise a child?"

"No, not really, but I'm sure I have enough to cover it all."

"No, Kye, I don't think you understand. It's thousands more a year in expenses. Whatever you are thinking it takes, times it by five. I learned the hard way."

"By five?" he said in disbelief. "It takes almost a hundred grand a year to raise her? Damn, do you feed her gold flakes for breakfast? Do you waitress with your top off to make that type of money?"

I couldn't stop my laugh, but I tried to hide it. "Okay, maybe not five times the amount, but it wouldn't surprise me if it was twenty grand a year to keep up with her."

"And what about you? Are we talking twenty grand or a hundred?" he asked with a laugh.

"A hundred. Look at this hair," I said with a grin, pointing to my hair that I have religiously cut in my own bathroom, and then to my nails, which currently had chipping nail polish I bought at the dollar store. "These nails? Easily two dollars a month."

He laughed harder. "Alright, so we have twenty and a hundred plus another thirty for basic living. Great, as of right now, we can easily live like that for a few years. Of course, we will have a few more kids, but I'll have to make more money in the meantime, so yeah, I think we're good."

"Ha. Ha. Not so fun when you add it up, right?"

"No, it's still pretty fun. I don't mind giving up all my money to have you two in my life. Although, let's factor out living expenses, I would love to see you spend eight grand a month. It's surprisingly harder to spend money like that when you have lived on pennies at any point in life. I think you'll find yourself scrambling to spend it."

"Kye, I was kidding. I live off more like eight dollars a month after bills and Bailey. Getting a fancy coffee is like a spa day."

"I feel like you aren't catching on that I am *not* kidding. Between the success at the garage, my career, and investing, I have plenty, Daze. Hundreds of thousands that you can spend how you want. And I'm set to make more money this year if I win some races and show up for these events. All my driving started paying really well after people saw that I was sponsored by Holt Racing. It's like that was a beam of light that I was worth a damn. All I've done for the last few years is drive professionally in some capacity, and people pay more and more for that each year. And there's not much to spend money on when you own your apartment, and half of everything else is paid for. I don't need much. I've gotten some sponsors for clothes, travel, cars, even ridiculous stuff like water. People will throw free stuff at rich people like they are poor. It's crazy. I could barely get help when I was a literal child with nothing, but now I get money and stuff handed to me without question."

"I'm sorry, hundreds of thousands?" I couldn't even comprehend it. Even before Bailey, when I started my career,

I was hoping for maybe sixty thousand a year. To make that much since we left each other couldn't be real.

"Yes, last I checked. Although Holt is very good at managing money, so it could be millions now. I don't know."

"How is that possible?"

He shrugged. "Like I said, I just kept recklessly driving and people liked that I would do ridiculous stunts. My friends make their own money, so I don't have to help them, and I have no other family. So the money has just been for me. I haven't wanted to move away from everyone and don't need much more than this place anyway, so I stay here. I don't know, the money just sat there. Then Holt helped me invest it into things and it kept growing without me doing anything. I don't need it all. I'd rather have you two around than a pile of money, so I don't know. Just spend it how and when you want."

"Kye, I can't just quit my job and spend your money. You worked hard for that. It isn't mine. We aren't even married. And what if we broke up? Then I would have no money, no house, and no job? Do you know how irresponsible that is?"

He put his chin in his hand with a smile. "Damn, I love how smart you are, even when it's working against me. If you're worried about breaking up, then we can put money in your personal account that I have no access to. Plenty to give you a year of living without me. I don't want you to feel like you have to stay with me just for money." His face scrunched at the words. "And as for not being married, we could get that done today if you would rather do that than go for ice cream."

"Can you please be serious?"

"Can you please take me seriously? I would marry you today if you wanted. At any moment, since the moment I knew I loved you, if you asked if I would marry you, I would have immediately said yes. You could have shown up without another word at any point in the past six years and asked if I would, and we would have already been on the way to the courthouse. Even if you said hey, can we have another 'fake' relationship and get married because I now have a child and need help? I would have said yes. There was never a point in my life after I met you that loving you was called into question for me. I knew I was just too fucked up to deserve to be in your life. If you would rather wait and have a wedding, we could do that, too." He sat back, the weight of his words making him take a deep breath. "For now, will you at least travel with me? I am booked a while out but can start turning things down before she starts school full-time next year. Then we'll be home more. I'll still have to leave sometimes to afford this apparent hundred thousand dollar a month lifestyle you live," he said with a smirk, "but I could be home a lot more, and you two could still come for weekend events, which a lot of them are, anyway. I know it would suck when I have to go for a week or two, but I think we could manage."

"You are serious?"

"Yes, one hundred percent serious. What part of this is the problem? Not working a job you hate, spending more time with Bailey, being with me?" It was like something clicked for him. "Wait, is that it? Are you doubting being with me?"

"No. No," I said more firmly. "That's not the problem. The problem is with me. That's a lot of change to take in all at once, and what if it's not the right thing for Bailey? What if she struggles without the structure we have now?"

"That child would thrive with no structure," he said, laughing. "If she could live in the woods as a wild animal, she would be thrilled. Seriously, though, if you see her struggling at all, you can come back and get into your routine. You can live here and I will just fly back every second I can. Plus, you love the crew. You could have the entire support team right at home. But I really don't think Bailey would struggle. There's plenty to do, and you two could see all the new places when you want. And best of all, I get you with me every night."

"And you just want a girlfriend and child all of a sudden? After years of bachelorhood, you're ready to settle down and be a family man?"

"With you? Yes. No question that I am. I haven't wanted to be alone, but when there is only one person you want to be with, it really makes your options limited."

"Kye, I was forced into this life before I was ready, and I know how hard it is. I couldn't ask that of you."

"I'm literally begging you for it right now. You aren't forcing anything on me, or asking it of me. I'm asking it of you. Anything, all of it." He got up, coming around and lifting me onto the counter. "Give me all of it, Daze. Don't make me have to live another six years without you, let alone six days. Don't make me have to live another day without you."

I chewed at my lip. There really was no one else I would want, and spending every day with Kye, traveling with him, felt like a dream come true. I could pursue my own dreams, Bailey could see more things and make friends. It was hard to think of the downsides, but I had to.

"Yes to the everyday with you, but you're going to have to give me a little bit to decide on dropping everything to travel around and spend all your money."

He grinned, kissing me once. "I really thought that would be the easy part, but okay. Fair enough, I did just drop a lot on you. Does this mean no to ice cream and bikes?"

"For me? Yes. You two can go, though."

He groaned, but nodded. "Happy to, although I was pretty

excited to have you pressed up against me on my bike all day."

"As tempting as that sounds, I can't leave Amber alone at the restaurant all night. Maybe you would be willing to do it twice in one week?"

"Whatever you want, Daze. Come on, we can at least give you a ride to work."

He leaned down to kiss me, squeezing my hand once before he disappeared around the corner.

It was hard to say no to all of it. Impossible even.

I had no reason to, and I realized fast that no part of me wanted to.

FIFTY-ONE

DAISY

THE NEXT DAY AFTER WORK, I got to the apartment to find the place empty.

Kye was supposed to be watching Bailey, and after my tires were slashed and the house broken into, my panic bubbled up immediately. I pulled out my phone, already hitting the button to FaceTime Kye.

He picked up in two rings, his smiling face filling my screen.

"Hey," he said, turning the phone down to Bailey quick and back onto him.

"Where are you?"

"Walking towards the apartments."

"And where have you been?" I asked, already heading back downstairs to the sidewalk.

"The tattoo shop."

My mouth fell open. "Excuse me?"

"We are right outside," he said. "I'll be inside in one minute."

He laughed, clicking the call off, and I wasted no time storming outside to meet them out front.

"You took her to a tattoo shop?" I was almost yelling, but I couldn't believe what he was telling me and I couldn't believe how cute the two of them looked. He apparently took her shopping too, because she had on new clothes. Her little shoes matched his and so did the hat, both of theirs backwards to match. Even her blonde hair matched his and I realized then that she looked like his. If we were walking down a street, I wouldn't think twice about assuming that was his kid. Even the relaxed way they were together made them look like family.

"Relax, Daze. It's one of the cleanest environments next to a hospital and the guys and girls there are great. She knew she had to behave and sat with me like a champ. Everyone loved her gymnastics routine too," he said with a smirk.

"I held his hand for the needles," Bailey said proudly.

"Yes, she did through the entire thing. And showed everyone your tumbling routine too, so that was a hit with them." He smiled down at her and back at me.

"You can't bring a child to a tattoo shop, Kye!"

"It's not like she got a tattoo and anyway, I needed the artist there for approval."

"The artist? What are you talking about?" Every part of me was about to explode with the cuteness that was Kye with a child and finding a reason to be upset was losing its appeal. "I swear if you let her tattoo you, Kye, you will both be in so much trouble."

He leaned down, whispering something to her, and she giggled before running to his other side and trying to pull up his shirt. Finally he helped and I could clearly see what the tattoo was, even covered in wrap.

It was the animal she drew on him with marker before. It was close to what she had drawn, a little perfecting from the tattoo artist, but overall, it was Bailey's drawing.

My heart raced and stomach dropped.

"You got that tattooed on you?" My voice squeaked, but nothing was processing. I struggled to find any coherent words.

"First my name on your hands and now this? Kye, this is too much. This feels like more than tattoos, this feels like..." My words died because it felt nearly unbelievable.

This made him really feel like ours.

He stepped closer, close enough that I could smell the musk of his body wash. The scent went to my head, and I leaned into him more.

This couldn't be real life. I couldn't be this lucky to find this type of love and have it come back to me.

The man I had loved from the day I met him, loved me back, and even loved my child.

And now he was two feet away, tattooed with my name on him and her drawing, asking me a question that I realized I was ignoring.

"What did you say?"

"I said," he leaned down, kissing my neck once, "what does it feel like?"

I hesitated. I already knew he wanted all of it. He made it clear that he wanted us together, but some part of me still feared the worst.

"Daisy, tell me."

Finally, I met his eye.

"It feels like you're ours. That we're yours. That maybe it's just a tattoo, but I've never been able to get one because that is permanent and then you go and tattoo us on your skin."

He just smiled. "That I can understand. I know I can go get a tattoo on a whim, but they do mean a lot to me. Looking down to see your name was the only thing that made me not feel insane after being gone for years. I would ask myself over and over how I could think of you so often. At least with this, I had an excuse to why I thought of you. I think I have been yours since the moment you pulled me in, told me I was now your boyfriend, and kissed me years ago. Tattoo or not. As for Bailey's tattoo, she is one of my favorite people and I liked her art. I can only hope to be hers, too." His hand trailed down my jaw and my head leaned back, giving him access to whatever he wanted. "Whether you want me or not, I could never be anyone else's."

I could barely believe his words. Dreams and nightmares of him saying these things to me made it hard to believe this was real. I grabbed onto his arms, trying to not collapse.

"Of course I want you. I only want you."

He kissed me hard, smiling as Ransom and Quinn's car pulled up.

Quinn rolled down the window. "Come on, you three. Head up to our place. We brought dinner."

I smiled, taking Kye's hand as he picked Bailey up.

I wasn't sure how life could get better than this.

THE NEXT DAY, I SAT BACK ON THE SMALL CHAIR THAT KYE had brought out into their garage for me. We had planned to go out tonight, but he insisted on taking his older car and it broke down before we even got out of the parking lot.

"You know, you have two other perfectly good cars to choose from."

"Yes, but this one is special."

"Special, but broken," I joked.

He turned back with a frown. "I can get it running with no problem."

"Tonight?"

He laughed, grabbing another wrench and leaning back over the engine. "Okay, that might be a problem."

"Well, then, I guess I will get comfortable." I hopped up on the back of the car next to him, already pulling out a book.

"You're staying?"

"Of course. We planned to hang out, and Bailey's with Fox and Ash. What else would I do now?"

He laughed, grabbing my hips and pulling me down from the car to the edge. "I have an idea of what you could do."

"Besides reading? What did you have in mind?"

He worked fast as he unbuttoned my shorts and pulled them down. His hands moved down my inner thighs, parting them so he could lean down between them. I closed my eyes, enjoying the lingering heat where his lips pressed against my thighs.

His tongue ran along me, making my back arch immediately. I laid back on the car, the cool metal making me jump at first, but his mouth came back down over me. He groaned against me, his arms wrapping around my thighs as his tongue pressed hard against my clit. My chest heaved as I struggled to get a full breath. Every nerve grew sensitive, and by the time he pushed two fingers into me, I was falling apart.

My body tensed. His fingers pushed into me again as his mouth clamped down on my clit. I broke, white stars bursting in my eyes as my body tightened around him. He slid me higher on the car, jumping up to crawl over me.

"Can you take more now?" he asked, laughing as he undid

his belt. "I don't even know why I asked. You always want more."

Before he could even get his jeans unbuttoned, my phone went off, the high pitched beep pulling me out of the moment.

"What is that?"

"An alarm, I think. Maybe it will stop."

We waited, but the beeping didn't stop, and I finally gave in, grabbing it to silence it.

"Shit," I said, seeing the notifications popping up. "It is the diner's alarm."

"What about it?"

"Carly gave me the login to take care of the alarm stuff until after the baby comes, but Mia, the other waitress, can never seem to set it right, so it goes off constantly lately."

"Do you need to go down there?"

I grabbed my phone, calling Mia twice before I realized she wasn't going to pick up. "Yeah, it should only take me a few minutes to reset the alarm. The place should already be shut down."

He was grabbing another set of keys and already heading to the door.

"Um." I stopped, pointing at the car he had been working on. "Based on the dark liquid pouring out of that car, I think you need to stay here."

"Shit," he said, heading over to grab something to catch it in. "Are you sure you're okay to go? I can get this stopped and come."

"No, it's alright. I'll be right back," I said.

"Alright. Here, take my car, the running one, and call me if you need anything." He leaned down, kissing me hard. "And hurry up, I wasn't even close to done with you."

I headed out, turning back to watch for one second as he

leaned back over the engine. His muscles strained as he fought with a bolt.

I was going to hurry. I was going to drive as fast as I ever had, if it meant getting back to that view sooner.

———

THE DINER WAS DARK WHEN I PULLED IN, LETTING ME KNOW that I was right. Mia had thought she was setting the alarm, but didn't. Hopefully, she at least cleaned the place up. I hadn't wanted to talk to Carly about her since Carly was a little busy with other things, but I think it was getting to the point I would have to.

I headed up, trying the front door, happy that it was locked at least. I tried the side door next, but it was locked, too. The alarm went off again, telling me it still wasn't locked up right.

A flash of white caught my eye, and I peered in the window more. At first, I couldn't understand. The blonde hair, the skirt and bare legs, the white of her shirt.

A girl was laid out on the floor, unmoving, with her face down. I couldn't see who it was and the blonde hair wasn't helping. Mia and Amber were both brunettes. I was already digging through my purse, trying to find my keys and my phone.

My hands shook as I pulled them both out, shoving the key into the lock and unlocking my phone.

The call connected just as I got inside.

"I need help," I said, trying to breathe as I turned the girl over.

It was Mia.

The rush of confusion made me stutter through the next few questions. Who was I, where was I, what was happening.

"I think she's dead," I said, the words echoing as I looked at Mia's face. I knew she was, but I could bring myself to confirm it.

"Okay, Daisy. They are coming. Don't worry." The woman kept talking, giving me directions until she finally told me to stand outside and wait.

I stumbled until I reached the cold brick wall outside, leaning against it as cars pulled up. My dad came up first, trying to pull me up, but I didn't move. He yelled out questions, and I tried to answer them, but I couldn't focus.

"Mark," he yelled. "Help her."

Mark crouched down in front of me, but I shook my head. "No, don't touch me. Go. She needs help, not me."

He stared for a few more seconds before getting up.

I didn't want my dad or Mark trying to help me. I didn't want anyone but Kye.

FIFTY-TWO
KYE

A HALF HOUR went by before I really started to worry. I'd
called her five times already, and thirty minutes to go reset an
alarm felt like a good enough amount of time that I wasn't
being an overbearing boyfriend.

I was already heading out to the dirtbike I had brought
down earlier when Carly texted.

CARLY
Get down to the diner. Now.

My heart stopped, and as bad as I wanted to take off, I
texted her back

KYE
Daisy?

CARLY
I don't know. We are heading there now.
Just meet us there asap.

I hit the gas, the bike screaming as I cut through a field
and made it back onto the road.

My heart hammered in my chest at the possibilities. There were only so many things Carly would text me like that about, and it didn't matter what happened exactly, it meant Daisy was involved.

I should have gone with her. I should have taken care of it, and not let her go out at night to check a fucking alarm alone. What was I thinking?

Was I really going to get Daisy back and then immediately let her walk into a situation that could get her hurt?

I hit another gear, pushing the bike as fast as it would go down the road that led to the diner.

The diner came into view, and I was almost expecting flames pouring out of it, but there were none. Nothing except red lights flashing on the brick building as the fire trucks, ambulance, and cop cars surrounded it.

My eyes scanned the entire place before I finally saw her blonde hair slumped against the wall, and for a moment, I wondered if she wasn't going to move. If she really was hurt, or worse.

My stomach churned as I got closer, until her head finally snapped up to look at me. I made it halfway into the parking lot, but she was already up and heading towards me. The bike fell as I got off and wrapped her in my arms, pulling her as tight as I could against me.

"What happened? Are you okay?" I pushed her back, looking over any part of her that I could see. "Are you hurt?"

She shook her head, stepping back against me. "No, not me. I'm okay."

I ran my hand down her arms, looking down at her tear-stained cheeks.

"It's Mia, Kye. She's dead."

My hands froze on her as I looked back at the diner. "How?"

"They don't know. I came and the doors were locked, but she was in there...dead."

"Come on," I said, already heading towards her dad's car. "We need to figure out what happens now."

My arm stayed tight around her, and her dad didn't fail to notice it. Daisy noticed it too, leaning against me harder and cursing.

"Did this really all have to happen right now?"

"I think your dad hating me is going to be the least of our concerns tonight."

"I doubt it," she said. "He's going to make it a concern."

"What the fuck are you doing here now?" her dad said, nearly yelling as we got closer.

Daisy froze at my side. "He came for me. To make sure I was okay, and I need him here."

"Why?"

"Because I just found my coworker dead and I would like someone to be here for me. Is that really an issue to you?"

He shook with anger, but looked back at the diner. "I have bigger things to deal with right now, but I can guarantee you both, we will be dealing with this."

"There's nothing between her and I that *you* need to deal with," I said, realizing Daisy wasn't going to say anything. I knew she hated the disapproval, and probably hated it even more when it was said right to her face, but part of me wished she wasn't so damn ashamed of me that she couldn't just tell him to shut up. "What happened?" I asked, trying to put all of our thoughts back on what was going on around us.

"Mia was killed. I won't be telling either of you more than that, but it doesn't seem like an accident of any sort. We...We have a few things that we need to piece together, and we're going to need you to come to the station tonight, Daisy. *Alone.*"

I smirked. "She doesn't have to go alone. You might need to talk to her alone, but she doesn't have to go sit there and wait alone." I couldn't stop it, couldn't help the words coming out of my mouth, already knowing he was going to be pissed about it. "I'm pretty sure her boyfriend is allowed to take her there and wait until she is done."

His nostrils flared. "Actually, she is a witness, and we need to make sure no one is feeding her what she *should* be saying. Mark will take you. You can follow on your…bicycle, if you want."

"I think I'll take my car, but thanks."

Her hand squeezed mine tighter. "But I don't want to go with Mark. I would like Kye to take me."

"Well, that isn't an option. We don't know who was involved in this yet," he said, looking at me. "And I can't risk anyone getting your story confused."

I leaned down to her, my lips at her ear. "It's okay. I'll follow behind you and be there at the same time."

"I don't want to go alone with Mark. *Please*, I can't," she whispered to me.

The fear and panic were clear, and I knew there was nothing that was going to stop me from being at her side.

"Alright, then, Daze. Let's get you to the station."

I opened the door, letting her into the back so she could be as far away from Mark as she wanted, and I pulled open the passenger door, sliding into the seat next to Mark.

"What the fuck do you think you are doing?"

"Getting a ride to the station."

"If you don't get out of this car right now, I'm going to—"

"What? Arrest me? That's fine. Then you'll have to put me back there with her."

His hands tightened on the steering wheel, nearly turning white, and I wondered what he really wanted to say to her alone in the car. If he thought talking shit about me for an hour or two would change her mind.

Daisy said he seemed upset about the breakup, but when he looked back in the rearview mirror at her, I didn't think she understood how upset he might be.

I understood it at the very least. Losing Daisy wasn't easy, and I didn't blame him for trying to get her back, but I was going to guarantee he didn't have a chance this time.

FIFTY-THREE

DAISY

KYE WATCHED me the entire ride. If he wasn't looking back at me, I could see him watching from the side mirror. With the way Mark was looking at me from the other side of the car, I was glad I asked Kye to come. I didn't know that I would have heard the end of whatever lecture Mark had to give me today. This was the first time that Mark and my dad had seen Kye and I together, and while they already suspected, I knew seeing it in person was going to cause issues.

And I was right, based on how my dad already reacted and how Mark wanted to react.

We rode to the station in silence, and I tried to think of anything I knew about Mia. I barely knew her. She didn't share much about herself, more about other people. I knew she lived with a roommate, and I thought she had a boyfriend, but again, she didn't say much about it.

Kye opened my door, pulling me against him as soon as I stood. As much as Kye liked pissing off Mark and my dad, I knew he wasn't doing it to make a problem, but to support me.

"Thank you for coming," I whispered.

Mark walked in ahead of us, but Kye pulled me back, turning me into his arms to cup my face and kiss me hard.

"Thank you for being okay, because I wasn't sure what I would do if you weren't," he whispered, kissing me again.

Before I could say anything, Mark was already storming back out and urging us inside.

He brought us to the waiting area, and Kye sat with an arm around the back of my chair.

I went to sit, but Amber burst through the door, already running to grab me.

"Oh my god, I'm so glad you're okay!" she yelled.

I hugged her back. "You, too. I'm glad you weren't there tonight."

"I almost was. Almost. Have they told you anything yet?"

"No. Nothing yet. Hopefully, soon. I can text you when I learn anything."

"Yeah," she said, nodding, but chewing her lip. "Yeah. I guess I will give my information and…go home."

Kye stood up, wrapping an arm around me. "No. Go home and get the boys. Scout and Chase are on their honeymoon and will be fine if you set up there for a day or two."

"No. I'm not stealing someone's apartment just because I'm a little freaked out."

He was already texting Scout to double check, but I knew her well enough that I knew the answer would be yes. Any of them would say yes. Even if I asked Kye for Amber to stay with us at his place, he would say yes.

I wrapped both arms around him now, holding him closer, just to remember this amazing man was real, and he was mine.

"When did Mia dye her hair?" I asked Amber. "I just saw her two days ago and it was still black."

"Yesterday. I thought it was you yesterday when I walked into work."

"Alright, Scout and Chase are fine with it. Go home, get your stuff and the boys, and come over for a bit. At least until we know what is going on."

Her shoulders sagged and she smiled. "Thanks. I appreciate it. I'll see you guys in a little bit, then?"

I nodded, hugging her once before she left.

"Daisy," Mark said, waving me over. "I need you in here alone."

Kye's hand tightened on mine. "If you have any problems," he whispered, "just scream, and I swear I will kick down that door for you."

I smiled, kissing him once before heading over to Mark's door. Even knowing Kye was on the other side of the door kept me calmer.

And it was Mark. At the very least, he cared about his job and would take this seriously.

He waved to the seat across from his desk before he pulled off his gun and a handful of keys from his pocket. He looked at me, flustered, as he threw the keys into a drawer along with the gun. The keychain flashed in the light, and it made me wonder if he was already seeing someone to have a keychain like that.

"How have you been?" he asked.

"I've been better. You?"

"I've been better," he said.

"Seeing anyone?"

His hand tightened on the pen he had poised to write, and his eyes narrowed. "After we broke up *two* weeks ago? No.

Unlike some other people, I don't go fucking around immediately."

My eyebrows jumped, and I sat back a little further in the
chair. "It's not like I went out and found the first guy off the
street to sleep with him. I'm sorry, but I've always loved Kye.
There's nothing wrong with you, Mark. I just can't help who I
love."

"Right." His jaw tightened, and he took a deep breath
before continuing. "Look, this isn't about us. It's about what
happened tonight. I need us to focus on that."

I nodded, feeling a pit of guilt in my stomach. I knew
what I did wasn't the greatest, but I couldn't help it. "Okay.
And I am sorry."

He sighed, running a hand through his hair. "I need you to
tell me everything you remember about tonight. Any detail,
no matter how small, could be important."

I recounted the night's events as clearly as I could, from
the moment I arrived at the diner to what I did after. Mark
scribbled notes furiously, his face a mask of concentration.

When I finished, he leaned back in his chair, tapping his
pen against his notebook. "Did you notice anything unusual
about Mia before tonight? Any strange behavior or
comments?

I shook my head. "No, not really. She seemed fine the last
time I saw her. She did dye her hair recently, which is drastic,
but that's about it."

"And you're sure you don't know anything about her
personal life? No ex-boyfriends, enemies, anything?

"I told you, she didn't talk much about herself. I know she
had a roommate and maybe a boyfriend, but she was pretty
private."

"She didn't tell you anything about her boyfriend? Nothing at all?"

"Not really. Just that she would see him once or twice a week, but didn't say much otherwise. Do you guys know anything?"

"Nothing yet. Where was Kye that day?'

My eyebrows furrowed as I looked at him. "With me? Why?"

"All day?"

"I mean, I was at the apartment for a while with Bailey while he was at the garage, and then I met up with him there."

"And was anyone else with him at the garage?"

"I'm sure one of the crew was there at some point. I don't know who exactly, though."

"So one of his closest friends will be the only one to give him an alibi for the hours when Mia could have been killed?"

"One of them, or me."

He was already standing up with a shake of his head. "All the people who would gladly lie for him if needed."

"What does Kye have anything to do with this? He barely knew Mia."

"We have reasons to think Kye could be involved, Daisy."

"How?"

"Because the last person Mia called was Kye, twenty minutes before she was killed."

FIFTY-FOUR

DAISY

TWO DAYS WENT by without a word from my dad or Mark about Mia.

Or trying to arrest Kye.

I tried to keep busy, but Carly had shut down the diner, not knowing when it would reopen. I think she was even thinking about moving it completely now.

I had spent every day with Kye. Either at the apartments or at the garage. But until they found out who killed Mia, he didn't want me out of his sight, and I wasn't inclined to fight him on it. There wasn't a single part of me that thought Kye did it. As ruthless as he could be, he wasn't going to kill some random girl for no reason.

I still hadn't asked him why Mia had called, though. I couldn't bring myself to wonder why he would have.

Kye had gone out today, doing a few errands for us so I could stay home with Bailey. Part of me knew I would be fine if I went with him, the other part was still scared to go out of the apartment. Someone had been after me. The tires, the break-in, and the worry that Mia's hair was blonde kept bothering Kye, which quickly bothered me.

He had said more than once that he worried they thought it was me, which meant me being under the equivalent of house arrest was fine with him.

I also couldn't figure out what else they would have on Kye that would really make them think he did it.

My foot tapped as I looked at my phone again. Kye hadn't said anything, which hopefully was a good thing. I couldn't wait any longer, though. I needed answers now, and I was sick of waiting. I couldn't sit here in silence, waiting to see if I would be attacked next or if Kye would be arrested.

I grabbed my keys and Bailey, heading down to Fox and Ash's apartment.

"Hey, I have to run out for a few minutes. Would you mind watching Bailey for a bit?"

Ash smiled. "No problem. You okay to go alone, though? Jax is here if you want a driver."

"You know what? That would actually be great, if he doesn't mind."

Jax walked out from the kitchen behind her. "Not at all. Carly's taking a nap, and I have nowhere to be. Where are we going?"

"The sheriff's station."

"Okay. Maybe I mind a little." He smiled, still grabbing his phone and keys. "Kidding, but can I wait in the car?"

WE PULLED UP TO THE STATION, AND I HOPPED OUT.

"Call me immediately and I will come in."

"Hopefully, no one but the receptionist is here. Can you

call me if any of the sheriff's cars pull up? Maybe even stall them?"

Jax grinned. "That, I can absolutely do."

I headed inside, waving to the receptionist, who was on the phone.

"My dad," I whispered, walking past her towards his office. It wasn't like me coming here was out of the ordinary, exactly. I came around even less now that I wasn't dating Mark, but no one seemed to care when I would come by before. I doubted the older receptionist would care now.

I slipped into my dad's office, moving fast to flip through all the folders on his desk until I found the one for Mia.

There were pages and pages of notes, each one more scribbled than the last, and I wasn't getting much out of it.

Another folder marked with my name caught my attention and I pulled it out of the stack. It was from when my tires were slashed and the house was broken into. I flipped through it quickly, not finding much. I almost shut it, but a photo of a knife caught my eye.

I recognized the wooden handle, the small engraved skull near its base.

It was Mark's knife.

Did that mean Mark slashed my tires?

And if he slashed my tires, was he also the one that broke into my house? I flipped through the papers again, not finding any evidence that it could have been Mark, but I had wondered why someone broke in and didn't actually take anything. I had been under the impression that I caught them mid break-in, but now I wondered if it was Mark. What had he been looking for?

I went back to Mia's folder, my heart racing and palms starting to sweat. I looked for any notes about her hair being blonde, but didn't find anything. Mark didn't take any notes of me saying that or my dad commenting. I looked out the window, my thoughts moving too fast now.

Was Mark even capable of murder?

He had never raised his voice or gave me any indication he would be violent, and what could Mia have done to push him to that?

I read more, making out a comment that my dad had made. "How did the killer lock up?" It was scrawled off to the side, and the realization hit me hard.

The keys Mark had with him that night weren't his. I had wondered why he would have a sparkly keychain, but he didn't. They were Mia's.

The thundering of my heartbeat filled my ears, making it too hard to listen if anyone was coming, but there was one more thing I needed to check.

My hands shook as I pulled out my phone, finding Kye's contact and hitting it open before flipping to the phone log my dad had printed. Lucky for me, he hated computers, so there were hard copies of everything now.

My hand trailed down the page until I got to the one he circled. The last call Mia made, which was noted as Kye's number. I looked between my phone and the page. It wasn't Kye's number. I hit Mark's name next—it wasn't his either.

That didn't explain why they thought it belonged to Kye, though.

JAX

A sheriff's here. Stalled as long as I could.
Get out of there.

DAISY

Coming.

I took a few photos of the pages first, making sure to get as much of the important things as I could before slamming the files shut and running out.

I passed one of the sheriffs as I walked out the front.

"Have you seen my dad?"

"Last I knew, he was going to arrest someone for the murder. Can't tell you much more than that."

My stomach dropped, and I picked up my pace. I ripped open the door to Jax's car, already yelling before I was inside.

"Go! We need to find Kye. I'm pretty sure Mark killed Mia and now he's going to pin it on Kye."

FIFTY-FIVE

DAISY

I HAD CALLED Kye five times as Jax headed towards the garage, but he never picked up.

"I'm going to kill him. Why is he choosing now not to answer my calls?"

"Maybe he's a little tied up."

"Is that supposed to be a joke about getting arrested? Are you thinking this is funny?"

"No," he said fast. "No, I just make jokes when I'm stressed. I can't help it," he said, nearly laughing. "I swear I'm not happy about this."

"You're laughing!"

"Not on purpose," he yelled back.

I sat back, calling Kye again. "Fine, joke all you want, but drive faster. I don't know what Mark's plan is. If he wants to pin all of this on Kye, he could do anything to him." Panic welled until my chest hurt. "Can you please go faster, Jax? What if he tries to arrest Kye? Or worse, kill him?"

"Why would he kill Kye?"

"Why would Mark, the guy that just killed a girl, kill Kye so that it's easier to blame it all on Kye so he can still go run for sheriff?"

He shifted again, the car picking up more speed. "Okay, point proven."

We turned onto the road of the garage, the red and blue lights already visible.

Jax pulled the car to a stop at the road, and I was already taking off across the parking lot.

Three of the sheriff's cars were there, and I could see Kye's car barricaded in against the garage.

The rest of the crew was standing near an open garage door, the shock so clear on their faces.

"When did they get here?" I asked, running up next to them.

"A few minutes ago. They are arresting Kye for killing her," Quinn said, the tears mumbling her words.

"What?"

Then I saw it. Mark walked over to Kye, who was calm and unmoving, until Mark grabbed him, ripping him backwards and pulling out handcuffs. Kye jumped back. The cuffs had to be his worst nightmare.

"No. I will go, but you are not handcuffing me."

"You killed a girl. Like hell am I *not* handcuffing you. Now hold still or you will be on the ground."

Kye's eyes widened and nostrils flared. I knew it was taking everything in him not to fight back, and I didn't know if he could handle being handcuffed, especially by Mark.

I pushed past the crew to my dad. Every part of me was a screaming mess of emotions, but one broke through.

I had to protect Kye. I sat around doing nothing the last

time this happened, and then Kye disappeared. I couldn't let it happen again.

"Stop. Stop this right now. You know he didn't do it."

I couldn't stand to see Kye like this. His eyes squeezed shut, and I knew it was because of how Mark was grabbing him, handcuffing him, leaving him defenseless to whatever Mark wanted.

"Mark has found evidence that he did it," my dad said. "I'm sorry, Daisy."

"Mark found it? The same Mark who has been stalking me? The one who slashed my tires, broke into my house, and I'm pretty sure killed Mia? That's the one who happened to find evidence against the guy I left him for?"

"What are you talking about, Daisy?"

"I'm talking about the knife that slashed my tires belonging to Mark, and why someone would break into my house to steal nothing, and that the phone call to Mia before she was killed was not Kye."

"What phone call?" Kye asked. "I didn't even know Mia."

"They have a phone call twenty minutes before she was killed and they say the number belongs to you, but I checked. It doesn't."

His eyebrows jumped up and mouth fell open. "Did you think it did?"

"No, of course not, but I kind of had to check to help you not get arrested."

He smiled, taking one small step away from Mark.

"What do you mean it isn't Kye's number? Mark ran it and showed me the printout. It's attached to Kye's name. Did you break into my office?"

"I walked in. I didn't break in. And it isn't his," I said.

"He probably just has a second phone you don't know about," Mark said.

"Then call it," Kye said. "Call the number. The phone would either be on me or in my car."

"Maybe you hid it," Mark said.

"I didn't know you two were coming. Why would I hide it?"

"Is this all a setup?" Mark asked. "Are you playing some stupid game so that your new boyfriend doesn't get arrested?"

He reached for Kye, slamming him down onto the car, even though he had already been handcuffed.

I headed towards my dad, his eyes following me as I walked to his side.

"No," I said, grabbing his gun out of his belt before he even knew. "Let him go. Kye isn't getting arrested because you're too damn lazy to do your job. I don't care if you don't like Kye. He didn't do it, and there is plenty of proof to show that."

"Daisy, stop! Stop!" my dad yelled.

"Daze, please, you're going to get hurt," Kye said.

I held up the gun, comfortable enough to use it after years of learning with my dad.

"Uncuff him," I said, keeping the gun trained on Mark.

My dad was yelling behind me, but I ignored him.

"Daisy, I am not uncuffing him. Do you know what he did?"

"I know what *you* did, and you will not blame him for it. Take them off. *Now.*"

Mark pushed harder down on Kye, but he didn't flinch, his eyes locked on mine. "You don't know what you're talking about, Daisy. You're trying to protect a murderer."

"I know it was your knife, Mark, and I know you killed

Mia. I saw her keys," I shouted, feeling the burn of tears in my eyes. "I'm not going to let you do this. Kye didn't do anything wrong."

"Shut up, Daisy. This is not your business."

"What keys?" my dad asked.

"Mia's keys. I thought it was strange that Mark suddenly had a sparkly keychain, and then I saw your note in the files. You didn't find out how the killer locked the door. Mark took her keys with him, and I saw them the night it happened, when we went to the station."

Mark's face twisted with rage, veins pulsing at his temples. "I found the keys in Kye's car today. I didn't have them that night."

"Yes, you did."I remembered the call and pulled out my phone. I had written the number down, and I entered it. "How about I solve this and call that number right now?"

"She is lying for him," Mark said.

I hit the call to connect, and as soon as I saw the panic in Mark's eyes, I knew my answer.

He did it.

Everyone went silent, the faint ringing of a phone filling the air.

My dad was already following it, heading straight for Mark's car.

Kye smirked. "Forgot to plant the evidence first, Mark?"

Mark picked up his head, slamming it back down onto the car. The crew started yelling, but I stepped closer, the gun still raised at him. Kye groaned, but his eyes were still open, and I hoped that meant he was okay.

My skin crawled for Kye. Every time he told me how he had been hit and beat was burned into my mind, and the pain of being touched now.

My dad held up the phone, the shock on his face almost making me feel bad for him.

"I didn't mean to kill her," Mark yelled out. "I thought it was Daisy. When I came up behind her, she freaked out. I was just going to try and talk to you more about this. She was fighting and screaming so loud that I threw her down to stop her. She hit her head."

Everyone was silent, waiting to see if he would say more.

"I don't get it, Daisy. We had it planned. Everything was working out. We were together, I was winning my campaign, your dad likes me. Why? *Why* would you leave all that for someone like him?"

"Because I love him," I said. My voice sounded far away, even to my own ears. Was he really saying that he accidentally killed Mia because he thought she was me?

"But why?" he screamed now. "What is he going to give you that I couldn't? Why would you want to give up everything we had for a guy who can't even stick around? Why do you think you can run around spreading your legs and come back to me when he leaves you again?"

He raised his gun, pointing it at me, and everything froze, my world crashing down with the realization that he could kill me right now.

My dad screamed in the background, but I couldn't make out what he said, everything sounding like I was underwater.

Bailey, Kye, the crew. It could all be gone in a second now.

Mark yelled, and I watched as Kye bent down, slipping his legs under the cuffs until they were in front of him.

Kye looked at me once before he reached up, slipping his handcuffs over Mark's head until they were in front of his neck.

Kye pulled back fast until the metal of the cuffs dug into Mark's neck. His gun waved around, and everyone ran, but I could only watch as Kye kept choking him. I raised the gun, ready to shoot, but there was no way to when Kye was so close.

Mark fought, swinging the gun back, attempting to hit Kye, but he ducked out of the way. Mark spun, dropping and getting out of Kye's hold.

Kye ran to me, and Mark turned, running towards the road.

"Mark," my dad yelled. "Stop right now."

There was no point, though. I would not let him get away. He tried to take it all away from me, and I knew how this worked. I knew how Dean got to walk away, with not a single consequence of what he did to me that night or the two thousand days that came after that without Kye.

Now Mark would, too.

I raised the gun again, pulling the trigger this time. Mark yelled as it hit his leg, making him drop to the ground in seconds.

"Daisy," Kye breathed behind me. "You shot him."

"I did. He will live."

"*Daisy*," he said again. I turned as his handcuffed hands came down over my head. "You just *shot* him."

"He deserved it!"

"He did. He for sure did. Look at you, coming to rescue me."

"Well, I wasn't going to let history repeat itself. I didn't want to stand around watching you get arrested. I didn't want you to feel like you had to run off again."

"I'm not going anywhere ever again. You're stuck with me in this town, chasing after you every damn day."

"Good. That's what I want. You're okay to be touched right now?"

He laughed, leaning down to kiss me once. "I'm going to need you to touch me everywhere. Erase it all for me, Daze."

"I think I can do that."His arms wrapped around me, pulling me hard against him. "I've told you before. Your hands always erase it. I need them on me forever. I need *you* forever. Come on, we need to see if we can go home."

FIFTY-SIX

KYE

I COULDN'T GATHER my thoughts fast enough, so I focused on Daisy's hands. Her fingers trailed up the middle of my back, moving over my shoulders and back down. I kept my eyes closed as I worked through the panic that still burned in my chest.

I had worked through so much of my issues with touching, but nothing would ever make someone that I hated hand-cuffing me feel okay.

"Hey," I said. "You doing alright?"

"I'm fine. Better now. Just making sure you aren't going to run," she said, holding me tighter.

My eyebrows jumped up, but she didn't look at me. "Run? The only place I would like to run to is our apartment, so we can be done with this shit and watch a movie."

"A movie? After today, you want to watch a movie?"

"Yeah, we're getting Bailey and watching a movie."

"Okay…but why?"

"Because ever since that night at the track, all I have

wanted to be able to do is sit with you two and watch a movie."

"What do you mean? With us two or the entire crew?"

I wrapped her up in my arms more. "Entire crew sounds great. Then this time, I get to show off my family and not get inundated with questions and pitiful looks that I don't have one."

"They did not do that."

"They absolutely did."

"You said, your family."

"Yeah. Now I have my own little family within my large, loud, endlessly growing family."

"I didn't realize we were now a family."

"I told you, I'm ready, Daisy. For you, for Bailey, for our own kids. You tell me the moment you're ready because I'm here waiting."

"I'm ready," she said, quickly. I smiled at the enthusiasm.

"Really? I thought you would need more time."

"No, not even a second. If it's with you, I'm ready now."

I spun her to face me, cupping her jaw and pulling her in to kiss me. "I love you, Daze. I've loved you, only you, every day since I met you, and I hope you are serious right now."

"Of course I'm serious. I want everything with you. I love you, too, Kye."

"Forever this time, no years apart."

"And no one getting in the way this time," she said.

"Then I think we need to go talk to your dad, and make sure we're done here so we can go home and get started on that," I said with a grin. "And maybe make sure he doesn't hate my guts enough to threaten you more."

"He will," she said. "I don't know if it will ever stop, but we can stop being around him."

We headed over to her dad, who was already scowling at me.

"You just tried to arrest him for killing someone when he didn't do it and your side lackey did, so unless you are going to apologize or tell us we can leave, I don't want to hear anything from you," Daisy said.

"Kye," her dad said, his face hard as he stared at us. "*Don't* leave town. We will have plenty of questions to ask."

"But?" Daisy asked.

"But for now, you can go. I have enough to sort out with Mark, so we can talk tomorrow."

My eyebrows jumped up, but I said nothing as he walked away. "Did your dad just say that he *didn't* want me to leave? Incredible. We are already making progress. Who would have thought it would only take me basically being framed for murder, only to find it was your golden hero of an ex-boyfriend for him to like me?"

"We really could have saved ourselves six years apart had we known this with Dean."

I laughed, pulling her under my arm and heading back towards the crew and the garage.

"Time to go home. To our home, and our girl." I leaned over and kissed her forehead. "I love you, Daisy. Forever."

She smiled, her eyes shining with tears. "I love you, too, Kye. Forever."

EPILOGUE

DAISY

I HELD MY BREATH.

Every turn that he took was sharper than the last. I couldn't even see the road, the rain and fog so heavy on parts of the mountain that I didn't know how he would see the next turn coming.

I knew he'd done this before. I knew he said he knew the road, but he was driving up the side of a mountain with zero visibility as fast as he could. I didn't know how I could be calm about this.

I sat with Bailey, watching the camera that was set up so that we could watch his car pass over the finish line.

My chest eased, and I could finally take a breath. "He made it."

Bailey yelled in excitement, jumping up to go play with the other kids now.

I watched the camera as he parked the car at the top and got out, walking around the front to the crowd of people.

A girl spun to face him, throwing her arms around him and making my heart stop. It wasn't that Kye couldn't hug other women, but watching it happen when I knew he didn't like many people touching him made my heart sink a little bit.

I waited as the crowd dispersed and Kye disappeared. I knew he would talk for a few minutes, and then make the drive back down to get us, but now I was already impatient to see him again.

Kye had said it could take a while for him to get back to us or get us to him, but it had been close to an hour now.

"Hey, that's Kye," Tara said, pointing to a car coming around the corner. I knew Tara well enough, at least enough through Ash. Her husband was good friends with Kye and on his team to set these races up. She had two amazing kids of her own that were more grown than Bailey.

"Hey, Tara. I'm really sorry to ask this, but could you maybe watch Bailey for, like, thirty minutes? I can pay you, if that helps."

A sly smile grew on her face. "Why? Is something wrong?"

"No, I just need to talk to Kye…in private."

She laughed. "Of course. And pay me? Babe, I have a husband that I still think is the hottest man in the world. How about I watch her now and you repay the favor with my boys when I need to *talk* to my husband in private one day?"

My mouth dropped, but I didn't have time to argue. "That's a deal. Are you sure you're okay with it? She can be a handful." We both looked to Bailey, who was playing with her boys.

"She's nothing I haven't handled. Two boys is a lot to handle. I won't underestimate her," she said, laughing. "Just go. We will be here when you get back."

"Thank you. Thank you so much."

Kye had made it to us, slowing down and parking, but I

jumped in the passenger side, realizing there was barely a second seat in his race car.

"Go somewhere."

"What?" he asked, looking around. "What are you doing?" He was laughing, but I ignored him.

"Go somewhere else. Go park somewhere private."

"Oh, fuck. Okay." He pulled back out. We were halfway up the mountain, but he pulled out to go down. He rounded the corners as people still packing to leave cheered at his car.

"Is private going to be too hard to find?"

"On one of the biggest race days of the year for this place? No, not at all."

He turned into one of the parking lots, pulling us to the back that was now empty. "At least you waited until the races were over. Everyone is already clearing out." He parked, angling the car into the corner.

"Can someone see us here?"

"I mean, probably, and it's not like we don't stand out, so you better do or say what you need to before someone walks over," he said, his eyebrows jumping as he smiled.

"You're terrible," I said, already climbing over to him. I sat myself between him and the steering wheel, the fit so tight I could barely move.

"Can you move the seat back?"

He laughed harder. "No. This is a built race car, the seats do not slide. Everything is bolted in place, so I have less of a chance of wrecking and dying."

"Not funny. I just had to watch you race yourself up the death mountain. Fine, we can make do like this." I lifted myself up, awkwardly pulling off my leggings.

"Damn, did watching me race make you this hot for me?

I'm going to race up this fucking mountain every day of my life."

"No. I mean, yeah, I liked that, too, but that wasn't all."

"Then what was it? So I can repeat it every chance I get."

"I saw that girl hug you," I said, coming back down over him, focusing on unzipping and adjusting his race suit, but he froze, grabbing my wrists to stop me.

"What?"

"You heard me."

His smile grew as he looked up at me. "And you were jealous because a girl hugged me?"

"Well, yes, I don't see that all that often besides the crew, so I just wondered who she was."

"You're hilarious. Jealous after three months together, and over six years of me being so in love with you, I haven't even slept with anyone else."

"Okay, so I'm jealous. I have a hot boyfriend who I can't keep my hands off, and I guess I'm assuming other women are thinking the same thing."

I finally moved the zipper all the way down, already knowing what he was wearing under this, which helped as I navigated it without being able to look down. Our bodies were pressed too close to see.

"Well, come on, Daze. We don't have a lot of time, and I'm going to need to see exactly how jealous you are," he said, kissing my neck.

"Obviously, that is the driving force behind all of this," I said, grabbing his cock and seating myself on it.

He laughed. "I really can't move much."

"That's fine." I moved, able to move up enough and fall back down onto him.

I moved slow at first, until I couldn't take it anymore, riding him harder and faster.

"I never want anyone else," he said, watching me. "I never want to be with anyone else. I'm sorry you had to think that, but any bad day or messy attitude or fight, it doesn't matter. I want you for all of them. You told me that you wanted me and my chaos. I want you and yours. You can be messy. I still only want you. Do you think anyone else could fuck me like this, Daisy? No one else makes me lose my mind like you do. Makes me cum like you do," he said with a groan. "Anyone else would pale in comparison. Everything about you is enough."

I yelled, my orgasm washing over me as he kept going, telling me everything I needed to hear as he showed me how true each word was.

"Daisy, someone is coming over here, so you need to quickly get your pants back on."

"What?" I fell over, reaching for my leggings as Kye fixed his race suit, tying the arms at his waist and then helping me adjust myself and get back into my seat.

He got out, talking to whatever guy had come over and asked for photos.

Being called out for wanting to go have sex with your boyfriend was embarrassing enough. Someone catching you was also embarrassing, but someone taking photos of a car that you just had sex in while he stands by it beaming was turning my entire body beet red as I slid down so far I was nearly on the floor.

Kye came back moments later. "What are you doing?"

"Hiding. I really do not need a stranger to have a picture of me all sexed up in your car."

"No? I would love that picture. I do need a new photo for my phone. According to you, that's how I get to boyfriend status."

"Yeah, years ago. We are not telling everyone in the world every time I want to go have sex with my boyfriend."

He grabbed for my hand, shifting the car with mine, and a huge smile.

"I love being called your boyfriend, but I really would like to upgrade the title. Also, I just got news that I won."

"What?"

"Yeah, fastest time."

"You won? Like, won won."

"Yeah, like, won won."

I jumped over the car, wrapping my arms around him with a shriek.

"We have to go up and get Bailey. Then go to the top."I nodded, still wrapped around him as he tried to drive. He groaned. "I hate to do this, but this car is not built to have passengers in my lap."

I laughed, pulling myself back into my seat. In minutes, we were back at Tara, with Bailey running to Kye's car as fast as she could when we came to a stop.

He scooped her up, kissing her head. "Hey, little bee," he said, and she smiled against him. Her arms wrapped around him, and it seemed like she was as obsessed with him as he was with her.

"Wow, Kye, you're screwed," I said.

"Oh, I know," he said. "I've known for a while now and am accepting my fate. Come on, let's get up to the top."

"That's right, we have to go celebrate you winning."

"I have you two. I already won."

He held Bailey, heading towards the car and waiting for me. My heart was exploding, though. We had both finally won. Fate had taken him away from me, but it also brought us back together, and now I knew I had found my forever.

EPILOGUE

KYE

<u>SIX MONTHS Later</u>

The street was already empty as I pulled my car up to the line. Maybe it was boring to some people to keep coming to the Thursday night races, but there really was nothing better than beating some of these younger guys who thought they could kick my ass without even trying.

The race started and was over before I even blinked. I won by a few car lengths and smiled as I pulled my car up next to the crew. Everyone was here tonight. The kids were at home, so the entire crew fanned out, smiling and laughing with each other.

Everyone, including Daisy.

I wasn't good at a lot of things, and this might be one of them, but damn if I wasn't going to try.

I revved the engine, feeling adrenaline and nervousness mixing in my veins. With one deep breath, I stepped out of my car and walked over to Daisy, my heart thundering in my chest. She looked beautiful like she always did, but tonight was different.

Because tonight, she would hopefully agree to be my wife.

It's not like it would be a surprise to her. I only told her every single day that I wanted her to marry me. I just didn't think she would be expecting a proposal here tonight.

The crew gathered around. They were all married now and were more than happy to help me propose to Daisy. Their cars circled around us, each one running colored lights and surrounding us in a vibrant rainbow of colors.

It was as pretty of a setting as I could come up with, and she seemed more than happy as she looked around.

"What's going on?" Daisy's voice was soft, her eyes full of curiosity as she peered down up me. I took a deep breath, trying to calm the nerves that threatened to make my hands shake. The hum of the engines and the glow of the colored lights wrapped around us, and I knew I couldn't do better than this.

Maybe I could have found another place, maybe I could have waited to do it in a damn field of Daisy's, but this felt right to me, and that's all I could do.

"You know I'm not always good with words," I began, earning a laugh from the crew gathered behind me. "But every day, I wake up grateful that you're in my life. You make me want to be better, to try harder, to love you the best I can every day. I only want to spend my life making you as happy as you make me."

A soft smile tugged at the corners of Daisy's lips, her eyes glimmering with unshed tears. "Kye..."

I lowered myself onto one knee, reaching into my pocket for the small box that held a ring with a light blue stone that I thought she would love.

"Will you marry me?"

She yelled out something, tears falling as she fell down, throwing her arms around me as she landed on my knees.

"Do you even have to ask? Of course, it's a yes. A thousand times, yes."

The crew erupted into cheers and applause, engines revving in celebration, as Daisy slipped the ring onto her finger. I stood up, pulling her close to me as we were surrounded by our friends.

A sense of peace settled over me. Daisy was going to be my wife, and I couldn't imagine a future without her by my side. The colored lights continued to dance around us, a beautiful backdrop to the start of our new chapter together.

"One more thing," I whispered, waiting as the kids got out of Fox's car. Bailey came out last, a bouquet of daisies in her hand. "Looks like you're stuck with me, little bee," I said as she ran over.

She screeched, jumping onto me as I lifted her up.

"I figured you would want her here," I said, "but I really thought you should say yes before I included her."

Daisy was crying now, grabbing Bailey from my arms and holding her close between us.

"We're together forever, Kye," she cried. "You're absolutely stuck with us now."

"Thank god," I said, kissing her once before kissing Bailey's head. "I don't know if I could be happy if it was any other way."

Two days later, I pulled up to the track at Holt, Daisy in my passenger seat.

I lined the car up before taking off around the curves and swinging the back of the car around each one.

Daisy reached out, her fingers digging into my forearm suddenly. "Kye, stop," she said, grabbing onto my arm. We were at the other end of the track, and she was currently looking more car-sick by the second.

I laughed, trying to ease her tension. "Alright, hold on."

"Kye! Stop!" she yelled, fighting the harness now. She had ridden with me plenty of times, and I wasn't expecting the sudden freakout.

I hit the brakes, letting the car jolt to a stop.

"What, did I freak you out?" I asked, pulling off the helmet. "It's been months, Daze. Does it scare you that bad?"

She fought with the harness and then the helmet before kicking open the door.

"Daisy, what's wrong? What are you doing?"

She, apparently, wasn't able to answer, finally breaking free and making it to the edge of the track just in time to puke.

I ran out, trying to help how I could as she kept puking, but there was nothing to do but let it happen.

Finally, it slowed.

"Water?" I asked.

"Yeah, here, come on." I picked her up and sat her on the back of the car.

"Here, water," I said, grabbing the bottle from the car and handing it to her. Her face went pale again, and for a second, I thought she might start puking up the water.

"I'm sorry, Daze. You've never had a problem. I didn't realize all the spinning would get to you that much."

"No, it's fine. Not your fault," she said through short breaths.

"I'm still sorry. Do you want to go lie down? There are plenty of places we can set you up for a minute until it stops."

"It's not going to stop."

"If I stop spinning the car, it will," I said with a laugh, trying to make her feel better.

She took a deep breath, looking back at the crew, who had to be wondering what was going on. "I had been looking for the right time to talk about this, but I think this is the best I could ask for in our lives, considering what this car, place, and people mean to you."

Worry and fear filled my gut. There was something dark that always lingered when you loved someone so much, the gnawing fear that anything could take them away. Now, I was worrying that something was seriously wrong.

"Best for what?"

"I'm not puking because you're spinning. I'm puking because I'm pregnant," she said fast.

The words sounded so foreign to me that I couldn't think of anything to say. There's wanting a child one day, and then there's the day that actually comes.

I stared, trying to think of any single word that could make her understand what I was feeling.

"I'm sorry," she said. "I know we talked about things, but your face looks horrified."

"No, no. Not horrified at all. This happened recently?"

"Very recently. Like, I still need to go get bloodwork done and confirm it. I was going to do that before I talked to you, but I also wasn't expecting to throw up, so things changed."

My face fell more, my heart racing now. "Fuck, Daisy. I just drove around with you like that. And you're pregnant? Fuck, I am so sorry. Are you okay? I'll go so slow back it will take us all day. I'm sorry." I pulled her into me. "You're pregnant, and I'm going to have a kid."

Tears were threatening me, and for a minute, I was pretty sure my heart was going to explode.

"Yes. Are you okay with this because I thought you would be, but now I'm a little unsure?"

"I'm more than okay." I buried my head in her neck, trying not to cry. "I'm so fucking okay I don't even know what words would describe it. I wanted kids, but there's never been anyone else I have ever even considered it with. I've been pathetically in love with you and couldn't imagine anyone else to have a family with, and now that's happening? Of course, I'm okay."

"Wow, good because I was a little worried there for a second."

"No, I just couldn't believe I just drove like that with you pregnant in the car. I'm still so sorry."

"It's okay. I knew you were being careful enough not to wreck. It's why I got in. I just wasn't expecting the nausea to hit like that."

"Fuck. You're never allowed in my car again. Do you want me to carry you back?"

"No," she said, laughing. "Just maybe slow and easy, please."

I held her closer, not able to pull myself away. For years, I cursed fate. I cursed the entire world for what it had given me in life, but now I knew better.

It wasn't reckless. It knew all along what I needed.

And what I needed, what I would always need, was Daisy.

JOIN THE CREW

Kate's Reader Crew (Facebook group)
facebook.com/groups/katesreadercrew/
Instagram: instagram.com/authorkatecrew
TikTok: tiktok.com/authorkatecrew
Facebook: facebook.com/authorkatecrew
Pinterest: pinterest.com/authorkatecrew/

OTHER BOOKS

Hollows Garage

Heart Wrenched - Ransom and Quinn's Story

Wrecked Love - Fox and Ash's Story

Racing Hearts - Jax and Carly's Story

Love Collided - Scout and Chase's Story

Reckless Fate - Kye and Daisy's Story

The Mavericks

Rook & Rebel - Releasing October 2024

Printed by Amazon Italia Logistica S.r.l.
Torrazza Piemonte (TO), Italy

61405692R00268